THE BRAILLE KILLER

AN ALICE BERGMAN NOVEL
BOOK ONE

DRAGUN

PUBLISHING

THE BRAILLE KILLER

Edited by Catherine Jones Payne
www.quillpeneditorial.com

Published by Drezhn Publishing LLC
PO BOX 67458
Albuquerque, NM 87193-7458

Print Edition - April 2020
Fourth Edition

Cover design by Dan Van Oss, CoverMint
www.covermint.design

ISBN 978-1-947328-11-2

BOOKS BY DANIEL KUHNLEY

MYSTERY THRILLER

Alice Bergman Novels
Birth Of A Killer (novella)
*The Braille Killer
The Night Mauler

FANTASY

The Dark Heart Chronicles
*† The Dragon's Stone
*Reborn
*Rended Souls

Scourge (novella)

* - Also available as an audiobook
† - Previously released as Dark Lament

Visit Daniel's website to find these books and more!
danielkuhnley.com

READ *BIRTH OF A KILLER* FOR FREE

Curious how Alice gained her sight as a teen?
Want to read about the attack that started it all?

Sign up and read *Birth Of A Killer*, An Alice Bergman Novella, and also get **EXCLUSIVE** access to additional Alice Bergman series content. Be the **FIRST** to get sneak peaks at my upcoming novels and the chance to win **FREE** stuff, like signed books.

Thank you for reading!

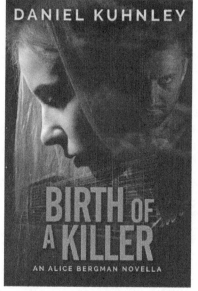

Be careful what you dream...

...when murder is on your mind.

Sixteen-year-old Alice is a ghost. Although born blind, the world is more blind to her than she is to it. Until the day she's noticed. By a bully.

She did what any girl would do...

...and wished him dead.

When a body is discovered, Alice fears the worst. Could she be to blame? No one would believe her even if she confessed. Because nightmares don't come true...do they?

You'll enjoy this supernatural serial killer thriller, because everyone enjoys a nail-biting mystery they can't put down.

Get it now.

Birth Of A Killer is the prequel to *The Braille Killer*.

AN ALICE BERGMAN NOVEL BOOK ONE

THE
BRAILLE KILLER

DANIEL KUHNLEY

CHAPTER ONE

I CANNOT PEEL MY gaze away from the manila envelope sitting in the driver's seat of my sedan. The single, calligraphic 'A' handwritten on its front is unmistakable. Immediately, I know what day it is, but I take my cell phone out of my pants pocket and engage the display to verify. It reads Tuesday, July 17 06:34. My fingers and toes curl and chills sweep through me despite it being ninety degrees already.

After ten years you'd think I'd never forget this day, or perhaps I would've added a calendar reminder on my phone so that I wouldn't. Yet I stand frozen in my driveway staring through my car window at an envelope I should've expected but didn't. In my defense, it's not an event that I ever wanted to be memorialized, but the bastard who's left it will never let me forget it.

I glance around, half-expecting him to be watching me—waiting for my reaction and getting off on it like the disturbed voyeur I imagine him to be. It sickens me that he's eluded me for so long, and so the chase goes on.

He's forced me to participate in his twisted little game. I never asked to be part of it, yet I obsess over it. I will not rest until I bring him to justice.

I take my keys out of my pocket. They jingle-jangle in my trembling hand like sleigh bells. I wish the envelope were from Santa Claus or some other imaginary entity full of jolly and kindness, but I know better. I settle on thanking the stars for the key fob that hangs from the keyring. If not for it, I'd be keying the side of my car trying to unlock it.

I press the right button on the key fob, but nothing happens. I press harder, then several more times, but the doors don't unlock. Anger stills my hand. Why does technology thwart me at every turn? It has my entire life, and I'd love a reprieve from it. Just for one day. This day. Is it too much to ask for?

I smash the button down one last time and the doors unlock with a *click*. Tension drains from my fingers and toes, but I know it'll be short lived. I pull the driver's side door open, grab the envelope and toss it onto the passenger seat, and then plop down in the driver's seat.

I thumb the lock button on the door several times, even after hearing and seeing the locks engage. A scream rises in my throat, so I force it back down like bile. He'll never hear my fear manifest.

My hands wrap the steering wheel and I stare at the brown stucco wall in front of me. I have no desire to open the envelope because it will contain another letter and some random-ass item that leads me straight back to where I am: *nowhere*.

However, my resolve is fragile, and my curiosity is piqued, so I snatch the envelope off the passenger seat and clutch it between my hands. I want to rip it open and dump its contents into my lap, but this one is different than the others. The ink used for the 'A' on its front is blood-red instead of the usual black.

My breath catches in my throat like half-swallowed food, and my heart knocks against my rib cage with such violence that it jolts me forward time and again. What does the red ink signify? My heart knows the answer, but my mind isn't ready to make the connection and draw the conclusion.

I turn the envelope over and carefully bend up the two metal prongs that secure its flap. I pull the flap open, reach inside the envelope, and pull out a bracelet of tightly woven strands of red and brown. The materials used are silky and fibrous simultaneously, their origins elusive.

Another friendship bracelet?

I examine it closely for clues but find nothing tangible. No tag. No message. A simple bracelet just like the first one. *Why would he send these to me?* I slide it back into the envelope, pull out the folded piece of yellowed, card stock paper, and place the envelope back on the passenger seat.

Unfolded, the paper stares up at me. Without lead, graphite, or ink marring its surface one might assume it to be blank, but it's far from that. Its message will pierce my heart just as the others have.

My palms, wet with perspiration, stick to its edges. I peel my right hand away and wipe it on my pantleg several times. The clamminess remains.

I take a deep breath and slowly glide my finger across the page. The words, strung together with braille letters meticulously pressed into the paper, pierce my heart and numb my mind.

> *A badge and a gun you possess*
> *But it's a heart you've never had*
> *The lies you tell make you far less*
> *And drive this hatter mad*

> *You should've listened to me*
> *But you blew your last chance*
> *You wouldn't pay the fee*
> *For your sordid little romance*

> *Now my patience has run dry*
> *And your time has just run out*
> *You'll no longer turn a blind eye*
> *To things that come about*

> *You will play into my plans*
> *And soon you'll see just how*
> *All the blood is on your hands*
> *And there's no stopping now*

As with all his letters, it ends with a threat of disclosure: *"This matter stays between us. Involve the authorities or anyone else and everyone you love will die."*

I groan and the paper bends where I'm clutching it. I want to wad it up and toss it into a burning trashcan down on South Central. I want to forget Denise ever existed, but I can't.

Why does her death still haunt me?

I didn't even know her, let alone kill her, yet I've clung to her existence for these last ten years. She's the thread that binds me to him, and he's the only person in the world that can explain why she chose me and why he helped her. This single event forces me forward on a path I might never have chosen, and I cannot rest until I meet its end.

I smooth the paper out where I bent it, fold it back up, and return it to the envelope. I close and secure the envelope and take a deep breath. *Everything will be okay.* By this point in my life I should know that lying to myself does no good.

I press the start button on my dash and the engine roars to life without hesitation. Honestly, I'm surprised. I switch on the AC, but nothing happens. I smack the top of the dash with my fist because sometimes it helps make things work, but not today. Not on July 17th. The damned thing's gone on strike.

Fifteen minutes later, I pull into the parking lot at the police station. I'm not sure how I even made it here, the drive just a blur. I shove the envelope under the seat and climb out of the car. My clothes are stuck to my sweat-covered body. I pull at my blouse and fan myself with it to try and get some air circulation, but the result is far less than I'd hoped for. *I'm glad I showered this morning.*

I walk inside and straight to my office, grab my mug off my desk, and head for the breakroom down the hall and to the left. The aroma of fresh coffee wafts in the hallway and tractor beams me into the breakroom. The coffeepot isn't on the warmer. Glass shards and puddles of coffee glisten on the countertop and across the floor. Officer Janis kneels with her back to me, picking up pieces of shattered coffeepot.

"What happened?" I ask even though the evidence is clear.

She looks up at me over her shoulder. "Stupid thing stopped dispensing water, overheated the pot, and exploded. Luckily no one was in here at the time. Heard the pop from my desk."

"Ugh. How am I supposed to survive the briefing without caffeine?" I eye the counter to my left. "No donuts either?"

Officer Janis shakes her head. "Nope. Bob's out sick today."

I groan. *The perfect storm.*

Like the rest of the police station, the breakroom is battle worn. Paint chips hang on the cinder-block walls in several places like scabs waiting to be peeled off. The carpet is ripped in places and completely gone in others, the pattern it once donned lost in the past. Brown stains dominate the yellowed, drop-ceiling tiles which were once a pristine white. All three tables sit on crooked legs, each wobblier that a Weebles doll, and the chairs are a hazard waiting to be had with cracked seats and unbolted backrests. Budget cuts have impacted everything.

Defeated, I retreat back to my office, drop off my empty mug, and head to the locker room. A few minutes later, I find myself staring into my open locker, my mind hung on the words of this morning's letter. *All the blood is on your hands.* Had he meant Denise or something far worse?

"Bergman." Lieut. Frost's voice startles me.

I glance around, knowing the exact reason for his visit. *No Seth? Where the hell are you?* No one else lurks about in the locker room.

Lieut. Frost strides toward me with dogged determination. His bulldog jaw is set and his ice-cold, brown-eyed gaze chills my core. *This day can't possibly get better.* I shake my head and slam my locker door shut.

Lieut. Frost pulls up next to me and suddenly I'm a dwarf from Middle Earth. I'm 5'7", but he's nearly a foot taller than me and twice as wide. He has the Superman look nailed, but there's no chance of him having a suit and cape underneath his drab attire. Every day he wears brown slacks, a white shirt with the sleeves rolled up to his elbows, and some sort of power tie. Today it's red and matches his cheeks.

Matches the ink on the envelope.

The smell of his cheap cologne snakes into my nostrils like octopus tentacles. I breathe through my mouth and do my best not to gag on its skunk-butt odor. Lieut. Frost's brow sinks, and his nostrils flare. He's clearly immune to his own stench. I stifle a snort by coughing.

His eyes narrow as he pushes his wire frame glasses up his nose. Even in that small act his bicep bulges underneath his shirt. I've seen him do it a thousand times, but I still stare with awe. He is an exquisite specimen of the human male and I cannot deny myself a lingering glance even though his personality repulses me even more than his cologne does. I lower my gaze.

"Bergman, where's that worthless partner of yours?" His gruff voice shakes my chest with a barrage of bass reminiscent of rap songs. It focuses my attention quicker than a dog sighting a squirrel.

I close my eyes and lean my head against the locker for effect. "Oh God, I knew I'd forgotten to do something. Ryan's car is in the shop. He asked me to give him a lift this morning." I slam my fist into the locker next to my head. "Dammit."

"You keep covering for him and it'll be *your* ass, Bergman."

I sigh and pull my head away from the locker. "I swear, Lieutenant, he really did ask me for a ride this morning. I totally spaced it. This one's on me."

He shoves a meaty finger in my face and shakes it at me. "Briefing room in thirty. Detective Ryan had better be there. Am I clear?"

Clear? Not through your cloud of cologne. I need to seek lower ground to survive. I hold my tongue and nod. It's a rare occasion, and I'm proud of myself for doing so.

Lieut. Frost shakes his head, a boulder atop his broad shoulders. "Save your smirks until after I've walked away. Makes your blatant lies a bit more palatable."

I nod again and then clear my throat when I hear the soft squeak of rubber-soled shoes on the other side of the lockers. Lieut. Frost doesn't react to the sound and instead storms away. I let out a deep sigh, breathe in through my nose, and regret it. The air still reeks of skunk butt.

I turn around and face the opposite end of the line of lockers. "You can come out now, Seth."

Seth Ryan's head pokes around the end of the lockers. "How do you do that? I didn't make a single noise when I came in."

I breathe on my nails and rub them on my shirt. "I told you I'm a certified ninja. I've got more than ten years of ninjutsu training." I move into an angry tiger stance and motion him forward. "Nothing escapes me. By the way, you need new shoes. The soles are wearing on the outside edge and causing you to walk bowlegged. I don't date cowboys, so you'd better get them replaced."

Seth rounds the corner and waddles toward me like a penguin-cowboy. A crooked smile mars his otherwise beautiful, hairless face. I conjure a smile as I roll my eyes.

His wavy brown locks hug the top of his head like a glove, and the sides and back are trimmed short. If he were allowed to grow it out, I think he'd look even sexier. He reminds me of Jon Bon Jovi, but only in looks. Seth can't carry a tune to save his life. Believe me, I know. Karaoke night at The Dive was a one-time deal. I'd never been asked to step off the stage in the middle of a song before. Awkward moment. Who knew a duet of *Close My Eyes Forever* would bring us to the lowest point in our relationship? I'm certain I did Lita Ford proud, and who could possibly screw up Ozzy Osbourne? *Seth. Only Seth.*

We still hang our heads in shame every time we pass by The Dive's doors, and we've never set foot inside its walls since. I think back on all the situations we've been forced into over the last two years that we've worked together, and I cringe. Hopefully Seth will never have to sing to save my life. His voice might kill me before my captors got a chance.

His tight blue jeans hug his muscular legs and drape over his black leather boots like curtains hung too low, and his black button-up shirt is untucked at the side and back. He always wears his shirt with two buttons undone at the top—a sight I relish. He's not a hairy man, so thankfully there's no tuft of hair poking out like the gerbil on Tom Selleck. A thick, silver necklace with a dagger pendant hangs just below his neckline. He's never without it, just as I am never without my cross-pendant necklace.

His cologne, Drakkar Noir, precedes him and chases away the nidorous scent that Lieut. Frost left behind. I breathe deep, every muscle in my body tenses, and I shudder with delight. Seth is my partner, both in work and in life. He is my foundation rock. My shelter. He holds the weight of the world on his shoulders so that I don't have to. He keeps the monsters at bay — at least the ones he knows about.

There are some things I keep from Seth, not for his sake but for mine. He knows nothing of my past, and I'll do everything in my power to keep it that way. He doesn't know about the ten letters I've received over the past decade either. I cannot risk losing him and everyone I love, so he never will.

Those letters are to be kept between me and the sicko who sends them. He's made it perfectly clear. I will catch him if it's the last thing I do. He's the reason I studied criminology, joined the force, and worked my way up to detective. In some twisted way I guess I can thank him for that.

Seth weaves his fingers into mine and presses me up against the lockers with my hands over my head. He leans down, and his hot breath moistens my skin just before his soft lips caress the side of my neck. I moan, louder than I'd expected and flinch. I scan the locker room and find we're still alone.

"Seth, we can't—"

He leans into me, nibbles on my lower lip, and pulls on it. I wish I could forget where we are and give into the moment but too many things niggle my mind. Anyone could walk in and see us together. His gun digs into my ribs a little, and perspiration trickles down my nape, under my arms, and into places I don't even want to think about.

The air conditioning units have been on the fritz all summer. It must be a hundred degrees in here. I doubt they'll ever get fixed.

I push Seth away with reluctance, but his hands stay locked in mine. I smile. "Save it for tonight."

He presses into me again. "What's wrong with right now?"

"Oh geez, get a room." Officer Todd appears in my peripheral view.

Seth backs away and releases my hands. I look over at Officer Todd. "Your timing is impeccable, Tommy."

Seth turns and winks at Officer Todd. "I'm afraid the show's over, buddy. Better get here earlier next time. Doors open at 6 am."

I roll my eyes at Seth. "The only times you've ever seen 6 am is when you've been awake all night."

Seth hooks his thumbs in his front pockets. "Pfft. Stay the night with me, and I'll be up anytime you want. Guaranteed."

Tommy's cheeks turn red and his gaze falls to the floor. "Don't you guys have somewhere to be? Some corpse to unbury or some killer to hunt down?"

Seth nods. "Every day, buddy. Death never sleeps."

Tommy shakes his head and walks over to his locker. He puts one hand over the lock so that we can't see his combination and spins the dial back and forth with his other hand. It clicks, pops, and then the door groans open.

Tommy's only been on the force for three weeks, but he's already made a lasting impression on me. His elongated forehead and alien-shaped face reminds me of Barney Fife from *The Andy Griffith Show*. Much like Fife, he's a beat cop down on South Central Blvd. Not a place I'd want to be assigned.

Thomas Terrence Todd. *What were his parents thinking?* He goes by Trip T in the rap world. My eyes tear up, and I snort so violently that it pangs my throat.

Seth frowns at me. "What's so funny?"

I shake my head and walk toward the exit. Sometimes it's the best thing to do. "Be safe out there, Tommy. I don't want you to be my next call."

He nods as I walk by. "You, too."

Seth follows me out of the locker room and down the main corridor like a leashed dog. *My leashed dog.* We're like *Turner & Hooch*. I snort again and cough. If he knew some of my thoughts, he wouldn't be so eager to stand at my side. Then again, I can't even imagine what goes through his mind at times. Don't think I want to.

We stop by our shared office and I freeze in the doorway. The light on my desk phone flashes like an ambulance and my breath catches in my throat. I look over at Seth's desk. His isn't flashing. My pulse begins to race and sweat beads on my brow. No one ever calls my desk phone anymore. I check my cell phone, but I've missed no calls and have no messages.

I walk into the office and round my desk. The stale, hot air weighs on me like a dense fog and I have to sit down to keep my legs from buckling underneath the crushing weight. My throat muscles contract, and I fight to catch my breath.

I look up. Seth is eying my desk phone.

His gaze moves to me and locks on mine. "Are you going to check it?"

I swallow hard and nod once, certain that if I were to answer vocally, I'd only squeak like a mouse. My breath catches with every blink of the red light and the tension in my jaw ratchets up another level.

Red… just like the 'A' on the envelope. I know it's him. It must be.

Seth settles in his chair and drums his fingers on the leather armrests.

I exhale, pull my desk phone close, and stare at it for several moments before finally picking up the receiver. I press the red button and enter my 6-digit code on the dial pad.

I stare at Seth as the message plays. Static crackles and pops for several seconds like it does at the beginning of a 45 record and then a music box begins to play in the background. I know it's a music box because I had one when I was little and because the metal strips flicking against the nubs on the metal roller are so distinctive. The tune it plays is familiar, but I can't recall its name or where I've heard it before.

A gruff, male voice talks over the music and pulls me down into the depths of my past. "Five one four three Elm Street. I took my time with her. She never saw me coming. Blind girls never do." He laughs. "Fifteen years old. She was ripe for the plucking. Sarah Johnson's blood is on your hands, Detective Bergman. How many more will you kill?"

The music stops, the line clicks, and then the message ends.

My fingers tremble as I press the button and delete the message. I set the receiver back down on its cradle and exhale. My heart thunders. *This day is unrelenting.* I pinch the bridge of my nose and lean back in my chair.

Several seconds go by as Seth's brow wrinkles and then furrows, and his eyes narrow until nothing but slits remain of them. "Well? What did the message say?"

The blood is on your hands. I look down at my crimson-stained hands and cringe. They're not actually red, but it doesn't stop me from picturing them that way.

I look Seth in the eye and tell him what he needs to know. "Anonymous call. A body's been discovered."

He slams his fist into the chair arm. "Damn. I'd hoped today would be a good day."

"So did I." I know how the rest of this conversation will go. I can feel it in my bones, and my heart's already aching. I know all the questions he'll ask me and the things I must withhold.

"Give me the breakdown."

I close my eyes. "A young girl. Early teens. Looks to have been raped."

"Damn." Seth slams his fist into his desk and my eyes shoot open.

A stack of case files tilts and then falls on the floor with a smack, and his phone's receiver jumps out of its cradle. He picks the receiver back up and slams it back home. It wouldn't surprise me if he cracked the whole damn phone.

Seth rolls his chair around the side of his desk and scoops up the splayed files. "You get a location?"

"Five one four three Elm Street." My eyes are open, but I stare into a world made of nightmares. Seth says something to me, but fear renders me deaf and his words fade into the ambient noise of buzzing fluorescent lights.

The blood is on your hands.

My stomach twists in knots, and I cannot move. My feet root themselves to the floor and my arms to the chair. I fight back tears of anger and shame from a decade's worth of neglected emotions.

When I return to our world Seth is on his phone with Officer Janis, reporting the tip. He hangs up and stands. "Ready to roll? Officers Spalding and Dupree are right down the street from the scene and forensics should be rolling up on it soon as well. They were just a block over wrapping up another scene."

I reach deep within and find the strength to rise from my chair. "After you."

As we walk out to the unmarked sedan my mind returns to the call. *Blind.* It's no coincidence. He's killed, and I know why. I cringe as a single thought sears my mind like a cattle brand and marks me as the monster I am.

She's dead because of me.

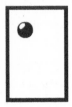

CHAPTER TWO

SETH ROCKETS THROUGH THE streets, squealing tires around corners and laying on the horn relentlessly. The veins in his neck and arms bulge like he's on a roid rage, and his knuckles are stark white against the black leather steering wheel, his fingers vise-gripped around it.

I keep one hand braced on the dashboard and place the other on Seth's leg. "Slow down, Seth. This is exactly why Lieut. Frost is on your case. Not every call we respond to is an emergency."

"You don't know that." His words push through gritted teeth. "I arrived moments too late once before. Never again."

For the past two years Seth has been everything to me. He came into my life when I was at one of my lowest points I can remember. I'd all but given up on finding the sicko that had haunted me for eight years.

It took Seth more than a year to open up to me about his sister's murder and even then, I had to pry the words from his sealed lips. I try my best to be there for him when he needs me, but I am a shell of a person as well. We are two souls filled with pent-up emotions and no outlet to relieve the pressure.

I squeeze his thigh. "I know, and I'm sorry, but getting there quickly today won't bring this girl back to life. She's already dead." Those last words drive a spike through my heart.

All the blood is on your hands.

Sorrow and rage brew in the pit of my stomach like a bad chimichanga, so I focus my thoughts on the people in my life that matter. Truth be told, there are only three of them: Mother, Seth, and Veronica.

My mother, Gladys, tells me often that Seth is a sign from God. Of course she thinks everything is a sign from God. I love her with all my heart, but she's a bit batty and drives me crazy with all her religious banter.

I believe in God's existence about as much as I believe in destiny or fate, and I've told her as much on numerous occasions. How she believes in something so intangible is beyond me. If he existed, I wouldn't be in this car right now chasing down a psycho who had raped and killed a blind girl.

I look down and see that I'm clutching my cross pendant between my finger and thumb. *When did my hand move from the dashboard?* I sigh and stuff it inside my shirt. Why I still have it and wear it daily eludes me. It's a meaningless symbol, but I can't seem to rid myself of it. It haunts me like the nightmares of my past. Like the psycho we're chasing now.

Veronica's my best friend. She has been for the past eleven years. She's a bit neurotic at times and I love her for it. She'd gladly be my better half if I were into that sort of thing but I'm not. I wish she'd move on and find someone who could return her love.

Seth slams on the brakes and I gasp as it snaps me out of my thoughts. I recover just in time to catch myself from rearranging my face with the dashboard but tweak my left wrist in the process. I shake off the twinge. Seth peels his hands off the wheel, slams the car into park, throws his seatbelt off, and is out the car door before I have a chance to take another breath.

The door thwacks shut, and it jolts me. I unbuckle my seatbelt, throw my door open wide, and let the darkness rush into me like it has the last several days. My vision darkens, my chest heaves, and I hear myself hyperventilating, but there's nothing I can do but wait it out. This seems to be my future. This is my cross to bear. My penance for surviving. The reason I wake up each morning.

All the blood is on your hands. I'm certain this one's on me.

The moment of darkness passes, and my vision returns. I pull myself from the car, step up on the curb, and push the door closed behind me. We aren't the first ones to arrive on scene. We might in fact be the last.

Dirt, rocks, weeds, and trash precede the three-foot-tall chain-link fence that surrounds the front yard of the house. The fence has seen better days; its top pipe is bent down in several places and a few sections of its chain-link are ripped open and droop down. *Frowns on sad clowns.*

The yard is comprised of dirt and weeds, with a few tufts of grass here and there. A skeleton tree looms over the left side of the house, a vampire ready to sink its teeth into its helpless victim.

The house, little more than a rundown shack, sits back on the lot about a hundred feet. Its dull yellow stucco is stained brown in several places from water damage and age, and several sections of the stucco are missing altogether. It reminds me of the marred face of a zombie from *The Walking Dead.*

The front-facing windows are missing their screens, and the glass is scarred in several places with lengths of aluminum tape that cover and bind the fissures in them. *Band-aids amongst gaping wounds.* The only thing fresh about the property is the yellow-and-black crime scene tape draped along the chain-link fence.

I walk over to the gate. It's unhinged at the bottom and is opened into the yard at an unnatural angle. Only the bolts for its latch remain. I look around, but the latch is nowhere to be found. To the right of the gate is a beat-up, gray mailbox that sits atop a metal pole rusted with age. The box is dented, and two of the four numbers on it have been lost with age, leaving only a one and a three.

Thirteen. We're on Elm Street, and the irony isn't lost on me. The day's certainly been a nightmare already and I know it's about to get worse.

Officer Dupree stands to the left of the opened gate, clipboard in hand. I lift the crime scene tape and stoop underneath it. "Morning, Officer Dupree."

He nods as he writes my name in the entry log. His eyes are red and a bit swollen. "This one's the worst I've seen." He has a daughter of his own about the same age, so his grief is understandable.

I return his nod and chart my course through the yard. Shattered concrete slabs, a semblance of what was once a sidewalk, lay before me. Weeds jut up from the cracks between and through them. I navigate the maze-like path toward the sagging porch. When I reach the porch, I turn around and take in the entire neighborhood.

Not a single yard is kept up. There are couches on curbs, washing machines and old refrigerators on what once were lawns, and trash and decay everywhere. Several cars line the street in various stages of disarray and disrepair, some of them with broken windows and flat tires, and a few stripped of their doors, fenders, and hoods.

One police cruiser sits in the driveway and another in the street to my left, behind Seth's unmarked sedan. Several people stand in their yards and others on their porches, all curious of the police activity but none bold enough to approach the outer fence.

None of them look like killers to me. Then again, anyone can be a killer given the right circumstance. I wonder if the psycho is watching right now. My skin crawls on my arms, and I rub them.

A funk I cannot quite identify permeates the air and wrinkles my nose. Perhaps it's all the trash and animal feces piled in the surrounding yards, but I can't be certain. However, I'm positive it's not the body awaiting me inside. That smell will be far worse.

I turn back toward the house and cringe, knowing full well what I'm about to walk into. The yellowish-white door stands open, its paint cracked, chipped, and peeling. Its handle hangs loose on stripped screws like a nearly severed hand. The porch roof sags nearly a foot in the middle, and I wonder if it'll give up the fight and collapse on my head when I walk underneath it.

I move forward and step up onto the concrete porch. A brown, rubber mat butts up against the small step that leads into the house. Worn, blackish-white letters spell out 'Willkommen' on its face. *German.* It reminds me of home.

I step across the mat and then up into the house. Immediately, I'm met with a heatwave of ripe odors ranging from sweat and BO to feces and urine. *How do people live this way?*

Dingy, dirt-colored carpet flows throughout the house, but there's more plywood showing through its gaping holes than actual carpet, and they're both covered in yellow, brown, and black stains left from God-only-knows-what. The filth is so thick, and the fibers are so matted that I'm uncertain of the carpet's original color or pile.

I navigate toward the back of the four-room house and that's when the pungent odor hits me like a brick to the face. I stagger from the stench, and I am forced to use the wall to guide myself down the hallway. Grime collects under my fingers as they slide along its rough, oily surface. I imagine I've left streaks along the wall, but I can't stomach the thought of looking back to confirm. Instead, I focus my mind on the task I've come here to perform.

Several officers stand at the doorway with masks over their mouths and noses. I don't blame them. I cover my nose and mouth with my shirt and my hand, but it only helps so much. My heart wrenches and my eyes tear up before I reach the bedroom.

Seth exits into the hallway just as I'm about to enter the bedroom and arm blocks me from proceeding. I look into his eyes; rage and sorrow radiate from them. Summer heat on asphalt.

"She's been dead about eight hours, and, with the excessive heat and no air conditioning, it's pretty bad." I give him the look, and he sighs. "Don't just rush in there. It's one of the worst scenes I've witnessed in a long time."

I nod with a half-smile and gently push his arm aside. He shakes his head at me, but he knows I have no choice. It's my job. I move past Seth and enter the bedroom with my eyes trained on the cracked and peeling ceiling.

Deborah, a forensics expert, gives me a nod. "We've swept the entire room and dusted every surface, but there's so much contamination in here I'm not sure we'll be able to get anything from it." Her voice is muffled through her mask.

I keep my eyes trained on Deborah, my mind still not ready to take in the scene. "Did you find anything I should know about? Anything significant?"

Deborah shakes her head and lowers her eyes. "Nothing. This guy is a ghost."

I nod. "Thank you."

She pulls rubber gloves off her hands. "Charlie walked through the scene with Detective Ryan and gathered all the shots and video. If you see anything that we missed please mark it and then send Charlie back in to photograph and log it when you're done."

"Will do." If I've learned anything in my two years as a homicide detective, it's the fact that there is always something to be found; some sort of clue. The twisted psychos that commit these crimes have a need to be understood—to be validated. Most of them want to be caught. This bastard is no different. His letter in my car proves it.

"The room's all yours, Detective. Please let the coroner know as soon as you and Detective Ryan have finished. And Detective, I wouldn't spend too much time in here. What's been done here is not good for the soul."

"Understood." I step out of Deborah's way as she moves toward me. She exits the room, and I close the door behind her. I take several moments to compose myself before taking in the scene, but I know that no amount of time will prepare me for what I'm about to see.

I lower my hand from my nose and mouth. The smell is so offensive that I gag with every breath, but I refuse to plug my nose again. I won't disrespect the victim. *Victim.* I chide myself. Victim is so impersonal given the circumstance.

All the blood is on your hands.

She has a name. *Sarah Johnson.* I force my gaze toward the tattered mattress that lies on the floor in the corner of the room, and then to her.

So young. So little. So like me.

She's lit up by police work lights. If not for the two sets of them we'd be in near darkness. No overhead light exists, and the single lamp next to the mattress lies on its side, its shade ripped, and its bulb shattered.

A lone window breaks up the wall to my left, but little light penetrates the layers of tape holding it together. Its small size and high placement fall short of current safety standards. A child would struggle to reach it or fit through it. An adult would likely get stuck.

The greenish-brown carpet doesn't match the rest of the house. It's gummed together in spots and covered in a thick layer of dust and hair. A yellow, tented marker with a black "1B" on it sits at the foot of the heavily-stained mattress, next to a mound of cigarette butts.

How long had he been here? The thought devastates me, and then I recall his words from the voicemail: *"I took my time with her."*

I walk over to the mattress, marked "2B," and every atom in my body cries out for her with an agony I've never felt before. My nails dig into my palms as I fight to hold back a torrent of tears begging to be released, but my sorrow is so deep that it quakes me to my core. I cannot stand any longer on shaky legs, so I kneel next to the mattress. Next to her.

I retrieve a pair of latex gloves from my pants pocket and struggle for several seconds putting them on. I hate wearing them, but I must follow protocol. The level of bacteria and disease carried by a dead body is significant, so gloves are a necessity. *I'm sorry, young one.*

My fingers tremble as I pull back bloodied, matted strands of blonde hair from her sunken white face. Her eyes have been removed and her nose crushed into her skull. I don't know if she suffered these wounds before or after death, but I know it's my fault. He did this to her because of me. Rage builds in my chest and tightens my throat. He will not get away with this. I won't let him.

Her deep-purple dress with tiny white flowers is covered with dried blood and ripped from sternum to pelvis, and her panties and bra have been removed. Her arms are folded across her swollen abdomen, and her legs are spread wide. It only takes a moment for me to realize that she's been positioned this way on purpose. Her arms and legs form an "A." *A for Alice.* I swallow hard. *Had anyone else noticed?*

As I examine her further, I notice several small rounded wounds that run down the inside of her left thigh. I look back at the pile of cigarette butts and understand what he used them for. As I look closer, I realize that they aren't just random burns. There are six distinct sets of wounds. A pattern. No, not just a pattern, but six letters written in braille. A message left for me to find. *A M E R C E...*

I rack my brain, but the letters hold no meaning for me. I need context around them. *What the hell are you trying to tell me you sick bastard?* I commit the letters to memory and then finish my examination. Nothing else stands out.

I move back to my left, toward her head, and settle next to her once again on my knees. Her broken face holds my gaze. *How beautiful you must've been.* How someone does something so heinous to such a beautiful little girl is beyond me. My heart aches for her and for her mother.

Something compels me to lean over and cradle her face in my hands. I've never had a compulsion such as this, and the thought of her cold, dead skin separated from mine by a thin layer of latex gives me pause. Touching her would violate every rule and protocol.

I want to rise and exit the room, but the compulsion grows stronger. There must be a reason for it, and I'm left with no choice but to obey it.

I do, and the entire room darkens around us until nothing remains but her and me. Never has this happened, and it scares the hell out of me, but there's no turning back now.

The smell of decay crawls back out of my lungs, retreats from my nostrils, and I breathe deep. I close my eyes and touch my forehead to hers, but it isn't cold and clammy as I would've expected. Instead, it is warm and soft.

My pulse slows and time itself seems to halt. My skin burns with fire and I feel a shift in myself in a way I cannot explain. It's unexpected and it startles me. I've never felt anything like it before. I open my eyes, but I can no longer see. I am blind, as she is.

A moment later, I realize that I'm no longer myself.

I *am* Sarah Johnson.

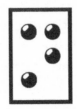

CHAPTER THREE

*I **HUDDLE IN THE** corner of my room on my mattress, scared to death of the bogeyman looming in the shadows. He visits me often and has never done anything to harm me, but tonight I sense something has changed. Tonight, he's dangerous.*

Somehow, he knows I can feel the change in him, and he moves toward me with lightning speed. I scream for my mom, but I know it's too late. He drags me from my corner by my feet and pulls me underneath him. He clamps his sweaty hand over my mouth and forces my legs apart.

"Scream again, Sarah, and I'll gut your mama too." Spittle peppers my face, and his rancid breath of pickles, garlic, and cigarettes chokes me.

I nod.

He growls at me. "You're nothing more than a birth defect that should've been aborted. A blind girl, invisible to the world. No one will even notice you're gone."

He moves his hand from my mouth to my chest, and I can finally breathe. "Please don't hurt my mom," I manage to say through waves of sobbing.

"Hush, little baby." His breath is hot on my cheek. "I'll sing a song for you tonight when your mama and I celebrate her freedom from you. She likes some good karaoke, doesn't she?"

He's a big, strong man, and he crushes me when he shifts his weight. "Don't you worry, darling, I'll show her a good time. Won't be a problem going down the rabbit hole like it was with Alice."

He grabs my mouth and squeezes my lips apart, and then he sticks his ashtray tongue between them. I reach out to fend him off, but my hands meet a rat's nest of sweaty hair and a thick scar that runs down the middle of his chest. Fear envelops me, and I become rigid. He grabs my arms, pins them underneath his legs, and then rips my dress down the front.

I cry out, knowing what's coming next.

My left cheek explodes with pain, and my head jerks to the right. "I warned you."

My groin warms as urine soaks my panties.

He breathes heavy. "You piss yourself?"

His hand grabs my crotch, and he rips my panties right off of me with a grunt. His hand returns to my face, his fingers wet with urine. I can smell it. I turn my head to the side, but he digs his fingers into my cheeks and pulls my head back straight. "You just cost your mama her life. How does that make you feel? Tell her. She's watching. She's listening."

I scream, but he silences me with a blow to the throat. I cough and choke, but I cannot breathe. I cannot move. He stuffs my urine-soaked panties into my mouth and clamps his hand over it and my nose. The acidic, ammonia taste makes me dry-heave, but I'm helpless to do anything about it.

My body jerks. My lungs burn. I fight for air. I cling to life. As long as I can. He won't relent. Light fades into darkness. I know it's over.

I don't understand. Why choose me? It's my fault. Somehow. Everything is. My fault.

Sorry. Mom. Forgive…

* * * * *

I gasp as my spirit returns to me, and I fall back onto the floor. *What the hell was that?*

My heart hammers in my chest and sweat saturates my clothes. Tears soak my face and my hair as though I've been out in the pouring rain. I am myself again, but the darkness of Sarah's world remains with me.

I peel off my latex gloves and massage my throat, the strength of his blow still fresh in my mind. Throbbing pain radiates from my left cheek and down into my jaw, making my teeth hurt. His rancid breath lingers in my nostrils, and his tattered hands still stroke my skin.

This is my fault. Your blood is on my hands, Sarah.

My head is splitting, but my vision has begun to return. The room blooms into focus, but I still cannot conjure a single explanation as to what just happened to me. I don't know if I should tell Seth about it either. I'm not sure he'd understand even if I were to. How would I even explain it to him? I cannot fathom a way.

The inside of my left wrist itches something fierce. When I start to scratch it, I notice that there's something on it. It feels sinewy like a raised scar. I hold it up to one of the floodlights so that I can get a better look at it.

I have a birthmark on the inside of my wrist that looks like a curved sickle blade resting over the top of an open eye. Usually it's a light shade of brown and smooth to the touch, but right now it's raised off my skin like a brand and has turned from light-brown to dark-red.

I'm lost as to what it might mean, if anything, so I turn my focus back to Sarah. I lean over the mattress and stroke her hair with my bare hand, the damned gloves having lost all meaning. "You're not alone, Sarah Johnson. You're not invisible, and I will never unsee you."

I curl my other hand into a fist. *And I will avenge you.*

I find my feet, stumble out of Sarah's bedroom in a daze, and lean against the wall in the hallway. Activity swarms the house like a beehive, but I pay it no attention.

Seth meets me in the hallway. "You okay?"

He tries to take my arm, but I push his hand away. "Not here."

I walk through the house and out the front door. Seth follows. The air, though not as fresh as I'd like, breathes life back into my lungs and revitalizes me.

We sit down on the edge of the porch, and Seth sweeps a few rogue strands of hair away from my face. He presses the back of his hand against my forehead. "You're burning up, Alice."

I nod and close my eyes. The heat burns straight through the back of them, all the way to the back of my skull. I squeeze them tight in hopes of generating some moisture, but all the tears I shed for Sarah have left them dry.

In my mind, I rewind the moments of the day back to our arrival on the scene. So many people had been watching from afar. Had one of them seen something? Could one of them be him? I had discounted him watching us earlier, but now I'm not so sure.

He watched Sarah for months. He wouldn't want to miss this. And, like Sarah and so many others, I think he wants to be seen. He wants to see our reactions too. *My reaction.*

I exhale and open my eyes. Seth still stares at me. "He's close, Seth. I can feel it." I look around. "Somehow, he's watching us."

Seth frowns. "How do you know the perp is male?"

I glare at him. "You really think a female would be capable of doing that to a child? Mutilating and raping her?"

His eyebrows rise, and he raises his hands. "Yeah, I see your point. All signs point to a male perp, but we're not certain she's been raped."

I know, Sarah, and I'll never forget what he did to you.

I stand, descend the two steps, and walk across the yard, my arms folded over my chest. I scan the street, the yards, and the windows of houses. Curtains covering the window on the house across from us sway a bit.

As with Sarah, I'm compelled once again to act. I don't understand what's driving me forward, but I race toward the house with urgency.

Seth follows me, his rubber-soled boots smacking the ground with each long stride. "Alice, wait up. Slow down."

I ignore Seth's request and reach the front door in a few more strides. I knock on the door but don't wait for an answer. Instead, I yell through it. "Detective Bergman, homicide. Open the door!"

I pummel the door with my fist so hard that it creaks open on the third blow. My hands tremble with rage. I draw my gun and then push the door open with the tip of my boot. I enter quickly and sweep the small living room with my gun. The room is barren, save an elderly man sitting in a wheelchair by a window to my right.

The man smiles, calmer than the situation should allow. "No need for a

24

gun, detective. I said the door was open." His voice is rough, and it prickles my skin.

Seth enters the house and pulls up next to me. "What the hell do you think you're doing?" he whispers.

I don't have time to deal with Seth, so I ignore him again. I keep my gaze on the man and lower my gun. "Are you alone?"

"Ever since my Eleanor passed." The man sucks on his lower lip for a moment and then looks right at me. Shadows streak his face. "Ten years ago today, if I remember right. Name's Russell. Didn't catch yours."

"Detective Bergman." I holster my gun and move toward him. The compulsive drive has faded, but rage still grips me and forces me to talk in short sentences. "About eight hours ago. Did you see anything? Hear anything? Anyone lurking around? The last few days? Someone you didn't recognize? Anything?"

The man chuckles but it sounds more like fits of coughing from lungs crippled by emphysema. "Darling, I'm not sure if it's the glaucoma or the cataracts that has bested my eyesight. Either way, there's not much I see too well these days. Was thinking about having a tea party. Would you like to join me, Detective? Everyone's invited, even the queen."

The queen? I growl and storm out of the house.

Seth is hot on my heels. "Alice, stop!"

I halt in the middle of the street and rage at him. "What the hell do you want me to do, Ryan?" I shake my finger at the Johnson's house. "Did you see that girl in there? Did you see Sarah?"

Seth frowns. "How did you know her name was Sarah? We didn't get an ID on her until after you went into the room."

I cross my arms, afraid if I leave them free, I might punch him. "What difference does it make how I know her name? Did you see what he put her through?"

"I did, and it sickens me." Seth grabs my shoulder, but I jerk away from him.

"Don't touch me, Ryan, not right now." My glare catches him between the eyes. Had it been a bullet, he'd be dead. "That bastard is out there right now taunting us. Laughing at us. Toying with us."

Seth rakes his head with his fingers. "I understand, but you can't storm into people's houses and shake them down. Besides, you know as well as I do that this isn't the kind of neighborhood where people willingly talk to the police. They don't trust us. They all feel like suspects."

"That's because they *are* suspects." Heat radiates from my cheeks, and my jaw is so tight that it aches. "I'll kick in every door on the block if that's what it takes to get information out of these people."

Seth sighs. "That wouldn't accomplish anything, and you know it. Besides, if you did happen to get some intel that way it wouldn't be admissible in court."

I grit my teeth. "Screw the courts. All I care about is catching this bastard before he has the chance to kill again."

"There's no way to know if he'll kill again. We have no motive or suspect yet."

"Someone does something that sick and you think they won't do it again? He took his time with her. You saw the pile of cigarettes." My face is so hot it feels sunburned.

"You need to calm down before you do something really stupid. What's gotten into you today anyway? You act as though this case is personal to you."

I glare at him. What am I supposed to say to that? *Yes, Seth, it is personal. Sarah's dead because of me. It's all my fault.*

Seth pulls back a little bit and cocks his head. The lines across his forehead deepen. "Is it? Is there something you're not telling me? Did you know this girl?"

He touches my shoulder and this time I don't pull away.

I shake my head. "No, it's nothing like that. I knew a girl when I was younger that was abused like Sarah. Thank the stars she wasn't killed."

I hate lying to Seth, but I know he wouldn't understand. How could anyone understand the things that I've seen and what I've been through? My headache rages and my head spins like a top. I need to sit down again. I return to the sedan, open the passenger door, and collapse onto the seat.

Seth opens the driver's door and slides into the seat. "You're not looking so hot. Are you feeling okay?"

"How can I be after all this?" I lean the seat back and settle into it. "Has anyone heard from Sarah's parents?"

He shakes his head. "I spoke with Officer Spalding while you were in the room with the victim. No one's heard from her mother, Yolanda Johnson, since she left work yesterday afternoon. Her father's not in the picture. Doesn't feel right, does it?"

We're taught to detach ourselves from horrific acts like what was done to Sarah, but I still hate that he calls her the victim. After my experience, I'll never be able to detach myself from Sarah; at least not until I've avenged her. I won't hold it against him though.

I stare up at the black cloth headliner. "She's dead, Seth."

"The mother?"

"Yes." I close my eyes and clutch my stomach as realization settles in. "He made her watch everything he did to Sarah."

Seth exhales with such force that his lower lip vibrates. "You said that with conviction. What makes you think that? Did you find something we'd missed?"

I recall the last moments of Sarah's life as though they are memories of my own. I still don't understand how I experienced what I did, but I don't doubt its authenticity. I didn't imagine it.

I was there. I was her. Her terror became mine. I experienced every sense that she did. I wish she hadn't been blind. If I could've seen what was happening, I'd be able to nail the bastard. "I can't explain it. I just know."

"If I've learned anything by working with you it's that I should trust your intuition. You're rarely wrong."

I push my hair back from my face and stare into Seth's mesmerizing grayish-blue eyes. Red veins fissure their whites like cracked eggshells but take nothing away from their beauty. "He's still watching. Waiting for us to make the discovery. It's part of his sick game. He must watch."

Seth scratches his head. "I'm not saying it's not true or feasible, but how?"

I bolt upright. My heart hammers so hard it quakes me. "Did anyone find a camera in the room?"

Seth's brow wrinkles. "Not that I'm aware of."

My headache rages, but I fight through it. "Was there a toy or stuffed animal close to the body?"

He tilts his head back a bit and looks to the ceiling for several moments before answering. "I don't remember, but you were in that room for a good twenty minutes. You tell me. You never miss a detail with that photogenic memory of yours."

He stares at me hard, his pupils dilated. I shrug. "I don't have a photogenic *or* a photographic memory, and, even if I did, I don't recall. Sarah drew me to her in a way I can't explain. I can tell you every detail about her. Every scar... bruise... laceration... but I just can't remember much about the room itself right now." I reach out and curl my fingers. "Something *is* there though. We just missed it."

"Are you thinking a nanny cam?" Seth drums the steering wheel with his thumbs. "Doesn't fit. They're too poor for something like that."

"Right, but I think it's something he would've placed in there." I look back at the house and my stomach wrenches. "He's been watching Sarah for some time. Weeks. Months. Maybe longer."

He sighs. "Again, you seem so sure of it."

I glare at him. "I'm *not* wrong."

He reaches over and squeezes my shoulder. "Okay. Guess we'd better get in there and take another gander."

I swing my legs out of the car and pull myself to my feet. My head pulses with pain and I become so dizzy that I cannot stand. I fall back into the car and darkness fills my vision.

Seth's around the car and by my side in a flash. His hand cradles the back of my skull. "Did you hit your head when you fell back into the car? You've got a good-sized lump going."

My teeth ache, and the left side of my tongue hurts. I can taste blood. "I'll be okay in a few minutes. I just got up too quickly and blacked out for a moment. I didn't eat breakfast."

"Yeah, heard about Bob being out."

My vision is still dark, but I don't tell him. If I did, he'd take me straight to the ER, and we don't have time for that right now. "I think you'd better go back in there without me. You know what to look for."

Seth leans in and kisses my forehead. "I'll be right back. Don't go banging on peoples' doors while I'm gone."

I smile, but I don't even know if I'm looking at him. "No guarantees." I lean back in the seat.

I hear him walk away, and I close my eyes. My chest tightens, and each breath is more ragged than the last. Sweat drips from my brow and slides down every crevice I have.

What the hell is wrong with me?

A hand gently shakes my shoulder. I startle and open my eyes to a blurred world. I blink several times, but the blurriness persists. I can just make out Seth's features. "Did you find the camera?"

"You're never wrong, Alice. I found a stuffed unicorn on a shelf in the corner of the room. I'm not sure how we missed it the first time. It was the only thing in the entire room not covered with filth.

"We found a camera shoved inside its head. More importantly, the little red light was still flashing. The tech geeks were able to enhance the signal and track it to an abandoned warehouse about three miles from here."

I massage the back of my neck with my hand. "How did they trace it so fast?"

"Fast? It's been forty-five minutes." He hands me a cold bottle of water.

I press the bottle against my forehead. "Thanks. I must've dozed off. I'm feeling much better now." I'm not, but there's no way I'm sitting any of this out. "Forty-five minutes is still fast."

"Yeah, they said something about the type of signal. Easier to trace than most because it used a unique frequency—"

I sit up in the seat. "Are we going or what? You can tell me all the geeky details on the way."

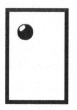

CHAPTER FOUR

SETH RUBS MY CHEEK with his thumb. "You look like hell. Are you sure you're up for this?"

I push his hand away. "I'm fine."

"You don't look fine. Your skin is flushed and you're squinting. Maybe I should get one of the officers to take you home."

I kick the underside of the dashboard. "The hell you will! There's no way I'm letting a headache stop me from going with you. I'm not missing this."

Seth raises his hands. "Okay, but if you still can't stand up when we get over there you're staying in the car. We don't know what we'll find in that place. It could be a trap."

"Fine." I'll be damned if I have to stay in the car. I'll drag myself into the building if I must.

I raise my seatback and buckle in. Seth closes my door, rounds the front of the sedan, hops into the driver's seat, and slams his door shut. He turns the key and the engine roars to life. He throws it into gear and gives it enough gas to squeal the tires and pin us against our seats as we jet forward.

I bob in the seat like a buoy as we round corners and weave through the morning traffic. My head still pulses with pain, but my vision has almost recovered. My stomach on the other hand is worse for wear, its contents sitting at the top of my throat begging to be purged.

A few minutes later, we skid to a halt in front of an old textile mill. Seth and I step out of the car, and I'm immediately thankful that I don't blackout again. Seth looks over at me, and I give him a nod. I take a deep breath to calm my frayed nerves.

The brick-and-mortar building before us is a menacing goliath, its height and breadth impressive. Six stories of brown bricks, each lined with long rectangular windows set high on each floor. Most of the windows are covered with decades of grime and a few are cracked or broken out completely. Graffiti covers several sections of its walls too, but even the graffiti's paint has become lackluster, aged many years.

A large sign hangs from the side of the crumbling building that says "Kyle's Textiles" in large, faded-out letters. The right side of the sign is broken at the top, splitting the sign so that the "iles" part hangs down at an angle.

A single smokestack rises above the six-story roofline, blackened with age. I imagine it hasn't seen action in at least five decades, long before my time. In its heyday I'm sure the building would've been a magnificent sight with its beautiful architecture and decorative millwork around its windows.

Vertical bell towers bookend the building, stanchions used to bring heavy loads to the upper floors via a hoisting mechanism. At the building's center, directly in front of us, is the mill's entrance. Three concrete stairs lead up to two massive doors, both ajar.

Six cruisers pull up next to our sedan, lights flashing and sirens blaring. I know we won't find the killer still lurking about, but why broadcast our arrival to the ends of the earth? I sigh aloud. Seth motions for them to cut their sirens off and then he draws his gun. I draw mine too.

Two medic transports pull up behind the cruisers. Within thirty seconds, everyone has assembled around Seth. "We have no idea what we might be getting into here, so everyone should proceed with the utmost precaution."

Seth and I lead the charge, approaching the parted mill doors with caution. Seth takes point and I cover him as he pushes the doors open further. They moan in protest as they swing wide, and the noise triggers a flurry of wings and a barrage of squawking. We both switch on our flashlights and move inside. Insurmountable layers of dirt, debris, and pigeon crap cover the floor, but there are no signs of human disturbance, so we move farther inside.

Seth halts and turns back to me and the others. "COMS on two, everyone. Let's fan out and cover the other floors. This is a big place, and I don't want to be here all day."

I nod and hear several clicks as everyone else sets their walkie-talkies to channel two. Mine is already set.

"Two officers per floor. Detective Bergman and I will cover this main floor. If you find something, let everyone know, and, whatever you do, don't touch anything."

The ten officers nod and move straight ahead toward the set of concrete stairs leading to the upper floors. A few moments later, Seth and I are alone. Seth moves to the left and waves me forward. I hesitate.

Something draws me to the right as a thought crawls into my mind. The killer has warned me to work alone. I doubt that's changed. "It'll go faster if we split up."

Seth turns and glares at me, but he knows I'm right. "Okay, but be careful. He could still be in here."

"I know. You be careful too." I move off to the right before he can change his mind.

Once out of sight, I click off my flashlight and holster my gun. I stop and wait several moments for my eyes to adjust to the dim light, and then I move forward through the maze of textile machinery and debris. Every fiber in this place has a story of its own, each of them sealed in the past where we cannot return. Soon, their stories will be linked to Sarah's mother as well.

Sixteen cylindrical steel kettles run the length of the building to my right. Each kettle towers many feet above my head and spreads twenty feet in diameter. A metal catwalk suspends from the ceiling and connects the kettles together, creating easy access to them.

I sense movement behind me before the deep moan reaches my ears. I whirl around and draw my gun in a single, fluid motion. Four feet away, a large, orange-and-white tomcat crouches next to one of the kettles, his hackles raised, and his tail fluffed out. A large puffed Cheeto.

I lower my gun and bend down on one knee. I extend my free hand toward the cat with my palm up. "It's okay, big guy. I won't hurt you."

The cat moans, but it creeps forward a foot and then another. That's when the realization hits me: its fur is matted with dried blood.

The cat lunges at me, and I swipe at it with my gun. My swing connects with the side of its head with more force than I intend, creating a loud crack and pop. "Ugh!" I shudder as the cat careens into the side of the kettle, drops to the floor, and lies still.

I switch on my flashlight and shine it down at the cat. Blood oozes from a gash on the side of its head and its chest isn't moving. My insides squirm with guilt, but the darn cat attacked me, not the other way around. I gather myself and continue across the mill floor.

At the back-right corner of the mill I come to a stairwell that leads to a lower level. I sweep my flashlight around the area. There are several sets of footprints in the dust leading toward and away from the stairs. Most of them are feline, but a couple of sets stand out. From the size and pattern of the imprints I estimate that they are a men's size eleven work boot.

Got you, you bastard. I take the stairs two at a time, mindful not to contaminate the prints we'll need to narrow the suspect pool. By the time I reach the bottom of the stairs I know I'm in the right place. The smells of grease, oil, and must, mixed with the ripeness of urine and feces, sting my nostrils.

I move forward and into the bowels of the engine room. Electric turbines the size of houses crowd the room and leave narrow passages between and through them. I thank the stars for my slender frame.

I snake my way through thirty yards of pipes, vents, valves, and hoses before eying an open space. As I draw near, the smell becomes overpowering. I cover my nose and mouth with my shirt as I exit from the jungle of pipes and into the open space.

Floodlights shine from each of the four corners, illuminating the entire area. I switch off my flashlight and place it back in its belt pouch. My walkie-talkie hangs from my belt and I touch it, but I'm not ready to call the others yet.

A lone metal chair sits at the center of the twenty-foot-square area, its legs bolted to the floor. A blonde-haired woman sits on the chair with her back to me. Leg irons bind her feet, its chain woven around the chair legs, and a leather strap pins her head to the chair's metal headrest.

I move around to face the woman. Parts of her face, neck, and chest are missing, chewed on and ripped from her body. The guilt of killing the cat upstairs leaves me as I exhale.

I cannot look away from the woman. Sarah's mother. Yolanda. Her eyelids are sewn open with black thread, and her tongue's been cut from her gaping mouth. Dried blood covers her chin, neck, and the front of her naked torso. I want to cover her, but I know I can't.

I turn around, not because I can't stand to look at her anymore, but because I want to see what he forced her to watch.

A monitor sits on the edge of a metal bench, situated right at her eye level. It hisses with static, its video feed dead, but I know what she witnessed. What she endured. It sickens me.

I turn back around and face Yolanda. Metal clamps secure her hands to the chair. I unclip my walkie-talkie from my belt and press down on the button to talk into it, but that's when I see it. That's when I see the piece of paper in her hand.

I release the button and hunker down next to the chair. I know I shouldn't touch anything, but my gut tells me that this note is for me. Me alone. I reach out and pry the thick paper from her hand and unfold it.

The note is written in braille once again, and I glide my finger across its pockmarked surface. It reads:

> *The Queen is red, your dress is blue*
> *Sarah's dead because of you*
>
> *Alice, oh Alice, you'll never learn*
> *To Wonderland you won't return*
>
> *White Rabbit says you're too late*
> *Another body will fill your plate*

Give up Alice, confess your sin
And you'll invoke the Cheshire's grin

Last night's pizza climbs into my throat and burns me with its acidic taste. I choke it back down, fold the note back up, and shove it into my back pocket. I stand and back away from the chair several steps.

My mind reels as I try to find a connection between Sarah and myself. Then a thought occurs to me. *What if I touch Yolanda the way I did Sarah?* The absurdity of it isn't lost on me.

I'm still uncertain about what happened with Sarah. I could be going crazy. Then again, maybe I *could* see Yolanda's experience as well. Based on her current condition she wasn't blind, so maybe I can get a glimpse of the killer through her eyes.

I retrieve a pair of latex gloves from my front pants pocket for the second time today and pull them on with a snap. My pulse races and my hands tremble. *For Sarah. For Yolanda.*

I step forward and cradle her face in my hands like I did Sarah's. I lean forward and touch my forehead to hers. Her skin is clammy but still warm, and the stench is beyond repulsive. I gag and choke on my own vomit until I can contain it no longer.

I pull back, but it's too late. Bile spews from my lips and covers Yolanda's face, neck and chest. I stagger backward, and the metal table's sharp edge bites into my lower back. "Aaagh!" I clutch my back. "Dammit!"

To my right, something clangs and clatters to the floor. I turn and see the damned tomcat on the table. His head hangs awkwardly to the right. Fresh blood drips from the left side of his jaw and pools on the table.

I unholster my gun and take aim at the little bastard. He howls and groans at me and rears back to pounce. His front paws push away from the table and I pump two rounds into his head before his hind legs uncoil. He flies backward off the table and lands on the floor with a soft thud.

I round the table and shake my finger at him. "You don't eat people!"

"Alice!" Seth's voice echoes through the engine room.

I hear footsteps approaching fast. "Over here." My voice rasps. "She's over here."

I cough and spit remnants of vomit from my mouth. I can't even imagine what Seth's gonna say when he sees what I did.

Seth enters the open area from the opposite end I'd come through, his gun drawn and ready. "I heard gunshots."

I lean against the metal table as my vision swims about the room. I close my eyes and choke back unwelcome tears. "The damned cat attacked me. *Twice*. It's been feeding on Yolanda."

"What the hell happened here? Did the cat vomit on the victim?"

I open my eyes and shake my head. My cheeks are scorching hot. "That... was me."

His voice raises an octave. "You?"

I nod. "I don't know what happened. It just came out of nowhere, and I couldn't hold it back."

Seth holsters his gun and bends over, his hands on his thighs just above his knees. "Are you okay?"

"Yeah, not sure what's going on though. I've been nauseous all morning."

His eyes widen. "You don't think—"

"I'd know if I was pregnant." The thought scares the hell out of me.

He motions at Yolanda and the fresh vomit. "What am I supposed to tell forensics about this?" He straightens and paces back and forth. "Dammit, Alice."

I stand up straight and look at him. My vision blurs again. If I didn't know it was him, I wouldn't be able to identify him. *What is wrong with me?*

I pull off my latex gloves and toss them on the table. "I know, and I'm sorry."

Seth rakes his head. "I should've insisted that you go home earlier. This is on me."

"Seth..." I want to tell him everything, but I'm in so deep that bringing him on board now would jeopardize his job and put Mother and Veronica at risk.

"What?" His voice stabs at me, and he knows it. He pulls on his hair. "Sorry, I'm just trying to work this out."

I round the table, stagger over to Seth, and grab hold of his forearm. He didn't seem to notice my lack of balance. "I'll talk to Deborah and Charlie. They'll be able to sort it out. In the meantime, we need to do some interviews. Neighbors, schoolmates, teachers. Someone must've seen something."

He peels my hand away from his arm. "Hell no. You're too close to the case and not thinking right today."

I plead with him. "Don't do this to me. I swear I'm fine."

"No you're not." His gaze is steel and his voice stern. "You've done more than enough interviewing and crime scene investigating for one day. You're going home. Officers Brex and Spalding will do the rest of the interviews and follow-ups."

I place my left hand in my back pocket and slice my finger on the edge of the folded piece of paper. I clench my jaw and curse under my breath. How could I have already forgotten it?

"You're right. I need to go home and get some rest. I'm about as stressed as I can get." I reach over and grab his right hand with mine. "I'm sorry about today. I promise I'll be myself again tomorrow."

His eyebrows rise. "It's about time you admit that you have faults."

"Trust me, I'm fully aware of them." I turn and spit on the floor. "I have a mouth that still tastes like vomit to prove it."

Seth leans over, kisses my forehead, and recoils. "Ew!" He scrubs his lips with the back of his hand. "What the hell did you get on yourself?"

There's no way I can tell him that I touched my forehead to Yolanda's, so I shrug again and lie once more. "In this place? God only knows."

A zombie moan escapes from Yolanda Johnson's parted lips, and Seth and I start.

"She's still alive?" I can't believe I'm asking. *How did I miss it?*

Seth checks Yolanda Johnson for a pulse and then grabs his walkie-talkie. "We need medical attention in the basement! We've got a live one! I repeat, we need medical in the basement!"

CHAPTER FIVE

AFTER A LONG SHOWER and an hour's rest, I find myself sitting in a chair inside my storage unit. I stare at the metal sheeting that makes up one of the unit's walls, but my thoughts are far from contemplating how they built it. Instead, my thoughts are focused on my failure as a detective.

I'm struggling with this case. With life. Everything is so difficult. How can I solve this on my own?

I'm running a marathon through quicksand, and every step I take I sink deeper. If I stop now, I'll never start again, and the thought is tempting. Let myself sink into the quicksand until it overtakes me.

But it's never that simple. Nothing ever is. At least one has died because of me, and I don't even know why. I cannot connect the dots between Sarah and myself, nor can I find a connection between her and this psycho killer.

I groan with frustration. Why I've kept all this from Seth is beyond me. He's my rock, but now I've done things that I can't come back from; things that would bring shame on him as well, and I can't do that to him. He deserves more. Someone better than me.

The badge I carry is no longer one of honor but of deceit. In a single day I've lied, cheated, and abused my authority. I've tampered with, stolen, and destroyed evidence all in the name of what? To hide my guilt?

Why have I done this to myself? How did I let this bastard crawl under my skin and compromise me with a few hollow words? He points a finger at me and I accept the guilt without question. What did I do wrong? Survive?

I can't even look Seth in the eye now without struggling for air, and it kills me. Tears wet my face, and I can imagine the godawful mess I must look like. I use the backs of my hands to wipe my eyes and cheeks, and when I pull them away, they're marred with streaks of black mascara. An image of my life. Beauty ruined.

I sigh and recline farther in my chair. Why can't I be the one to just give up? Why was I chosen to carry this burden? I'm not strong enough. I'm only one person, not an army. Why should I continue? What's the point of it all?

I know the answer, but it does nothing to ease the burden. *For Sarah. For Yolanda. For all the girls he's yet to kill.*

I shiver as though I sit naked in the snow in deep winter. I pull the hood of my jacket over the top of my head, stuff my hair into it, and draw the strings taut. When I rented out this storage unit seven years ago, I knew I'd made a great decision: a climate-controlled, interior unit. Plus, the owners ripped off Tolkien for its name: Dunharrow Storage. How could I go wrong?

This unit serves as my refuge from both the dry desert heat and Mother. It also provides a place to store the collection of letters and items left for me by the psycho who stalks me, and it's a place where I can pore over all the details I've connected to said psycho through a decade of investigation without being disturbed.

It's no paradise though. It's small, dusty, and drab, and I can hear the rodents crawling through the walls behind the sheet-metal. Also, the lighting is poor at best. I've gone through more batteries than I can remember to keep my lantern powered. However, it's still a place of my own. No one knows about it but me.

It's late, but there's no time for sleep. He's out there right now preying on some other girl. How could I sleep? I might be the only one who can stop him. The blood is on my hands, and I can't allow it to continue to flow. I cannot rest until I find him.

Papers and pictures cover my desk and fill the boxes that line the wall to my right, an array of chaos I've collected over the last decade. I've yet to make sense of any of it, but tonight I'm determined to organize it all and find a pattern.

On the way over to the storage facility I stopped at Home Depot and bought a six-foot by four-foot corkboard, a box of inch-and-a-half sheet metal screws, and a pack of thumbtacks. I rise from my chair, retrieve the small drill from its box in the corner of the room, and use it to mount the corkboard to the sheet metal wall behind my desk with six of the screws.

I step back and examine my work. The board isn't perfectly straight but will serve its purpose. I'm sure this violates my rental agreement in some way, but I really don't care.

I draw a question mark on a small piece of paper and tack it to the center of the board. It will serve as the hub for connecting everything I know about the Braille Killer—it's the name I've given him.

I rummage through the boxes on the floor and dig out an envelope dated July 17, 2009—written in my own handwriting. I unbind the envelope and pull out a piece of yellowed, card stock paper. I carefully unfold the paper and place it against the back of the envelope. There are no ink or graphite marks anywhere on the paper. Instead, it's written in braille, and, based on the accuracy and spacing of the raised letters, I believe a braille typewriter produced it. Unfortunately, that kind of typewriter is quite easy to obtain and virtually untraceable.

I stare at the paper for several moments. My heart races just as it did the day I received it. My stomach curls in knots and lurches as I slowly glide my finger over the paper's raised bumps. Gooseflesh covers my skin as the words come to life in my mind:

She is dead because of you
And my heart's been set afire
If you confess, it will do
It's all that I require

You claim it was an accident
But we both know the truth

You're so far from innocent
Your survival is the proof

You've nothing more to fear
Unless you cannot see
The path has been made clear
A map to help find me

I shudder. Why am I to blame for her death? *Because she was in love with me?* It's not my fault, but it doesn't stop the guilt from strangling me. I close my eyes and take a deep breath, but all I see is Sarah's broken body. I clench my fist and push the guilt back into its cage where it belongs.

I open my eyes, reach into the envelope again, and pull out a photograph of a girl named Denise Chavez. In the photograph Denise is splayed on the floor, face-up. Her head is turned sideways at a grotesque angle, her neck broken. A pool of blood surrounds her head and shoulders like a crimson bridal veil—a stark contrast to the surrounding white porcelain tile.

Her scream pierces my ears again like it did that day, a short outburst before a sickening *crack* and *thud*. I wince and stutter backward to my desk and lean against it. *It was an accident.* I force myself to break free of this endless cycle of guilt and stare at the photograph.

Denise is wearing a pair of tight blue jeans with holes in the thighs and knees, and a white, short-sleeved blouse with a V-neck. Rings in various shapes, colors, and sizes adorn several of her long, slender fingers. A thin silver necklace wraps her neck, its puzzle-piece-shaped pendant lying in the pool of blood next to her. The silver pendant has a heart embossed on its center.

I turn the photograph over. It has a date embedded in its lower right corner: 2008/07/17 4:14pm. *Ten years ago today.*

I pin the letter and photograph to the top-left corner of the corkboard with a pushpin. It's a start to the puzzle I've yet to solve. The need to sit and brood over the clue nearly overwhelms me, but I force myself to push it aside. I need to see the entire picture. Complete the puzzle.

I return to the boxes, find the envelope marked July 17, 2010, and pull it out. I unbind the envelope and squeeze it open. A silver necklace slides out and nearly hits the floor before I hook its chain on my finger. I lift it up and let it dangle in front of my face. The puzzle-piece pendant twists back and forth several times before settling. I look between it and the picture on the corkboard and confirm that it's the same necklace.

Every time I see these items, my mind cycles over the same thoughts and questions the same things: had he been there that day and removed it from her then, or did he remove it from her later?

He must've been there. Who else would've taken the photograph?

Nothing ever changes and nothing new arises, but I must follow the ritual. I obsess over them for several minutes, but I cannot break their cryptic code.

I push the necklace over my wrist and then take the accompanying piece of folded paper out of the envelope. The letters are the same each time: raised braille lettering on yellowed, card stock paper without a single mark of ink or graphite. I read the letter again with my finger:

You took her from me; she wasn't yours to take
You're a cheater and a liar, nothing but a fake

Alice of Wonderland, you cannot be
Blinded by words, you will never see

Scratch the surface and take a peek
To find what isn't yours to keep

All the clues, they lead to me
Confess your sin and be set free

I pin the letter to the corkboard, next to the first letter, and then I hang the necklace from the pushpin. I move back over to the boxes and busy myself finding the third envelope before I have a chance to contemplate the two clues. A minute later, I hold an unbound envelope in my hand marked July 17, 2011.

I remove the contents from the envelope: a folded piece of paper and a newspaper clipping about Denise's death. I set the envelope on the desk with the others and hold the newspaper clipping up to the light.

I read the article aloud, thinking it might help me catch something I've overlooked when I've read it in the past. "Denise Chavez, a 19-year-old female, plunges sixteen feet to her death outside of her therapist's office. The police have ruled it an accident, but some are wondering if she jumped from the banister. Dr. David Strong, Denise's therapist, would not comment on the matter, citing doctor-patient privilege. The only other witness at the scene was a blind girl. Denise, a ward of the state, has no known relatives, associates, or friends. Her remains will be cremated at the Valdez Funeral Home on Tuesday, July 23, 2008."

I set the clipping down on the desk and sigh. *Nothing new.* I unfold the accompanying paper and drag my finger across the words:

> *Two years have passed and not a single peep*
> *You're more helpless than Little Bo's lost sheep*
>
> *Blind as a mouse, is there anything you see*
> *I've left all the clues that will lead you to me*
>
> *No accident threw the princess off the wall*
> *So don't pretend you didn't cause her fall*
>
> *Just admit that you have sinned*
> *And all of this will come to an end*

Frustrated, I grab a pushpin and stab it through the two papers and into the corkboard next to the last one. Its end catches my thumbnail and drives underneath it. "Ouch!" Blood seeps from under my nail and drips on the floor before I can get my thumb to my mouth. I suck on my thumb for a solid minute before the throbbing pain subsides.

I want to punch the wall, but past experiences remind me of how that will turn out. Instead, I find the fourth envelope marked July 17, 2012 and rip it open. All its contents spill onto the floor, so I discard it on the floor as well. I bend over and pick up the folded piece of paper and high school photograph.

The large photograph has North Highlands HS 2008 Senior Class embossed on it in gold lettering across its bottom. There are seventy of us in the picture. I've counted numerous times. We're standing in front of and on top of a set of aluminum bleachers out by the football field. I'm in the picture on the bottom left, standing on the grass. I'm not quite facing forward, and I'm not looking toward the camera either. It's a typical picture of me. On the second row, two people to my left, is Denise. She's facing forward, but her eyes are angled toward me. A heart's been drawn around her and me with fire-engine-red lipstick. I want to rip it up, but instead I pin it to the corkboard next to the other items.

I unfold the paper. The uniform braille lettering flows underneath my finger like water from a faucet, but the words are anything but refreshing:

Two little lovebirds standing on a field
One gives ground but the other won't yield

Why must you continue to pretend
That you didn't kill your lover friend

You couldn't handle forbidden love
So you made that final shove

Admit it, Alice, her blood you spilled
And when you do, I'll be so thrilled

Like Hansel and Gretel, you'll get yours too
Just follow the crumbs I've left for you

I pin the paper above the class photo on the corkboard. How long had Denise been in love with me? She never said a word to me. I didn't even know who she was until the day she died. She was as invisible to me as I was to everyone else, save Veronica.

Had Veronica kept it from me? She can be the jealous type.

Speaking of Veronica, it's been several days since I've heard from her and it worries me a little. We talk almost every day or at least message each other. I take my cell phone out of my pocket. The display reads 02:14. I've got zero bars. I always forget that I have no service when I'm holed up in my storage unit.

Veronica works graveyard shifts, so there's no point in calling her now. I slide my phone back into my pocket and eye the boxes against the wall. Papers and envelopes still spill from them. *Have I even made a dent?*

My stomach rumbles. It scares me how often I forget to eat. Even worse, my throat is parched. I can't remember the last drink I had other than the bottle of water Seth gave me yesterday morning.

Time for some Slice 'N Drive. It's the perfect stop for late night pizza. You roll up to it like an ATM machine, select your toppings, and get hot and fresh slices in one minute. My mouth is watering already.

I pull off my jacket, exit my storage unit, and lock up. I take the elevator down to the first floor and walk twenty paces along the dark corridor before the lights finally flick on. The motion sensors work about as well as the security cameras dangling from the ceiling.

Outside, my sedan is the only car left in the parking lot and sits beneath the single functioning light. I head toward my car and halt just beyond the loading zone awning, half-way between the building and it. The interior light is on. The hairs on my nape rise with my pulse. I'm certain it wasn't on when I arrived.

I draw my gun and flashlight and approach the car with caution. The rear passenger door is ajar. Each heartbeat crashes in my ears like thunder as I lean forward and peer inside the window.

CHAPTER SIX

MY HAND TREMBLES AS I pocket my flashlight and yank the car door open. A traitorous seatbelt buckle lies across the doorjamb. "Stupid seatbelt." It must've caught in the door when I grabbed the Home Depot bag earlier. I holster my gun, move the buckle out of the way, slam the door shut, and climb into the driver's seat.

Fifteen minutes later, I'm back in my storage unit scarfing down two slices of pepperoni pizza and guzzling a 44oz Mountain Dew. Normally, my storage unit would be the last place I'd choose to eat food, given the present company of mice, spiders, and roaches. However, I can't afford to waste more time. There can't be another Sarah.

I pop the last bite of crust in my mouth, throw the garbage in one of the Home Depot bags, and start rummaging through boxes again until I find the envelope marked July 17, 2013. I unbind it and open it up. It contains just a single piece of yellowed, card stock paper; it's the letter and the clue.

Unlike the other nine letters I've received, this one's printed on letterhead from Blackwell's Asylum and Home for Children, an orphanage abandoned in 2012. I broke into the orphanage right after I received the letter and found a vault of records hidden in the subbasement of the building. Some of them dated back all the way to the late eighteenth century. Among them I found a record for Denise Chavez from 1990. Her mother was a drug addict and prostitute who died in childbirth. Her father was unknown.

The braille on this paper is a bit harder to read visually because many of the words are typed through the letterhead. I glide my finger across the small bumps:

> *Death for a birth?*
> *Such a tragedy*
> *But death for sight?*
> *Yet you still can't see*
>
> *While one girl lives*
> *The other lies dead*
> *A killer she's made*
> *Her hands stained red*
>
> *Admit your guilt*
> *For the things I've seen*
> *No more waiting*
> *It's time you come clean*

I pin the letter to the corkboard and then retrieve the envelope marked July 17, 2014 from one of the boxes. Inside the envelope is another letter and a plastic baggie with a crushed fortune cookie inside it. I unfold the letter and scan it with my finger:

> *If you crack it open*
> *To see what's inside*
> *You might just find*
> *It has nothing to hide*
>
> *If I crack you open*
> *What would I find?*
> *A liar, a traitor*

A girl who is blind

I stick the letter up on the corkboard and then unzip the baggie. I fish out the rectangular piece of paper from the bottom of the bag and look at the fortune. It says: *"Murder is a passion of the heart. I know how passionate you are."* I turn it over and read the back: *"Lucky Numbers: 1 37 45 62 89"*

Every time I look at these items and letters my frustration skyrockets. Ten years and I've yet to crack his twisted codes. I often wonder if there's anything to be found in them. I shove the piece of paper back in the baggie, seal it, and pin it to the corkboard.

I sit down for a few minutes and rub my eyes. With every passing hour I find my vision blurrier, and thoughts of going blind paralyze my mind. The last thing I want is to live in darkness again. If I do, I don't think I'll ever find him.

But he'll find me.

I want to give up and go home, but that would serve his purpose and not Sarah's. Not mine. I must see this through. I must get organized.

I retrieve the envelope marked July 17, 2015. Inside is a swatch of red fabric with tiny yellow roses. The swatch is scented with a perfume I've come to identify solely with Denise. Its fragrance has faded over the last few years, but the smell will never fade from my memory. It will forever haunt me.

I unfold the accompanying letter and read it with my finger:

A swatch and a scent
Both beyond compare
She wore it and rubbed it
All through her hair

She spent hours getting ready
Yet you never knew
A beautiful young woman
She did it for you

But you're an evil little brat
So twisted and trite
You threw her over the banister
Just out of spite

You deserve to be punished
But I have a heart
Just tell me you're sorry
And make a new start

I don't think it's possible to understand the mind of a psycho. How does one equate love with lust and torture? And how does an accident become more than just that? I cannot add reason to the unreasonable. I'm not sure why I ever try to.

I put the letter and swatch up on the corkboard and retrieve the next envelope. July 17, 2016—package number eight. I don't need to open the envelope to know what's inside. Just thinking of it leaves me cold and nauseous. It's part of the puzzle and I know it must go up on the board, but I'm not sure I can stomach seeing it every time I walk into this storage unit. I'd rather see a thousand grisly images than it.

Reluctantly, I pull up the two metal fasteners and open the envelope. I carefully pull out the folded piece of paper, making sure that the photograph stays inside for now. I unfold it and stare at the words. I don't need my finger to read the braille, but I can't help doing it anyway.

I close my eyes and let the words sink into my mind as my finger glides across the paper:

I've tasted of your fruit
And you're rotten to the core
You'll spread your legs for anyone
You're a dirty little whore

She gave you her love

And you cast it aside
If I opened you up
I'd find nothing inside

You were a bad apple
Right from the start
A hollowed-out cavity
You're missing your heart

For once in your life
Stop telling the lie
And if you refuse
Another will die

Don't make me beg
Don't spoil your chance
Confess to me now
Before the end of our dance

My throat tightens and tears well in my eyes. Angry tears. "You did this to me, you son of a bitch. I didn't ask for any of it."

I shove my hand into the envelope and pull out the photograph before I change my mind. However, I'm not ready to look at it, so I turn it upside down. I stare at the date embedded in its lower right corner: 2008/04/18 9:34pm.

My breathing turns ragged and I tremble. No amount of therapy will ever rid me of the hate, anger, and shame that this photograph conjures in me. I was so young, innocent, and vulnerable. How did they single me out when I was supposed to be invisible? What the hell did I ever do to them?

I set the envelope and paper down on the desk and sit down in my chair. I turn the photograph over in my hand and stare at it. Not really at it but through it. If I were Superman, I'd use my heat vision to burn it up. Or at least I'd have his strength to endure its content.

I focus on the photograph as best I can with my diminishing vision. I was only sixteen when it was taken. An innocent young girl. I'd never kissed another person other than my mother before. That day they stole things from me that I'll never recover.

My hands shake with rage and several tears splatter across the photograph. It takes every ounce of my willpower to keep from ripping the damned thing to shreds. I take a deep breath, wipe my eyes, and focus on the details.

In the photograph I'm lying on my back on an unfamiliar bed, completely naked. Denise lies next to me on her side, also nude. She's pressed up against me, straddling my right leg and spooning my side. Her right hand is planted firmly on my crotch. My right breast is covered by her arm, but my left breast is cupped in her left hand, my erect nipple pinched between her thumb and forefinger.

Denise is smiling at the camera, her tongue resting on the corner of my open mouth. My eyes are rolled back in my head, and my face glistens with tears.

Did she somehow think I enjoyed this?

It isn't visible in the photograph, but they'd tied my hands behind my back and forced my legs apart. I fought them hard, but there are only so many punches one can take to the gut and groin before giving in. My threshold was twenty-seven. I'm not sure how I held out that long. Perhaps adrenaline from the sheer terror that consumed me.

The photograph blurs further as rivulets flow from my eyes again. I need a break from my past. I need some fresh air. I need a cigarette and I don't even smoke. I've only tried smoking a cigarette once in my life. Maybe I should try again.

I get up, pin the letter and the photograph to the corkboard, and remove my jacket. I switch off the lantern, roll the storage unit door up just enough to slip underneath it, and then shut and lock it. I take the elevator down two floors and exit to the right.

At the end of the corridor I step through double-doors and into the night. The warm air hits me like a gale. The smell of sagebrush tickles my nose, and there's nothing refreshing about it. I hate summers in the desert. There's often no reprieve from the heat.

Within a few minutes my armpits are sopping wet. Sweat drips down my nape and runs between my breasts as well. I fan myself with my top, hoping to generate some kind of breeze, but the attempt fails magnificently.

I walk beyond the concrete-and-steel awning that stretches across the front of the building and take my cell phone out of my pocket. 03:28. I've got full bars, but still no messages.

I can't help but wonder what happened with the interviews. Seth usually keeps me in the loop and I feel a bit agitated that he hasn't. Then again, I've cut him completely out of what I'm doing. How hypocritical am I?

I contemplate calling Seth, but I'm not sure what I'd say to him right now. I just want to hear his voice. Instead, I shove my phone back into my pocket and pull my hands up into my armpits like I always do when I need comfort.

Unfortunately, the wetness of them leaves me wanting to gag. I pull my hands away and wipe them on my pants. Winter can't come soon enough.

I walk back to the building's entrance and the automatic doors slide apart. A rush of arctic air blows my hair back and I lean into it, but it only lasts a moment before the outside air suffocates me again.

I walk back inside the building and toward the set of elevators at the far end of the corridor. I hear the doors close behind me with a whoosh and it sends chills up my spine. I stop and look back, but there's no one behind me.

I find my reaction to the doors a bit odd, but it's been a terrible and strange day. Then, just as I'm about to move on, I glimpse a man standing in the corridor to my right. He stands about three yards away from me, next to an open storage unit on the left, and is side-lit by a set of dysfunctional, overhead lights.

I glance his way, and he smiles at me, but it's not the kind of smile a female wants to receive, especially when she's alone. It's more of a snarl, the left side of his lip drawn up a bit. He undresses me with his dirty eyes.

His orangish-brown overalls look as though they've missed laundry day for an entire decade, and the left side is undone and hangs down his front. He isn't wearing a shirt, and tufts of brown hair poke out the sides and top of the overalls. He's a tad on the chubby side, but his arms are well defined.

His puts his finger in his mouth and digs around between crooked teeth. The thought of where his finger's been does nothing for my full stomach, but I can't make myself turn and walk away. He's frozen me with fear—fear of turning my back to him.

He pulls something long and stringy out of his mouth with his finger and thumb, tilts his head as he examines it, and then puts it back into his mouth. He chews on it a bit and then swallows with a loud gulp.

This is why I shouldn't be here at four in the morning.

My feet dance with the urge to run, but I just stand there, a captive to this man and his disgustingness. He doesn't speak or move toward me, but his gaze moves to my chest. He smiles again.

I think there's something wrong with his face, but I can't quite tell. Perhaps it's the shadows playing tricks on my eyes, but I can't be certain, especially with my blurred vision.

He reaches into his overalls pocket, pulls out a pack of cigarettes, and pounds the bottom of it until a cigarette slides partway out of the torn top. He lifts the box to his mouth, wraps his lips around the end of the cigarette, and pulls the box away.

He tosses the empty box into the open storage unit and then takes a lighter from another of his pockets. He lifts the lighter up to the end of the cigarette and, with a couple flicks of his thumb, it bursts to life with a two-inch, blue-and-yellow flame.

The flame lights up his entire face, revealing the true horror of what he is. I fight to conceal a gasp as my heart thrums in my ears. Scars cover his face like moon craters, and the only thing that comes to mind is Freddy Krueger from *A Nightmare on Elm Street*. Had he been wearing a green and red striped sweater I would've seriously freaked. Even so, I've been reminded of those movies twice in one day and I can't help but wonder if it's not a coincidence.

I swallow my fear and head toward the elevators before I find myself frozen there for eternity. I look back twice, but he's not pursuing me. I reach the elevator and press the button repeatedly, annoyed that it didn't open on the first press.

Gooseflesh crawls on my nape and I tremble. I can feel him approaching, even though he moves like a ninja. I twist around, gun drawn, but I'm all alone. The elevator dings behind me and I cry out, nearly squeezing off a round into the ceiling.

I turn back toward the elevator. It stands open and empty in front of me, but I can't move forward. For the third time today, I am compelled to act without reason—a feeling deep within that forces me forward down a path I might not have chosen. Alas, I cannot deny that there's something more to the man. Something disturbing. *I must confront him.*

I lower my gun, but keep it drawn as I make my way back over to the side corridor where he stood. I come around the corner, both hands on my gun, but the corridor is empty. Dim lights flicker overhead, and all the units are locked down tight, including the unit he had open—109.

I dash toward the end of the corridor and pull up just before moving into the intersecting corridor. I swing wide as I sweep my gun left and then right, but the corridor is empty. Further down and to the right I hear the familiar whoosh of the front doors.

I bolt down the corridor, round the corner, and nearly kill myself when I collide with a long-bed hand-truck. Its metal edge catches the tops of my shins and I fly forward face-first like Superman onto its wooden-planked surface. The impact knocks the air from my lungs and my gun from my hands. My gun skids down the corridor and comes to a stop underneath a tan, rubber-soled boot. To make matters worse, an orangish-brown cuff hangs down over that rubber-soled boot.

Dammit!

Bursting shards of pain in my shins fight me like a pack of half-skinned cats, and I cannot fathom moving a single inch at the moment. I squeeze my eyes tight to try and manage the pain, but it makes no difference.

When I open my eyes again my gun is gone and so is the rubber-soled boot. I roll over on my back and he's standing over me, that twisted grin from before plastered on his face. My gun is in his hand and he has it pointed at my chest. Of all the ways I've imagined dying this isn't one of them.

I give him my best scowl. "What the hell are you waiting for?"

He cocks his head, ejects the cartridge, clears the chamber, flips the gun around, and offers it back to me. "Too many accidents. Wouldn't want to be the next one." His deep southern drawl spins my head.

I reach up and take my gun back. I don't understand what the hell's going on, and my mind has gone blank.

"Something's got you all riled up now, hasn't it? You look more spooked than a fraidy cat on Halloween. Something's done stole your voice." He looks down at my legs. "How about them shins of yours? Pants are done soaked through with blood."

I wave him off with my hand. "Give me some room."

He takes a few steps back, his arms raised. "Hey, I'm only here to help, little miss. If you don't need it, I'll be on my way."

I sit up and look at my pants. He wasn't lying, they're wet with blood. My shins throb with every beat of my heart. I try to raise my right pantleg to assess the damage, but it's already stuck to my leg. I wince.

He bends down and looks me straight in the eye. "Need help getting somewhere? I'm quite a bit stronger than I look."

His gray eyes fluctuate in and out of focus, and I sense another blackout coming on. *God, not right now.* The entire room starts to spin, and the lights become so bright that they feel like they're stabbing the backs of my eyes.

I'm more stubborn than Mother's ranting of God, so I pull myself to my feet. I stagger forward, lose my balance, and he grabs me by the arm. I go to pull away, but the floor's no longer under my feet. Darkness swirls at the corners of my vision and there's nothing I can do but close my eyes.

I feel his arms holding me, one under my back and one under my knees. The smell of cigarettes on his clothing is enough to get a nicotine fix, and it makes my head spin even harder. I don't trust him, but I'm in too much pain and far too dizzy to even contemplate where I might wake up or if I ever will.

"Three. Four. Seven," I say.

"That I can do." His breath smells of garlic and pickles, and alarm bells ring in my head, but I can't remember why.

My body sways back and forth in his arms as he lumbers through the corridor. A few moments later, I hear the ding of the elevator and then the doors sliding open. He steps inside, I hear the doors shut, and then we rock a bit as the elevator begins its ascent to what I surmise will be the third floor.

Again, we rock as the elevator grinds to a halt. It dings once more, and the doors slide open. He lumbers forward, and I direct him to the left. Thirty seconds later we come to a stop.

"Three forty-seven," he says.

The world is still dark around me and my head spins like a top. I'm not sure how much more I can take before my head explodes.

"Put me down." He obliges, and I steady myself against the wall. "I think I can manage from here."

"You sure? I can get that door open for you no problem."

"No." I say it with so much force it nearly knocks me back a step. "Sorry, I'm just not myself today. Like I said though, I can manage."

"Don't you worry yourself one bit, little miss. I've got a body or two hidden away myself if you know what I mean." He chuckles, but my skin crawls.

I turn away from him and toward the lock on my storage unit door. "Thank you. Have a good night."

"You're welcome, little miss. Best you watch where you're going next time. Accidents can be a nasty little thing. Suppose you know all about that though, don't you?"

I think his comment is a dig at me, but my head's spinning too much to even contemplate it. I can't think of a way to respond, so I don't. Instead, I fumble with the lock. Luckily for me the numbers are in braille, so I don't have to see what I'm doing.

From the corner of my eye I can just make out that he's walking away, but my head is throbbing so much that I don't even hear his feet hit the floor. I slide to the concrete floor and lean against the steel roller door.

I hear the ding of the elevator, and then his voice echoes in the corridor. "Sweet dreams, *Alice*."

CHAPTER SEVEN

HE'S AFTER ME. HE'S *always after me. No matter how far I go I cannot escape him. I've run so long that my lungs are on fire and my chest heaves like bellows stoking the fire.*

He's a demon lurking in the shadows, his sulfuric breath billowing out around him like a poisonous cloud. Every drag from his cigarette lights the dark with its cycloptic red eye, winking hatred and promising pain.

Down the alley I fly, a streak of fear wailing like a lone siren in the dead of night. The noise attracts him, but I can silence myself no more than I can stop breathing. His attack is inevitable, his wings pounding the air like a galloping horse.

He's nearly upon me, so I tense to lessen the blow. Never did I imagine the force of tightening my muscles would lock my legs so completely, but it does, and I careen face-first onto the asphalt.

The palms of my hands shred like grated cheese as I slide several feet. Bits of rock, glass, and debris cut into my cheeks, my nose, and my forehead. The crack of splintering bone reverberates in my skull and my nose explodes with pain so intense that I can't even scream.

By the time I flip over he's upon me, his weight crushing me into the ground. His razor-sharp talons slice through my clothes and dig deep into my flesh. Rivulets of blood run down my nasal cavity and into the back of my throat, pooling there and choking me with their coppery taste.

I gag and cough, but something keeps me from turning my head to the side. It's in that moment I notice he's wearing a bomb vest. Its countdown timer has just reached the end and it beeps incessantly.

The heat hits me before the flash or sound of the blast.

* * * * *

I snort, cough, and kick my legs but the devil is gone. Darkness surrounds me, and I can't remember where I am, but then the lights above me click a few times and come back to life. My head throbs, and the fluorescent lights don't help one bit.

Somehow, I've managed to wedge my head between the wall and my storage unit door. *Explains why I couldn't turn my head.* I push myself out of the corner and manage to sit up. My neck is beyond stiff, and the left side has a crick in it that I fear may never work itself out, but I dig my thumb into it anyway.

My phone's alarm blares from within my pocket, piercing my ears with every beep. I take my phone out to turn off the alarm and check the time, but the screen's impossible to read. I look down the corridor and then up at the ceiling. Everything's blurrier than I remember.

On top of it all, my shins hurt like hell. I draw my knees toward my chest and pull my pant cuffs up to inspect the damage. A crusted, bloody line runs perpendicular on each shin. Well, more like a crevice than a line. Black, purple, and blue bruises spread outward from each wound a good three inches.

Then the night hits me once more: Tan, rubber-soled boots. Cigarettes. A pockmarked face. A stranger who knew my name. *Did I tell it to him?* Right now my memory is about as good as stilts made of wet noodles.

"My gun." My voice sounds like a frog giving its last croak before being dropped into a pot of boiling water. "He handled my gun... but so did I." I pray that I can salvage even a partial print.

I pull myself to my feet and use the storage unit door to steady myself. An urgency grows within me. I need to go through the rest of the evidence

I've collected before Seth and I review the forensic and coroner's reports. I need to be fresh on the facts so that I miss nothing.

I drag myself over to the elevator, take it to the first floor when it arrives, and head toward the front of the building. I exit and move out past the awning. It's still ninety degrees. I don't think this heat wave will ever end.

I dial Seth on my phone and he answers on the second ring.

He groans. "Do you know what time it is?"

I've clearly woken him, and it makes me feel a bit good. I'm such an evil person sometimes. "No, but if I were to guess I'd say about six forty."

"To the second. I've been in bed for about twenty-three minutes now." He yawns. "Sorry... what do you need?"

I pace an area about two yards wide. "Did you find anything else after you dropped me off at the department yesterday? You never called."

"I did call. Twice. Left you two messages. Went by your house too." He pauses for a moment. "Where the hell have you been? Your mother said you never went home last night."

"I'm sorry, Seth. I stayed over at Veronica's. I haven't been feeling well since yesterday. My head's killing me. I haven't had a migraine like this in a long time. I should've let you know."

"You should've let your mother know. She was beside herself with worry after I showed up looking for you."

Damn. I pull my hair out of my face, but the light breeze blows it right back where I moved it from. "Look, I'll let you get back to sleep, but I just wanted to tell you that I won't be in today. Gonna try and sleep this thing off. Just call me when the reports are in."

"Fine. Say hello to Veronica for me."

"Will do. Love ya."

A long silence hangs on the line, far greater than the physical distance between us. He chuckles. "Love ya back."

I roll my eyes. "Jerk."

I end the call and text Veronica to make sure that she'll corroborate my story if asked. Then I pull up Mother's number and stare at it. *Am I really in the mood to deal with her? No.* I lock my phone and slide it back in my pocket.

Coyotes yip in the distance. It's my cue to head back inside. I do, and the cold air swarms me once again when the doors slide open. It chills the sweat on the nape of my neck and under my arms. I'm in heaven for several moments.

I return to my unit, unlock the door and lift it open, and then close it behind me. I slide the inside locking bar into place. I installed it myself so that no one can disturb me while I'm here.

My shins ache and remind me that they need attention. I reach inside my bottom-left desk drawer and retrieve the first aid kit. Thankfully, I'm prepared for just about anything with all the supplies in my storage unit.

I pull out a bottle of hydrogen peroxide and a package of cotton balls from the kit and clean my wounds with them. The peroxide bubbles violently for almost a minute. God only knows the things that hand-truck has hauled. I can't allow myself to think about it. I finish cleaning the wounds and return the supplies and the kit to the drawer.

I sit down on my chair and study the corkboard hanging on the wall. The contents of eight envelopes are pinned across its top. At its center is the piece of paper with a question mark. I grab a pen off the desk and jot down everything I know about him underneath the question mark:

FACTS ABOUT THE BRAILLE KILLER:
1. Scarred chest
2. Hairy
3. Smokes cigarettes
4. Likes pickles and garlic—or garlic pickles
5. Friend or relative of Denise Chavez
6. Knows braille
7. Hates blind girls - calls them abominations

The only item of significance I see in the list is his relationship to Denise. How could he be so close to her and still be a ghost? Everything I dug up about her failed to lead me to him. What else do I have to go on? *Unit 109.*

My pulse races as I scribble down things I know about him:

FACTS ABOUT UNIT 109 OWNER:

1. Badly scarred face

2. Smokes cigarettes

3. Breath smells of garlic and pickles

4. Southern drawl

5. Crooked teeth

6. Wears tan, rubber-soled boots

7. Orangish-brown overalls

8. No shirt, hairy chest

9. Has storage unit on first floor - 109

10. Knew my name

I step back and eye the board again. Many things match between the two lists and no item in one list excludes the other. Number ten on the second list shakes me to my core. How would the man from unit 109 know my name unless he's the Braille Killer?

He wouldn't.

I sit back down on my chair and let the weight of the revelation settle. There are numerous storage facilities in town, and he just so happens to pick the one that I use? It isn't a coincidence. *The bastard is fearless.*

I check the time on my phone and it's 07:24. It's too early for the storage office to be open, so I dig into the boxes lined up against the back wall again. I find and pull out the envelope marked July 17, 2017. The familiar, handwritten, calligraphic 'A' is centered on its front.

I turn the envelope over and unbind it. I lift the flap and shake its contents out onto the desk: a letter and a friendship bracelet. I reach over and grab the sack sitting next to the desk. It's one I brought in with me last night.

In the sack is the envelope that was left in my car yesterday morning. I snatch it out of the bag and quickly unbind and open it. I pull out the red-and-brown friendship bracelet and compare it with the black-and-tan one from the previous envelope. The size and pattern of the weave are identical. Intricate. Meticulous. Hand-made. They're like silk between my fingers.

He took his time making these. Why? What do they symbolize? My mind is a wasteland of lost thoughts.

I set the bracelets down on the desk and pick up the letter from 2017. I unfold it and stare at the blurry braille letters until my eyes begin to cross. Unfortunately the words never focus. I close my eyes, take a deep breath, and read it with the tip of my finger:

With sight reborn
A friend is lost
But you didn't mourn
So what's the cost?

An eye for an eye
Or something more?
Should the innocent die
For a sinful whore?

Follow the path
And meet my demands
Or suffer my wrath
It's all in your hands

It's your curtain call
I've told you what to do
Will you take the fall?
The ending's up to you

I open my eyes. Everything's laid out right there on the page in plain English. Sarah Johnson's blood covers my hands. Had I solved these stupid riddles and tracked him down years ago she'd still be alive. I might as well have killed her myself. In the back of my mind lives a demon who tells me as much. *You're one heartless bitch, Alice.*

My hands are shaking so bad that I'm afraid I'll rip or crumble the letter if I hold it any longer. I set it on the desk and double over in my chair, my stomach riling with a guilt I'll never outlive.

I cover my face with my hands and tears soak them. However, in my mind they're covered with Sarah's blood. I wipe them on my shirt and stain my shirt crimson.

I scream so violently that the entire building trembles on its foundation. Not literally, but I imagine my scream can be heard across the third floor. Perhaps even the second. I don't care who hears me. I just want to purge my guilt and pain. I want to take down this bastard before he kills again.

I sit up, wipe my eyes, and grab a tissue from the box on the back left corner of my desk. I blow so hard into the tissue that I'm surprised when I find no gray matter amongst the strings of snot within its folds.

My eyes sting and I rub them. It reminds me that he removed Sarah's eyes. I can't fathom why he would remove them. A trophy perhaps? Or maybe he eats them. The thought does nothing for my appetite.

Enough of this.

I take the two friendship bracelets and letters and pin them to the top of the corkboard alongside the other eight letters and items. He waited ten years before his first kill. But why?

My heart stops and my breath catches. Is Sarah really his first victim or just the first he wanted me to see? The notion unsettles me. "My God..." *Are there nine more Sarahs out there butchered in my name?*

I cannot shake the thought from my mind, but I won't allow it to paralyze me either. I was just as much a victim as Sarah was. I grit my teeth. I'm better than this, and I'm stronger than he knows. I just need to solve the clues he's left me.

What I really need is someone to share the burden with. I know why I couldn't confide in Seth or Veronica from the start, but he's changed the rules, hasn't he? He brought the police into it, not me. After what I did yesterday, I can't bring Seth into it now. I've overstepped boundaries.

"But Veronica..." Would she understand? Would she be able to handle the weight of it? She's a strong woman like me, but she's never been exposed to the horrific things I've seen.

One thing is certain: Mother would never understand. As much as I love her, I cannot confide in her — in anything. When I have in the past it's always come back to bite me in the ass. What she knows, Father Rogallo knows. She keeps nothing from him, and he has no qualms confronting me about anything she's told him. Mother, her priest, and her God will never know.

I grab one of the boxes off the floor and set it in my chair. It still contains several items I've collected over the last decade. As I pull each item out, I pin it to the corkboard underneath Denise's picture.

Some of those items include: a handful of newspaper clippings about her death, the police and coroner's reports on her, and Dr. Strong's testimony on what he witnessed when he came out of his office after she died.

Then there's the notes on the queries I conducted after her death, including her place of work and friends. I can't help but chuckle when I think about the absurdity of it. I posed as a journalist to get information about her life and I was only sixteen. Why anyone talked to me about her is beyond me. Perhaps it helped them cope with her passing. Either way, I'll never know.

Emptied, I toss the box on the floor by the door. I grab another box and set it in my chair. The only thing left in it is my old diary. I take it out, toss the box over by the other discarded box, and sit down.

It's been several years since I've cracked it open. Its beige leather cover is without blemish, and the embossed gold lettering on the bottom right corner still proudly bears my name: Alice Marie Bergman.

A single piece of leather woven through a golden buckle holds the book closed. I unbuckle it and open it to the first page. The top of the page has a date scrawled in red ink: Sunday, July 20, 2008.

So many thoughts circled in my head that day and the three days prior. Seeing for the first time should've been the most exciting thing to ever happen to me, but guilt and shame and anger overwhelmed me. Mother thought it would be good for me to write down the things I was feeling and going through so she bought me the diary. It was one of the few things she suggested that actually helped me cope.

I read the first entry:

After sixteen years my eyes have finally been opened but

thoughts of what they did to me erode my joy even as I write this. It's been three days since Denise's death, and my life will never be the same again.

The nightmares cease to haunt me, but I can still feel his curly chest hair wrapped around and between my fingers when I close my eyes at night. And the thick, knotted scar that splits his chest down the middle like a living Frankenstein will remain with me forever.

I will hunt him until my last breath if I must. He will not win. I won't let him.

My throat tightens, and I feel empowered by the words as they churn in my mind. At sixteen I knew my life's mission, yet I forget it so often. I cannot allow myself to forget it again.

I flip to the last entry in the diary and my heart is already aching before I've laid eyes on it. I know the words too well. They haunt me still.

In black ink at the top of the page: Sunday, July 17, 2016.

It's a single entry:

why did they do this to me? Why show me now? I never needed to see it. I didn't need proof that it happened. I lived through it.

Dammit! I wish I was blind again.

A large inkblot follows the entry. I remember breaking my pen in half that day. I'm tempted to break the pen sitting on the desk, but I know it will do little good. He's left a body. There must be evidence.

One thing's clear: I need to get into unit 109 and soon.

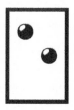

CHAPTER EIGHT

THE OFFICE WINDOWS OF Dunharrow Storage are dark, but I knock on the glass anyway. I wait several minutes even though I know no one's inside. There never is. I knock again, wait another minute, and am satisfied that I'm alone.

I traverse the corridor, hang a right at the first offshoot, and stop in front of unit 109 on my left. The overhead lights flicker like oversized fireflies, and three of the four bulbs in the fixture above me are blackened and dim.

Multiple cameras monitor the long corridor at twenty-foot intervals, but they're all pointed straight at the floor and dangle from their wires. My instincts tell me that I should just walk away from the unit but that's just not who I am. I have a job to finish no matter the cost. *For Sarah.*

The unit is padlocked, but the lock isn't engaged. It could be my lucky day, or it might be a trap, but I'm not in the mood to call it in and wait for backup to arrive just to find out that the storage unit is empty. Besides, I have no logical way of explaining why I'm here, and I sure as hell can't tell them the truth.

My vision is blurry, so I wipe my eyes with my shoulders, but it makes no difference. I should've fetched a stronger pair of glasses before coming down here. There's no time for it now.

I pull my shirtsleeve down over my hand, remove the lock, and set it on the floor. I disengage the slide bar, bend down, and lift the rollup door. It's stiff at first and the wheels shriek with protest.

The noise is alarming, and I almost freeze, but I realize there's no point in stopping now. If anyone's heard the noise, they've chosen to ignore it. By the time I raise the door to my waist it quietly rolls the rest of the way up on its own.

The worthless corridor lights fail to penetrate the veil of darkness that shrouds the unit, and my clouded vision only compounds the issue. I unclip my flashlight from my belt and switch it on. Dark fabric hangs from the ceiling like blackout curtains, concealing the contents of the unit from prying eyes.

I draw my gun and switch off the safety. My heart races but my hands are steady. I'm built for this. I take a deep breath and probe the fabric with the end of my flashlight. Toward the far right side I find a split between its layers.

I don't know what to expect behind these curtains and my gut says it will be certain death, but I move forward anyway, slipping through the opening with my flashlight and gun leading the way. Once beyond the curtains it's nothing like what I expected.

The unit is wider and much deeper than mine, a ten-foot by twenty-foot behemoth. The walls, ceiling, and floors are painted black, but they're much more than that. It's hard for me to be certain because everything is so blurry, but it looks like every surface is covered with depictions of constellations and planets. It's both mesmerizing and disorienting and I feel like I'm floating through space.

I holster my gun and drift toward the back of the storage unit as I take it all in, but then my gaze locks onto the full-length mirror propped up against the far back wall. Like a tractor beam, it pulls me toward it. Its beauty is so profound that I'm lost for words.

I stand before the mirror, so close my nose nearly touches it. I'd miss all the detail if I were to stand back farther. Its four-inch-wide frame is like nothing I've ever seen before. A network of thick vines and leaves the size of my hand comprises it, but its golden, reflective sheen defies all logic and captivates me.

Were it not for its reflectiveness I would've guessed it to be carved from some kind of wood. However, I've never seen any wood like it before. It produces a faint odor of cedar and pine with a pungent twinge of mildew and seawater.

I trace the frame with my flashlight beam. Randomly placed symbols are carved into the frame all around the mirror. Some of them I cannot decipher but many I know: a leaf, a claw, a flame, a gust of air, a water droplet, a sun, a mountain, an optical triangle, an eye, a heart, a lightning bolt, a metal bolt or screw, a sundial, a scroll, a book.

My beam illuminates the lower right corner of the frame. "Auh!" My gaze locks onto the familiar symbol and I drop to my knees. I draw nearer and compare the birthmark on the inside of my left wrist to the symbol. It's an exact match: the curved sickle blade over the top of an open eye.

Awestruck, my mind explodes with questions: Why is this mirror here? Where did it come from? What do the symbols mean? Why do I have this birthmark and why is it on the frame? What does it have to do with me and the Braille Killer?

I cannot fathom the answers, but I must know. I stare at my blurred reflection until my eyes burn. *Who am I?* I have no answer, but I don't think I've ever known. I've been lost to this obsession for the last decade.

I reach out and touch the mirror. Its surface is hot, but not in a way like anything I've ever experienced. Its heat crawls beneath my skin and into my veins like liquid sunshine and courses through my body. I cannot pull my hand away, and I don't want to.

Feelings I don't understand awaken and stir inside me like a maelstrom. My heart flutters, and a longing for something or somewhere that I cannot grasp fills me until I erupt with emotions. I quake and sob and laugh simultaneously. I cannot put these feelings into words or even thoughts because they're so foreign to me. All I know is that something beckons me and I'm desperate to know its source.

I got so caught up in the moment that I didn't realize I'd closed my eyes. When I open them again, my gaze doesn't meet my reflection. Instead, I'm staring into an unfamiliar bedroom. I gasp and my heart stops.

Everything is perfectly clear through the mirror. I look behind me and confirm that the storage unit is still a blurred mess. I turn back to the mirror.

A young girl, perhaps thirteen or fourteen, sits on a daybed in the corner of the room. Her pale, flawless skin reminds me of a porcelain doll, and her long brunette hair is pulled back into a single braid and rests over the front of her right shoulder. A red bow is tied around its end.

Silver hoop earrings, each with four ball-shaped beads, dangle from her petite, rounded ears. The edges of her mouth are curved up slightly, and her pink lips glisten with lip-gloss. High, softly pronounced cheekbones and a narrow chin with a dimple at its center complete her v-shaped face. By any standard she's beautiful.

She holds an open book in her lap. Her eyes are closed, but her left finger sweeps the book's page with fervor. My throat tightens. *She's reading braille.*

Her smile broadens, and she laughs with such joy. Her laughter fills my ears and my throat tightens further. How is this possible? How can I see or hear this girl through the mirror?

I knock on the solid surface that separates her world from mine. "Hello? Can you hear me?"

She doesn't respond or show any signs that she's heard me, so I say it again, louder. She flips the page and reads on, oblivious to my beckons.

My legs tingle and ache when I move them. They've fallen asleep. *How long have I been watching her?* I shake my legs for a minute to get blood flowing in them again and then move to get up, but that's when her eyes open.

She turns and stares directly at me with her cloudy, brown-eyed gaze. "Even though you're as silent as the stars I can feel you." She cocks her head and her forehead wrinkles. "But you're not like him, are you?" She smiles, and the aura around her brightens. "You must be some kind of angel. How do I know?" Her expression turns grim. "Because he's the devil."

Another voice comes through the mirror. "Priscilla, dinner is ready. Stop playing with your imaginary friends and come downstairs."

Priscilla smiles again, but it fades. "I hope it's you who visits me tonight and not him. He scares me, and I don't know what he wants from me." She sets her book aside and slides off the side of the bed. "Bye for now."

She moves beyond the mirror's limited view and I'm left panting like a dog in the summer heat. I lower my hand from the mirror and Priscilla's room fades to darkness and then back to my blurred reflection. The intense heat coursing through me dissipates as well, leaving me chilled once more.

I take my phone out of my pocket and check the time. 17:14. I rise from the floor and head toward the front of the storage unit. Just as I'm about to part the thick fabric I hear footsteps approaching in the corridor. They stop abruptly just on the other side of the curtains.

I slow my breathing, pocket my phone, and click off the flashlight as quietly as I can. I clip the flashlight to my belt, draw my gun, and back up until my back is against the wall. Then I move into the small opening between the rollup door rail and the front wall.

The fabric parts, and a head pokes through the narrow opening. The flickering corridor lights bounce off the bald scalp like a mirrored disco ball. *It's not the man from earlier, so who the hell is it?* I squeeze tighter to the corner.

Something spindly skitters across my nape and left shoulder and it takes everything I have to keep from shooting out of the corner in some sort of African dance move.

"Mr. Hallard? You in here? George?" The bald man steps through the curtains and into the unit.

The fabric falls back into place behind the man and brings darkness to the unit once again. It takes several moments for my eyes to adjust to the dark, but I can still hear him.

The man turns and looks directly at me. The arteries in my neck leap several inches with every beat of my hammering heart, and I can hear nothing above its deafening drumming. I hold my breath, fearing he might not only hear me but smell my dragon breath.

The man reaches out and nearly grabs my chest as he probes the wall. I shift my gaze to the wall and see the light switch he's searching for. His fingers find the box first and then the rectangular stub protruding from it. He turns his attention back to the unit as he flips the switch.

Several lights down the center of the unit click, buzz, and then come to life. The purple glow of blacklights surprises me, but then the room comes to life in a whole new way and I'm left dumbfounded. The imagery on the floors, walls, and ceiling glow like the astral bodies they represent and seem to pull away from the surfaces that they are painted on.

I can't fathom the hours someone spent painting this place with such painstaking detail. However, the way they laid everything out strikes me as odd. I'm certainly no astronomer, but I should be able to discern something as iconic as the big dipper at a minimum, yet none of it is familiar.

The man grunts and takes a few steps forward. I exhale softly and take another breath, and that's when the dust begins to tickle the hairs in my nostrils. I wrinkle my nose and scrunch my face, but the urge to sneeze only grows. I holster my gun and wipe my nose with the back of my hand, but it makes no difference.

Finally, the man walks deeper into the unit, so I decide to take the opportunity to slip out of the corner and through the folds of fabric. To my chagrin, several things manifest from this decision. I manage to brush the light switch with my arm and flip it to the off position. Then I cannot hold my sneeze back any longer and nearly punch a hole in the side of my head when I jerk it sideways and right into the track of the metal rollup door.

The ruckus I've caused by the sneeze, the switch, and the blow to the head stuns me almost as much as it does the bald man. When I do manage to pull myself from the corner and move to escape from the unit, I get myself hung up in the folds of fabric and nearly rip the whole damned thing down, bar and all, as I struggle to free myself from its clutches.

"Who's there?" barks the bald man. "No sense pretending you ain't."

I stop struggling and the fabric loosens its grip on me. I step back into the unit and flip the switch back on. The lights buzz with life again and cast their purple hue throughout the unit. The bald man still stands several paces away and makes no attempt to close the distance.

My cheeks burn with fire and I wonder if they're glowing red under the blacklights. I raise my hand and tilt it to the side. "Hello."

The man crosses his arms over the top of his plump belly. "Who are you, and what in God's creation were you doing standing in the corner?"

"I'm sorry, sir." I move toward the man and stop about two feet from him. I stick out my right hand, my left ready to draw my gun at a moment's notice. "Detective Bergman. You are?"

The man eyes my hand for several moments before finally deciding to accept it. He unfolds his arms. "Bill." His hand swallows mine by sheer girth, not because he has long fingers. "Bill Braggard."

His hand is cold and clammy, and he gives mine the dead fish shake. Why people feel the need to do that is beyond me. It's creepy and a bit gross.

I take my hand back and casually wipe it on my jeans while I engage him in conversation. "This your unit, Bill?"

He glances around a bit and grimaces before answering. "No, ma'am. Talent went into these walls. You think I got that kind of talent?"

I shrug. "I don't know anything about you, Bill, so I'm not sure I can make a determination like that yet."

"Pfft. You summed me up as soon as I stepped through those curtains." He reaches down and jangles the ring of keys hanging from his belt, eying my holstered gun nervously. "What kind of detective are you?"

"Homicide."

His eyes widen a bit, and he cranes his head back. "Homicide... you looking for something specific? Did something go down here I should know about? I manage the place."

Manager. I smile to myself. *Guess it's my lucky day after all.* "Not sure yet, Bill. I'm looking for George Hallard. You know him?"

"I know most of the regulars around here. George has been renting this unit for what... seven years now?"

Seven years? My pulse races. "Know how I can find him? Does he have an address on file or something?" I can hear the desperation in my own voice, so I take a deep breath. The last thing I want is to call it in. "A phone number would be just as good."

"Bergman... Bergman..." He taps a plump finger on his lower lip. "You have a unit in the building as well, correct?"

"I do."

"Third floor if memory serves me."

"Yessir, that's right." I turn and walk toward the front of the unit. "Can we get back to Mr. Hallard? You'd be doing me a huge favor." I stop, turn my head, and offer him my best smile. "I don't forget favors, Bill." The sexiness in my voice creeps me out knowing its target.

Bill grabs his keys and swallows hard. "A favor? But I'd need a warrant."

I move in on my prey and stroke his cheek with my thumb. "I understand, but those things take time. I don't have that kind of time." I lower my hand and nibble the corner of my lower lip. "I guess you don't want me to be indebted to you, do you?"

His cheeks flush red. "I do. I'll get you what you want." He hurries forward, brushes past me, and parts the sections of fabric so that I can easily make my way out.

"Thank you, Bill." I touch his shoulder as I exit the unit and wait patiently while he switches off the interior lights.

He pushes through the folds of fabric like a birthing calf, his brow glistening with beads of sweat. Thankfully, he knows what deodorant is and the smell is almost pleasant.

Bill reaches up, grabs the thick fabric strap hanging from the bottom of the rollup door, and pulls it all the way to the ground with one big tug. It's actually quite impressive. It never takes me less than two or three tugs to get my unit's door all the way down.

He shoves the slide bar home, picks the lock up off the floor, and places its end through the eyehole. However, he doesn't close the lock. He smiles at me and I frown.

"George never locks the unit. Says he keeps it open in case someone wants a peek. I do have to say it's pretty eye-catching. Should offer paid tours or something."

"No doubt there. And that mirror…" I shake my head.

"Mirror?" Bill guffaws. "That old thing ain't even worth the plywood it's mounted to. Don't know why he keeps it in there. Certain no one will ever attempt to steal it though."

Plywood? I probe deeper. "You don't like the frame?"

The lines in his forehead deepen and his entire scalp creeps forward. "Are we talking about the same mirror? The one at the back of the unit?"

I bob my head. "Was there another?"

He tilts his head and then his eyes widen. "Oh, I see. You're jerking my chain."

I turn and stare at the door as though it will turn transparent when my x-ray vision kicks in. Alas, it does not. What I don't understand is what the hell I saw in there.

Bill saunters down the corridor and takes a left at the end. "You coming, Detective?"

I reel my eyes back inside my head and chase down Bill. By the time I round the corner he's standing at his office door, rummaging through the mass of keys on his keyring. I pull up next to him.

He scratches his head and lifts the keyring in front of his face. "I know it's one of these. Not sure why they all have to look the same."

I notice there's a blue sticker placed just above the office door handle. One of the keys on Bill's keyring has a sleeve over its top that matches the blue of the sticker. Being a detective and having deduction skills like no other person on the planet I surmise that it's probably the key he's looking for.

My spine prickles. *Is he stalling?* What purpose would it serve? *Is he in league with George?* I can't see it. Everything the Braille Killer does is planned out. Meticulous. Bill is none of that. Pushed hard enough, I think he'd crack. Not the kind of guy one would rely on.

I shake off the notion and point out the suspect key. "How about that one there?"

He eyes the key for such a long time that I wonder if he's transitioned into a waking coma. Finally, he grunts and nods at the key. "Suppose it could be the one."

I am completely dumbfounded. I can do nothing but shake my head. He's a perfect example of the rapid deterioration of society as a whole.

Bill slides the key into the lock and it magically turns, unlocking the door. He turns to me and smiles. "I guess you really are a good detective."

Within a matter of ten seconds he's managed to leave me dumbfounded twice. It must be some kind of record. "The keys are color-coded, Bill."

He looks at the ring of keys. "Probably, but I'm color blind."

Color blind? Now I feel terrible. "Sorry."

We step into the office and I'm inundated with the smell of Funyuns and old pizza. I stagger back a step, ill-prepared for the sudden trip back to college. Empty soda cans are stacked on the desk in columns, several of them reaching the ten-foot ceiling. Discarded candy wrappers litter the floor like confetti. I literally have to shuffle my feet so that I don't have to judge the distance to the floor through the piled mess.

"Sorry about this." He shuffles through the trash like walking through snowdrifts. "Won't lie, this is a bit embarrassing. Don't usually have guests in here."

I hold my tongue because the words that come to mind would do me no favors and I still need his help. Instead, I wrap my arms around myself and pray that the health risk of standing in this pile of filth is worthwhile. Either way, I'm in need of a sterilization scrub down.

Bill moves farther into the office and disappears into a back room. "Things aren't quite organized in here, so it might be a bit before I find Mr. Hallard's information."

Given the state of the front office, this revelation shocks me to my core. "My time is in your hands, Bill."

I take my phone out of my pocket and squint at the display. 17:58. A single signal bar. Nine missed calls, four from Seth and five from Mother. Seventeen text messages from Veronica and Seth, and six voicemails.

Mother's number comes up first in my contact list. I sigh and press call. I can only imagine the barrage of guilt she'll lay on me when she picks up. Five rings later it goes to her voicemail. My entire body relaxes. *She must be at work.*

I wait until I'm prompted to leave a message. I take a deep breath. "Hello, Mother. Heard you were looking for me. Sorry I didn't leave you a note. I've been working a case all night. Should be home tonight. If not, I'll call. Love you."

I press end, dial into my voicemail, and skip through the first five messages, all of them from Mother. The last message is from Seth. I press one and listen:

"Alice where the hell are you? I stopped by Veronica's apartment and you weren't there." He pauses for a few moments and sighs loudly. *"It took a lot of coercion, but Veronica finally told me that you were never there last night. Where are you, Alice? Are you okay? What's going on with you? Call me back when you get this."*

I press end on my phone and exhale. I don't blame Veronica for cracking. Seth's very good at his job. So good that I'd give anything to bring him in on all this. I wish I could've right from the start of our relationship. I put my life in his hands daily. How could I not trust him with this?

I know the answer, but it has nothing to do with trust. His help isn't worth losing everyone I love. There's more to it than just that though. A single picture that now hangs on the wall of my storage unit shames me and forces me to keep this secret to myself. An image of an innocent girl who couldn't fight back.

I'm not her anymore.

It's not the fact that I'm naked in the picture that shames me. It's not that I'm with another girl or that she's touching me places no one ever had before. I'm not into girls and would never willingly participate in something like that, but that isn't it either. It's the fact that I was powerless to stop it.

Now, I feel the same way about Sarah. I had ten years to stop him before he took Sarah's life. Her blood will always be on my hands. I cannot allow him to take the life of another girl next July 17.

He will not win.

Bill grunts like a hog, and his flatulence echoes from the back office like a foghorn. A deep brown fog, I'm certain. I can't help but snort.

I retreat a few steps and lean against the doorframe of the outer office. I'm certain it's crawling with germs, but the thought of touching any other surface in the entire office riddles me with nausea.

I scroll through my seventeen text messages while I await Bill's search into uncharted territories. Several of them are Veronica responding to the text I sent her early this morning:

Wednesday, July 18, 2018

06:48

Anyone asks, I stayed with you last night. :A

07:12

V: roger roger where u at girl?

07:29

V: u been dissin me last several dayz wassup?

10:47

V: we need ta rap bestie miss u buzz when u can

12:14

V: crap crap crap! boytoy at da door!

12:48

V: folded bestie sorry! hope ur ok

14:15

V: no joke u gotta bring me up ta speed

14:16

V: cant handle bein outa da loop

Veronica has been my best friend for twelve years, and I need her more than ever. I send her a quick response:

18:12

I'll bring you in on everything soon. Promise. :A

Veronica responds almost immediately:

18:13

V: thank god ur alive!

V: u better!

18:14

V: got uglies lined up if u dont!

Uglies. I can't help but smile. It's one of the few jokes between us that never gets old. I skip reading Seth's messages and pocket my phone. My attention no longer occupied, I notice that the back office is eerily quiet.

I move toward the back office, traversing the debris. My feet slide across the papers and wrappers; it's like walking on ice. "Bill, are you still with us?"

I hear a snort and then a cough. I reach the doorway and peer into the back office. The state of it is far worse than that of the front office. Stacks of papers, books, and boxes rise from the floor like skyscrapers, filling most of the room. I can't tell how far back the room extends because there are so many stacks.

Two pathways disappear into the paper city. I take the first and it leads me back around to a cot and portable television. I reverse my steps and take the second path. It leads to a small desk at the back of the office. Bill sits in the undersized chair behind the desk, and the side of his head rests on the desk's edge.

I kick the side of the desk with my boot. Bill startles, gasps, and sits straight up. He raises his arms and looks up at me with deer eyes.

I glare at him. "What the hell, Bill?"

He rubs his eyes and nose with his hand. "Doc says it's narcolepsy. So sorry about that. Got a bit too comfy."

I shake my head. "I saw the cot. Are you living here?"

He pops up from his chair like a jack-in-the-box and grabs my hand before I have a chance to retreat. "Please, Detective, don't say anything. They don't pay me much, and I've got nowhere else to go."

Tears well in his eyes and I don't know what to say to him. I look down at his fat, sausage-fingered hand wrapped around mine like a greasy taco shell from an open-all-night fish taco stand and all I can think about is the germs and where that hand has been. To compound matters, I see that his fly is wide open, and his yellowish-white skivvies are hanging out.

I focus my gaze back on his face and the five-o'clock shadow that's several days old. Then to the pea-sized mole trapped between the right-side of his nose and his cheek. Then to his eyes once more: small, hunter-green irises and beady little pupils against a canvas of pink with red veins.

I cannot pull my hand away from his. Not because he's made it physically impossible but because if I were to pull it away, I'd risk him breaking down into a blubbering mess of tears and snot and never giving me the help I came for. So, I bite my lip and place my other hand over the top of his.

Unfortunately, I didn't foresee what would happen next. Who could've? In the blink of an eye, Bill pulls me close with his sausage nubs and plants his dried-out, cracked lips on mine.

I can't recall how long I stood there lip-locked to a scruffy blowfish before regaining my composure and dignity. I pull away and slap him right across the face. It smacks loud like a cap gun, and Bill staggers backward. His hand shoots to his fire-engine-red cheek and he just stands there in shock, his eyes wider than I thought physically possible.

"What the hell was that?" I stock toward him and he retreats behind his chair.

"I thought we were having a moment." He bites his lower lip. "Weren't we?"

I thrust my arms in the air. "A moment? Are you being serious right now? There's no chance you and I will *ever* have a moment. What's wrong with you?"

Bill holds his breath and his chest convulses. His entire body quakes and bubbles of snot expand out of his nostrils. He grabs his head and screams so loud that I retreat several steps. He grabs the back of his chair, hoists it above his head, and throws it against the wall behind him. I jump with the crash and my hand shoots over to my holstered gun.

Bill drops to his knees and beats the side of his head with his fist. "You're stupid, Bill. Stupid, stupid, stupid."

I bend down but keep my distance. "You're not stupid."

He stops and looks up at me, his eyes even more bloodshot than before. "Mother passed a few months back. She was my entire world. I don't know what to do. How am I supposed to go on, Detective?"

Snot hangs in his scruff and tears shine on his cheeks. "How can I pretend everything is okay when all I want to do is die? My heart is in a thousand pieces and there's nothing anyone can do or say to bring her back. Why did she leave me? What did I do to drive her away? Is God punishing me,

Detective? Am I that bad of a person that he took my mother from me?"

God.

Why do I find myself caught-up in matters of a pretend deity on so many occasions? I look down at my chest and stew in a brew of my own making. My traitorous fingers have latched onto my cross pendant once again. I'm like a junkie, always seeking it for a fix, but it does nothing for me.

God.

I'm at a loss as to where to go with this, so I close my eyes for a moment and conjure Mother's holier-than-thou religious spirit.

"God works in mysterious ways, Bill. Perhaps he's testing you to see if you're worthy of what he has planned for you. Had you thought of that?" I can't believe the garbage I'm spewing, but Bill seems to be eating it up like a spoon-fed baby.

Bill wipes his face and eyes and cocks his head. "Testing? For what?"

"To help me, Bill." I eye my pendant again. "Help me stop a rapist and murderer."

He frowns and holds his chin. "Are you saying that God killed my mother so that I'd help you?"

"Didn't he? Would you have been here today if she were still alive?"

Bill slowly shakes his head and his eyes light up with understanding. "Guess not. I only ever worked evenings before she died. God *does* work in mysterious ways…"

I can't believe my illogical logic is working, but who am I to say what should or shouldn't work? I stand. "Exactly. I need your help, Bill. Do you know Mr. Hallard's address or not?"

Bill pulls himself to his feet and rummages through a stack of papers on his desk. "He paid cash when he first rented here, but we require an address on the lease form. No exceptions."

"And you have the form?"

Bill picks up a piece of paper and cocks his head. "Curious."

"Can I see that?"

He hands me the paper. It's a lease form for George Hallard as far as I can tell, but with my blurred vision and such bad handwriting I can't make out the address. I should've grabbed a pair of glasses from the box marked "glasses" in my storage unit. I've got more than a hundred pairs, each with a differing prescription.

I hand it back. "Can you write that address down for me?"

"Sure." He grabs a piece of paper and tries to scribble down the address, but his pen doesn't work. He tries several others without luck. He grunts and hands the lease form back to me. "Return it to me as soon as you can."

"Thanks, Bill." I turn to leave.

"Detective?"

I sigh and turn back. "Yes, Bill?"

He crosses his arms. "You don't care to know what's curious about it?"

I shove the piece of paper into my pocket. "Shoot it to me straight, Bill. What is so curious about his lease form?"

"He paid for seven years upfront."

"Seven years? That is a bit curious. I doubt many people do that."

Bill nods. "Yeah, that alone *is* curious, but what's more so is that his lease is up today."

I choke on my own spit and lurch into a coughing fit. My vision goes dark for a moment and the next Bill's pounding my back with his palm. I raise my hand, and he stops pounding, but not before he's dislodged the fillings in my molars.

I cough several more times and manage to sputter "I need some water" between them. Bill is a jackrabbit in his own environment and has a cold bottle of water for me in less than fifteen seconds flat. I don't know where he produced it from, and there's no way I'm gonna ask. He twists off the lid and hands it to me.

I take a few swallows, catch my breath, and then down the rest of it in three big gulps. I can feel a pocket of air trapped deep in my throat, so I push it out with a large belch.

"Yeah!" Bill raises his hand up and I oblige him with a high five. I couldn't leave him hanging with all he's been through.

I hand him the empty bottle. "Thanks, Bill."

He tosses it on the floor, and I shake my head. *Could've done that myself.*

He shrugs and smiles. "I'll work on cleaning this place up tomorrow. Next time you're in here you won't recognize the place."

Next time? There's no chance in hell of that happening. I nod, turn around, and do my best to traverse the treacherous terrain through the back and front offices without killing myself in the process. When I reach the corridor, I can't shake this niggling thought that I've missed something.

I head straight back to unit 109 again and the door is rolled up. Nausea rears its head in the pit of my stomach. I grab fistfuls of black fabric and yank as hard as I can. The fabric rips in a few spots and then the entire ensemble comes crashing down, steel bar and all. The sound is deafening. I retreat just in time to escape the bar crushing my head.

My ears ring and my heart hammers. I draw my gun and flip the light switch on, but it doesn't help my blurred vision. The shapeless shadows are as still as death, and I can't make out any details beyond ten feet.

I'm confident I'm alone, but jangling keys and pattering feet approach. "Alice are you okay?"

It's Bill. Sounds like he's out of breath. The noise probably frightened him as much as it did me. He rounds the corner to my left and I proceed into the unit and toward the back. Several steps in and my heart crashes to the floor just like the steel bar.

The mirror's gone!

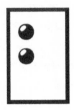

CHAPTER NINE

I SIT IN MY sedan two doors down and across the street from 12136 Mockingbird Park Dr., the home of George Hallard. The clock on the center console reads 20:12, but the numbers are already starting to blur. Two hours ago, these glasses worked perfectly. It won't be long before I need a stronger prescription.

I know nothing about George Hallard, but my gut says that he's the bastard responsible for Sarah Johnson's death. I don't believe in coincidences, especially when they begin piling up. He's racked up too many for me to ignore. He rented a storage unit in the same facility as mine right around the same time I did. He paid cash in advance for a seven-year lease. He knew my name. He left his unit open so that I'd see the mirror and Priscilla.

It can't be coincidental. *George Hallard must be the Braille Killer.*

I desperately want to call Seth for backup, but how could I possibly explain what led me here? "Hey, Seth. Met this creepy guy at the storage facility I've never told you about. He left his unit unlocked. I trespassed, saw a mirror and a vision of a blind girl in her room in it, and tracked down the address of the owner. Want to come find out if I'm insane or not?"

I'm in so deep down this path of deception that there's no turning back now. I should've run a background check on George, but I didn't want to lose the element of surprise and have him get away. I fear this might be my only chance to nab him before he kills again. If it's him.

The thought of being blind again leaves me cold.

I don't want to live in a world of shadows again, but I'm starting to learn that just about everything in my life is beyond my control. I am nothing more than a pawn in some game of chess, made to move ever forward despite knowing my end is fast approaching.

I push those thoughts to the back of my mind and focus on the double cheese Happy Burger in my hands. I melt into my seat a little further with each bite. Never has one of their burgers tasted so good. Then again, I've had nothing to eat in the last eighteen hours.

At this point, anything would probably taste like the world's greatest food. Well, probably not Bob's Chinese Food or Game Time Pizza with the cardboard crust and rubber cheese, but just about anything else.

I wash down my last bite of burger with a long swig from my strawberry milkshake. It's so thick that my brain's in danger of getting sucked through the straw instead of it, and I wouldn't want it any other way. I reach into the bag on the passenger seat, grab a handful of fries, and then a car pulls into the driveway at the Hallard residence.

I drop the fries back in the bag and brush off my fingers and hands with a napkin. Recycled materials sound great in theory but are pretty worthless in reality. I toss the wadded napkin in the seat and finish wiping my hands on my jeans. I unholster my gun, eject the magazine and verify that it's fully loaded, and slide it back in.

I holster my gun, take a deep breath, and exit the car. I sprint across the street, sticking to the shadows as much as possible, and approach the house. A four-foot-high red brick retaining wall hugs the raised yard and works against me. I can't see the parked car, the walkway, or the front door.

Across the street, a man jogs my direction with his dog, a beautiful mastiff. He doesn't even glance my way, but his dog does. I wonder if the dog knows something is about to go down. If so, he doesn't seem to want to get involved. When they pass by, I can almost make out the lyrics to the music the man's listening to because he's got it turned up so loud.

Half a block up on my side of the street is an elderly woman. She's heading in the same direction as I am, scooting her walker down the sidewalk at a snail's pace. I can almost feel the vibrations of the aluminum legs with each scrape. The noise wears on my already frayed nerves.

Atop the retaining wall at the front of the yard is a three-foot-high, white, iron fence with squared lances across its top. A stairway with four stairs splits the raised yard and climbs up into it. White, iron handrails flank the stairs.

A thought in the back of my mind keeps niggling at me. In all the time I've spent trying to figure out this stalker-turned-killer, I never once pictured him living in an upscale neighborhood like this or in such a nice house.

The yard is perfectly manicured. Through Sarah's memory I remember his broken nails cutting into my skin. A man so unkempt couldn't possibly live here, could he? It doesn't fit his profile.

I proceed up the stairs with caution. My right hand rests on my gun, ready to draw it in a moment's notice. If he does turn out to be the Braille Killer, I'm not sure what I'll do. I can't think that far ahead right now.

No one lurks in the shadows in the yard, and no one peers through the windows. A single window is lit to the right of the front door, but all the other windows at the front of the two-story home are dark.

The front door sits about six feet back from the front of the house, squeezed between what I imagine are the living and dining rooms. The roof extends over the open area, creating a dark alcove ripe for monsters. The overhead light is off, leaving only the doorbell to light the darkness.

I reach for the doorbell button and my phone buzzes in my pocket, sending my pulse racing and me gasping for air. *Get a grip, Alice.*

I breathe deep and push the button. A melody of chimes sounds deep in the house and I wait. Around me, the world ages decades. I reach to press the button again, but then the overhead light turns on. A lock turns, then another, and then a chain falls, knocking on the doorframe a few times as it settles.

The door whines and swings open a few inches. A red-headed woman peers around the side of the door.

"Can I help you?" Her voice is muffled a bit through the glass storm door.

I reach back, take my credentials out of my back pocket, and hold them up to the glass so the woman can see them. "I'm Detective Bergman. May I come in for a few minutes?"

The woman opens the door all the way, squints at my badge for several moments, and then looks at me. "Homicide? What's this about?"

I step back and return my credentials to my back pocket. "I have a few questions to ask the two of you. It will only take a few minutes of your time. I promise."

She unlocks the storm door and pushes it open. "Doesn't it seem a bit late for a house call, Detective?"

"I'm sorry, ma'am. I wouldn't be here if it wasn't urgent." I step around her and into a grand foyer.

It reminds me of the entrance to a five-star hotel where you'd pay a thousand bucks per night. It pulls me right out of my comfort zone and into a place of angst. I didn't grow up wanting of food or shelter, but we never had money to waste. If we had, it would've gone straight to the church or to charity.

Directly ahead of me lies a marble staircase that curves around the wall as it rises toward the second story, and its intricately detailed, rod iron banister looks like it came from some European castle. Its cost probably exceeds that of my car parked down the road.

The woman closes the door and leads me into a living room the size of Mother's entire house. Grayish-tan hardwood runs throughout the room, covered in places with lavish Egyptian rugs and furniture straight out of the palaces of movies. A large fireplace on the far-left wall demands attention with its gray-and-white swirled marble façade stretching to the ceiling.

She gestures toward a black leather couch. "Please, have a seat."

"Thank you." I sit on its edge. It's far more comfortable than I imagined it would be.

She folds her hands in front of her. "May I offer you a drink?"

The smile she wears looks more like an elaborate mask that she puts on for company than it does anything genuine, and her cold, green eyes look right through me as though I'm an apparition.

"No thank you. I've little time as it were."

She settles down on the matching leather chair that sits perpendicular to the couch. "I am Grace." Her gaze dips to the floor for a moment and her lips purse. "You may proceed with your questions."

I nod curtly. "When was the last time you or your husband visited your storage unit at Dunharrow —"

"I'll stop you right there." She crosses her arms and looks down her nose at me. I can tell she thinks herself superior to me. "If you are a detective, then do some detecting. Do we look like the type of people who would rent out a storage unit? I think not. Own an entire franchise perhaps, but never rent."

The tone in her voice is so condescending that I want to jump up and slap her. Knock that stupid smiling mask from her narrow, angled face. Instead, I move forward with what I came to find out.

I clasp my hands together. "May I speak with your husband? Perhaps the unit is something he's never mentioned to you."

She scoffs. "Absurd. He doesn't lift a finger without my knowledge and approval of it." She spreads her arms wide. "I own everything you see here, Detective."

The longer I sit here the less impressed I am with this woman. "Perhaps that's true, but I'm going to have to insist on speaking with George. It is George, correct?"

Grace rises from her chair like a skeleton from a grave, her hands locked on the armrests and her arms ratcheting herself up. "If you insist on talking to my half-wit husband, I will call for him, but his answer will be the same as mine."

I stare at her so hard that my lip nearly curls into a snarl. "Please do. Half-wits are more my speed."

She glares at me for several seconds, huffs, and walks out of the room. I can't help but smile.

Grace's voice echoes through the house. "Erma, fetch your brother for the detective. And make it quick. I've grown tired of her presence already."

"Yes, Grace," says another woman.

I stand and stretch my legs. My migraine is on the cusp of returning and the floaters have already begun swimming across my blurred vision. I walk over to the marble mantle and pick up a picture. *Grace.* I set it down and look at several others. They're all of Grace. How can someone be so full of themselves?

"Ah, Detective. Bergman is it?"

My hand moves to my gun as I turn to face the approaching man.

"Hold on, cowgirl. No need for that." He raises his hands in the air in submission. "I'll go with you willingly if it'll get me away from the wife for a night." He winks at me. His brown eyes are warm, and they smile even though his mouth doesn't.

Dammit. It's not him.

I move my hand away from my gun and offer my hand to him when he reaches me. He takes my fingers, turns my hand over, and kisses the top of it.

"I'm George Hallard, and you're the hottest homicide detective I've ever met."

My cheeks burn, but I roll with it. "Guess you don't get out much. You should see my partner."

He laughs heartily. "Truth be told, you're the first one I've ever had the pleasure of meeting. If I'd known they came in models like you I might've killed the wife long ago just to get you over here."

"You keep it up and I might have to arrest you for conspiracy to commit murder."

"I like you, Detective Bergman." He points at me, winks, and clicks his tongue. "I know you're in a rush, so let's cut to the chase. The old ball-and-chain said you have some questions about a storage unit?"

Ball-and-chain. No love lost for his wife. "Dunharrow Storage. Know of it?"

He doesn't flinch or hesitate. "Nope. Should I?"

I pull out the folded lease form that Bill lent me from my left back pocket, unfold it, and hand it to George. "Look familiar?"

George pulls out a pair of reading glasses from his shirt pocket and puts them on. "Well I'll be boondoggled. That sure is my name and address, but it's not my signature." He hands the paper back to me. "Seeing as how you're a homicide detective I suppose you found a body there?"

I look back at all the pictures of Grace on the mantle. "I can't discuss the details of my case but suffice it to say I'm hunting a man who has no regard for life."

George nods knowingly. "I can understand that. Marry a woman like my wife and you'll begin to wonder if you've got some sort of death wish."

I frown. "So why do you stay with her if you're so miserable?"

His eyes brighten. "My daughter. Well, technically Grace's daughter. Grace adopted her when she was only a week old. She's the light of my life and the bane of Grace's existence. I'd travel to hell and back for that little girl."

I smile. "It's always about the kids, isn't it?"

"Well, that and my sister Erma. Without her, Priscilla would probably be in some sort of boarding school for the blind."

Priscilla? My skin prickles and I shudder.

George cocks his head. "You all right, Detective? Your complexion has gone from rosy-red to sterile-white. How about you take a seat?"

I close my eyes for a moment and wave my hand at him. "I'm okay. I've had little sleep in the past few days and it's catching up to me."

He removes his readers and puts them back in his shirt pocket. "With your line of work I imagine there are many sleepless nights. The darkness brings about all kinds of evil."

"No joke there. So I'm following you correctly, Priscilla's the name of your daughter?"

"Yes ma'am." He shakes his head and smiles. "Fourteen and a prodigy on the piano. Can't even imagine trying to learn to play the piano with sight. How she does it blind is beyond me. She's going to be the next Stevie Wonder or something."

I move close and take his forearm. "Can I meet her? Is she here?"

George pulls his arm back and steps backward. "Kind of an odd thing to ask, don't you think? She's just a girl. Why are you really here?"

"I can't explain it, but I think your daughter's in danger."

George's eyebrows rise. "Danger? From what? She never leaves the house. Grace won't allow it."

My mind is reeling. What can I say to make him understand the gravity of the situation? I have no choice but to tell him the truth. At least part of it.

"The man I'm chasing likes to kill young blind girls. I came here tonight thinking I'd finally found him, but now I'm certain he's led me to your daughter. I think she's in danger."

George's eyebrows dip over the bridge of his nose and he nods slowly. "I heard something on the news about a blind girl being killed. It's tragic for certain but what does that have to do with my Priscilla? How would this guy even know about her?"

I shrug and put my hands on my hips. "I don't know how he finds his victims, but what do you think led me here? A storage unit he leases under your name. That's what. Would you chalk that up as a coincidence? I certainly wouldn't. Are you willing to risk the life of your daughter on it?"

George groans. "I hear what you're saying, and you've certainly raised my hackles with alarm, but you must see it from my point of view. I have a daughter who literally never leaves the house and you're telling me that some killer is out there waiting for the right moment to invade my home and take her from me? How could he possibly know she exists?"

His argument is sound, and I have no proof to the contrary, but the past two days have led me here. How can I convince him of something I don't understand myself? "I don't know, but I'm certain he's coming for her."

George thrusts his arms in the air and his voice raises several octaves. "Do you understand how insane you sound, Detective?"

I pace in front of the fireplace. "You're right, Mr. Hallard. I do sound insane, even to myself, and I don't know what I can say to make it sound any more plausible. But I wouldn't still be here if I didn't think that it was a viable threat. For all we know he could work somewhere where he has access to information about blind people like a hospital or care facility. Please, for the sake of your daughter, trust what I'm telling you. Don't leave her alone until we catch this bastard."

"She's not lying, Daddy."

George and I turn around simultaneously. Priscilla stands by the couch in her jammies, a matching set of white shorts and t-shirt with purple, yellow, pink, and red flowers on them. A brown braid rests on each of her shoulders and hangs to her midsection.

George moves between her and me. "What are you doing down here?

You're supposed to be in bed."

"And I was in bed until she came inside the house. I knew she was here, and I had to meet her."

George walks over to Priscilla and drops to one knee. "What are you talking about, darling?"

My hands are shaking, and I can't stop staring at the beautiful young girl. She reminds me of myself. So young and innocent. How could anyone think of hurting her?

Priscilla reaches out and touches George's face. "She's my guardian angel. I saw her in my room earlier today."

"She what?" George turns and glares at me. His cheeks are as red as the Devil's. "Get the hell out of my house before I call the police!"

I stand there like a statue, unwilling to move. I must understand how Priscilla sensed my presence. It could be the missing link to finding the Braille Killer.

"Daddy—"

George raises his hand. "Enough, Priscilla! Go to your room now."

Grace walks back into the room. "You heard your father, Priscilla. Obey him or you'll be punished." She points a long, skinny finger at me. "You. Out. Now."

I dig in my heels. "I'm not leaving here until I'm certain you understand the threat against your daughter."

Grace crosses the room in a few strides and gets right in my face. "Oh, I'm well aware of the threat to our daughter. I'm looking right at it. Either you show yourself the door or I will."

I know I should walk away, but there's too much at stake. "I'd like to see you try."

Grace looks back at George. "Take her upstairs, George. I'll handle this."

George nods, grabs Priscilla's arm, and escorts her out of the room.

Grace returns her cold, dead gaze to me. "You come near this house again and I'll have you arrested."

My fist itches to clock her smug face. "You're a heartless woman. If I have to come back here to collect your daughter's body, it's you I'll be coming after.

Her blood will be on your hands."

Grace slaps me right across the face. Her talon nails cut like razorblades. "How dare you come into my house and threaten my family. I'll have your job for this. Do you hear me?"

I wipe my cheek and look at my hand. There's no blood, but it feels like there should be. "I could arrest you right now for assaulting a police officer, and you're threatening *me*? Keep pushing it and I'll take you to the station right now. Is that what you want?"

Grace's nose wrinkles and her jaw quivers, but she keeps her mouth shut. I wish she hadn't. I storm toward the front door and knock a picture of Grace off an end table when I walk by. It crashes to the floor and the glass shatters, but I keep moving.

I yank the front door open and shove the storm door out of my way. "You haven't seen the last of me."

I'm halfway down the walkway when the front door slams behind me. Rage shakes me to my core. How can they be so indifferent toward their child's safety? I turn around and look up at the windows on the second floor. One is lit, and a piece of paper is pressed against it. Circles within rectangular patterns. *Braille.*

I hold my breath and the entire world seems to come to a halt around me. The breeze in the trees falters, dogs cease to bark, crickets stop chirping, and the beat of my heart fades into nothing.

I am as still as stone. A gargoyle perched on the walkway. Nothing exists but me and the five words written on that piece of paper. They repeat in my mind like the static at the end of a record. A young girl's plea for help.

Five words that I understand better than anyone else: "*Don't let him take me.*"

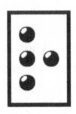

CHAPTER TEN

RAIN DRIZZLES FROM THE sky like a faucet that won't turn off, adding to the weight I already carry. Priscilla lay in my arms, rigid, cold, dead. My feet march up the sloped road, my legs pumping like those of a machine, without feeling and unrelenting.

People line the street on both sides, cloaked in red robes and chanting in a tongue I don't recognize. Some spit at us and others throw bottles, rocks, and other debris, but it doesn't slow me down. I am on a mission, my gaze locked onto an old, marble structure in the distance.

Up ahead is a massive expanse of grass, headstones, and crosses, fenced and gated in black iron. The large gates are spread wide like arms of love, welcoming the dead into damnation.

I stride through them and they bang closed behind me, but I do not flinch. I keep moving forward up the hill until I reach the crypt. I lay Priscilla on the ground and glare at the black-and-gray marble doors.

Each door is half his face, scarred and leathery cheeks and demon eyes that glow with fire. I step over Priscilla's body and pull the doors apart. A heat more intense than any I've ever known blasts me with its full force, but I do not waver. The smell of sulfur burns my eyes and nostrils, but I do not blink.

Flames flicker from the depths of the pit concealed within the crypt. Hell's fire for the Devil himself. Through the flames I see a number smeared in blood on the back *wall: 56.*

I turn, pick up Priscilla's body, and then toss her into the fiery pit. The flames awaken her soul, and she screams like a wraith. The number on the back wall changes to 57.

"How many more will it take to make you stop?" I scream.

A voice rises from the depths, shakes the ground like an earthquake, and vibrates my eardrums. "You had your chance, Alice. Their blood is on your hands, and there will never be an end to the killings."

"No!"

I leap into the flames and descend like a heat-seeking missile. Far below I see nothing but darkness, yet flames surround me. Priscilla is a hundred yards below me, her arms and legs flailing. Her clothes are aflame, and her screams flow from her charred lips without pause.

I tuck my arms to my sides and descend faster, closing the distance between her and I in just a few seconds. At the last moment, I open my arms and spread my legs and then wrap them around Priscilla when we collide.

She squirms in my arms and beats my chest with her forearms. "I thought you would save me."

I look into her dead eyes. "I have saved you. I'm right here. I won't ever let him hurt you."

"How can you be so blind, Alice? As always, you're too late. I'm already dead."

Her body turns to ash in my arms and I'm left clutching the air when I fall right through her. "Priscilla!"

The pit's bottom materializes below me—an endless matrix of razor-sharp stalagmites. I close my eyes and pray to a god I've never believed in.

* * * * *

My mattress sinks as I crash down on it. I gasp for air. Sweat soaks my sheets and I'm burning up. My pulse races faster than I thought possible. *Priscilla...* The only way I'll be able to save her is to catch *him*.

Sunlight fills my room, but I can't make out anything. I rub my eyes and pluck the sleep from their corners, but everything is still a blurred mess.

I roll over in bed, snatch my glasses off the nightstand, and shove them on my face. The room becomes less blurry, but not enough to make me happy. I wonder how much longer I have before I'm completely blind.

My phone vibrates on the nightstand and saves me from a pity party. I reach over and pick it up. It's Seth, so I answer it.

"Hello?" My voice croaks like a bullfrog.

"You still sound like hell, Alice." Seth's voice soothes my ears.

I lay back and stare at the ceiling. "You think I sound bad? You should see what I look like right now. You'd never lay eyes on me again if you did."

"Yolanda Johnson's awake."

My throat tightens with excitement. I sit up and kick the covers to the foot of the bed. "Sounds like you're driving. You on your way here?"

"Yeah. You up for a trip to the hospital?"

"I will be in fifteen. To be honest, you might have to drop me off in the psych ward when you go though."

"You are a bit crazy, but that's what I love about you. No chance I'm leaving you there. We're like Adam and Eve. Unseparable."

"Inseparable, genius."

"Whatever. I'll be there in five."

"Well you just might catch me in the shower."

"I look forward to it." I can tell by the sound of his voice that he's smiling.

"You'd better hurry then."

"Pedal's to the metal, babe."

"Bye." I press End and the line goes silent.

I return my phone to the nightstand, crawl out of bed, and strip off my t-shirt, socks, and panties on the way to the bathroom. I reach around the front of the shower curtain and turn the water on, and then I sit down on the toilet.

My head aches like I've been out drinking all night, and my brain is on a carousel from hell, spinning back to Priscilla and my crazy dream over and again. *Am I too late to save her? Fifty-seven victims… Will I ever find this bastard?* I shouldn't think like that, but my mind is… well a mind of its own.

I finish peeing, grab a couple ibuprofens from the medicine cabinet, swallow them down, and then hop in the shower. The cool water feels good on my hot skin. I lather up and scrub down until my skin is red and raw, but no amount of scrubbing will ever cleanse my hands of Sarah's blood. They'll be stained crimson for eternity.

I turn off the water, exit the shower, and grab my towel. I dry off as best I can, wrap the towel around my torso, and tuck the end in underneath my arm so it doesn't fall off. I move over to the sink, see the words "You're too late, Alice" written on the fogged-over mirror, and gasp.

I stagger backward, ram the door, and stab my shoulder with the corner of the towel rack. I squeeze my eyes shut and hold back a slew of profanities teetering on the tip of my tongue. Three successive raps on the door startle me further.

"Alice are you okay in there?" It's Seth.

I look back at the mirror, but the words are gone. "Yeah, my foot just slipped on the floor when I stepped out of the shower." I lean forward and inspect the mirror, but there's no sign of any words ever being there. I can't help but wonder if they ever were.

"I'm okay." Physically anyway.

"You sure? I can come in there and check out all your parts to make sure everything is still in working order."

I wipe the fog from the mirror with a dry washcloth and inspect my speared shoulder. There are a few broken blood vessels but nothing more. It'll make for a nice bruise in a day or so. "You do, and we may not make it to the hospital."

He sighs loudly. "Okay then. It's all work and no play with you. I'll be in the living room."

Eight minutes later, I find him sitting at the kitchen table chatting it up with Mother while she dries dishes with a towel. Sometimes I wonder if she loves him more than I do. "Let's go, Charming."

He winks at Mother. "Sleeping beauty has risen. Guess it's time to make our rounds."

Mother sets the glass and towel down, grabs Seth's hand, and pats the top of it. "May God bless your day, Seth. Keep that crazy girl of mine safe for me."

"Yes, ma'am. God willing."

I roll my eyes and walk into the living room. "I'll be outside."

When I open the front door the sweltering heat rushes in and I'm falling into the pit of Hell again. "God I can't wait for winter."

I step outside and onto the concrete sidewalk and I swear my shoes melt right onto it. The sunlight is nearly insufferable with my mild migraine, and the tint on my glasses is far less than what my eyes require. Beads of sweat begin forming on my brow and under my arms.

I shake my head. "What was the point of the shower?"

Seth smacks my butt and steps around me. "At least you don't stink... yet."

I swat at him, but he's far too quick. I start to smile, but the idea of having a bit of fun is crushed by thoughts of Sarah and Yolanda and the pain and suffering they endured. I shuffle over to the car, my mind wrapped around the dreams, letters, and that mirror from storage unit 109.

Seth fires up the engine before I've settled in the seat, and we've cruised halfway down the block by the time I get my seatbelt latched.

Seth's hand moves to my thigh. "Talk to me, Alice. You've been distant ever since we got the call about Sarah Johnson Tuesday morning." The concern in his voice fills me with shame. "What's going through that head of yours? Where've you been the last day-and-a-half?"

Most of the time I'm begging him to talk to me, but right now I wish he'd just shut up and drive. If I tell him any of it, he'll have me committed. I put my hand over his and squeeze it.

"Please don't ask me about that, Seth. You wouldn't understand. I'm not even sure I do. When I get it all figured out, I'll tell you everything. I swear. Just be patient with me and promise you'll be here for me when I need you."

Seth rips his hand out from under mine, brakes for a car that pulls out in front of us and lays on the horn for a good five seconds. The driver in the other car sticks his arm out the window and flips us the bird. Seth reaches for the switch to turn on his lights and siren, but I grab his hand and pull it away.

"It's not worth it, Seth. Be angry with me if you need to, but don't waste your time on that loser. We've got much bigger things to deal with right now."

The tension in his hand dissipates. "Fine, but I'll remember his plates. When I see him again, I'll let him have it."

"I'm sure you will."

We turn into the St. Thomas Medical Center parking lot and Seth slips into the last of the police parking spaces at the front of the building. He kills the engine and swings his door open. It bumps the car next to us and the car's alarm blares. I grab his forearm.

He looks at me and groans. "What?"

"Did you bring an extra notepad and pen?"

He's one of the few people I know that has dimples when he frowns. "For what?"

"Yolanda's tongue was removed, remember? She's gonna need something to write on."

"Damn. I've got the extra pen." He scratches his head. "I'll see if there's a notepad at the nurse's station. If not, I'll grab one from the gift shop."

I release his forearm, open my door, and stand up. The entire structure of the hospital sways in my vision, but the darkness stays at bay. I close my door and stumble over to the curb.

Seth grabs my arm. "Dammit, Alice. You need to see a doctor."

I glare at him. "Thank you, Captain Obvious." I don't know why I'm trying to sabotage our relationship, but I think it's working. "Sorry."

He helps me up onto the curb. "How about we go over to the ER and get you examined?"

I start to shake my head but think better of it given my current state. "Not a chance. They can't help me."

"Sometimes you can be so stubborn." He holds my arm and leads us toward the entrance. "I've never seen you wear glasses before. Do you normally wear contacts or something?"

I lean my head on his shoulder. "Something like that. I'm sure I look like a total dork. They're making me a bit dizzy. I think the prescription in them is old, and the sunlight makes it worse. I'll get it taken care of this afternoon."

An ambulance pulls up under the covered drive and a tall man climbs out of the passenger-side door. I see his scarred, pockmarked face and I freeze for a moment.

I reach for my gun, but Seth grabs my hand. "What are you doing?"

I look to Seth and then back to the paramedic, but his face is no longer scarred. The man nods at me and walks to the back of the ambulance.

What the hell is wrong with me? I take a deep breath. "I thought I saw something for a second. It must be these damned glasses."

"Well I can't have you drawing your gun at apparitions. Do I need to relieve you of your weapon?"

I roll my eyes. "You're a genuine comedian today. Rare form."

"It's not a joke, Alice."

"I'm good. I promise." I pull on his arm and we start forward again.

The automatic doors slide open as we approach the entrance, and we continue inside without missing a beat. The lobby is enormous, and the ceilings are nearly impossible to find, looming eight stories above our heads. It's dizzying even under normal circumstances.

Everything that can be is painted in some shade of brown, including the metal furniture. No splashes of color can be found anywhere unless you include the off-white couches near the coffee bar. Even those are a stretch though.

I let go of Seth's arm. "I'll be okay from here. What room is Yolanda in?"

"S1309 in the south wing. It's on the third floor."

I smile at him. "I'll meet you up there. Go find that notepad."

He salutes me, and we separate. My heart still races from the incident with the paramedic, and my anxiety continues to rise. By the time I reach the south wing I'm constantly looking over my shoulder. Everyone I encounter stares at me like I'm some sort of alien, and those that are congregated together speak my name with hushed voices and eye me as I walk by.

I pull on the collar of my shirt, but I still can't breathe. The walls are closing in around me and I run toward the cluster of elevators. I smash down the up arrow, but the thought of being trapped inside the elevator terrifies me. I see the sign for the stairs, so I head for it.

I shove the door open and traverse three flights before I realize I'm being followed. Bang, bang, bang their footsteps echo. I turn and look back, but it's too late. He's upon me.

Big tan boots with rubber soles. He's wearing scrubs and a blue cap, and a white mask covers his face, but I know it's him. I grab the mask and rip it from his face.

The man gasps and so do I. His face is as smooth as a baby's. I drop the mask and rush up the last flight of stairs before he has a chance to confront me. I yank open the door to the third floor and step inside.

My heart beats so hard that it aches, and there's more tension in my muscles than strings wound too tight on a violin. I stumble down the hallway until I find a bench I can sit down on. I barely make it down before my legs give out.

I close my eyes, but there's no escape from the demon in my mind. *You're too late, Alice. You'll always be too late. Their blood is on your hands. On your hands. Your hands.*

A hand rests on my shoulder. "Are you okay, miss?" A woman's voice.

I open my eyes and look up at the nurse. Her dark-brown eyes exude love and kindness. "Not today, but I will be." I can't believe I just said that aloud.

She hands me a tissue and sits down next to me. "Did you lose someone close?"

Tears stream down my face and reappear as fast as I can wipe them away. "I did, and I'm about to lose another."

She puts her arm around me and I lay my head on her shoulder. She reminds me of my grandma. "Loss can be devastating, but know that God always has a plan, even in the most tragic of losses. Look to Him and you will get through this. That, I can guarantee."

Something about her takes away my inhibitions and frees my tongue. I can't help myself. "I don't believe in God. In any god."

She pats my back. "It's okay, sugar. You don't have to believe in Him for His plan to work. He works through us despite our shortcomings. Seek Him, and you will find the light. The darkness never prevails. Think about it. A sliver of darkness does nothing to dissipate the light, but a sliver of light in the deepest darkness can be seen far and wide like a beacon. Give in to that light and you'll find answers to questions you didn't even know you had."

"I don't think I can. I wouldn't know where to start."

The woman laughs, and it sounds like beats of pure joy. "It must start from within. Recognize that you can't go through it alone. Be open to a higher power and purpose in your life. It takes faith. Just because you can't see something doesn't mean that it doesn't exist. You must decide to believe. Change your mind and you can change the world."

She removes her arm from around me and I daub my eyes dry with the tissue. When I look over there's no one next to me. I stand and look around, but she's nowhere to be found. I'd be worried about my mental stability, but I haven't felt better in the last two days. Talking with her vanquished my anxiety and paranoia.

I stroll down the hallway toward the nurse's station. I reach the station and lean over the counter. A young Asian woman sits at the desk and stares at her computer screen. Well, I'm guessing she's young, but they always look young. Asians seem to age better than most.

The woman is so involved with whatever is on her screen that she doesn't even notice me. It makes me think of Sarah and of myself in high school. *Living ghosts.*

I clear my throat, and her eyes look up in my direction.

"Can I help you?" Her attention returns to her screen.

I drum my fingers on the counter. "I hope so. I'm looking for one of the nurses on this floor."

She sighs. "Name?"

I can't help but strive to annoy her further. "Detective Bergman."

"Their name, not yours," she says flatly.

I shrug. "That's the thing. She didn't mention her name."

The woman leans back in her chair and crosses her arms. "Well then what can you tell me about her?"

I cock my head, purse my lips, and look to the ceiling for a moment. "She's a bit chubby, but not excessively fat. She has a big smile and pretty, white teeth. Oh, and a laugh that'll fill you with joy."

She pushes her glasses up her nose with one finger—her middle one.

"Don't waste my time."

I guffaw. "Oh, I'm sorry. Did you not ask me to tell you about her?"

She uncrosses her arms, and stares at her computer screen again. "Move on before I call security."

I drum my fingers harder until she looks up at me again. "How about I give you a description? I'm looking for an older, black woman with silver hair and freckled cheeks. Does that help?"

She shakes her head. "There are only two older woman nurses on this floor. Neither of them is black. Have a nice day, Detective."

Did I imagine her too? I pull a wadded tissue out of my pocket. *Well, I didn't imagine that part at least.*

"And you're certain about that?"

She sneers at me. "Do you think I'm uncertain of anything?"

I lean farther over the counter and read her nametag aloud. "Chen Liu. I've formed many opinions of you but I'm too much of a lady to voice them."

She glares at me, but my attention's drawn to the ding of the elevator down the hallway. Seth steps out of the elevator and heads my direction. He holds up a notepad and smiles.

I smile back. "Wasn't sure you were gonna show."

"I can't lie. Thought I might leave you here. Touch and go for several minutes." He halts in front of me. "By the way, I think you look sexy in your glasses. Kinda got that Diana Prince look."

I chuckle. "Wonder Woman? Don't I wish."

He cocks his head. "We've been apart a whole ten minutes, but you seem to be more yourself again. What happened? Got lost, found the chapel, and found God?"

Sometimes he reads me better than anyone should be allowed. "Closer than you might think." I wink at him and then walk down the hallway to a room on the left with a placard that says S1309. I enter the room.

He follows me in. "I'll never understand you women."

"Truth."

I walk over to Yolanda's bed. She lies there with closed eyes. Scabs cover her eyelids and eyebrows where the stitches had held them open, and black-

and-blue bruises paint her wrists and forearms.

Stitches bind two inches of her left cheek together, just below her ear and close to the corner of her mouth. Another set of stitches runs from the corner of her right eye and down her cheek about an inch-and-a-half. The right side of her neck is also stitched together in a scribbly 'y' shape. I remember that part of her left breast was missing as well. I can't imagine the physical pain she suffered, but it doesn't compare to what that bastard made her watch.

Seth gives me the look. "I'll do the talking."

I nod.

Seth leans against the bedrail. "Mrs. Johnson? Are you awake?"

We both watch with bated breath as she stirs. Her eyelids flutter and then slowly open. She blinks several times.

Her blood-shot eyes make mine water. I wonder how long they were kept open. Do they eventually stop burning once the tear ducts run dry? I doubt it.

"I'm Detective Ryan and this is Detective Bergman. We'd like to ask you a few questions so that we have a better chance of catching the bastard who did this to you and Sarah. Are you feeling up to it?"

She blinks and nods slightly. Her hand moves to the bed controls and she presses the button. The bed slowly rises until she's in a semi-upright position. Seth hands her the notepad and a pen.

Seth leans forward. "How long did he have you there, Mrs. Johnson?"

Her hand trembles as she draws a question mark on the first line.

"Did he take you from your house?"

She writes "yes" on the second line.

"Can you tell us anything about what he looks like?"

Yolanda points to the "yes" and then flips the page over. Within a few strokes of the pen I realize that she's drawing us a picture.

I touch Seth's arm. "I need to sit down for a few minutes."

He nods, but his eyes never leave the notepad. "Do whatever you need to do. I'm not going anywhere until she's done."

I walk into the hallway, sit down on the bench, and close my eyes. When I open them again my phone tells me it's been twenty minutes. The crick in my neck confirms it.

I stand and enter room S1309 again. Seth's back is toward me and he's talking on the phone. I walk over to him and peer over his shoulder.

In Seth's other hand he holds a piece of paper with a man's face drawn on it. Narrow face. Shoulder-length hair parted on the right. Dark, brooding eyes set underneath thick eyebrows. A hooked nose. Crooked mouth with crooked teeth. Goat patch on his chin. A small hoop earring in his left ear.

I thought I knew the face of the man we're hunting. I came face-to-face with him at Dunharrow Storage. I had no doubts about what I saw that night. However, the caricature Yolanda's drawn looks nothing like him, except for the eyes. They both have eyes of a killer. My mind cannot process the discrepancy between the two.

Did I hallucinate it? My shins would argue I didn't. But the details…

I walk over to the chair on the other side of the bed and sit down. I don't understand at first, but then a revelation comes to me.

My God… are there two of them?

CHAPTER ELEVEN

I ARRIVE AT SETH'S condominium complex a little after five o'clock in the evening and sit there for a good ten minutes, reluctant to leave the comfort of my air conditioned car.

It's as hot a day as I can remember, the temperature teetering on 120 degrees. Radiation plumes rise from the asphalt a good three-and-a-half feet, transforming the parking lot into an undulating black sea. A red hue would be far more appropriate and a better warning to those daft enough to traipse around on the magma lake.

I switch off the ignition and cringe as I open the door. I swear it's like opening the Ark of the Covenant in the movie *Raiders of the Lost Ark*. My skin starts melting, bubbling, and burning.

My rubber-soled shoes gum and stick with each step, and by the time I finish crossing the parking lot toward Seth's building it feels like my skin is sloughing off in chunks and splattering on the asphalt and concrete like scoops of melted ice cream.

I grab the metal door handle; it's a pan straight from the oven, roasting my fingers and blistering my palm in the two seconds it takes to pull the door open. I crawl inside, little more left of me than bones and tendons. *Roadkill.*

The lobby is an oasis at its cool hundred degrees and I drink it in until reality sets in. My top is heavy on my shoulders, weighted down with buckets of sweat, and I can't keep my jeans above my waist. I look like a gangster holding up my baggy jeans as I strut across the lobby toward the bank of elevators.

Most days I'd take the stairs, but this isn't one of them. Today it's all about survival. I imagine there'll be several reported deaths by dehydration in the morning. Few people think these days, especially about how deadly the heat can be.

By the time the elevator doors slide open on the tenth floor I'm in desperate need of a cold shower and a gallon of water or some electrolyte-filled sports drink. I'm certain Seth has none of the latter.

I weave my way down the hallway until I reach number 1042 on my right. I press the buzzer and wait patiently while I dehydrate further. Rivulets of sweat course through my hair, run down my face and neck, and traverse every single crack and crevice on my body.

My panties are wedged deep and pasted to me like a wetsuit, and my socks are soaked through. It wouldn't surprise me if my shoes squish when I walk like they tend to do after fording puddles on a rainy day. What I would give for a downpour right about now. Then again, the humidity might kill us all.

Of course I'm sniffing my armpits when Seth opens the door. What else would I be doing?

"Dang, Alice. You jog over here?" He pinches his nose. "Ugh! You got that wet cougar smell."

I punch his arm and push past him. "You keep that up and you won't be getting any of this wet cougar." I head straight toward his bedroom.

He shuts the door, locks it, and follows me. "Not so certain I *want* any of that in its current state. Not sure you qualify as a cougar unless twenty-six is the new cougar age. Is it?"

"If it were, I wouldn't be going for an older man like you." I sit down on the corner of the bed and pull off my shoes.

Seth stands in the doorway. "Suppose that's true."

I peel off my socks and t-shirt.

Seth's eyes widen. "What are you doing, Alice? I thought you came over here so that we could go over all the reports, not to have sex."

I shake my head. "Trust me. This is anything but a sexual advance."

I unhook my bra from the back, slide my arms out of it, and toss it on top of my discarded t-shirt. I stand back up, unbutton my jeans and let them fall to the floor, and literally peel my panties off.

Seth ogles my naked body. "You could've fooled me."

"Keep your pants on and fetch me a change of clothes. I'm gonna hop in the shower for a few minutes to try and cool off." I walk into the attached bathroom. "And please turn the air up."

"I've got it cranked as high as it will go. Don't think we'll get much more relief with it so hot outside."

"Hell isn't as hot as the parking lot is out there." I walk into the glass-enclosed shower and turn the cold water on full blast, but even it doesn't stay cold long.

Seth stands in the doorway to the bathroom now, eying my breasts more than my face. "No kidding. You should've felt it in here when I got home. It's chilly now compared to that."

I close my eyes and let the lukewarm water soak my head and shoulders. The tension and heat dissipate. When I open my eyes again, I see that Seth is still standing there like a young boy sneaking a peek at his dad's porn magazine. "Clothes, Seth. This isn't a peepshow."

He grins. "My place, my rules."

"You might want to refer back to what I said when I got here."

"You know that's unfair. You're asking the impossible. I've seen the boobs. Once the boobs are out, all recollection is null and void. Not only that, but when you talk with your shirt off, it's equivalent to you repeating the word 'boobs.'"

I really don't understand the obsession with breasts. They're nothing more than fatty tissue and an outlet for delivering nourishment to infants. Everyone has them, some are just severely underdeveloped, especially in men—fit men that is.

I turn off the water, cover my breasts with one arm, and reach for a towel. "Clothes, Seth."

Seth frowns and then his expression turns to concern. "What did you do to your shins?"

I look down at my shins for several moments while I try to come up with an answer he'll believe. "Tripped in a parking lot earlier today and came down on the curb right across my shins. Hurt like hell for about fifteen minutes, but they're okay now."

"How can you claim to be a ninja and be so clumsy?" He shakes his head, smiles, and walks away.

I towel off, but the sweat is already surfacing again. At least I'm not immersed in it like before though. I hang the towel back up, comb through my hair a few times, and roll on some deodorant.

"Clothes are on the bed," yells Seth.

I throw on the fresh, over-sized clothes. Even washed, they smell like Seth. I slip my shoes back on and head out of the bedroom and into the living room. Seth sits on the edge of a tan, leather couch, rifling through stacks of papers and folders spread across the top of a rectangular coffee table.

I plop down on the couch next to him. A bottle of light beer sits on the coaster in front of me. It's sweating as bad as I was earlier. My mouth waters at the thought of having something to cool it down. I take the bottle and drain it three-quarters of the way down before returning it to the coaster. Water would've been better, but I'm not complaining.

I grab one of the folders and slide back on the couch. I adjust my new pair of glasses on my nose and open the folder. Inside the folder is the coroner's report on Sarah Johnson. I flip directly to the external examination and skim through it. Everything noted is consistent with the last moments I experienced as Sarah. Ligature marks on the neck indicate strangulation of the victim. Bruising of the abdomen. Fourteen burns on the inside of the left thigh consistent with those left by a cigarette. Forced, sexual penetration is evident, but there is no indication of foreign fluids.

I'm reliving her fear and pain with each detail in the report, and I can't read through any more of it. I close the folder and toss it back on the coffee table.

Seth broods over the CSI report from the Johnson residence. "I just don't get it. The victim is sexually abused, but there's no semen, pubic hairs, or anything else from the perp at the scene. Not a single fingerprint other than those of the victim and her mother. How is that possible? Was she raped by a ghost?"

My thoughts return to the mirror in storage unit 109 and it makes me imagine things I know to be impossible. The experiences I had with the mirror and with Sarah Johnson are also impossible, yet I'm certain they happened. I don't believe in ghosts, but perhaps a demon?

"I don't know about the fingerprints, but perhaps he used some sort of tool to rape her."

"The guy can't get it up? That might explain some of the evident frustration he displayed in hurting her."

The idea of him being impotent resonates with Sarah's story and my own. I'd never contemplated it before, and now I feel adequately dense. What else have I missed in the last ten years?

"You see those wounds on her thigh?"

See them? I felt them! "Yeah, cigarette burns."

"Right. The report says there's a pattern to them. Braille letters." He looks at me and I nod. He sets the paper down. "You already knew that though, didn't you?"

I'm not gonna lie to him about it, but I won't elaborate on what or how I know either. "Yes."

I can see the tension building in Seth's jaw. "Why would you keep something like that from me? Why didn't you report it?"

I don't blame him for being upset with me. The lies keep stacking up and it's making me sick.

I shrug. "Honestly, it slipped my mind. You saw the state I was in on Tuesday. I wasn't my usual self. Besides, I didn't report any of it. I went home right after we found Yolanda, remember?"

The tension eases in Seth's jaw. He sweeps his hand through his hair. "Yeah, okay. Sorry. All this evidence, or rather lack of, frustrates me. We've got nothing to go on but Yolanda's drawing, and even that's questionable."

I touch his leg. "I'm right there with you, but there must be something in here that we missed."

"The word burned onto the victim's leg is 'amerce.' Any idea what that means?"

I nod. "Only because I looked it up on Tuesday. It means to punish with an arbitrary penalty."

"So he punished her? For what? What the hell could she have done to deserve what he did to her?"

I swallow hard and focus my attention on the beer bottle. "I don't know. Perhaps killing her is punishment for someone else." *For me.*

Seth scratches his head. "Someone else?"

I pick up the bottle, suck it dry, and spring off the couch. "Gonna grab another one. You need another?"

"Sure… Someone else… You think the killing has something to do with Yolanda?"

I know the truth behind the Braille Killer's motivation, but perhaps he has something against Yolanda as well. I can't be the only one who has ever pissed him off. "Sure. It might be the reason he made her watch. If that's true, then we need to dive deeper into Yolanda's life. What did she do to this guy? How do they know each other? This kind of killing is personal and takes a lot of planning."

"No kidding. I looked through the CSI report for the mill earlier, and you won't believe what they discovered there."

I return to the couch with two fresh bottles of beer and hand one to Seth. "Try me."

Seth pops the cap on his beer and leans back. "Remember that cat you shot to death?"

Echoes of the tool falling off the workbench ring in my mind. "Psycho cat more like."

"Well, that bastard made a freaking video of what he did."

"A video?" My interest piques.

Seth sips on his beer. "Yeah, turns out the cat belonged to the Johnsons. It'd been missing for almost two weeks. Sarah and Yolanda had put up fliers for the missing cat all around their neighborhood."

I frown. "And the damned cat just happens upon the mill where Yolanda's held captive and decides to snack on her?"

"No." His expression turns grim. "The bastard set up a cage for the cat inside the mill and kept it caged for those two weeks. He starved it to the brink of death. Then, after he'd abducted Yolanda and taken her to the mill, he cut off part of her breast and fed it to the cat."

I gasp. "My God, that's on the video?"

"Yes." Seth exhales. "He must've turned the cat loose right before he went to kill Sarah. The poor thing was starved mad, smelled the fresh blood on Yolanda, and did what it needed to in order to survive."

I sigh. "And then I killed it."

Seth snorts and shakes his head slowly. "And then you killed it."

My stomach roils. "Did they find anything else? Was the killer on the video?"

"Nope. This guy's too careful. No fingerprints anywhere in that mill other than yours and Yolanda's."

"What about the footprints I discovered down the back stairway?"

Seth peels back part of the label on his beer. "All destroyed by the medic team. Not sure how helpful they would've been anyway."

"Damn." I take a swig of my beer, swish it around a bit, and swallow it down. "This guy *is* a ghost."

Seth sets his bottle down. "Yup, a damned ghost. There were a couple of noteworthy items that came up in the interviews though."

I straighten. "Oh? Like what?"

Seth leans over the table, rummages through the papers, and picks one up. "This is from the neighborhood interviews around the Johnson's house. Tell me what you notice."

He hands me the report and I look it over several times. Nothing stands out other than nobody saw anything. We already knew that would be the case though in that neighborhood.

"What am I supposed to be finding?"

He takes the report back. "That's just it. Remember the house you stormed into Tuesday morning?"

"Vaguely. I remember there was an old man in a wheelchair. I was so pissed at the time that I don't recall much else."

"Well, that house isn't on the list."

I snatch the report from his hands and scan it again. "What the hell? Why didn't they go back over there?"

"That's just the thing. They did. Officers Brex and Spalding said that the house was abandoned. Absolutely nothing inside. They also asked the neighbors about the house and confirmed that it hasn't been occupied in over six years."

"And the old man?"

"A ghost as well."

"How does an old man in a wheelchair just up and disappear?"

"Good question. I have another mystery for you."

I groan and toss the interview report on the table. This case is nothing but mysteries. "Might as well hit me with it. The first building you toppled over didn't kill me."

"Yolanda insists the killer left a note in her hand."

My heart stops beating. The room shrinks around me and the temperature skyrockets. My chest tightens to a point where I believe my ribs will crack if I make a sudden move. I cannot breathe. Don't want to.

Seth says something, but it's a distant rumble in my ears. The world tilts downward and my head finds the edge of the table before I can react.

The next thing I know, I'm waking up on the floor and my head is throbbing. Seth crouches next to me.

He speaks, and this time I can hear him. "Are you okay, Alice?"

I squint, the overhead lights like tiny suns in my eyes. "I think so."

He puts his hand to my cheek. "You're burning up, and you've got a pretty good knot right at your hair line."

I lick my lips. They're dried out and as rough as Bill's were. "I think I'm just dehydrated. Can you get me some water?"

"Sure." He gets up and heads into the kitchen.

I sit up, and rock myself to try and ease the pain. The last thing I want is to be one of the ones they talk about on the news in the morning. I can hear it in my head: *"Detective Alice Bergman dies from heat exhaustion and from lying to everyone she's ever met. Gonna be a scorcher where she's headed. She's survived by her mother who talks to God like he actually exists."*

Seth returns with a large glass of water and hands it to me. He settles down on the floor next to me. I gulp down the water like a landlocked fish.

He puts his hand on my leg. "I had Deborah from CSI return to the mill and sweep it again, but she still didn't find a note."

I empty the glass and set it on the floor. "If there was a note, maybe it got lost in the chaos with the medic team. Could've fallen out in the ambulance or in the parking lot or any number of places."

Seth strokes my hair with his other hand. "I don't know. I guess it doesn't matter at this point, but I can't help but wonder what it might've said."

I lean my head on his shoulder like I did with the nurse at the hospital. The words from the note dash me like sea waves. *Dead bodies... So much blood... Another body on your plate... Confess...* "Psycho rambling most likely." The slow, rhythmic beat of his heart calms me.

"I hope it wasn't a clue to the killer's identity." I flinch but he doesn't seem to notice. He stretches out his legs and rotates his ankles. Both of them pop. "I just hope this attack was personal like it seems to be and not the beginnings of a killing spree."

I close my eyes. "Me too."

I hate myself right now. How will I ever come clean about all the things I've seen and done without incriminating myself in the process? More importantly, how will I live with myself if another body turns up before we nail this bastard? I'm sick of thinking about the case and getting nowhere.

Seth knows me better than anyone. He often knows what I need before I do. His fingertips glide across my back and up the back of my neck, releasing tension with each stroke. My throbbing forehead fades into the past.

I needed a distraction to get my mind off of things for just an hour or so and Seth's delivered. I nuzzle his neck and breathe in his cologne; it's ecstasy. I slide my hand underneath his shirt and rub his muscular chest. His skin is warm and baby soft.

I nuzzle his armpit and breathe deep. He always smells so good no matter how much he sweats. I slide my hand down his chest, across his rock-solid abs, and inside the top of his jeans. He doesn't even flinch.

I push my hand farther down and look up at him. "Can I use my raincheck now?"

The corners of his lips curl upward. "I'm sure you already have your answer."

I twist around and sit on his lap, my hand still in his pants. "Here, or in the bedroom?"

He bends down and kisses the crook of my neck. "Anywhere, as long as it's with you."

I look around. The case files are spread everywhere. Sarah's pictures, both alive and dead stare up at me from the table. "The bedroom."

"The bedroom it is."

I'm not sure how he manages it, but he stands with me on his lap and my hand still in his pants. I lock my legs around his and he hobbles into the bedroom. He flips the light switch off.

I reach back and flip it back on. "You know the rules. Lights on or no fun. Besides, I want to see you. I need to see you. I don't want to think about or see anything else."

He walks over to the bed, twists around, and falls backward onto it. "I'm all yours, lover."

The poor thing doesn't know what he's gotten himself into until I grab his shirt and rip it open. Buttons fly everywhere. He gasps, but I'm just getting started.

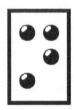

CHAPTER TWELVE

IT'S 8AM ON A Friday and Seth and I are cruising down South Central Blvd., headed toward the Johnson neighborhood once again. We've got the drawing Yolanda provided us in hand and will question the residents one last time.

I still can't wrap my mind around the idea of there being two suspects. It doesn't fit the profile or narrative I've built over the last decade. Then again, my hunt has been fruitless. Even so, what would be the motivation for the two of them to collude on something so heinous? Did they both know Denise?

The real question burning a hole in my mind is why Sarah? What ties her to me? Her house is all the way across town from where I live, and the police station is smackdab in the middle of the two. I'm certain that the connection is obvious, but I can't figure out what I'm overlooking.

Seth turns left on 43rd St. and the scanner lights up. "10-24! 10-24! Code three! South Central Blvd. and 41st. Goodtime Liquors and Convenience Store."

I grab the mic. "H19 to Nest."

Seth flips the lights on, brakes hard, and cranks the wheel to the left. The tires screech on the asphalt as the car whips back the other direction. Seth guns it and the tires squeal, catch traction, and propel us back toward South Central Blvd.

"This is Nest. Go ahead H19."

"10-77. ETA 1 minute."

"Affirmative H19."

"Roger."

We slide sideways halfway through the intersection before the tires grab the asphalt, and then we fly down South Central Blvd., zigzagging through morning traffic. We hit 41st and Seth swerves across two lanes, cuts between two cars with inches to spare, whips the car over the rough curb and into the Goodtime Liquors parking lot, and skids to a stop on the seen-better-days asphalt.

This is the first shooting and robbery in progress I've been to in three years. My hands are shaking, my heart's kicking in my chest, and my vision's a bit blurred, but the adrenaline rush kicks in and sends me into overdrive. Seth and I both pull on bulletproof vests, exit the car, and draw our guns.

Shards of glass pepper the sidewalk from the shattered front doors. Officer Todd lies halfway through the left door in a pool of blood. He isn't moving, and I pray he's still alive. Two people hunker down next to their cars, one praying to their God and the other with their cell phone out, trying to capture the events on video so they can share it with the world.

Sirens wail in the distance, but there's no time to wait.

Bang! Bang! A bloodcurdling scream erupts from within the store.

Seth and I stay low as we approach the front of the store. He motions for me to head around the back, so I do. Graffiti covers the side and back of the store and discarded needles are everywhere.

A homeless man is passed out drunk by the back entrance, a bottle still in his hand, and another rummages through the dumpster at the back of the lot, his butt showing through the worn-out seat of his pants. He must be deaf to have ignored the gunshots.

I nudge the man by the door with my foot, but he doesn't stir. I reach down and shake him by the shoulder, and he finally shows signs of vitality. "Move on, buddy. It's not safe here right now."

He reluctantly gets up, stumbles across the parking lot, and parks his butt next to one of the concrete parking barriers. The other man exits the dumpster, eyes my gun, and dives back in. I test the door and it's locked. I imagine it's locked all the time with the druggies, gangbangers, and homeless hanging around.

I turn to head back around to the front of the building, but then the door flies wide open. It catches my shoulder and knocks me sideways. By the time I reorient myself, there's a Latino man coming out the door, his arm around Seth's neck and a gun to Seth's head.

I aim my gun at the man's blurry chest and back up several steps. "Drop your weapon or I'll shoot!"

The left side of the man's face is tattooed. His lips are split, and fresh blood runs down his chin. "You drop yours, or this prick is dead!"

Seth's right arm hangs limp and his right cheek is bleeding. He glares at me. "Take the shot!"

Darkness swarms at the edges of my vision. If I take the shot, I might lose Seth. If I lose Seth, I'll never forgive myself. I breathe evenly and steady my hands. "I said drop it!"

The guy spits blood on the ground and moves farther behind Seth. "You ain't got the balls, puta."

I aim right between what I believe are his eyes and squeeze the trigger, twice. *Bang! Bang! Bang!* Both men cry out and drop to the ground like dead weight.

Three bangs, but I only fired twice. I can't allow myself to think about the third shot. I close in on the man, but not before he fires several rounds at me. *Bang! Bang-bang-bang!*

My torso jerks to the left and then the right. I stagger back a step but manage to keep my feet under me. Pain blossoms in my chest and both shoulders, but I have no time think about it. I pray the shots hit my vest. I squeeze off another round—*Bang!*—and the kickback sends me in a tailspin. I'm certain I missed. The man pulls the trigger twice more, but his gun just clicks.

I stagger forward like a drunk, stand over him, take aim at his leg, and pull the trigger. He screams something at me in Spanish, grabs his crotch, and curls into a fetal position. I kick his gun away and keep my eyes and gun on him.

I can see Seth from the corner of my eye. He's lying face-down. "You all right, Ryan?"

Seth doesn't respond and my stomach lurches. I'm tempted to put a bullet in this gangbanger's head and call it a day, but I'm no killer. Then again, if Seth's dead because of him, nothing will stop me from taking his life.

"Drop your weapon and put your hands in the air!" Two officers round the far corner and halt, guns drawn.

I toss my gun in their direction and try to raise my arms, but I can't fight the pain. "I'm Detective Bergman. I've been shot three times in the chest, so I can't raise my arms."

"Bergman?" says one of them. "What the hell you doing way over here on South Central?"

I don't recognize his voice or either of their faces, but my vision's so blurry at this point that I'm not sure I'd recognize anyone.

"Right place, wrong time." I motion toward the guy in the fetal position. "That's the perp. I think I might've shot him in the balls. Don't think he's going anywhere." I nod in Seth's direction. "My partner's been shot. Can I check on him?"

"Yeah, sorry." They holster their guns and approach.

I move over to Seth and kneel next to him. "Detective Ryan? Can you hear me?"

He doesn't respond. Darkness swallows my vision, leaving only a pinpoint of light at the center. I locate his neck, check for a pulse and find one, but I also find lots of blood. "He's unconscious and losing blood. We need a medic!"

"Davis, this is Brex. Send one of those ambulances around back. We've got another officer down."

"Rolling around back now."

I clamp my hand over the wound on Seth's neck. "Don't you even think about leaving me, Ryan."

CHAPTER THIRTEEN

THE AMBULANCE WAIL ECHOES that of my aching heart. Seth lies still on the gurney, an oxygen mask over his mouth and nose and a saline IV injected into a vein in his right arm. According to the monitors, his pulse is weak but steady.

I'm sitting in the ambulance on Seth's left side, my hands wrapped around his left hand like vise-grips. If I hold on to him hard enough, long enough, he won't slip away. At least that's what I keep telling myself.

Angela, the paramedic EMT, sits on the other side of Seth, monitoring his stats. Her jet-black hair would be darkness itself, except for its radiant sheen. It's a scientific fact that black hair doesn't exist and those we see with it actually have extremely dark-brown hair. I'm not sold on it though. I think she's an anomaly.

Her eyes match her hair and offer no distinction between iris and pupil. She's a wraith clothed in dark-caramel skin. If she's come to collect his spirit, I will battle her to the death. The only issue I'd have would be finding something made of silver in the ambulance to pierce her heart with. It seems I'm ill-prepared once again.

I cannot imagine life without Seth. He's the only thing that tethers me to this godforsaken world. Sure, I have Veronica and Mother, but I hang on to my humanity only for him.

And Sarah.

The ambulance pulls into one of the emergency bays at the back of St. Thomas Medical Center. The back doors swing open before the ambulance even settles, and we're greeted by a horde of medical staff. Angela updates them on Seth's status as they pull him and the gurney out of the ambulance. They've already wheeled Seth inside by the time I exit the vehicle.

I reach up and verify I'm still wearing glasses. *God, I wish I wasn't.* Everything's so dark and blurry that I struggle to put one foot in front of the other.

"Let me help you inside." Angela takes my arm.

The wraith has become my angel. "Thank you, Angela."

"Detective Bergman correct?"

"Yes, but you can call me Alice."

"Alice in Wonderland. I love that story."

All the Alice references from the decade of notes flood my mind and I tense.

"Oh, I'm sorry. You probably get that a lot, don't you?"

I take a deep breath and lie to her. "It's okay, Angela. I didn't tense up because of what you said. I'm just sore from taking those bullets."

"Oh, right. Those vests save so many lives. Glad you were wearing yours."

"Me too."

I hadn't realized how hot the morning had become until the double doors whoosh open and greet us with an arctic gale. I savor the moment, but it doesn't last. We walk into the emergency room waiting area and Angela leads me over to the reception desk.

"Thank you, Angela. I think I can manage from here."

She releases my arm. "You've got it. Try not to go down anymore rabbit holes and let me know if you find the looking glass."

My skin crawls on my bones. "What did you say?"

"Sorry, they're just more *Alice in Wonderland* references. Sometimes I can't help myself."

"The looking glass..." I can't help but picture the mirror from storage unit

109 and my experience with Priscilla.

"Yeah, my favorite of the stories. Wouldn't it be cool if we could actually travel through mirrors?"

Is that how he does it? Travels through the mirror? It sounds completely crazy, yet it makes perfect sense. Well at least in a horror movie. Then again, I still can't wrap my mind around what happened with Sarah or the mirror. Maybe I'm trapped inside one of my nightmares again and none of it's real.

But I'm not.

The thought of using the mirror is ingenious. I smile at Angela. "That would be something."

Set aside its absurdity and the evidence is compelling. No one would ever see him coming or going unless they were there in the room. In my heart I know it must be true, but the implications drive the contents of my stomach into my throat. *How will we ever find him or stop him?*

Angela leans on the counter with her elbows, her head cupped in her hands. She smiles at the elderly man on the other side. "Eddie, you make sure you give my friend here the royal treatment. Anything she needs."

"Only for you, Angie."

Angela walks back toward the emergency entrance. "Be safe, Wonderland."

"Wonderland, eh?" Eddie chuckles. "Angie must like you. She don't give out nicknames to just anyone."

I lean on the counter, more for support than anything else. "Look, Eddie. I'm sure you're the nicest man in the world, but I've had a really bad week and today just caps it off. Can we skip the small talk and you just give me updates on Seth Ryan and Officer Todd?"

"Not a problem..."

"Detective Bergman." I flash him my badge.

"Thank you, Detective. Please call me Reginald. We'll keep this simple and professional."

"Only Eddie for her. Got it. What are their statuses, Reginald?"

"You can call me Eddie if you'd like to, but my name *is* Reginald."

If I were a cat, I would've run out of lives long ago because of my obsessive curiosity. "Why does she call you Eddie then?"

Eddie scratches his freshly-shaven chin. "Something to do with an iron maiden. To be truthful, I don't know what it is she carries on about most of the time."

In spite of everything I'm wrestling with both mentally and physically, I can't help but snort a little. "I guess I can see the similarities, Eddie."

Eddie bangs on the keyboard with surprisingly spry fingers. "Okay, I see that Officer Todd is in surgery. No idea when he'll come out of that. Hmm... looks like Seth Ryan hasn't been admitted yet."

"Not admitted?" I can't breathe. The thought of Seth dead devastates me, and I cling to the counter. "Why?"

"Doesn't say. Sometimes they won't check people in if there are no beds available." Eddie looks around. "How about I buzz you into the ER and you can go see for yourself?"

I look around too, but my vision's shot. "I would be ever grateful."

Eddie stands and pats my shoulder. "Don't mention it."

I nod.

"Seriously, please don't." He moves around the desk.

"Lips are sealed, and the key's been tossed in the river. Promise."

"Good." He takes my arm. "You look like you could use some help."

I admit it's not my best day. "I appreciate it."

He leads me toward some doors to the right. "Right this way."

He waves his badge over the reader attached to the wall and the doors swing inward. He releases my arm. "Go do some detecting, Detective."

"It's Alice and thank you."

"Ah, Wonderland makes sense now. Not sure I'll ever figure out Eddie though."

I walk into the ER. The sense of urgency hangs in the air like a fog. Nurses and doctors hustle about, and I'm lost. How will I find Seth when I can barely see well enough to walk?

One of the ER security officers walks up to me. "You can't be in here, ma'am."

"I'm looking for Seth Ryan. He's one of the police officers that was shot."

"You family?"

"More than family. I'm his partner."

He looks around and then leans close. "Follow me. If anyone asks, tell them you're his wife or sister or something."

He leads me through the ER and to one of the curtained-off sections. He pulls the side of the curtain back. "Right in here."

I step under his arm and around the curtain. "Thank you, sir." He nods and releases the curtain, and it falls back into place.

I turn around and Seth is sitting up on a gurney. Tears of joy erupt from my eyes and stream down my cheeks. Tension I didn't know I was carrying falls away.

Seth sneers at me. "Surprised you'd show your face after shooting me."

I wipe my cheeks and give him the evil eye. "Came to finish the job."

He holds his arms out toward me and I rush into them. "I thought I might've killed you."

"Hate to break the news to you, but I don't think it was your bullet that hit me, killer."

I remember the third shot. "Tried my best though."

He kisses my cheek. "I'm ready to bust out of this joint."

I pull back. "Bust out? You just got here twenty minutes ago. They haven't even admitted you yet."

"And they won't. Bullet just grazed my neck. Missed all the veins and arteries. A miracle, really. They patched me up with a few stitches and a bandage and now I'm good to go."

"You were out cold, Seth. Your vitals were almost non-existent." I ball my hands. "You're not going anywhere if I have my say in it."

Seth shakes his head. "Turns out you don't, and they need the bed anyway. Besides, I was out cold because I knocked my head against the asphalt. No concussion though."

"Ugh! You're as stubborn as they come, aren't you?"

"The stubbornest. Besides, we have a killer to catch. Ain't happening from a hospital bed."

One of the nurses pulls the curtain open. She smiles. "You're good to go,

Mr. Ryan."

I move out of the way and Seth swings his legs off the side of the gurney. "Any word on Officer Todd?"

Her smile fades. "I'm afraid his injuries were too severe. The doctors did everything they could but couldn't stop the bleeding in time."

The lights in the room dim and the air becomes so thick that it's hard to breathe. I move back over to Seth and we hold each other. I know I'm selfish, but I thank the stars that it's Officer Todd who's dead and not him.

Seth rubs my back. "You did get this guy, right?"

"Right through the shoulder... and the groin."

Seth squeezes me. "You're hardcore, Bergman. I love you."

"Love you back." We part, and I back out of the way so that he can get up.

Seth stands and pulls off his hospital gown. He's only shirtless underneath it. He walks around to the other side of the gurney, grabs his bloody shirt off the stand, and eases into it. He takes all his effects and stuffs them into various pockets.

He comes back around the gurney and takes my arm. "Let's bail before they change their minds."

We walk toward the exit. "We'll need to call for a ride."

Seth stops in front of the ER doors. "You didn't drive my car over here?"

I couldn't drive right now if I wanted to, but he doesn't need to know that. "There's no way I was gonna let them separate us. I rode in the ambulance with you. Held your hand the entire way here."

Seth sighs. "Figures. I'd imagined a supermodel was holding my hand."

I can see in his eyes that he's hurting. We didn't know Officer Todd very long, but it doesn't always take long to form a bond. Joking is Seth's way of coping with loss and I'd never deny him that outlet.

I play along. "You're saying I'm not one?"

"Are you kidding me? You've got way too many braincells to be a supermodel. You'll have to dumb it down quite a bit to even have a chance of competing."

"But am I sexy enough to be one?"

"There's no way I'm getting out of this conversation unscathed. How about them Diamondbacks? Playing pretty well, right?"

I punch his arm. "Might as well reserve a bed here for the night. You're gonna need it."

Seth presses the exit button on the wall and the doors swing inward. "Only if you share it with me."

I smile. "Fat chance of that happening."

We walk out the doors and across the lobby. The front doors slide open with a whoosh and the heat laps at my face. I turn and wave toward the reception desk. "Found him, Eddie. Thanks!"

"You betcha, Wonderland. Have a good day!"

My stomach groans. I don't know when I'll ever have a good day again.

We walk out into the ambulance bay and around to the front of the hospital. The heat is miserable again, but not quite as bad as it was yesterday. It's still early though. Given time, I'm sure it will be sweltering.

Seth pulls out his phone and sets up a ride for us through a mobile app. I take my phone out and look at the screen. I've got three missed calls from Lieut. Frost. I dial my voicemail and listen to the first message left at 10:14:

> "This message is for Detective Bergman. This is Lieut. Frost. Can you please come over to the station when you get a free moment? Thank you."

The second message, left at 12:19, is more abrupt:

> "Hello, Detective Bergman. Lieut. Frost again. Please come to the station as soon as possible."

The third message, left at 14:18, is direct:

> "Come to the station. We've been waiting for you."

I delete the messages, hang up, and put my phone back in my pocket. I look up and Seth's staring at me. I frown. "What?"

"You got trouble in paradise?"

"Frost."

He raises a hand. "Say no more." He looks at his phone. "Ride is on the way."

Ten minutes later, we pile into the back seat of Tyler's car and head toward Seth's condo complex. Tyler's a chatty fellow, but neither of us are in the mood to converse. After several minutes of one-sided conversation Tyler finally gets the hint and leaves us in peace.

We pull into the condo complex and there's a police cruiser waiting outside Seth's building. "What the hell's so urgent?"

Seth looks at me. "Guess they really want you to go in."

I'm pissed, and it reflects in my voice. "Guess so. Not sure what's so urgent that it can't wait."

We both thank Tyler and exit the car. I walk Seth over to the building doors but don't go inside.

Seth holds my hand. "You don't need to rush off, Alice. Come inside and sit for a bit."

I look back at the cruiser. "You know I can't do that. I've gotta go in."

He shrugs. "Fine. Call me later?"

I kiss his cheek. "Sure will."

I walk over to the cruiser and peer through the window. As far as I can tell it's Officer Spalding sitting inside. It's hard to tell though because my eyes are so blurry. Thank God I have a stronger pair of glasses in my car.

The window rolls down. "Detective Bergman. I've been tasked to escort you to the station. Back door's unlocked."

I smile. "You're a good man, Officer Spalding, but I'll take myself in if that's okay with you."

"Not a chance. I have my orders."

I look skyward. It's nothing but a bluish-gray smear. All my surroundings are gummed splotches of colors. "Alright. Let me grab something out of my car and I'll be right back."

He nods. "Make it quick."

It's a struggle, but I manage to find my sedan in the parking lot by pressing the panic button. I open the door and wait a minute for some of the pent-up heat to disperse before climbing in. When I do, I make the mistake of grabbing the steering wheel and it burns my hand.

"Ouch!" I pull my hand away.

Whoever thought it was a good idea to settle in the middle of the desert should be hung. I'm not sure how Mother wound up out here in this godawful place either.

I open the glovebox and pull out four pairs of prescription glasses. They're my last four pairs. I take off the ones I have on and toss them in the glovebox. I try on the others in succession. The last pair I put on has the strongest prescription available, and my vision's still blurrier than I'd like with them on, but I have no other choice. They'll have to do. I have no idea what I'm going to do tomorrow when I can't see at all.

I throw the other glasses back in the glovebox and push it closed. I look up and see that Officer Spalding has pulled around and blocked me in. "Guess he doesn't trust me."

I admit the thought did cross my mind to ditch him.

I get out of the car, slam the door, and walk around to the opposite side of the police cruiser. I open the back door and slide onto the plastic seat. I can tell it's not going to be a fun ride for my butt. I close the door and buckle in.

I close my eyes. "Ready when you are."

We take off and I can't help but think that this might be my future one day. The past always finds a way of rearing its ugly head when least expected, and I've done more than my share of lawbreaking recently.

CHAPTER FOURTEEN

THERE ARE ONLY A few cars at the station when we pull into the parking lot. Officer Spalding drops me off at the front of the building and I thank him for the ride.

I walk through the front doors and the mood is more somber than on any other day I can remember. Officer Janis sits at the front desk, her eyes bloodshot and her nose red. I know she and Officer Todd were close, and, based on her reaction, I wonder if there was something going on between them. I can't bring myself to say anything, so I just nod in her direction and move on down the hallway.

At the end of the hall I take a left and traverse the stairs to the second floor. Lieut. Frost's office is the first door on the left and the door is wide open. I knock on the door frame and peer inside but he's not there. At the end of the hall is a conference room. The shades are drawn, and the door is shut. They never are unless something is going on inside.

I walk down the hall, knock on the conference room door, and crack the door open. Lieut. Frost and a few others are sitting around the rectangular table. Lieut. Frost waves me inside. I go in, shut the door, and sit down in the first available chair.

Lieut. Frost sits across from me. The smell of his godawful cologne hits me, and I want to gag. Officer Brex sits to his left and Officer Jaramillo to his right. I don't know how they can sit so close to him without choking to death.

The three brooding men set my fingers tapping. I'm a deer caught in the headlights and I'm sure I look the part. Whatever this is can't possibly be good.

Lieut. Frost's glare is softer than normal. "First of all I want to commend you on detaining the perp at the Goodtime Liquors and Convenience Store. Your quick action in that pressure situation saved the life of Detective Ryan."

My mind trips over itself. *Did Lieut. Frost just pay me a compliment?*

I let out the breath that I didn't realize I'd been holding in. "Thank you, sir. I did my best. I'm just sorry we didn't arrive there in time to save Officer Todd's life."

Lieut. Frost exhales. "As are we all. Now, to the bad news."

My throat tightens. "Bad news, sir?" The words squeak out like a mouse.

Lieut. Frost leans forward, rests his arms on the table, and clasps his hands together. "You're aware we have policies and procedures that must be followed."

My hands become so fidgety that I place them in my lap to keep from distracting the entire room further. "I am, sir."

He continues, "Because you were involved in an OIS I have no choice but to put you on administrative leave."

"Sir—"

Lieut. Frost holds up his hand. "This is not open to discussion, Detective Bergman. I understand that the shooting was justifiable, and I'm certain you'll have no remorse over it, but that does not preclude us from following proper procedure. An officer involved shooting must be dealt with properly, no matter the circumstance. You will see the department psychiatrist, as required. Once you've done so, you will attend a mandatory two-week training, and then be reevaluated by the department psychiatrist before returning to duty."

Heat burns in my cheeks. "Sir, you can't do this. Detective Ryan and I are right in the middle of a case."

Lieut. Frost pinches the bridge of his nose. "I understand your frustration, Detective Bergman, but my hands are tied. Detective Roland will assist

Detective Ryan during your absence. When you're fit to return for duty you'll be put back on the case if it isn't solved. That's all I can do for you."

I rise from my chair. "Detective Ryan isn't being put on administrative leave? How does that make any sense? He was shot for God's sake! This feels like some sort of witch hunt."

Lieut. Frost glares at me. "Sit down, Detective. You know as well as I do that this is no witch hunt. I have as much respect for you as I do anyone else in this department."

I sit back down, more so because I'm dizzy than to follow his order. "I know you do, sir." I close my eyes for a moment and take a deep breath. "It's been a really long day. Just forget I said that."

He nods. "I understand, and there's a good reason why Detective Ryan will still be working. As stupid as it may sound, he didn't fire his gun. Because of that, he isn't required to be put on administrative leave for an OIS. You should be happy about this because that means that he can continue working the case."

"I really am happy about that, sir. Elated, to be honest. He's the best homicide detective I know. I've never worked with Detective Roland before but I'm sure he's good too. We've got a lot of good people here."

"I couldn't agree more." He clears his throat. "Now, unless there's something else you'd like to discuss, I believe were done. Please make sure you report to the department psychiatrist as soon as possible. The sooner you do, the sooner you'll be back at work."

"Yes sir." I rise from my chair once again and cling to it for dear life for several moments. "I'll report to the psychiatrist first thing in the morning." I cannot allow myself to fall apart right now. My head is swimming and another migraine is coming on like a runaway locomotive and Lieut. Frost's cologne has done anything but help.

I exit the room and close the door behind me. The musty, swamp cooler air is almost crisp in comparison but even it does little for my head. I take a deep breath and stagger forward a few steps.

The hallway sways back and forth, and the lights are so bright that I have to close my eyes. I feel my way down the hallway and to the stairs at the far end. I hold onto the railing as I descend, and when I reach the bottom I have to sit down on the last step. But the rest is short-lived.

Nausea ripples through my stomach and I bolt for the locker room, praying no one's in my path because my eyes are closed. Thankfully I have the layout of the building memorized. I make it to the locker room and into an empty stall just in time to purge the contents of my stomach into the awaiting toilet.

My head's stuck in a never-ending tailspin and nausea keeps me perched in front of the toilet. I retch twice more and then follow it up with bouts of dry-heaving. By the time I feel confident in leaving the stall my abdominals are on fire and my throat crackles with stomach acid.

I remember that I have some migraine medication in my locker, so I head over to it. Officer Dupree is standing at his open locker, staring at it like it's the most foreign thing he's ever seen.

My locker is next to his, and I open it. "You all right?"

"Just don't understand who would want to hurt Officer Todd. He was one of the nicest people on this godawful rock."

Officer Dupree sniffs and I realize he's been crying. "At least I shot the bastard who did it. Twice. Once in the balls."

"Good you did that, but it ain't enough." Officer Dupree slams his locker door shut. "That thug don't deserve to live."

"I know how you feel Jim, but his life will be hell on the inside. He's a cop killer now."

"True dat." He starts walking off then stops. "Gonna make a call to some of the boys on the inside. When they're done with him, he'll never be able to sit right again."

He exits the locker room and I smile. If people knew the conversations that went on inside these walls we'd all be out of jobs. I pop a few pills, shut my locker, and sit down on the bench.

It's time to move forward, and the only thing I can do now is what I've been doing for the last ten years: work the case on my own. *Until I can't.* Tears moisten my eyes and I rub them away before they have a chance to fall.

How much longer do I have before going completely blind? The question trembles my lips and tightens my chest. I need to get home before the mess inside me breaks containment. God forbid the guys here see me break down.

Once I do go blind, I'll have to confide in someone. *But who?* Seth isn't an option. That only leaves Mother and Veronica and I'm not sure either of them is strong enough to handle it. I'm not even sure I am.

* * * * *

I stand out front of the police station at the bottom of the concrete stairs. My glass bottle lenses have begun to fail me, the world a blurred mess through them. I'm certain by tomorrow I won't be able to see at all.

Veronica pulls into the parking lot in her fully restored, white 1987 Mazda RX-7 and pulls up to the sidewalk. It's been decades since I've seen her—okay, almost a week—and I can't wait to catch up with her. So much has happened over the last three days and she knows nothing about it. My heart flutters like it did on the first day of college.

I open the car door and I'm immediately greeted by Guenter, her ever so excitable Maltese. Veronica scoops him up off the gunmetal-gray leather bucket seat and I drop down into it. The seat cradles me like an old glove.

Veronica strokes Guenter's head. "What's with the Diana Prince disguise? Trying to fend off the hotties?"

I exhale loudly. "I wish that were the case. Turns out Seth finds me sexier in them. The entire plan kinda backfired if you ask me."

She lets Guenter go and he's in my lap quick as a bullet. His little tongue laps at my hand, my arm, and then my face like they're bowls of water. I can't help but giggle. I think I might've missed him more than her.

Veronica reaches over and touches my leg. "You're just too sexy, girl. Next time try the fake zits and the fart spray. If that don't drive them away, nothing will."

I shake my head, lean over the center console, and hug Veronica. "I've missed you so much, Vee."

"Back at you." She kisses my cheek. "I know you're all secretive these days but finding out that you've kept Seth in the dark as well surprised me. I thought you guys shared everything with each other. Is everything okay between you two?"

I lean back in the seat and Guenter continues his exfoliation treatment on my arms and hands. "Never better. I've just been working some things out that have nothing to do with him."

She sweeps her long blonde hair off her shoulders. Her hair is so gorgeous it makes me sick. I wish I could grow mine out, but department regulations won't allow it.

She pats my leg. "So where we headed? Back to your pad or over to mine?"

"Actually, I need to go see an old friend. Mind taking me over to Rico's?"

Veronica turns in her seat and eyes me like a raptor. I can see the cogs turning in her mind. "Rico's? The white cane shop? What do you need to go over there for?"

"What if I told you I'm going undercover to try to stop a killer?"

Veronica frowns. I can tell she's not quite buying it. "Undercover? Is that why you're wearing the glasses too? For this undercover job?"

I hate lying to her, but I'm not quite ready to tell her the truth yet. How do you tell your best friend that you're going blind? "Yeah, from what I understand there have been some pretty cool advances in technology over the last ten years, as far as canes go."

Veronica guffaws. "Rico? Seriously? He's as likely to be into technology as the Pope is porn. I just can't see it."

I nod like a bobble head doll. "Unbelievable, but true—the part about Rico that is."

"Huh. Never would've guessed. Rico's it is."

I strap in and she puts the car in drive. We exit the parking lot and head northeast on Carmichael Drive. Traffic is fairly light for late Friday afternoon and it makes me wonder where they've all gone. There's nothing ahead of us but empty streets, green lights, and palm trees.

Fifteen minutes later we pull into the parking lot of Rico's Cane Shoppe. The square building is about as old as Veronica's car, but, unlike her car, it's never had a facelift. The beige painted cinderblock walls look like they have a bad case of leprosy, their paint chipped and peeled everywhere.

The once beautiful mural depicting a blind person using one of Rico's canes to traverse the landscape has all but faded into oblivion, and the sign above the door that used to read "Rico's Cane Shoppe" now reads "Ric's a hoe." A fitting sentiment to this rundown neighborhood. It is the epitome of the red light district.

I unbuckle my seatbelt, open my car door, and look over at Veronica. "I'll be back before you know it."

She gives me the bug eyes. "Pfft, you crazy, girl? It's a hundred and fourteen degrees out here. My butt would melt to the seat and then I'd be walking around the rest of my life with car seat butt! No, no, no, my butt is going inside where there's air conditioning. Guenter's coming inside too of course."

It's not ideal, but I don't blame her for insisting on coming in too. "Okay." I hand Guenter to Veronica and work my butt out of the seat. I grunt as I pull myself up.

The doorbell plays a jingle when we walk inside the shop. The melody is familiar, but I can't place it. Moments later, Rico walks through the black curtains hanging behind the front counter. I smile at him, certain he'll never recognize me from so long ago.

He shimmies around the side of the counter and approaches us with outstretched arms. "My Sweet Lord, if it isn't Alice and her trusty sidekick Veronica!"

He embraces me, and the smell of cherry vanilla tobacco on his shirt brings back memories I'd long forgotten. "Still smoking the pipe I take it?"

He chuckles. "Some things never change, hijita." He hugs Veronica and then steps back and eyes us both. "I'd say the two of you don't look like you've aged a day, but I believe that would be an insult in this case. You've both grown into such beautiful young women." He puts his hand next to his mouth like he's whispering a secret to us. "Best be careful in this neighborhood." He gives us both a long wink.

Veronica shakes her head. "You're as bad as they come, Padre."

She calls him Padre because he used to be a priest, but he gave up his white collar to sell wares for the blind community several decades ago. It was a smart decision at the time because we have one of the largest schools for the blind in the country here. From the looks of it though I'd guess online sales have nearly killed him. He sold me my first cane and every one of them since. I'd never think about going anywhere else.

"I call it as I see it." He smiles. "Gave me the opportunity to start an outreach program though. We meet here every Wednesday evening. I've managed to help a few of the girls stop hooking. It's made me a bit unpopular with the pimps though." He waves his hand. "Never mind that. You came here with a purpose."

He looks back and forth between me and Veronica and frowns. "Something here ain't the same. I could be mistaken, but I don't think that little pup there has seen a day of service." He draws closer to me again and moves his head from side to side like a cobra being charmed. I follow his movement with my eyes. "Praise the Lord! You can see, can't you Alice?"

I smile. "For the last ten years now."

"But... how? Thought there was no hope for you ever gaining any sort of vision."

"As you and Mother would say, 'It's a damned miracle!'"

He shakes his head. "You and I both know that isn't true. The damned part anyway." He crosses his arms and grins. "Wow. So happy for you, hijita!"

My cheeks catch fire, and I look down at my shoes. "Thank you, Rico. It's definitely been an experience I never thought I'd have."

"Well deserved. God is good." He retreats to the backside of the counter and waves us over to him. "Come on over here and tell me what I can do for you."

We walk over to the counter. I glance at Veronica. She shrugs, and her eyebrows nearly touch the low ceiling. I lean on the counter and give Rico my best deadpan stare. "I'm looking for something *special*."

Rico cocks his head. "And what kind of *special* are we talking? Digital? GPS?"

"No, not that kind of special. I'm working a case where I need to go undercover as a blind person. I need *protection*." I lean forward and whisper, "You know, a cane with *abilities*." I air quote the word abilities.

Rico looks around cautiously. "Where did you hear that I sold such things?"

His hand is on the counter and I place mine over it. "I'm a detective, Rico. I detect things."

His eyes widen. "Detective? As in private or police?"

"Homicide. Two years now."

He blows air out of his mouth and it vibrates his lips. "Well that is something, isn't it Veronica?"

"She's the best. At least that's what her boyfriend partner says."

I turn and glare at Veronica. She just winks at me. Guenter whines and wiggles in her arms.

"Boyfriend partner..." Rico whistles through his front teeth. "Dangerous combo there, hijita."

I raise my hand and smack it down on the counter next to Rico's. "No more stalling, Rico. It's time you show me your special collection."

He looks at Veronica. "Do you know what she's talking about?"

Veronica backs away from the counter. "I think I'll sit this one out." She touches my arm. "Guenter and I will be over there on the couch."

Rico nods slowly. "Wise choice, hijita."

I snap my fingers. "I'm not a little girl anymore. Don't treat me like one or I'll bring some of my uniformed friends with me next time."

Rico grimaces. "Oh that hurts. Threats from my little Alice. Never thought I'd live to see the day."

I glare steel at him. "I'm not messing around."

He thrusts his hands in the air. "Okay, okay. I fold." He looks toward Veronica. "Would you mind locking the front door and switching the sign over to closed?"

"Sure, Padre."

He stares hard at me for several moments. "Come around the side of the counter. I will show you my *special* collection of canes."

I turn and give Veronica the "if I'm not back in twenty call the cops" look and then circle around the end of the counter. "I'm trusting you with my life, Rico. I need something *extra* special."

"And I'm trusting you with my reputation." He pulls back the black curtain that separates the front of the shop from the back and holds it open. "Step on through." I do.

In the back of the shop are several workbenches with various tooling, some of which I recognize. There are machines that sew, stamp, and dye leather for the custom dog harnesses he sells and other machines that work with various metals to weld, mold, bend, and hollow out shafts for white canes. There are several dog harnesses and canes lying around the shop in various stages of completion. Rico handcrafts everything he sells in the shop right down to the stitching of the harnesses and the binding of the cords in the foldable canes. It's impressive, especially for a one-man operation.

The entire right and left sides of the shop are nothing but floor-to-ceiling cabinets full of various supplies. We walk over to one of the middle cabinets on the left. Heavy chain and a padlock the size of my hand secure the doors. Rico unlocks the lock with a key from the glob of keys hanging on a three-inch-diameter keyring on his belt. He unthreads the two-foot length of chain and hands it to me. It must weigh at least ten pounds. I set it on the floor behind me.

My lips are wet with anticipation as Rico takes hold of the two door handles. When he pulls them open, I blink several times, my mind unsatisfied with what my eyes see. Two canes hang by their cords from hooks on the cabinet's back wall, but they look just like the ones he has out front.

Rico steps out of the way and gestures toward the two canes with his hand. "Here they are. Beauties of my own design. They're the only canes I own with *abilities*."

I shake my head and set my jaw. "How are these any different than the others?"

He wags his finger at me and his eyebrows rise. "Ah, but that's the beauty of these two. Their subtle yet deadly differences will go unnoticed by most. Have a closer look."

I lean into the cabinet and pull the closest one off its hook. I wrap my fingers around the cane's leather-wrapped handle and close my eyes. It's been a long time since I've held one, but muscle memory takes over and, as strange as it sounds, gives me a sense of home.

I open my eyes and inspect it closer. There's a subtle, nearly undetectable break in the handle. I place a hand on either side of the break and twist counterclockwise on the left and clockwise on the right. With a bit more torque the two sides begin to unscrew from each other. With the threads clear, I pull on the top part of the handle and it slides out from the rest of the cane. A thin, long blade is attached to the handle end and shines under the fluorescent lights of the workshop.

I slide the blade back into the cane and screw the handle back together. "This is a nice application but perhaps a bit clumsy to utilize in the middle of an attack."

Rico nods. "Agreed. You might find the other one more to your liking."

I hang the cane back up and unhook the other one. It has the same feel that the first one did but there's no break in the handle. I run my fingers down its length but find no breaks of any kind. However, there's a slotted hole in its tip. I look at Rico and he just smiles.

My eyes race back to the handled end and the cord tied through it. The cord doesn't slip straight through the handle like they do on most single piece canes. Instead the cord angles down into the handle. I wrap the cord around my left hand and fingers and hold the cane in my right hand. I yank on the cord and a long, thin blade springs out of the bottom of the cane, turning it into a spear. The blade is about the same size as the one on the other cane.

Rico steps back as I whip it around. It feels natural and balanced in my hands, almost like a katana. I pull on the cord again, but the blade doesn't retract. I try again, a bit harder, but get the same failed result.

I look back at Rico. "Better, but how does the blade retract?"

Rico steps forward again and holds out his hand. "Let me show you." I hand him the cane. He wraps one side of the cord between his fingers. "Double release, single retract." He pulls the one side of the cord and the blade slides back into the tip of the cane. "Either side will retract it."

I hold out my hands palms up. "That is exactly what I came here for. I'll take it."

He lays it in my hands. "It's…" His gaze locks onto my left wrist and his smile fades. His brow furrows and his eyebrows dive toward his nose. "Hijita?" His eyes lift and peer into mine.

The workshop fades until we're left standing alone on a dark plane. I've never felt more open or vulnerable in my entire existence. My soul is left bare to his gaze.

Suddenly I'm an awkward teenager again, fidgeting with my hair as I stare at the inside of my left wrist. "Mother says it's a birthmark."

"A mark for certain, but not of birth. Perhaps a better term would be birthright."

I stare harder at my wrist. *Birthright?* I don't understand.

I gasp like waking from a dream and the workshop surrounds us again. The cane is no longer in my hands but hanging in the cabinet once more. Rico shuts the cabinet doors. I blink several times with utter confusion.

I close my eyes and take several deep breaths. "What just happened?"

He ignores my question. "Would you mind handing me the chain?"

The chain? The haze in my mind fades. I pick the chain up from the ground and stare at it. I can't look at Rico right now without blushing. "Did I do something wrong?"

He takes the chain from me and threads it through the cabinet door handles. "No, hijita."

I close my hands, lower my arms, and stare at the concrete floor, still unable to look him in the eye. "I thought you were going to sell me the cane."

He binds the chain with the lock and slams the lock shut with a grunt. "So did I, but we can never fully grasp the plans of the Almighty One until the moment is upon us."

I force myself to look at him again. "What plans?"

His grin stretches from ear to ear and his cheeks glow with excitement. "I've waited a long time for your arrival."

The aftereffects of my migraine still creep behind my eyes and slither through my mind. I rub my temples. "I don't understand. I've been here before, Rico. Several times in fact."

"Yes, but you weren't quite you yet."

His words spin my head about like a top and the rumblings of the approaching migraine thunder in my mind. "I don't understand anything you're saying. Are you speaking English?"

"What I speak of is of no consequence right now." He claps his hands together and my head nearly explodes. "It's time I show you the basement."

Just when I thought things couldn't get any stranger with Rico they turn toward the absurd. "Basement? These old shops are built right on top of the lava bluffs. Digging out a basement would be beyond expensive."

"In those terms I'd agree, but sometimes there are ways around such limitations." He leans close. "Are you ready to see the basement? Few ever have. Fewer have returned." He winks at me.

I raise my arms. "I think I'm good. I'll just take an ordinary cane and be on my way."

He beckons me closer. "Hijita I have what your heart desires, but your lips are too afraid to ask for it. Come and see for yourself."

My left wrist itches and I'm suddenly burning with fever. My mind fills with whispers of a past I could never have lived and a need to visit the basement wells within and consumes me. "Yes." My voice pants with desire. I *must* see the basement.

He leads me over to the back corner section of the right-side cabinets, opens the last cabinet door, and reaches up inside of it. I hear a soft *click* followed by grinding gears, squeaking pulleys, and whooshing gas shocks. The entire middle section of cabinets, about twelve feet long, slide out from the wall about five feet, revealing a narrow stairway leading down into the darkness.

I stand there, mouth agape. I'd expected a simple door with a stairwell, not some elaborately hidden dungeon. My pulse rises. *What is he hiding down there that requires such secrecy?*

Rico places his hand on my shoulder and his eyebrows furrow. "This stays between us, hijita. Understand?"

I nod, words still lost from my tongue. I'm certain I'll never view Rico the same way again.

He walks over to the stairway. "Follow me."

CHAPTER FIFTEEN

RICO AND I BEGIN our descent of the dark stairwell. A few steps down and the basement lights come alive, dispelling the darkness. I gasp, ill-prepared for the automatic lighting, but the light eases my tension. However, my heart still thumps like a rabbit's.

There are fifteen steps down to the basement floor. When we reach the bottom, the cabinets above slide back into place over the stairwell. I take a deep breath, but I can't shake feeling trapped inside a dungeon with no escape.

The single room basement is roughly an eighty-foot square, and its fourteen-foot ceiling is much higher than what I would've expected. Nine two-foot-square cinderblock support columns are evenly distributed throughout the room, supporting the foundation of the main structure above us.

A ten-foot glass cube sits in the center of the room, demanding the attention of whoever enters the basement. It has captured mine, so I walk over to it. Its four sides, top, and bottom are solid glass and its corners are slightly rounded. I cannot find a single seam on its smooth surface. It's a glass bubble.

I look back over my shoulder at Rico. "What's the purpose of this thing?"

Rico rubs his hands together. "An invention of my own. Be patient and I'll give you a demonstration of what it can do."

I pull myself away from the cube and snake my way through the room. Glass enclosures fill every void and give the room a Smithsonian Museum vibe. Each enclosure contains a single item and each item is like nothing I've ever laid my eyes upon.

Headdresses of gold and precious stones. A pair of tan, leather gloves with matching belt and five throwing knives that dart back and forth within their enclosure. A recurve bow and arrows that are ancient, yet advanced with spring-loaded heads and titanium shafts. Iridescent shards of glass shimmer in the light. Their large, scaly shapes conjure dragons in my mind. The sheer number of items is mind-numbing.

The content of another enclosure catches my eye and draws me toward it. A titanium war hammer with a long, black handle lies within its glass walls. One end of the hammer's head is a long blade, razor-sharp and curved like a talon, and the other end is squared with nine pyramid-shaped spikes. I'm certain its weight would crush a person's skull with a single blow. The flat side of the hammer's head is stamped with a black sun, and golden, luminous letters run the length of the hammer's handle, etched into it with machine precision. I've never seen a language like it, yet it's familiar.

Rico's hand settles on my shoulder. "It's called the *Hammer of Light* in our tongue. A beautiful, horrific weapon."

Rico's secret vault of priceless artifacts. I fear I've never known the real Rico.

I look up at him through blurry eyes, but it's not the blurriness that leaves me full of wonder. Physically, he looks like the same Rico I've always known, right down to the shoulder-length silver hair, gold capped tooth on his lower right canine, and Jesus Freak tattooed hands. But he's no longer the man I know, or at least not the one I thought I knew. There's a mystery to his aura that I never saw before today.

I turn away, wipe my eyes, and then continue to explore the room.

Rico trails me. "All of these enclosures contain items that I've obtained or invented. You'll find no match to any of them in *this* world."

I'm drawn to an enclosure in the far corner of the room and all the others fade from my memory like remnants of a fleeting dream. The enclosure contains a black-and-gold rod that's about four-and-a-half feet long. Black leather strips are tied to its end through a small hole at its center. Its shape is reminiscent of a white cane. I press against the glass, my eyes begging for a closer look.

"Is this what I think it is? A modified cane?" I look over at Rico.

His eyes sparkle like black diamonds and his toe taps the floor to a beat only he hears. I've never seen him so excited about something. "This is my pride and my crowning achievement. I call it *Aaron's Staff.*"

"*Aaron's Staff ...*" I stroke the glass with my fingers. "Can I try it out?"

His foot taps faster and he strokes his chin. "Like many other items in this room, it has a mind of its own, so to speak. You'll know if it's right for you when you touch it."

I put my forehead against the glass and long for its touch. "This is exactly what I came here for, Rico. I don't think I can leave here without it."

"We'll see about that. Many have sought it out, but no one has laid claim on it." He touches my shoulder. "Stand to the side and I'll remove it from the case."

I take several steps sideways. "Is this far enough?"

Rico looks over at me. "Perfect."

He reaches into his pocket and pulls out two clear, rubber gloves. He pulls them on, snaps the fingers into place, and then rolls up his left sleeve. A strange wristband wraps his wrist. It's shiny and solid black and looks like a wristwatch but has no display. He presses his gloved right thumb on the wristband and holds it there for several seconds. Then, the wristband lights up with blue LEDs.

I can't help but move closer. My heart pounds and my pulse races with anticipation of what he'll do next. He reaches into the enclosure—literally through the solid glass—and removes *Aaron's Staff* from it. I blink several times, my brain unable to process what my eyes just witnessed.

My hand crumples against the side of the glass enclosure when I try to stick my hand through it. I grunt and shake off the sting. "What the—"

Rico chuckles. "Pretty darn cool isn't it?"

I rub the back of my hand and stare at the glass. "It's like freaking magic. What is it?"

He pushes his free hand right through the glass again. "It's something I like to call nano-glass."

"I've heard some of the geeks at work talk about nanotech, but I'm not entirely sure what it is." My stomach flutters, and my voice climbs a few octaves. "How does this stuff work?"

He pulls his hand back out. "Grab hold of my hand." I do, and I feel an electrical charge flow into me. It's very subtle, but undeniable. "Now, take your other hand and touch the glass."

I reach out and touch the glass with my trembling fingers. It still feels solid.

"Good, now push your fingers through it."

I apply more pressure to the glass and it stretches like rubber around my fingers. I push harder, and the glass gives way like a bursting bubble, but it doesn't shatter. Instead, it curves around my fingers and then my hand as I push my hand farther inside the enclosure. I move my arm around and the hole follows it.

I feel like a kid in the candy store with twenty bucks to spend. "Rico, this is amazing!"

He smiles. "Let go of my arm."

My eyes bulge. "What? No! Why would I do that?"

His eyebrows cave over the bridge of his nose. "Trust me, hijita. I would never ask you to do anything that would harm you."

A wave of chills and nausea sweeps through me and my stomach gurgles. *You're stronger than this, Alice.* I exhale and release my death grip on his arm. The glass solidifies around my arm and traps it inside. I panic and latch onto Rico's arm again. My arm flies from the enclosure and yanks my entire body backward with it. Rico full-on belly laughs.

I slug his arm. "That's not funny!"

He points at the glass. The hole I put in it is knitting itself back together like water filling the bottom of a bucket. Within a few seconds the hole is completely repaired.

I step back, my arms akimbo. "Explain yourself, Rico. How does a priest turned vendor for the blind get into things like this?"

"I wasn't always a priest, hijita. Let's leave it at that. One day I may tell you more, but this isn't that day."

"Fine. Can you explain how the technology works?"

"That I can do." He holds up a finger. "Let me turn this thing off." He presses his thumb against the wristband again and waits until its blue lights fade. "Perfect."

He touches the glass. "This nano-glass is a composite of silica sand and nanites. Nanites are tiny, two-state robots that can be controlled with current. Their two states are active and inactive." He taps the glass. "Right now they are in an inactive or solid state. When current is applied to them, they switch to an active or fluid state."

My brain is already starting to hurt thinking about what he's trying to explain. "How do they turn into a fluid if they're tiny robots?"

"Fluid, as in moveable with applied pressure, not as in liquid."

"Oh, okay. I think I understand. And the current?"

"Extremely low-voltage electricity. Like a battery."

Suddenly I remember the staff he's holding, and the nano-glass seems trivial. "I think I got it. Can we move on to that staff of yours?"

He eyes the staff in his left hand and then me. "How risk averse are you?"

I shrug. "Depends on what we're talking about."

He holds the staff up. "The gloves I'm wearing protect me from its power. If I were to touch it with my bare hands it would throw me across the room. It's not designed for me."

I swallow hard. "What are you saying? It'll do that to me as well?"

His bushy eyebrows rise, and he shrugs. "Maybe, maybe not. There's only one way to tell without it hurting you too severely. Are you willing to risk it?"

Is this really what I came here for? A cane that'll throw me across the room? I don't even know what it's supposed to do. But it's so sleek and beautiful. How can I resist it?

I dig deep and conjure courage and strength I didn't know I possessed. "Yes."

He sucks on his lower lip and then smacks his lips together. "Perfect. Let's move over to the cube in the center of the room."

We walk over to the cube. "I'm guessing that this cube works just like the nano-glass enclosure?"

"Precisely. Let me turn on my wristband again and we'll step inside the cube." A few moments later his wristband is glowing blue again.

My throat tightens, and my lungs seize. My voice rasps from my lips. "How will we breathe in there?"

He takes my hand and squeezes it. "Relax, hijita. The nano-glass composite isn't solid, so oxygen can pass right through it."

I nod, but I still can't breathe. He steps through the glass and into the cube and pulls me inside with him. He lets go of my hand and lays *Aaron's Staff* down.

He takes my hand again. "You're turning red. You need to breathe."

I exhale, forgetting I'd stopped breathing. I take another deep breath and exhale again. My pulse slows and the thrum in my ears dies down. I hear myself say, "I think I'm ready."

Am I?

Rico lets go of my hand and steps outside of the cube. I push against the glass and it's solid.

"Now what?"

Rico slides his thumb across the wristband and the blue lights turn green. He places his palms on the glass. A subtle vibration works its way into my bones and then ceases. I push against the glass again and it bends outward like elastic.

Rico smiles at me. "If the staff rejects you, you'll be thrown across the cube. However, the cube is strong enough and thick enough to absorb the impact. I won't lie though. You'll feel it for several days afterward. Think of it like a fifteen-mile-per-hour collision. Hard, but not bone shattering."

"Okay. I think I can handle that."

"Then go ahead and pick up the staff."

I bend down and stare at the staff for a solid minute. Rico says nothing. He's far more patient than I am. I take five quick, successive breaths and grab the staff by its handle. Lightning rips into my flesh. I scream and drop the staff, but it doesn't throw me across the cube. I look at my arm, expecting to see plumes of smoke rising from singed hairs, but I find no visible damage.

"Again," says Rico. "You've made it farther than anyone before you."

Easy for him to say. I feel like a snake charmer in training, already bitten by the snake and awaiting death to set in. I also wonder how many others have tried before me. I guess it doesn't matter.

I gather my courage once more and pick up the staff again. This time I hold fast to it and ride out the initial barrage of chain lightning that courses through my body. It's hot, just like what I felt when I touched the mirror in storage unit 109. It speaks to me on a level that transcends language and harkens back to an awakened memory of a life I never lived. We are two shards of a severed soul. Reunited. Made whole.

Like a samurai sword, I twist and jab and parry and stab the air with it. It has perfect balance. I move in circles, dancing in cadence with my heartbeat. I'm uncertain if I lead it or if it leads me, but it doesn't matter. We are one. A pairing of two broken things now made whole together.

I come full stop in front of Rico, staff held above my shoulder and ready to strike. His eyes are wide with wonder and fear. I imagine mine look like those of a tiger stalking its prey. I lower the staff. It's the perfect height for me as a cane. We were truly made for each other.

Rico clears his throat. "Now, would you like to know what else it can do?"

I look at the staff. It's perfect as is. What more would I need? Then again, maybe it's something I don't even know I need yet. "Yes," I purr.

He points at the staff with his head. "There's a recessed button on top of the handle. Press it."

I find the button and press it. The staff turns from a rigid cane to a flowing whip. I turn and quickly strike the air with it. The air cracks. I do it several more times, enamored by the feel and sound of it. How I've lived my entire life without this weapon is beyond me. Blind or not, it won't leave my side again.

I pant with excitement. "Is there more?"

He nods. "Turn the top of the handle ninety degrees counterclockwise."

I do and the entire length of it glows blue and crackles like ice cubes when you pour warm liquid on them. Again I turn and whip the air. Not only does the air crack this time but it ignites with blue electrical sparks. It leaves me breathless with each crack, and somehow weaker.

"Think of that like a stun gun, but twice as powerful."

I whip the air several more times, but then my legs give out and I collapse. Like a flash of light, my joy is surpassed with fear. "Rico, what's happening to me? I can't feel my legs."

"Don't worry, hijita. You will regain your strength. What I failed to mention is that the energy it uses for the charge comes from you. Every time you crack that whip it zaps more of your energy. Use it wisely and sparingly."

I turn my head and look up at Rico. It's about all the energy I have left. "Did you *fail* to mention it on purpose?"

He nods, but he isn't smiling. "I wanted you to experience what it feels like and to know your limits before you went out into the world and discovered it at an inopportune moment."

My body feels akin to a puddle of mud. "Mission accomplished. Now what?"

Rico removes his hands from the cube wall. "I'll be right back. I've got a little something that will give you a boost, but it's a highly addictive substance. Don't even ask me if you can take any with you. The answer will be no. I only keep it on hand for times like this."

I suck a string of drool back in my mouth. "Well. Not going anywhere. Take your time." I can barely get words out between breaths. "Might check on Veronica. Probably wondering. What's taking so long. Might be panicking. If she's snooped around. And didn't find us."

"I'm not headed up there, but I'm certain that she and Guenter are doing just fine."

"How do you know?"

"Let's just say that the time we spend down here has no consequence on the time they spend up there."

I'm so worn out that my mind can't wrap itself around what he's saying. "Tell me later. Rico."

He nods and disappears from view. I hear him rummage through some drawers, curse under his breath, and rummage some more. I lie here, my mind fractured between wanting to know the truth about Rico and fearing what that truth might reveal about him and me both. The nanotech line he fed me doesn't sit well with me but what do I know? Certainly nothing about that.

I will come back and demand the truth from him one day, but with everything going on in my life I don't think I could handle it right now. I'm struggling to keep my head above the water as is. Bringing Veronica into my circle of one scares the living crap out of me. I can't stomach the thought of losing her friendship, but I can't move forward on my own either.

Rico returns and walks right through the sheet of nano-glass. He kneels next to me and shoves a small, white square into my mouth. Its texture and consistency are like rice candy, but it tastes like a turd. I gag several times and fight the urge to spit it up but finally get the entire thing down. Had it been any larger I would have balked. I rake my tongue against the bottoms of my upper teeth, but the taste lingers like a rank fart.

When I can finally speak without gagging, I do. "What the hell was that?"

Rico stands and backs away from me, clear outside the cube. "Five... Four... Three... Two... One..."

Tremors quake my entire body and my veins explode with fire. My mind races and I can't keep up with all the thoughts bombarding me from more directions than I can count. I'm up on my feet in the blink of an eye and dancing around like I've got fire ants in my pants. Another second, and the feeling subsides but now I've got enough energy that I could run several marathons back-to-back without breaking a sweat. I bounce off the cube walls like I'm a living ball in the game *Pong!* I can't stop myself and I don't want to because I might explode like the cap off a bottle of shaken cola.

Minutes later, my pulse and my movement begin to slow, and my thoughts become rational and coherent. I settle in the middle of the cube and stare at Rico. "I have no idea what you gave me, and I don't care, but never do it again."

Rico places his hands on the cube. "Pick up *Aaron's Staff* and come out of there."

I stand and pick up the staff. I turn the top clockwise ninety degrees and depress the button on the top of the handle. The staff straightens and stiffens. Rico pushes his hand through the glass. I take it, walk through the cube wall, and then let go.

I'm half-tempted to poke him in the side with the staff but I refrain. Instead, I raise the staff and twirl it around. "What do I owe you for this?"

Rico raises his hands. "It's not mine to sell, hijita. You are its rightful owner."

"How will I protect others from accidentally touching it?"

He presses his thumb on his wristband and waits until the green lights fade. "The power it contains is your own."

I look at the staff. "I don't understand."

"That initial shock you received from it was nothing more than it binding to your DNA. It will never work for another again."

I frown. "But you said you wear those gloves so that you can touch it and that others were thrown across the room by it."

He nods. "I did, and they were."

I grip the staff firmly. "So why didn't it bind to them or you?"

He folds his hands behind his back. "Those who tried to wield *Aaron's Staff* before you only believed in the words I told them and not in themselves like you do. I choose to keep myself separated from its power over me because I understand my weakness. I feed on power. That is one reason I sought after God. To still my heart and remove the temptation of power."

My heart flutters but my throat tightens. *Am I worthy of such power?*

Rico takes my hand and leads us over to the stairwell. There's a button on the wall. He presses it and the cabinets in the shop above slide to the side.

I cannot help but wonder if this new cane is somehow tied to the mirror in storage unit 109, and if they're both tied to this basement. He takes the first step, but I pull him back down. "Wait…"

He cocks his head. "What is it?"

"I discovered a mirror the other day with symbols around its frame. One of them matched my birthmark." I close my eyes and reach forward, picturing myself there. "When I touched the mirror my reflection disappeared, and I could see into someone's room. A young girl. She was blind, but she knew I watched her. She spoke to me."

I open my eyes and Rico's staring hard at me. His brow is wrinkled like a pug's and his jaw is set, but he says nothing.

His glare leaves me cold. "Do you know of it?"

He nods. "The Shadow Mirror." He crushes my hand in his and I rip it from his grasp.

"The Shadow Mirror... what is it?" I wring my hand to ease the pain.

His words are venomous and ripe with spittle. "An abomination. Tell me where you found it."

I touch his shoulder and the tension eases from his jaw. "It doesn't matter. It's no longer there."

He pulls a card from his back pocket and hands it to me. "If you ever see it again call this number. Day or night."

The card is creased and worn. It says "Steven's VCR Repair" across the top in gold lettering. Below that is an image of a VCR tape and a phone number. I flip it over but there's nothing on the back.

He shakes his head. "Don't ask. Just use it if needed."

The layers of this man named Rico are unending. I'm not sure I'll ever know who he truly is. I have so many more questions for him, but I cannot allow myself to dwell on it further right now. There's a monster out there killing because of me and it's my job to stop him. I don't think anyone else can.

"One day I will return and you're going to tell me everything."

He dips his head. "When you are ready, it will be my honor, hijita."

We ascend the stairs and exit from behind the cabinets. Rico goes over to the last cabinet and presses the button hidden inside of it. The cabinets slide back against the wall and click into place. Rico closes the cabinet door and we return to the front of the shop.

Veronica and Guenter still sit on the couch. She's reading an issue of *People* magazine. She looks up from it. "Wow, that was quick."

I look over at Rico and he winks at me. I think I might be the only one in the room who doesn't understand. I take my phone out of my pocket and look at the time. It says we've only been here for twelve minutes.

I look back at the black curtains that lead into the back area of the shop and shake my head. It's another question for another day. They seem to be piling up as of late.

We bid Rico farewell and pile back into Veronica's RX-7. The streets and the world fly by in a literal blur. Veronica starts up several conversations, but I offer up little banter of my own.

My mind is lost somewhere in another world where time moves independently from our own world. Even in this other world I'm repeatedly drawn to a single question: how will I find and stop the Braille Killer when I know I'll wake up blind tomorrow?

CHAPTER SIXTEEN

I STAND AT THE mirror in storage unit 109, leaning on my cane and watching her like he does. She looks so peaceful lying in bed, her arms neatly folded over her abdomen like a corpse at a viewing. Her chest rises and falls slowly and her eyelids twitch, her eyes moving back and forth under them. She's dreaming, but is it of him or of me?

Through the mirror I see a shadow on the floor creeping toward her and panic sets in. I beat on the mirror with my palms, but she does not wake. I bang harder and scream until my throat is raw, but she does not stir.

He creeps closer and my heart beats faster. He's nearly upon her and there's nothing I can do but watch. Now it's not just his shadow I see but also him. He turns and grins at me with yellowed teeth. Even through the mirror I can smell garlic, pickles, and ash.

He reaches down, opens her mouth, and stretches out her tongue, but still she does not wake. In his other hand he holds a lit cigarette. He laughs like the devil himself as he smashes the fiery red end of his cigarette onto her tongue. It hisses like a snake as it burns through her tongue, and the smell of burning flesh joins the smell of him.

Still she sleeps on, and I wonder if she's truly alive. Tears streak my face and I cannot stand to watch any more, yet I cannot turn away. His cigarette moves from her tongue to her face. Over and over it hisses and burns until her face is left scarred and unrecognizable.

He turns and looks at me, death gleaming in his eye. "Now her face matches mine. The daughter I could never have."

I look away for the briefest moment and he's lunging through the mirror. I turn to the side just in time and he sails past me like a ghost ship. I whip around and swing my cane, but he catches it in his hand and yanks me toward him. I let go of the cane, but my momentum carries me right into his arms.

He wraps me with arms of steel and I cannot move. I scream and kick but fail to connect with any force. He picks me up and drives me to the ground with such force that my ribs crack. I cannot breathe, but my cane lies at my side. I grab the cane, turn the top of the handle ninety degrees counterclockwise, and push the button on its end.

I fight through the pain and roll, whipping the air as my back meets the ground. The whip cracks the air like a clap of thunder, and blue bolts of energy light the dark room. Before the whip has a chance of retracting, he grabs it and wraps the end of it around his hand. He pulls so hard that my right shoulder rips out of its socket with a loud pop. I scream and let the cane go.

He depresses the button on the top of the handle and the whip turns back into a cane. He bends the cane over his knee several times, breaks it into many pieces, and tosses it through the mirror.

He laughs at me. "Did you really think your silly little cane would work against me?"

Each breath racks me with pain, rendering me a mute, so I nod.

He picks me up by my throat and I'm too weak to resist or fight back so I latch onto his arm with my left hand. My right arm hangs limp at my side like dead weight. He squeezes hard and my air pipe collapses. I cry out in pain, but no sound leaves my lips. I wheeze and grit my teeth, knowing that he's not done with me. God, I want it to end.

He walks back over to the mirror and holds me out so that I can see it too. He touches its surface and Priscilla's room morphs into a vaporous black hole in space. With his other hand he peels my left hand from his arm. He cocks his arm back that holds me and throws me through the mirror.

I scream but the hollows of space suck away the sound like a vacuum. I toss and turn and tumble and the mirror pulls farther away. He stands there laughing at me *and watching me float away. I can feel myself freezing from the inside out and everything grows black as my eyes become solid.*

My world is dead and so am I.

* * * * *

I gasp and crash onto my bed like I always do after a nightmare, but this time the darkness lingers. My head spins like I'm still in motion, drifting through space without destination.

Sunbeams penetrate my fortress of darkness, casting finger shadows across every surface they contact. I stare up at what was a popcorn-textured ceiling just a handful of days ago. Now it's nothing more than blurs of shadow and light.

My covers abandoned me sometime during the night and the air conditioner is running full blast, explaining the coldness I feel deep in my bones. Pins and needles stab my right arm when I move it from behind my head. It throbs and aches as blood flows into it again.

The only thing from my nightmare that lacks explanation is the dull pain in my ribs, but then I remember that first touch of *Aaron's Staff* and the paces it put me through last night.

The dream study I participated in during high school pays off once again. I can explain almost everything a person experiences when they dream. It's become my own personal superpower. I take a deep breath and sink into the mattress.

I reach over and grab my glasses off the nightstand. When I slide them on, they don't even sharpen the shadows. I pull them back off and throw them across the room with a grunt. A loud, hollow thunk tells me I struck the closet door with them, but it doesn't lift my spirits.

My life is in a downward tailspin and I've lost all control. The ground is fast approaching and soon I'll crash and burn. When I do, I fear there will be nothing left of me to recover.

I've been on administrative leave for a week now, but it feels like an eternity. The mandatory training wastes four hours of my life daily. The only saving factor is that they're online audio courses, so I can listen to them from home while lying in bed or on the couch.

What sucks is that I still have another week before I can be reevaluated by the police force psychiatrist, Dr. Trisha Zarko. She's a nice enough woman, but it's all a waste of my time, policy or not.

None of it will matter if I'm still blind.

The Braille Killer is out there and I'm twiddling my thumbs in bed, sitting through pointless training videos, and rehashing notes and artifacts with meanings that have eluded me for a decade. I am pathetic, and I will sulk in my misery for another week.

I pick up the phone to check in with Seth but the doorbell rings. I press a button on my phone and it beeps, prompting me to give it a command. "What time is it?"

"Zero eight twenty-four," it replies.

Why would someone be at the door this early? I'm not expecting any deliveries and even if I were, they never arrive before noon. I pull myself out of bed, slip on my bathrobe and slippers, and run my fingers through my hair as I walk from my bedroom to the living room. I cross the living room and unlock the door.

When I open the front door sunlight scorches my eyes. I shrink away from it like a vampire, but it seems to follow me. The sun never shines in this direction, so it must be reflecting off the window of a vehicle parked on the street. I shield my eyes with my hand. "Yes?"

"I'm looking for a Detective Alice Bergman." It's a male's voice. Deep, but not Barry Manilow deep, with a slight southern twang. A reformed Texan.

I step over the threshold. "You've found me. What can I do for you?"

"I have a package for you. Please sign to confirm receipt of delivery."

I reach out and he hands me an electronic tablet. I locate the rectangular box with my hand, scribble my name into it with my finger, and hand it back to him.

"B-e-r-g-m-a-n?"

I nod. "That is correct."

He hands me a large padded envelope. "Thank you, ma'am. Have a nice day."

I raise my hand. "Wait a minute."

His shoes squeak on the sidewalk when he turns back. "Yes ma'am?"

"Does it say who the package is from?" I cross my fingers underneath the package.

"No return address was provided, ma'am, and we have anonymous drop-offs all across town. The only thing I can tell you for certain is that it came from somewhere local."

My pulse rises. There's only one person in the world that would send me an anonymous package. A thought sparks in my mind. "Is there a way for the person who dropped it off to track its delivery or be notified once it has been delivered?"

"Yes, ma'am." He moves closer. I can smell mint on his breath when he speaks. "We have a tracking system that can be accessed via a tracking number. You can also provide an email address and we'll notify you of delivery. No email address was provided for this delivery though. The sender would have to check our tracking system manually."

Damn. So close. "Thank you so much for the information." I extend my free hand. "And you are?"

A gloved hand folds around mine and shakes it. "The name's Jess, ma'am. From Speedy's Courier Service." He lets go. "We'll bike it or hike it to any location in town."

I smile. "Thank you, Jess. Have a good day."

"You too, ma'am." I imagine him tipping a big old cowboy hat toward me even though I'm certain he's wearing a bike helmet.

Jess trots off as I close and lock the door. I walk over to the couch and sit down. If the envelope contains what I think it might, my day will take another turn for the worse. I'm not sure how much more I can handle before it breaks me. I have no doubt that's the point.

I take a deep breath and open the large, padded envelope. I reach inside of it and my fingers scrape across thick, meat-market paper that kind of crunches when you bend it. The all-too-familiar texture of the manila envelope leaves me numb. I can't see it for myself, but I have no doubt that there's an 'A' on its front. The only question is whether or not the 'A' is written in black or red ink. My heart wishes for black, but my brain thinks red.

I pull the inner envelope out and discard the padded one on the coffee table. A red splotch stands out against the orangish-yellow manila envelope. My heart cries out and my hand curls into a fist. *Damn.*

I stand and retreat to my bedroom with it. I close the door and turn the lock even though I'm home alone. I retreat to my bed and clutch the envelope with shaking hands.

My thoughts flash back to the mirror in storage unit 109 and I can't help but imagine him watching me now. I cringe as his wretched gaze violates me. Tremors quake me in violent waves like I'm having an epileptic seizure, but it's far worse than that. They reach into the farthest depths of my mind and pierce my soul.

I close my eyes and focus on my breathing. I cannot allow him to do this to me. I am stronger than this. I must be for Sarah Johnson and for myself. Together, we will defeat him.

I reach over and open the top drawer of my nightstand. I retrieve a pen from it and scribble July 27, 2018 on the envelope so that I won't forget it later.

I toss the pen back inside the drawer and then close the drawer. I locate the flap and then the metal clasp on the envelope and bend up the tabs. I unfold the flap and reach inside. Like the last two before it, this envelope contains a hand-woven bracelet and a letter. I leave the bracelet inside the envelope since I can't see to examine it, but I take out the letter and unfold it.

As with the other ten letters, this one is written in braille. I glide my finger across the raised bumps and the canvas of my mind ignites with letters and words:

The roses are red
And the violets are blue
One girl is dead
Oh wait, there's two

The body count will rise
While you idly stand by
Entangled in your lies
So many more will die

One by one
The girls they fall
What's done is done
You'll murder them all

The darkness inside
It clouds your sight
It's a great place to hide
But you'll never see light

You once were blind
And now again
It's not your mind
But your sin

Return to the start
Where things came to be
Follow your heart
And you'll find me

I showed you the path
I gave you the key
Now they'll suffer my wrath
Until you confess all to me

The words sink in and still my beating heart. *Two girls.* My eyes moisten, and I blink back the tears. I will not allow myself to wallow in self-pity anymore. It's time I shift my mind from what he wants me to think to what is true.

I didn't kill Denise and I didn't kill these girls. They certainly died on my watch, but their blood isn't on my hands. It can't be. I'm not the psycho singling them out and killing them. He is, and he will pay for it.

My phone buzzes on the nightstand and whips my head around. I set the letter down on the bed and pick up my phone. "Hello?" I hear a deep sigh on the other end and I know it's Seth. "Seth, what's wrong?"

"My God, Alice..." His voice trails off.

I'm pretty certain I know why he's called me, but I wait for him to collect himself and give me the news.

He clears his throat. "Another body's been found."

Another Sarah. Why couldn't I be wrong? I groan. "When?"

"Just a few minutes ago. I'm heading out the door as we speak."

"Pick me up on the way?"

"Alice..." He sighs again, his voice distant. "You know I can't do that."

"Seth, you know I'd never ask unless it was important. I need to see the body."

"I'll bring pictures by later if you want, but I can't take you over there. We'd both be fired or at least kicked off the case."

Pictures are not what I need, especially since I couldn't see them anyway. "No, pictures won't be good enough. I need to physically see the body."

"You're not making any sense, Alice. Are you feeling okay?"

"Never better, but..." How can I tell him about my experience with Sarah Johnson's body without sounding crazy? *Is it possible?* I still can't wrap *my* head around it.

"But what?"

I have no choice but to tell him, and I hope it doesn't push him away. "There's something you need to hear that will change the way you think about everything."

"Really? Seems like a pretty tall order." If skepticism were an odor, I'd be inundated with it.

In my mind I return to Sarah's house. "Do you remember me going into the bedroom where Sarah Johnson was murdered and closing the door?"

"I do. Thought it was a little odd." His horn blares, and he mutters something indistinguishable.

I'm in Sarah's bedroom, kneeling next to her. "Yes, but what I'm about to tell you is going to sound so absurd you'll think I've gone mental."

"You're starting to scare me, Alice." He sighs. "What did you do?"

"When I was in there, I became overwhelmed with a need to touch Sarah's face. I cradled her face in my hands and touched my forehead to hers."

"What the hell, Alice? Why would you do that?"

"That's not important. What is important is what happened when I did."

"My God, the germs and bacteria."

I exhale. "Just listen, Seth."

"Fine. Go on."

"When I did that, something crazy happened. I don't know if our spirits connected or what, but for several minutes I became Sarah Johnson and lived out her last moments with the killer. I was there, Seth. I felt his cigarette burning my leg. I smelled his garlic, pickle, and cigarette breath when he bent over me. I heard his voice when he spoke. The ripping of my dress and me wetting myself. I felt and experienced *all* of it."

Nearly a minute goes by before Seth finally responds. "That's impossible, Alice."

I want to scream and throw my phone across the room but that would only make things worse. "Don't you think I know that? Why do you think I kept it to myself until now?"

"Let's pretend what you're telling me is true."

"It is, dammit! You know me, Seth. I don't make crap up like this."

"If you did experience this, then tell me what he looks like. Did Yolanda's drawing look the same?"

"I couldn't see anything, Seth. I *was* Sarah. She's blind, remember. I can give you detailed smells, touches, tastes, and sounds, but nothing visible."

"What you're telling me is beyond impossible. Why should I believe you?"

"Give me a minute to think about it."

"I don't see how you could say anything to change my mind."

"I understand, but I'll think of something. For the moment, how about you tell me what you know so far about the new victim."

"Fourteen-year-old female. Blind just like the last one."

"Who called it in?"

"The father. He went upstairs to check on her because she hadn't come down for breakfast and found her dead."

I can't imagine how terrible it would be to find your child not just dead but murdered. My heart breaks for the man. "What's her name?"

A mental image of Priscilla Hallard rises to the front of my mind: pale skin, a long brunette braid, and eyes the color of English tea.

I mouth Priscilla Hallard as Seth says her name. "Cara Strum."

It takes a few moments for my brain to process the discrepancy. "Say that again?"

"Cara Strum. Does the name sound familiar to you?"

I shake my head. Nothing I've learned over the last ten days fits together. Why did I see Priscilla in the mirror if she wasn't to be the next victim?

"Alice? You still there?"

"Sorry. No, it doesn't sound familiar."

"Well that's all I've got so far. Need to go. Rolling up on the scene now."

"Wait! I have the answer."

"Shoot."

"First, promise me that you'll take me by the morgue later to see the body if what I tell you pans out."

"Fine. I promise. Now hurry it up."

"The killer said many things while I was… joined with Sarah, but one thing in particular stood out. I'm certain Yolanda would remember it. It's also something that I'd have no way of knowing. She didn't mention it in her interview."

"Okay. You've got my attention. What is it?"

"He said: 'I'll sing a song for you tonight when your mama and I celebrate her freedom from you. She likes some good karaoke, doesn't she?'"

"That is random. I'll have one of the guys check it out."

"Don't wait, Seth. I need to see Cara's body."

"I'll get on it as soon as I'm done with you."

"Alright. Call me as soon as you're done there."

"You know I will, partner."

"The morgue is a date then." I cringe and wish I could take back those last words, but I learned long ago that there are no backsies in conversation.

The phone goes silent for a moment and then the electronic voice says, "Call ended."

I lie back on my bed again. *Yolanda don't let me down.*

CHAPTER SEVENTEEN

I SIT ON THE couch in the living room and pretend to watch a rerun of *Leave It to Beaver*. I've seen the episode a dozen times, so I laugh at all the right moments even though I can't see a thing. Mother sits in her favorite chair humming the tune to *When the Saints Go Marching In*.

She always hums when she knits, but she's a one-trick pony. I've never seen her knit anything other than afghan blankets. I don't know how many afghan blankets it takes to qualify as too many, but we've got enough of them to cover every square inch of flooring in the house, possibly more than once. I'd say we've crossed that threshold.

"You working on another blanket?"

"There's a drive at church tomorrow afternoon to collect pantry and winter items, so I'm knitting a couple of blankets."

"In July? Seems like an early start for the winter season, but what do I know?"

"You can never be too prepared, Alice. God prepared for His son's death from the very beginning."

Every conversation with Mother leads to God and Jesus within three or four sentences without fail. I honestly wonder if she gets some sort of kickback for it. An extra dose of the Holy Spirit or something.

"Couldn't you just take some of the ones we have around here? I think we have a few spares."

"Why would you ever take used items to the church? The people we serve are in need, Alice. They deserve something new, not some used old blanket."

I rub the afghan draped over the back of the couch. It's silky soft. "I don't think used or old fits the description of any of our afghan blankets. Most of them have never seen a lick of light since their creation."

"I take pride in my work, and knitting brings me profound joy, especially when I'm doing it for the Lord. Speaking of work, how much more leave do you have before you go back?"

Mother's always fishing for information about one thing or another. It's a bit annoying at times, but I've grown accustomed to it over the years. I pull my feet up onto the couch. "Not sure yet. I have another week of online training classes to watch before I can go back and get reevaluated to return to duty."

"I'll send a message to Jesus asking him to make sure that everything works in your favor and you return to work soon. I've got his personal number, so to speak." She laughs, but the sound she produces is closer to that of a cackling old witch.

I wish I had a glass of water to throw at her. It wouldn't surprise me if she melted into a gelatinous puddle of blood, flesh, and bones like the witch from *The Wizard of Oz*. At least that's what would've happened in my version of the movie.

"You dial Jesus up so often that I'd imagine He's blocked your number by now." I laugh, but Mother doesn't.

I can feel the heat of her glare on my face. It's like Superman's heat vision, only stronger. "Don't you be making jokes about our Lord and Savior. He died for you, young lady."

Your Lord and Savior. That's what I want to say. I've said as much in the past, but I'm ill prepared for that kind of conversation tonight. "I'm sure Jesus appreciates a good joke. After all, His father created humor, right?"

"You're never too old for me to bend you over my knee and paddle your rear. Keep that in mind before you open that sassy mouth of yours."

I'm close to earning my first black belt in ninjutsu, but even that wouldn't save me from Mother's wrath once it's been invoked. I believe she has some special ability to channel the wrath of her God. I wisely change the subject. "I've barely seen you the past few weeks. Seems our schedules have been at odds with each other."

"At odds because you're avoiding me." Her raptor gaze strangles me even though I can't see it.

I can't deny avoiding her, so I change the subject once more. "How's work at the library?"

"You know better than anyone that my work stays at work. It is nothing more than a means to living."

Why do I bother? I can't compete with her priest. Or Seth for that matter. "You're right, Mother. Sorry I showed interest in your life beyond the church walls."

"Speaking of church, perhaps you should shift that interest toward something important like attending church with me. Father Rogallo would be pleased as pudding to see you again."

I saw that beady-eyed old man once in the last decade and he was anything but pleased to see me once he found out I could see. He took me aside and accused me of selling my soul to the devil. I assured him that I hadn't because it was an impossible task selling something to a non-existent entity. His face turned as red as the devil himself. It wouldn't have surprised me to see horns rise from his temples and a spear-tipped tail whip around the side of his leg. If Mother knew what I'd said to him that day she would've disowned me on the spot.

The doorbell rings and I look in Mother's general direction.

"Well don't just sit there, Alice, answer the door. I don't accept callers this late in the evening. Perhaps you shouldn't either."

If she only knew. I smirk as I rise from the couch and navigate the dark landscape toward the front door. I arrive without incident, unlock the door, and pull it open.

I pray that it's Seth, and his rapturous cologne confirms. "You coming in, or we headed out on our date?"

"Please don't call this a date." Seth kisses my cheek. "Good evening, Gladys."

"You best marry that girl of mine and start calling me Mother."

I roll my eyes. This conversation happens so often I feel like I'm trapped in a time loop like Bill Murray in the movie *Groundhog Day*. I reach out and hook Seth's arm. "Let's get a move on before they close the place down."

I wave toward Mother. "Don't wait up. Might not be back until late."

"May Jesus protect you both," she says.

"Thank you, Gladys. It's always a pleasure seeing you, no matter how brief the time."

"As is with you, son."

I force Seth out the door and close it behind us. I fumble with my keys for several moments before finally finding the right one. I lock the door.

"Why are you so certain that your information checked out with Yolanda?"

"You're here, aren't you? You would've just called otherwise."

"Suppose so, but I still don't understand how you got that information. I can't wrap my mind around what you told me. It's just too unbelievable. However, I've got nothing to lose taking you to see the body. Anyone can visit the city morgue, so Lieut. Frost would have no reason to reprimand either of us."

I smile and offer Seth my arm. "Be a gentleman and walk me to the car."

"That's not your style, Alice. You're miss independent, remember?"

"Most of the time I am, but tonight I want to feel pampered. So take my arm and walk me to the car, rock star." I snort.

He takes my arm. "Fine, but you agreed we'd never talk about The Dive again."

I snort again. "Didn't mention it."

He guides me over to the car, opens the door, and helps me down into it. I tuck myself in and he shuts the door. The seat buckle is still warm from the day but far from scalding as it so often is. I buckle myself in and take a deep breath.

Seth opens his door and rocks the car when he climbs into the driver's seat. He slams the door and the car rocks again. His seatbelt whines as it unwinds, and then the buckle clicks in place.

Seth starts the car, the gears clunk as he puts it in drive, and I'm pinned against the seat as we pull away from the curb. He knows no speed but fast unless it has to do with relationships. In that case, he'd give a sloth its run for the money for the slowest-moving-creature-on-the-planet race.

Most of the time when we sit in silence, I'm comfortable with it, but tonight it's first-date awkward. I think he senses that something has changed with me. He wouldn't be wrong.

I break the ice. "What did you find at the scene earlier?"

"We're not starting there, Alice. In fact, I'm not going to tell you anything about the second victim. If you can do what you said with the body, you won't need me to tell you anything."

I cross my arms and stare straight ahead. "Fine. You want more proof then I'll give it to you."

His hand touches my leg. "Your mother might be oblivious to what's going on with you, but I'm not. Talk to me, Alice. Tell me what's on your mind and what's wrong with you.

"I feel like you've been avoiding me ever since you were put on administrative leave. You're also the most observant person I know, but you've said nothing about the beard I've grown over the last week."

I reach over and touch his face. The coarse hair has already grown past the stubble phase. I fight back a torrent of emotions, but I cannot contain the entire storm.

A tear slips down my cheek. I wipe it away, but not before the car jerks to the right. My hand grabs the "oh crap" handle that hangs above the door and I lean forward as the car screeches to a halt.

Seth leans over and pulls me into his arms. "Talk to me."

I cannot find the right words to explain what's happening to me, so I just blurt out, "I'm blind."

Seth pulls back. "What do you mean you're blind?"

"Literally, Seth. I can't see a thing. I started losing my vision the day Sarah Johnson was murdered."

"Why didn't you say something? Have you seen a doctor?"

"Yeah, on Monday. I saw three different doctors. They ran a bunch of tests on my eyes, did a brain scan, and several other tests. Everything came back normal just like it did ten years ago." I punch myself in the leg. "I don't know what the hell is wrong with me, and you're the first person I've told other than the doctors."

He takes my hand in his. "I'm so sorry. Tell me what I can do."

I hate feeling helpless. "Pretend I can still see."

"You know that isn't normal, right?" The concern in his voice pangs me.

"Nothing about me has ever been normal. There are things about my past that I've kept from you. I tell myself that it's better you don't know because I don't want your pity. Now I realize that it makes me feel like I'm less of a person and I don't want you thinking the same thing of me."

He strokes my head. "There's nothing you could tell me that would alter the way I see you or change how I feel about you."

"Do you remember the other day when you asked me if Sarah's murder was personal to me?"

"Yes, and you told me it wasn't."

"I know I did, but I lied to you. It pained me so much to lie to your face like that, but I didn't know what else to say."

"What are you saying, Alice? You know her?"

"No, it's nothing like that. It's personal to me because she was blind. I was also blind, Seth. The first sixteen years of my life I only knew the world through touch, sound, smell, and taste."

Seth exhales. "Blind..."

"Yes. I immediately understood her life better than most."

"So how did you gain your vision? Drugs? A procedure?"

"I don't know for certain how it happened. Could've been any one of those. I fell and hit my head ten years ago and when I regained consciousness, I could see a little. Over a few days, my vision improved."

"Alice... why would you keep that from anyone?"

"I didn't think they'd let me on the force if anyone knew I was blind most of my life."

"Honestly, I'm not sure what they would've said." The inflection in his voice belies his words.

"When I woke up this morning and was completely blind again, I didn't know what to do. How can I go back to work this way?" I sob once and catch myself.

Seth hands me a tissue. "You can't. You need to inform Lieut. Frost as soon as possible."

"If I do that I'll be off the case for good and probably out of a job."

"What alternative is there? You can't fake having vision forever."

"I know, but I need some time to figure this out."

Seth groans. "I won't say anything, but I won't lie for you either."

"I'm not asking you to lie for me. Just don't shut me out, Seth. I need to see this case to closure and I need you."

He kisses my forehead, my left cheek, and my lips. "I'm not going anywhere, and we'll continue to work the case together from my place."

His words bring me solace, but the task ahead keeps my heart grounded. "Good. Can we start by going to the morgue now? I still need to see Cara's body."

"Is there anything else you want to tell me first?" A hint of accusation mires his soft tone. "Are you holding anything else back?"

Everything in my storage unit comes to the forefront of my mind. "No." I tell myself that this lie is for his own good, but waves of guilt thrust my heart against the rocks and tear me apart inside. I vow to never lie to him again.

Ten minutes later we arrive at the City Morgue. They're conveniently located right across the street from St. Thomas Medical Center. I remember it being a drab red brick building with a small blue sign next to the front door that reads "City Morgue." I guess people prefer to forget these kinds of places exist. I don't blame them.

Seth moves around the car and helps me out. We walk over to the front entrance and Seth presses the button for assistance. Someone's always here working, but normal visiting hours are eight to five. A few minutes later, one of the morgue attendants comes to the door.

I assume Seth flashes the person his credentials because the door creaks open. "Welcome, Detective Ryan." It's a woman's voice. She sounds Russian.

"Evening, Sasha." Seth leads us through the door and down a long hallway toward the positive temperature cold chambers. Goosebumps form on my arms. I should've brought a jacket or sweater with me. I always forget how cold they keep this place, but it makes sense.

We reach the cold chambers and another morgue attendant greets us. "Ah, Detective Ryan. I've been expecting you, and your timing is impeccable." This man has a Boston accent. It's surprising how much you can tell about a person just by their voice.

"Mr. Massey. It's good to see you again. I gather you have everything prepared for us?"

"I do. You'll find the body of Cara Strum in exam room three. I've just completed the autopsy report on her. I've also taken the liberty of leaving a copy of it for you in the exam room."

My stomach aches with nerves. "Thank you, Mr. Massey. Will you be joining us?"

"No, Detective Bergman. You and Detective Ryan will be on your own."

Breathing becomes a bit easier. "Very good. Busy night?"

"Quite so. An apparent turf war left thirteen dead. Sasha and I will be working through the night."

"I heard about that," says Seth.

I nudge Seth. "Let's get this over with, Detective Ryan."

We exit the cold chambers and make our way down the hall to exam room three. Seth closes the door behind us. Nausea swirls in the pit of my stomach and my hands are shaking. What if my experience with Sarah Johnson was an anomaly? Or what if she created the link and not me?

Seth leads me over to a table and sets my hand on its troughed, metal edge. "Everything's covered except for her head."

I hug myself, chilled from both the room and the thought of touching this young girl's corpse. With Sarah it was different. I could see her, and she became someone to me, not just some cold vessel of flesh and bone. But I don't know Cara.

Seth touches my shoulder. "Are you ready?"

I shrug. "I don't know. Now that we're here I'm not sure I can do this."

"I can leave the room if it would help."

I reach up and put my hand over his. "No, please stay. I need you here."

He kisses the top of my head. "What can I do then?"

"Tell me about her. What does she look like? What is she wearing? Anything at all that will help me connect with her."

"In the photos her dad showed us, she was one of the most beautiful young girls I've seen. She has a rich brown complexion and a starfield of brown and black freckles on her cheeks. Her round face is complemented by poufy lips, a short but cute nose, and big brown eyes.

"Her hair is styled in a bob just above her slender shoulders. Her entire body is slender, even for her age, but the expressions she produces in her photos tells you that she's one ornery girl. You'd never know from the photos that she was visually impaired."

An image of Cara forms in my mind and settles my nerves. "Thank you, Seth. That helped me more than you know."

I lower my arm and latch onto the lip of the table. The cold steel bites at my fingertips, but I push the thought of it to the back of my mind. "You might give me some room now. I'm not sure what's going to happen."

Seth's boots echo on the tile floor as he steps back several feet. "Do your thing."

I take a pair of latex gloves from my pocket and snap them on. I hate their rubbery smell and the fact that my hands sweat in them within seconds of donning them, but I've yet to find an alternative.

Even though I can't see, I close my eyes. I slide my palms across the table until I reach Cara's shoulders. They're covered by a sheet that feels more like a shower curtain than anything else. I move my hands closer together and touch her cold, slender neck. My fingers move up her neck, to her jaw, and to her round cheeks. It feels like I'm holding a large ice cube between my hands.

Show me Cara. Let me feel what he did to you. I lean forward and rest my forehead against hers. Seth gasps and I don't blame him. I'd gasp myself if I were in his shoes.

Cara's skin softens, and her cheeks warm my hands. As with Sarah, I feel that unexplainable shift in myself again. I open my eyes and know that I am no longer myself.

I *am* Cara Strum.

* * * * *

I always know when he arrives. The room blooms with garlic and pickles and cigarettes. I smell them now. I smile at the corner of my room, where the shadows are the darkest, because that's where he always comes from and it's the polite thing to do.

His visits have become more frequent and he stays longer each time. I wonder why that is. What's so fascinating about a girl like me? I guess it doesn't matter because he's the only friend I have.

Sometimes I speak to him, but he never replies. In fact, he never makes a sound. My silent friend could be a mute, but I'm doubtful of it. Sometimes I wonder if he exists at all.

My bedroom door whines and clicks shut. I sit up straight in my bed and pull my covers up to my mouth. My bed squeaks and bounces and I turn into a pillar of stone.

I finally find my voice, but it's shaky, stuttered, and little more than a whisper. "Ha-ha-have you c-come out of the sh-sh-shadows?"

He sits right behind me on the bed. His mouth is right next to my ear and his hot breath tickles when he whispers. "Yes, Cara."

I cannot keep from shaking. "Who are y-you?"

His hands wrap my waist, work themselves underneath my shirt, and slide up the sides of my ribcage, pulling my shirt up with them. They're rough hands, like sandpaper. Terror grips me so completely that I cannot open my mouth to scream. I cannot even cry.

His hands are on my breasts and then under my armpits and then around my throat. He squeezes so hard that I cannot breathe. My survival instinct kicks in, but is it too late?

My arms flail over my head as I try to grab, scratch, and claw anything I can. I snag something on a broken nail and pull back as hard as I can. I feel it pull like the finger of a rubber glove and then it rips.

"You'll pay for that." He squeezes harder until something pops in my throat.

He shoves me forward on the bed and smothers my head in the covers. Something sharp slices my back and my arms and legs go limp. He rolls me over and my arms flop like a ragdoll. I can breathe again, but it hurts so bad. I try to scream, but no sound comes out.

He strokes my head. "You want to know who I am? I'm the exterminator. I rid the world of cancerous freaks like you. You don't deserve to live. You make those like me feel special until you know what we look like and then you laugh at us just like the others. You're the birth defect, Cara, not me. The proof is on your wrist."

Tears streak the sides of my face. I feel his hands on my abdomen. His fingers under the top hem of my panties. He grabs them and rips them off of me. I am helpless to do anything but wheeze and whimper.

He takes my hand, lifts it to his face, and rubs my fingers against it. It's smooth and slick. "You see? You girls smile for this."

I doubt anyone smiles for him.

My hand slides down to his neck and I feel a ridge across it like a scar. He curls my fingers underneath the ridge with his and we pull upward together. I don't understand what's happening at first, but then I realize he's been wearing a mask.

He shoves my fingers against his face again but this time it's leathered and pockmarked. "No more smiles. She has no more smiles for me."

In some sick and twisted way I feel sorry for him. I know what it's like to be rejected.

My hand flops back on the bed when he lets it go. He pounds on something that sounds hollow. Then I hear the strike of a match and smell it. Then the smell is replaced by that of a cheap cigarette.

He moves away from me and pushes my legs apart. I beg God to make whatever is about to happen stop, but He cannot hear me without my voice.

I cannot move but I can still feel pain. The inside of my right thigh erupts with scorching pain. I scream in my mind as the stench of burning flesh fills my nostrils. Again and again, he burns the inside of my leg. I beg God to make it stop and this time He listens. The pain dies out and a peace like I've never known fills me until I'm overflowing with joy.

The darkness surrounding me turns into a light so brilliantly bright that it rivals the sun. I reach toward the heavens and beg to be taken home.

* * * * *

I straighten and gasp as my spirit returns to me. Seth's right there to catch me as my legs give out.

"I've got you, Alice."

He pulls me to the examination room floor and holds me in his arms until I gather back my strength. I'm a wretched mess, covered in a film of sweat and tears and chilled to the bone.

I said I wouldn't cry again, and I haven't. The tears falling from my eyes aren't mine but hers. Ones she never had a chance to shed. The bastard is malevolent and more sadistic than I could have ever imagined.

"Seth, we can't let him kill again. We've got to stop him." He wipes the tears from my eyes, but new ones replace them.

"You know we're doing everything we can. Hell, I brought you to a morgue so that you could experience the last moments of the victim's life." His voice tells me he still doesn't believe. "What more can we be doing?"

I swallow, but the large lump of guilt lodged in my throat makes it difficult. "I don't know, but I did learn something from this experience."

"You did? What's that?"

"He wears masks. I can't be certain, but I think they're made of latex."

"And you think that's why no one's seen the man based on the picture Yolanda drew?"

"Exactly. She doesn't know what he looks like any more than we do. That's why he didn't fear her living. In fact, I don't think he ever intended for her to die."

"Why is that?"

"Because he's targeting blind girls for a specific reason. He wears the mask to hide his deformed face."

"So we're looking for someone who's physically deformed… but what if he wears a mask all the time? How will we ever find him?"

I squeeze my head between my knees. "I don't know. We're definitely missing something."

"A lot of things. Like motive."

"He burned the inside of Cara's right thigh. Is it braille like what we found on Sarah's left thigh?"

Seth leans back. "How did you know it was her right leg?"

"Dammit." I glare up at him even though I can't see him. "What will it take for you to believe me?"

"Give me time. It's a lot to take in." He squeezes my shoulder. "Is there anything else you can tell me?"

The inside of my left wrist itches something fierce. When I start to scratch it, I notice it's raised again like it was the day I became Sarah. *What in the world does it mean?* It must be related to the visions, but I can't fathom how or why.

It reminds me about what the Braille Killer said to Cara. "Does she have a birthmark on her left wrist?"

Seth gasps. "You really *did* experience something?"

He makes me want to scream. "I'll take that as a 'yes'."

"Yeah, but I don't recall what it looks like. Want me to check?"

I sit up straight. "Did Sarah have one too?" I don't remember the coroner's report saying anything about a birthmark, but it could've been missed. In my mind I return to her room again and see her arms crossed over her abdomen. *Damn.*

"I don't know. Is there some significance to it if she does?"

I shrug, but the answer is clear if she does. It would tie her and Sarah to me in another way besides being blind. Its meaning is beyond me though.

We sit in silence for several minutes before Seth speaks again. "I don't understand how it's possible, but I believe you now. And, to answer your earlier question, there was a word on Cara's thigh. It says B A L I N G."

"Baling? As in evading responsibility?"

"I guess so."

"Amerce baling…" I tap my fingers on my leg. It helps me think sometimes. "…to punish with an arbitrary penalty and to give up on or abandon something, as to evade a responsibility."

Seth slaps the floor. "What the hell is that supposed to mean? Are these words supposed to be some sort of label or brand? Sins of their parents or something like that?"

"Like in the movie *Seven*?" I ask.

"Yeah, like that. Maybe he's a religious nutcase or something."

The meaning of the two words punches me in the gut and takes my breath. I know the Braille Killer has directed them at me. It's another way of him telling me that he killed these girls because of me. In his twisted mind I've evaded taking responsibility for Denise's death for a decade.

A new revelation hits me even harder. He's targeting blind girls because I was blind when Denise died. Those girls represent what he despises most: *me*.

What I can't figure out is his affinity for Denise. What created such a strong bond between them that would drive him to kill? I must get back to my storage unit and study the notes more. I need to ditch Seth and I feel horrible about it.

"He may very well be a nutcase, but I'm starting to feel like one too. Can you drop me off at Veronica's? This whole dead body vision thing has wiped me out. I think I could sleep for several days right now." But there's no time for sleep.

Seth stands and helps me to my feet. "Sure you don't wanna crash at my place? I don't mind."

He puts his arm around me and we head out of exam room three. "Any other day I'd jump at the chance to sleep with you, but I can't tonight. Those visions of what he did to Cara are haunting me already."

"Veronica's it is then."

Veronica's...

Ahead of me is a road I don't want to travel: revealing the truth that I've kept concealed for a decade. A truth that leaves my skin crawling every time I think about it. A truth that shames me to the core. A truth that has already left one girl dead. A truth that I am a killer even if I didn't physically commit the crimes. No matter how much I scrub my hands, they will never be clean again.

I'm not looking forward to filling Veronica in on all the details of my stalker, the Braille Killer. I hope she'll forgive me for keeping her in the dark for so long when I do though. I already feel bad about unloading on her and we haven't even arrived at her place yet. Unfortunately, I can't think of any other way to continue my investigation without her. She'll be my eyes once again, just like she was in high school.

We'll be the real life *Cagney & Lacey*. Kinda.

CHAPTER EIGHTEEN

I LAY BACK IN Veronica's wicker papasan chair and I can feel the threads of sleep pulling me down. Guenter's fast asleep on my stomach and chest. The poor little guy must've had a rough day to be so zonked out. I stroke his head and back. She had him groomed earlier today and now his fur is soft and fluffy like cotton candy and clouds.

Veronica works the graveyard shift during the week at St. Thomas Medical Center as a NICU nurse, so she's used to being up all night. I expect her to emerge from her bedroom like a vampire soon. When she does, I'll spring the news about being blind on her like a fully-wound jack-in-the-box.

Guenter wags his tail and whimpers. He's probably dreaming of chasing a dirty old cat. He loves hating cats almost as much as I do. He reminds me so much of Artemis, the guide dog I used to own. Not in shape or size but in personality. Guenter's one of the gentlest dogs I've ever met. Artemis passed away four years ago. That day was one of the hardest of my life. She was my best friend for so many years and my eyes still mist every time I think about her.

"You traitorous little thing."

I smile. Dracula has emerged. "You talking to me or Guenter?"

"Guenter. He must've bailed on me when you arrived earlier." The seat cushion moans when Veronica plops down on her brown leather recliner.

"Do you blame him? The cute guys always flock to me."

"You wish! You'd better watch it, or I'll start lining up the uglies for you again."

"So…" So much for a jack-in-the-box. "I have a confession."

Veronica shifts in her chair. "I likes me some confessions. What you got, girl?"

"I can't… I'm…" Man is this hard.

"Do I have to go over there and beat it out of you? You know I will."

My chest tightens, and I think I might start crying. "I'm blind. There, I said it."

Veronica laughs really hard. When I don't join her it morphs into a chuckle and then stops altogether. "You're serious, aren't you?"

My body jerks as I try to hold back the tears but it's a quick battle and I don't win. I sob and cough, my words spewing out in bursts. "I woke up yesterday and couldn't see anymore."

Veronica gets up off her recliner, picks Guenter up off of me, and sets him on the floor. He whines and barks once. She crawls into the chair with me and we hold each other. She strokes my hair and I cry into her shoulder.

"I'm so sorry, Ally. Have you told Seth or your mother?"

I sniff. "Only Seth. I had no choice but to tell him because I needed a ride. I'm pretty sure Mother knows though. You know how she is."

"It didn't just happen overnight, did it?" I know that tone. It's more of a statement than a question.

"It started about ten days ago."

"That explains the glasses and cane. I knew something was up. Why didn't you just tell me?"

"I've been so busy and under so much stress the last two weeks that I didn't want to talk to anyone about it. I've been having migraines and thought it might be related. I was hoping it'd just go away."

"Have you talked to your doctor about it?"

"Ugh. You sound like Mother, Vee."

She squeezes my head in the crook of her arm. "Don't lump me into that camp just because I care about you, Ally."

"I'm sorry. That was insensitive of me."

"Dang straight it was." She kisses my forehead.

"I saw several doctors last week. Nothing's changed. No answers."

"Sorry, girl. If I think of something, I'll let you know."

"Vee… there's something else I need to tell you, but I'm not sure if I can."

She pulls away and strokes my cheek. "There ain't nothing you can't tell me. You know that. We be like yin and yang. Butter and toast. Peanut butter and chocolate. Pepperoni—"

"Yeah, I got it after the first pairing of things."

"So lay it on me then. What's got you so wound?"

"It all has to do with work and the case Seth and I am working. And me."

"And?"

"What I'm about to tell you stays between us."

"As in you, me, and Seth?"

"No! As in you and me. What I'm gonna tell you Seth doesn't even know. He can't know. Do you understand?"

"I hear what you're saying, but it doesn't compute. Seth is your partner and boyfriend. If this is about work and the case you're working, shouldn't he know?"

"No. I mean yes, most of the time. Not this though." I sigh. "Forget it Vee. I don't want to get you involved either."

Veronica nudges my shoulder. "Oh hell no. You don't start something heavy like that and then get to brush it under the rug. You lay it on me, or you'll be spending the rest of your life tied to my bed until you do. I'll go *Misery* on your ass if I have to. We clear?"

"Fine, but you gotta promise you'll never tell Seth even if he begs you or threatens to torture you."

She presses her forehead against mine. "Never a soul. Girl Scout Cookie honor or whatever."

"Do you remember what happened to me ten years ago?"

"Yeah, you got your sight. How could I forget?"

"Yeah, but do you remember Denise?"

"The girl that died at your doctor's office, right?"

"Yeah." I close my eyes. "Ever since that day, I've received a package on the anniversary of her death. The package always includes a note in braille and some sort of picture or object."

Veronica jerks back and the entire chair tilts sideways before righting itself. "Okay, not only is that creepy, but why wouldn't you let me in the loop on this?"

"I didn't want to freak you out. Besides, I don't think about it very often." It's not entirely untrue.

"How long have I known you, Ally? Thirteen years or so? I know when you're lying. You don't look at me."

I open my eyes. "Better? It isn't for me. Still can't see you."

"You know what I mean. Just continue."

"Okay, so each letter is like a poem, and the poems always blame me for Denise's death and tell me I need to confess."

"Damn, that's messed up. That chick fell to her death on accident."

"I know, but I haven't gotten to the worst part of it."

"Well spit it out."

"The note last year told me that it was my last chance to confess. The note this year said the blood is on my hands. The same day a young blind girl was murdered."

"Holy…"

"Yeah, exactly. Ten years and then he murders someone. I can't tell Seth now because of everything that's happening. I wish I'd told him two years ago."

"Wow. Don't know what to say to that."

"Yeah, but it gets worse."

She squeezes my thigh. "How the hell does it get worse from there?"

"I removed evidence from a crime scene."

Veronica sits up. "What the—"

"And this morning I received another package and another dead girl surfaced. I don't know what to do anymore."

"You've gotta tell Seth, Ally."

"No! That's why I'm telling you. So Seth doesn't need to know."

"And what am I supposed to do about it?"

"Help me solve the case and nail this bastard."

"And how are we supposed to do that when you're on mandatory leave?"

"I've got a storage unit..."

"You've got a what?"

"Yeah, it's got all the letters and objects the killer has sent me over the last ten years." My voice is full of desperation, but it's all I have left at this point. "I need you to help me go through it all again so that we can figure out who he is and where to find him before he kills another little girl. I need your eyes, Vee."

"What you need is a psychiatrist."

"Are you gonna help me or not?"

"Ugh." Veronica gets up and the chair shakes. "Do I really have a choice at this point?"

"Nope. That's why you're my bestie."

"Until the end, my friend. I think *I* might need to see a shrink by the time this is over."

I laugh. "Luckily for you, I know a good one."

Veronica exhales loudly. "I'm guessing you want to go over to that storage unit of yours tonight."

"The case won't solve itself."

"Fine. Let me throw on some clothes and we'll go have ourselves a merry old time." I hear her pad away.

I shout, "Love you, Vee." I imagine she gave me the one-finger salute, but I wouldn't stake my life on it.

Guenter jumps back up in the chair with me and nuzzles my neck. "And I love you too, little guy."

* * * * *

Veronica's arm is locked around mine. "This place is freaky, girl. You've been coming here for ten years by yourself?" Her voice is barely a whisper over the buzzing lights.

Our footsteps echo down the corridor and we sound like a heard of goats, bleating every time the lights flicker. I clutch Esther in my free hand — that's what I've decided to name my new black cane. I didn't like the name Rico had given it. Too manly. Too not me.

"Seven years, and it's definitely creepier when you're blind." My mind focuses on storage unit 109. "Be on the lookout for anyone hanging around or following us."

"You asking me to haul your butt back out the front doors?"

"We'll be fine."

We stop, and Veronica presses the button for the elevator. It dings and opens immediately. We clamber into it and the doors close behind us.

"Third floor," I say.

Veronica presses the button and the elevator jerks as it begins its ascent. Ten seconds later it comes to a halt. I've ridden the elevator in this facility enough times to know that we've stopped way short of the third floor.

The doors slide open. "Good evening, ladies."

Veronica squeals and nearly jerks my arm off. I raise Esther, ready to strike.

"Whoa, I'm so sorry. Didn't mean to give you a fright."

My heart is racing, but I know that voice. "Bill?"

"Oh, hey Alice. Good to see you again. Who's the beautiful woman hanging on your arm?"

I lower Esther. "This is my girlfriend Veronica."

"Pleasure, I'm sure," says Veronica.

"Oh, wow. Didn't realize... well, you know. Hey, I'm not judging though. Makes sense now with what happened before."

I roll my eyes. "Don't be a twit, Bill. We're not lesbians." *At least not both of us.*

Veronica kisses my cheek. "Says you." I can only imagine what kinds of gestures she's making.

"You alright, Alice? You seem different somehow."

"Long day, Bill. You gonna get in or just stand there?"

"Oh, right. Sorry. Headed down. I'll catch it again on the way back. Stop by anytime."

The doors slide closed and we're ascending once again. "Don't ask, Vee."

"No wonder you've never brought Seth over here." She nudges me in the ribs. "Got an ugly on the side. What happened *before*?"

I'm about to lay into her in our playful banter way, but the elevator lurches to a halt, dings, and the doors slide open. "Saved by the bell."

We exit, and I guide Veronica to the left. "Three forty-seven is my unit."

"Oh, you got something? Bring it, girl."

"I could take you down so far that you'd be looking up for days just to see the surface. Even my uglies are better than your have-nots."

"Burn—" Veronica yanks me to the side of the corridor. "Keep walking," she whispers.

My pulse rises. Why does this place have to be so creepy? I reach for my gun but of course it isn't there. Not only am I blind but I'm on administrative leave as well. What kind of irresponsible dolt would let me carry now? Then again, Esther is the deadliest weapon I've ever wielded.

Veronica pulls me to a stop. I can feel her breath on my ear. "I think the creeper's gone," she whispers. "Hand me your keys before he decides to come back around."

"I can open it. The dials are in braille."

"Keys are faster."

"Fine." I pull a wad of keys from my pocket and she takes them from me. "It's the one with the trapezoid-shaped top."

"Got it."

"Once we're inside the unit we can lock it from the inside."

"That seems a bit odd. Why would they lock from the inside?"

"I modified it so that no one can disturb me."

I hear the lock click open and slide through the metal ring. "Or kill you."

Veronica hands me the lock and keys. She grunts, and I hear the door roll up. I duck inside the unit and move out of the way. The door rolls back down and thuds against the concrete floor.

"There's a bar on your right attached to the door. Do you see it or feel it?"

Veronica grunts and hits the door a few times. "I think I found it."

"Good. Shove it toward the wall."

The sound of metal scraping metal fills the enclosed space and ends with a *thunk*. "You've gotta find a better place, Ally. I will *not* be coming back here with you."

"Help me solve this case tonight and we won't *need* to come back."

Veronica grabs my hand. She's trembling. "Ugh. I ain't no Nancy Drew, but I'll do what I can to help."

"Vee, what did the guy in the corridor look like?"

She shudders. "Girl, my skin's still crawling. He was beyond a creeper standing in the shadows. He made that Bill guy look like the nicest, sexiest man on the planet."

"Sounds pretty bad. Sometimes it pays to be blind. Did you get a look at his face?"

"More than I wanted. Almost lost it when I saw his Freddy Krueger mug."

I freeze and can't breathe.

"Ally are you okay?" She touches my shoulder and I flinch.

My grip on Esther tightens. "We need to go back out there and find him."

Veronica drops my hand. "The hell you say? I ain't going back out there until it's light outside."

"We have to, Vee. I think he might be our guy. Besides, there aren't any windows in this place."

Veronica groans. "I'm sorry, but I didn't sign up for chasing down psycho killers in some creepy-ass storage facility. I'm a nurse, Ally, not some badass ninja detective like you."

I sigh. She has a point. "You're right. Do you have a cell signal in here?" I'm pretty certain of the answer she'll give me, but she does have a different service provider than me.

"No service," she whispers. "This just keeps getting better by the minute." She squeezes my forearm hard. "We'll die in here, won't we? No, don't answer that."

"You're gonna be just fine. Take a deep breath."

She takes several deep breaths. "How am I supposed to help you do anything in the dark?"

I peel her hand off of mine. "Don't move. I'll turn on the light."

"I'm sorry, but it would suck to be blind."

I walk over to my desk. "I never thought it was that bad growing up, but I had nothing to compare it to. However, after having sight for the last ten years, I'd say there are advantages to both."

I locate the battery powered lantern and switch it on. "Welcome to my secret world."

Veronica gasps. "Holy cow, Ally! A real life crime board. I feel like I'm on an episode of *Castle* or something."

I smile. "Some things on TV are actually credible. Crime boards like this one organize case facts and help make it solvable."

Veronica grabs my arm. "You and Denise? I don't understand, Ally. We need to have a serious talk."

"I know, Vee." Searing pain ripples through my entire body. "There were some things that happened in my life that I could never tell you about."

"I get that we all have secrets, but this is crazy. I had no idea you were ever into girls, especially not ones like her." I can feel the hurt in her voice just as much as I can hear it. "You should've told me."

"Take a closer look at that photo. Do I look happy?"

She lets go of my arm and walks over to the board. "You're... crying. What happened?"

"Remember the week of school I missed toward the end of our senior year?"

"Yeah, you said you had the measles or something."

"I know what I told you, but I lied." I sit down in my chair. "Denise and this guy I'm hunting raped me and beat me so bad that I spent an entire week in the hospital."

"Why didn't you tell me? You know I would've been there for you."

Tears well in my eyes. "I was so embarrassed and ashamed of what they did to me that I repressed the memories."

"And that's why you were seeing Dr. Strong, isn't it? It was never about the dream study."

"Honestly, it was both. I started having such bad nightmares that I was afraid to sleep for several months. Music is the only thing that saved me. The therapy helped unlock my memories."

Veronica walks over and smooths back my hair. "Well I'm glad that bitch died. If she hadn't, I'd go hunt her down right now and take her out."

"Now you understand why I have to find this guy?"

The steel in her voice calms me. "Completely. Walk me through each of these letters. Maybe I can help you discover something you've overlooked."

I wipe my eyes and stand. "I've read and analyzed every word of those letters so many times but there seems to be no real substance to them."

"We don't think the same way though. That's the reason you got me involved, right?"

"That, plus you can see."

"There's that too. How about we start with you reading the letters since I don't know braille."

I walk over to the corkboard and begin reading the letters from oldest to newest. Several times Veronica stops me, and we ponder the meaning of a verse but neither of us comes to any sort of revelation on any of it.

I kick my chair into the desk. "This is what happens every time. Nothing but brick walls. I feel like torching the place and just walking away."

Veronica hugs me from behind and rests her chin on my shoulder. "You and I both know there's no quit in you. You'll get this figured out. I'm certain of it."

I lean my head against hers. "And how many more girls will die in the process? He seems to be killing another girl every ten days. It's all my fault and I feel helpless to stop it."

"The only possible way this could even be remotely your fault is if you *did* kill Denise. If you didn't, you should tell the police. Or at least Seth. You didn't though, right?"

"Sometimes I wonder if I did. Maybe this psycho is right in blaming me."

"I know for a fact that you didn't even if she deserved it. You're not that kind of person. You value life, even for those undeserving of it."

"I didn't know how she was involved in all of this until I received that picture of her and me. Maybe I knew subconsciously." I raise my arms. "I don't know."

She kisses my cheek. "You look beyond beat, Ally. We should go back to my place so that you can crash for a few hours."

"You're right. I can't even think straight right now."

"When did you sleep last?"

"I don't know. What day is it?"

"Officially, it's Saturday morning. Three o'clock."

"Saturday?" All my days have blurred together without having a job to go to. "Let's get out of here."

"It ain't light outside yet, but I can't take much more of this place either. It's like a steel coffin. Let's bolt." Veronica moves away from me and slides the bar back on the door.

I switch the lantern off and there's a rap on the door. Three successive knocks. Veronica swears, and I tense up. I move toward the door, Esther in hand.

"Alice, it's Bill. You in there?"

"Open the door, Vee. I've got a man to beat with my cane."

"Not if I get my hands around his neck first." Veronica rolls up the door.

"What the hell, Bill? You mental or something?"

"Sorry, Alice. I just saw George Hallard leaving the building and wanted to make sure you two were okay."

"Aside from you scaring the crap out of us, we're fine," says Veronica.

"Good, good. You find his place the other day?"

"I did, but it wasn't the man I was looking for. The George Hallard I met said he didn't know anything about a storage unit."

Bill's keys jangle. He seems to play with them when he's nervous. "Well that just about takes the cake. Who's the man that comes in all the time claiming to be George Hallard then?"

"That's a good question. Why was he here anyway? Didn't he move out of here the day we spoke?"

"That was only the one storage unit. He has two others here."

"And you didn't think to tell me that the other day?"

"You were only asking about the one. Didn't know you cared about the others."

Veronica guffaws. "Is this guy for real? Are you really that dense, Bill?"

I reach out, find Veronica's arm, and hold it. "It's okay, Vee. Bill lost his mom and has had a rough time of it since. Go easy on him."

"Hey, this is your circus. I'm just here for the spectacle."

"Did you happen to catch what he was driving?" I ask.

"Oh, yeah. Wouldn't ever forget a ride like that. 1968 British Triumph T120 Bonneville. Maroon and white tank with black trim. Chrome pipes. Black leather seat. Mmm, she was a beauty."

"Did you get a look at the plates?"

"Plates? No, barely got a peak at the bike."

"Damn." It's time to regroup and focus on what we do know. "Where are those additional units of his?"

"One's right around the corner over here and the other is on the top floor. Refrigerated unit."

"Refrigerated?" asks Veronica. "What would someone store in a unit like that?"

Bill whistles. "Everything you could think of and more. Food. Furniture. Paint supplies. Motorcycles. Some people use them for tire storage as well. Guess it saves them from dry rot during our hot summers."

I let go of Veronica's arm and step out of the unit. "Can we get into them?"

"You know the drill. Show me a warrant and I'd be happy to."

"Fine." I turn toward Veronica. "Let's lock up and get back to your place. We've got a lot of things to figure out."

CHAPTER NINETEEN

IT'S MONDAY MORNING, AND every step is a potential minefield at the Bergman house. Mother's in a tizzy over a death at her church. Apparently, one of the parishioners dropped dead in the row in front of her right in the middle of Sunday morning mass. I told her that it was a perfect place to kick the bucket, but she didn't find that funny. In fact she got downright nasty about it.

What I really think is bothering her has nothing to do with the death at church. I think she's upset with me for not saying anything about being blind again. I'm not really sure how she could blame me though. Every time I try to talk to Mother about anything serious, she winds up bombarding me with talk of God. I don't want to talk about God. Ever. Avoidance has been the key for me for the last week, but now there's no getting around the fact that I can't see at all.

"You win, Mother." I step into the kitchen, slide one of the chairs out from under the kitchen table, and sit down.

"What game are we playing this time, Alice? The one where you keep lying to me or the one where you finally tell me the truth?"

I rap my knuckles on the table. I know it drives her crazy, but I can't help it. I'm honestly not trying to upset her further. "I'm blind again. Just like before."

"I know. You have been for the last several days." She's either peeling potatoes or carrots, but I can't tell which by the sound. "What made you decide to tell me now?"

"Circumstances. I figured I couldn't bang around here forever without you noticing. I also wasn't ready to admit it to myself. I'm at a loss as to what's going on with me and it scares me. I've gotten so used to seeing that I don't know if I can handle being blind again."

"You don't need to be strong all the time. I'm here for you, Seth's here for you, Veronica's here for you, and so is God. We can be your strength if you'll just let us in."

I lean back in the chair and balance on its back legs. "How do you do it? How do you continue to have faith in your God when everything you know and everything you care about dies or crumbles around you? How do you not blame Him for it? If He truly is the God of the universe and controls everything, then isn't He also to blame for everything? How is it possible for Him to be one and not the other? The Creator but *not* the Destroyer. How do you explain that?"

The peeler stops, the chair next to me slides out from under the table, and mother sits down next to me. I drop the front of my chair back to the floor. I don't need her to touch me to feel her presence. I've felt it since the day I was born. It's in this moment that I realize I need her more now than I ever knew. Her leg touches mine and I tremble.

Mother takes a deep breath and I can't help but hold mine. "God is omniscient and omnipresent. He is the Alpha and the Omega. He knew the end before the beginning ever started and everything else in between. He *is* the Creator *and* the Destroyer, but not out of hate or spite but of love. He is just and righteous. Every decision we make forms our path, and the path to Him is narrow, so we might falter from time to time and find ourselves caught in the briar patch when what He wanted for us was to be basking in the light of His presence.

"When Adam and Eve ate of the forbidden fruit in the garden of Eden it set in motion a chain of events that still affect us. In that moment, sin entered the world and through it death, disease, and evil. God knew this would happen from the beginning and laid out plans to send His only begotten son, Jesus Christ, to this earth as a human to take away sin.

"Jesus lived a sinless life, preached the truth of His father God, and paid the ultimate sacrifice for it. Thank God that He did. He conquered death and opened a pathway to God. Not only did He create this pathway, but He made following it so simple. Believe in Jesus Christ as the Son of God and accept Him as your Savior. That's all there is to it."

I shift on my chair. This talk always makes me feel so uncomfortable. "If that's all there is to it then why do you jump through so many hoops for your church? Why do you go to confession and confess your sins to a man? Can you not speak to God and Jesus directly? Is that not what your Bible teaches?"

Mother pats the top of my hand. "Don't confuse what's obligatory with what's given freely. I don't do works to get into heaven but because I'm going to heaven. And the purpose of confession is to be held accountable for what we do, not because we can't talk to God directly."

The air seems to have thickened, each breath more difficult than the last. My palms are wet with sweat, and my left leg bounces without restraint underneath the table.

I can't take any more God talk, so I move to change the subject. "I guess we'll have to agree to disagree for now. What I'd really like is to try and figure out how I move forward. Where do I go from here? If my sight isn't restored again then who am I? I'll no longer be able to be a homicide detective. I don't know how to be anything else. I have no other value."

She puts her arm around me and pulls me close to her. "That's nothing more than the devil talking, Alice. Every breath you breathe adds value to this world. You affect those around you in ways you'll never see or understand, including me. You may choose to walk in darkness but you're still the light of my life. You are my daughter and you're the most precious thing I have on this earth."

I lay my head on her bosom. Her heart beats slowly. Softly. It calms me. "Why do you think this is happening to me?"

She strokes my head and rubs my back like she used to do when I was little and scared. "It could be any number of things. I can tell just by yours and Seth's demeanors that work has been really stressful as of late. I don't know what case you're working, but it seems to be pulling you down into the darkness with it. On top of that, you also lost a coworker. That's difficult for anyone to handle."

"That's all true but I don't think that's the issue. I started losing my vision before any of that started."

"Then perhaps it's one of the treatments you underwent. Maybe one of them helped you and now its effects have worn off. Or maybe one of the various surgeries helped bring your vision back and now it has reverted somehow. Have you contacted any of the doctors who treated you?"

"I'm going to see Dr. Strong again."

"The shrink? And what do you hope to gain by seeing him again?"

"If it really is stress related, I thought it might help. He helped me learn to cope with things in the past."

"Well then I suggest you give him a call and set up an appointment. In the meantime, I suggest you pray about it. God is the king of miracles."

"How about you pray about it and I'll see Dr. Strong? Besides, I have an appointment with him today."

"I started praying for you the moment I found out I was pregnant, and I've never stopped."

I take a deep breath and exhale. "Thank you, Mother."

* * * * *

I step through the double doors of the Westin Medical Group complex and it's 2008 again. The bitter scent of coffee wafts in the air, but it doesn't cover the acidic smells of ammonia and bleach. I sweep Esther back and forth as I ford the sea of porcelain tile. My heels click with each step like a prancing dog.

I reach the curved stairway without issue and grab onto the banister. Its smooth, wooden surface caresses my fingers like fine silk, but the euphoria is fleeting as my mind conjures images of Denise's broken body lying on the floor. Her glassy eyes stare up at me as her bloody headdress spreads ever wider.

Her arm rises from the pool of blood and she points a crooked finger at me. Her lips move but she makes no sound. It doesn't matter though because I know what she's saying. She accuses me just like he does. "You did this to me, Alice. I'm dead because of you."

I rush up the stairs, tripping over the treads several times. I crash to my knees just as I reach the top and topple over. It's roughly the same spot where I hit my head ten years before. I rise, brush off my knees, and straighten my clothes. I pick Esther up off the floor and make my way to the first office on the right.

The door is open, so I knock on the wood-cased doorframe. "Dr. Strong?"

"Please come in Ms. Bergman and shut the door behind you." His rich tenor voice eases my nerves.

I walk inside and shut the door behind me.

"Straight ahead seven paces and the couch will be on your left. Nothing lies between you and it."

"Thank you." I forge ahead, Esther whipping left and right.

Esther strikes the side of something solid and I assume it's the front of the couch. Dr. Strong confirms it. "You're there."

I ease down onto the couch and slide back on it just a bit. "Thank you for seeing me on such short notice, Dr. Strong."

"I'll admit I was quite surprised when I received your message this morning. Normally you would've waited several weeks to get an appointment, but it seems that the fates favor you. My late cancellation Friday evening was from a patient who never misses their appointment."

I lay Esther on the couch and clasp my hands in my lap. "Their loss is my benefit."

"Let's hope so. Shall we begin the session?"

My nerves have returned in full force, but there's no going back now. "Ready when you are."

Dr. Strong clears his throat. "Good. How about you tell me why you're here today, Alice."

Why am I here? To understand why I've gone blind again. "Do you mind if I give you a little back story first?"

"This is your session, Alice. Tell me whatever you feel is necessary so that we can get to the root of why you're here today."

"It's been ten years since I last saw you." The veins in my neck pulse with such violence I imagine my head jerking with each heartbeat. The silence in the room is deafening and it stretches beyond measure. *I don't think I can do this.* I grab Esther.

"How about I put on some background music?" His chair squeaks when he rises from it. "Still a fan of Red?"

"Yes." I clear my throat. "Thank you."

The song *Breathe Into Me* begins playing and I sink into the couch. Nothing used to get me through my nightmares except music. I relinquish my death grip on Esther.

Dr. Strong returns to his chair. "Maybe we should start with why you canceled all of your appointments right after your accident."

I couldn't face coming here again after that day. Is that what he wants me to say? It is, but I can't bring myself to admit it to him. If I did, I'd have to face the truth of it myself.

I continue, "July 17, 2008. Do you remember that day?"

His pen taps along with the music's beat. "As though it were yesterday. Some things are unforgettable, especially the death of a young woman. How did that make you feel?"

"At the time? Indifferent to be honest. We went to school together, but I didn't know her, and I was dealing with my own issues. You remember me suffering an injury to my head, right?"

"I do."

"Well, over the next few days following that injury I gained my eyesight."

"Wow! That's remarkable."

"It is, but I'm uncertain if it was the injury that brought my vision back or if it was the assortment of treatments and procedures that I underwent that finally started working."

"But you're blind again. What happened?"

The couch becomes concrete beneath me and I struggle to find comfort within its embrace. "Honestly, I have no idea. I started losing my vision two weeks ago, and now I've been fully blind again for the last several days."

"I am so sorry, Alice. How does it make you feel? Being blind again."

I grind my teeth together hoping to stave off the wave of emotions crashing down on me. "Terrified. Forsaken. Alone. A ghost amongst society. An outcast. I'm everything I never wanted to be again."

"Have you been having suicidal thoughts?"

Tension stiffens my jaw and works its way to the back of my skull. "What? No. Never. I'm not that person."

He scribbles down notes. "Okay, good. So what would you like to get out of this session?"

"I've been under a lot of stress lately with work. There are things happening beyond my control."

"Well, let's start there. What do you do for work?"

"I'm a homicide detective."

"A homicide detective? I never would've guessed that given your background. I can only imagine how stressful that kind of job must be seeing the worst in humanity day after day. Can you give me an example of something that's happened beyond your control at work?"

I ease back on the couch and lean my head back. "Ten days ago I was put on administrative leave and it pisses me off."

"Because of your blindness?"

"No, because I shot a perpetrator while on duty."

"I see. Is there anything else going on with work?"

"The current case my partner and I are working is hitting very close to home. We're hunting a man who kills blind girls."

"And how does that make you feel, Alice?"

My hands ball into fists at my sides. "How the hell do you think it makes me feel? Those girls could've been me. In a way, they are me, and I've been helpless to save them."

"And do you blame yourself for their deaths?"

"How can I not? The longer it takes for us to catch him the more victims we'll discover."

"I think I'm starting to form a picture here. What else has been happening, Alice?"

"The nightmares have returned, but this time they're all about the killer and his victims."

His pen scratches the paper with fury. "Are you not sleeping, like before?"

"That is one thing that differs from the past. I don't seem to be having any issues sleeping. Just the occasional nightmare."

"What about your family life and relationships? Has anything changed there since I saw you last?"

"I do have a boyfriend, and he's the best thing that's ever happened to me. Believe it or not, my mother loves him too."

"And what about your father? I don't recall you ever talking about him. Is he not in the picture?"

Rage swells in my chest and I can't contain it when I speak. "My father's a worthless piece of crap who tried to get my mother to abort me. Thank God my mother said no and left him. What kind of father doesn't want their child? Apparently, mine."

"Do you feel better getting that off your chest?"

"It's not a secret that I hate my father, so no, not really."

"Have you ever met your father?"

"No. Mother would freak, and I have no desire to do so."

"Have you ever spoken to him and confronted him about your feelings toward him?"

I reach over and touch Esther. She may only be a cane, but she comforts me nonetheless. "Why would I do that? He's nothing to me."

"It's hard to imagine that you feel nothing for him when your voice and gestures tell a different story. Would you like to delve into that a bit more? Explore your feelings?"

I'd like to kick you in the teeth right now. I grip Esther tight. "No. Look, I'm not here because I have daddy issues. Can we please move on?"

He scribbles more. The pen he's using has an annoying squeak to it. It's almost as bad as fingernails on a chalkboard. "Noted. Is there anything else bothering you?"

"That about sums everything up. So, in your professional opinion, what the hell is wrong with me? Why have I lost my vision? Please don't tell me you're at a loss as to what might be wrong. I can't hear that again, especially from another doctor."

He clears his throat. "I certainly have some thoughts as to what might be causing your blindness. However, I pride myself as a psychiatrist who cares deeply for the person on my couch and I wouldn't be doing my job if I wasn't thorough. I believe you're holding something back."

I still my hands but my legs twitch about. "Believe what you want. I've got nothing else for you."

"Very well." Dr. Strong shifts in his chair. "I think there are several factors contributing to your condition. Some of this you may not like hearing, but I'm going to tell you anyway. Most of what you've told me relates to a literal loss of control or a feeling of it. The first contributing factor could be the relationship with your father. There have been many documented cases where a person has lost their vision because of the lack of a relationship with one or both parents. Specifically because they feel unloved or even hated.

"I believe this kind of vision loss might stem from feeling invisible, like you do. Subconsciously, they want the world to be invisible to them so that they don't have to deal with their feelings. I think meeting your father could be a good first step in gaining some control of that part of your life. Confronting him about how you feel will go a long way toward not acting like a victim."

I shake my head, frustrated. "I'm sorry, but that makes no sense to me. First of all, I'm not acting like a victim. I don't give a damn about the man. Second, how would my father have anything to do with my blindness? I've been blind since birth."

"That would certainly be true when you were first blind but we're talking about the sudden onset of blindness that started a few weeks ago. At any rate, I think it's time to move on. The second contributing factor could be a form of PTSD brought on by your shooting of someone."

"I don't buy that either. I have no remorse from shooting that thug. In fact, I wish I'd killed him. He shot and killed one of my fellow officers." The thought of that thug wasting tax payer money while rotting in jail eats at me. I clinch my jaw, but it's not enough. Esther's in my hand and I smack the couch with her. *Thwack!* "He has no right to live anymore. Besides, I was already going blind by the time that happened."

He taps his pen on his notepad. "Ah, I see. Another point where you were in a situation beyond your control. Your words and your body language don't jive, Alice. There is definitely something there beyond the anger. You might want to work on that with your police psychologist if you're not willing to do that with me."

I cross my legs and fold my arms over my chest. "I'll take that under advisement."

"Noted. A third contributing factor could be the case you're on. Stress plays a large part in our overall health, and you've been under an excessive amount."

"Yes. That's the only thing I could think of as well, but I think I started going blind before I ever got the first call for this case. I admit that the timing's a bit fuzzy though."

"Yes and add to that the facts that your case involves blind girls and that you were abused when you were younger. It's impossible for you to not take it personally."

I nod, unable to speak.

"Have they ever found the person that assaulted you?"

I shake my head as anger wells in my chest.

"How does that make you feel knowing you were violated, and that person walks free?"

I explode from the couch like a bottle rocket. "I've dedicated the last ten years of my life to finding this bastard! He's the reason I studied criminology and why I became a detective. The homicide part was just an accident."

"Okay, Alice. I understand your frustration and anger, but I must ask you another question. Please don't try to answer it right now. It will be something for you to contemplate."

I sit back down. "Fine. What is it?"

"It seems like you've tied your abuse to this killer you're hunting. I'm not saying they belong together, but you've associated them with each other. Are you certain your need to solve this case is for the victims' families or is it for yourself?"

My first instinct is rage, and venom seeps into my tongue, but I hold it. As the moments pass the feeling quells and I'm left wondering if he's got a point.

He continues, "The fourth and final contributing factor to your blindness could be that whatever treatments and procedures you had in the past have finally worn off or failed. I know you went back to see your doctors, but perhaps they missed something. No doctor, including me, sees everything. However, I don't think you see it as a viable solution. If you did you wouldn't have come here."

I shrug and nod. "Probably true."

"I have two recommendations for you. The first is that you seek medical attention for your blindness again, and the second is that you confront your father about your feelings and take control back. I know you find it irrelevant, but sometimes these issues are triggered from the strangest things. Things we deem invalid or impossible. The mind is a very powerful instrument and unaddressed issues often manifest physically."

Dr. Strong's watch beeps, and I know our session has come to an end. I'm not sure I feel any better now than I did before I came here, but at least I can check it off my list of things to do. I grab Esther and rise from the couch.

"Thank you, Dr. Strong. It's been a pleasure talking with you again."

"You're quite welcome, Alice. I hope our session has given you insight and a path forward. I'd like to see you again in two weeks, and I want you to promise me you'll confront your father."

I nod. "Two weeks, but no guarantees with my father."

Esther guides me across the room, out the door, and over to the landing. I touch the railing where Denise fell over. I wish her death had been the end of everything. *But it was only the beginning. Why isn't life fair?*

The last thing I want to do is seek out my father. It's absurd. I know it is, yet I still wonder if Dr. Strong is on to something. Meeting my father scares me. My hands tremble with just the thought of it. What if he hates me or still wants me dead? I need to do what I do best: investigate his life and find out who he is before I decide if I want to track him down. In truth, I don't want to confront him.

God, I hope he's dead.

CHAPTER TWENTY

IT'S TUESDAY AND SETH and I cruise down Main Street on the way to his condo. I'm hoping he can help me find the truth about my father. Mother wouldn't divulge any details other than my father's name, so I don't know what else to do but dig into his files and records. Thank God I have Seth and that he understands my need.

It's another scorcher outside, but I've got my window rolled down anyway. I love the feel of the wind in my hair even if it is a hundred and fifteen degrees. Seth has the AC cranked up all the way, so we're good.

I stick my hand out the window and the air bobs it up and down as it rushes by. It makes me feel like a kid again. I wish we could go faster but I'm sure Seth is exceeding the speed limit already. The only problem with having the window down and the AC cranked is that it's nearly impossible to carry on a conversation.

I'm reluctant to roll up the window but I'm in the mood to talk, so I sacrifice my enjoyment and pull up on the switch to roll it up. The wind noise decreases by several decibels by the time the window is fully closed. I hadn't really noticed how loud it was before.

I slip off my shoe and put my foot up on the dashboard. "Any more news on Cara Strum?"

"Not a thing. I hate to say it, but we've hit a brick wall. This guy is smart and elusive. We've got next to nothing to go on and the only thing that links her to Sarah is that they are both blind."

"And the birthmarks—if Sarah had one." I rub my shins. They are still sore from the hand truck incident.

"Perhaps, but I still don't understand what the significance would be. Anyway, if this guy sticks to his MO of killing every ten days, then we'll have another body on Monday. I don't even want to think about that."

"What are we gonna do Seth? We can't just let this guy keep killing girls."

"I agree, but what would you have me do different? This town is chock-full of young blind girls. We don't have a force big enough to watch them all."

"I know. I just wish there was a way to narrow down his victim list. There must be something about these girls that we're missing. It doesn't seem to be anything physical, and the two girls were worlds apart when it comes to living conditions. But there's gotta be something."

Seth pulls to a stop, puts the car in park, and turns off the ignition. "We will find him, Alice. Either we'll crack this case, or he'll mess up somehow. It's inevitable. Nobody is perfect."

"I'm sure you're right. I just wonder how many more girls will die before it happens though." I open my door, grab Esther, and climb out of the car.

Seth comes around the car and takes my arm. "None, if I have anything to say about it."

Seth escorts me across the parking lot, through his building, and into his condo.

I wrinkle my nose. "Smells like old pizza and beer in here."

"Sorry about that. The last few days have been really long. Detective Roland and I have been going crazy trying to figure this case out."

I smile. "Kind of feels like you've been cheating on me."

"Well you're the one who went and got yourself put on administrative leave."

"Should've been you on administrative leave. You're the one that got shot *and* the one who told me to shoot the guy."

"I see. You're jealous of me working with Detective Roland. I bet you wanted him all to yourself. Got a thing for him, don't you?"

"You keep it up and you'll never see this office slut naked again."

"Whoa, that's going a bit too far."

"What is? Calling myself the office slut?"

"Nah that part's pretty accurate. It's the never see you naked again part that concerns me."

"Good. We can introduce ourselves to the world of blind sex, but not until after we find out everything we can about my father."

"I'm not blind. Are you saying we can turn the lights off for once? It'd level the playing field, so to speak."

Lights on has always been a requirement when we've had sex. My heart begins to race just thinking of doing it in the dark, but I am blind now. What do I have to lose besides my sanity? "I guess so."

"I'll hold you to that."

We move over to the couch and sit down. Seth's laptop has one of the loudest keyboards on the planet. Every keystroke clicks like a dragon's claw on a marble floor.

"What did you say your dad's name was?"

"Isaiah Mallard, if Mother can be believed."

"Mallard like a duck?"

"Yeah, but not Howard."

"Isaiah Mallard it is... and don't be so hard on your mother. I'm kinda fond of her." Seth's two-finger typing is like slow-motion rapid fire on the keyboard. *Tick-tick. Tick. Tick-tick-tick.*

I lean back on the couch, grab one of the leather pillows from its corner, and hold the pillow to my chest. It's not as cold as I'd like but it's better than nothing.

"Hey, looks like we got a hit, but..."

I wait a few moments, but Seth doesn't continue. "But what?"

"According to the records database, there's only one Isaiah Mallard in the area and he didn't exist before 1990."

"So what are you saying? He was two years old when I was born?"

He nudges me with his shoulder. "Of course not. What I'm saying is that he must've changed his name in 1990."

"My father changed his name? Why? What drives a person to do that?"

"Who knows? I guess you'll have to ask him to find that out."

"What did he change it from?"

"Let me check public records." The keys tick away for several moments. "Hmm… I can't find one."

"That seems odd. Why would he not show up?"

"To hide his past. I know a guy who can look into this a bit more. I'll give him a call and see what he can dig up for us."

"Perfect. You take care of that real quick and I'll go crawl into bed." I reach over and rub his leg. "Don't take too long or I might start without you."

"Two minutes."

I get up off the couch and stroll into the bedroom. I slip out of my shoes and my clothes, pull the covers down to the bottom of the bed, and lie on top of the sheets. My pores bleed perspiration and my heart gallops like thunder in my chest.

The thought of sleeping with Seth while I'm blind terrifies me. Perhaps it's because the only experience I've ever had doing so was with Denise and the Braille Killer. No matter what the reason, there's no way I can tell Seth. I'll find a way to fight through my panic attack.

Seth enters the room and closes the door. He breathes heavily. I hear him unbuckle his belt and unzip his pants. He grunts twice, and then his shoes smack the wall with a *thud*. I thought my pulse had been racing as fast as it could already, but the thud sends it into overdrive.

The bed shifts when he plops down onto it and my body turns rigid. His hand caresses my stomach and I can't help but whimper. I know Seth's cologne and love the scent of it, but right now all I can smell is garlic and pickles. He works his hand up my left side and over the top of my breast and I hold my breath to keep from crying out.

His lips caress the side of my neck and I shudder. I'm not sure how much more I can take before my heart explodes in my chest. Chills shake me, and I can't breathe as I wait for his hands to close around my neck.

"Are you cold?" he asks.

I nod, not knowing what else to do. He pulls the covers over us and rolls on top of me. His toes worm their way between my ankles and slowly spread my feet apart. I hold my legs closed with all the strength I can muster and brace myself for the bombarding punches to the gut that I know are coming.

He kisses my neck, my shoulders, and the tops of my breasts. I gasp for air and he moves lower, thinking I'm on the brink of ecstasy when in fact I'm dying inside. He moves so low that my insides squirm like they're infested with maggots.

When I can take no more, I reach down and pull him back up from the dark depths. He rises and settles on top of me, his hairy chest pressed against mine. My hands are pinned between us and I can feel the knotty ridge of scar tissue between my fingers. I scream inside.

It's happening again!

In my fit of terror, I lose track of myself for several minutes and resurface only to find my legs spread wide. I cannot close them because he lies between them. Tears wet my cheeks and fill my ears until I can hear nothing but the beating of my heart.

I crawl inside myself and pray that this isn't the end for me. I count and count and count until I lose track of where I am and then I start over again. How long this lasts I'll never know, but he finally rolls off of me and to my right side. I turn away from him and pull my legs up to my chest.

He wraps one muscular arm around my waist and pushes the other underneath my neck. He pulls me close and holds me against himself. "Alice you're soaked with tears. Are you okay? Did I hurt you?"

"No," I lie. Fear strangles me, and pain crushes my heart. "You just make me so happy."

He holds me tighter and touches me again, a reminder that lying never helps anyone. All I can do is retreat within once again and give myself to him one last time.

I'm uncertain if it's been minutes or hours, but I find myself alone in the bed. I roll to the side of the bed, swing my feet onto the floor, and sit up. My head aches from crying. I stand, gather up my clothes, and retreat into the bathroom.

It burns when I pee, and I wonder if he's cut me somehow. It sucks being blind and unable to do simple things like self-examinations. I wipe, flush, wash, and then dress. I splash water on my face and rub it into my hair but the feeling of being violated lingers in my mind. One thing's for certain: I'll never sleep with anyone ever again while blind.

I return to the living room and Seth's on the phone. From the one-sided conversation that I hear it sounds like his guy has found more information pertaining to my father. I return to the couch and wait for Seth to finish on the phone.

My thoughts return to Sarah and Cara, my kindred spirits. In a way I envy their deaths and it scares me. They'll never have to relive those moments with the Braille Killer ever again, but I'll remember them for the rest of my life and relive them in my nightmares.

Should I tell Dr. Strong?

Seth hangs up the phone and moves next to me. "I've got more info about your father. Ready for it?"

My voice is hoarse and I whisper-bark "yes" like a dog with its vocal cords snipped.

"Isaiah Mallard was born Philip Isaiah Sudermann in 1972. What's even more remarkable is that according to his birth records he was born blind."

I gasp and jerk back against the couch. "Blind? My mother never mentioned that he was blind."

"I know, and in 1990 he had a driver's license. That means that he wasn't blind anymore. What are the odds of you and your father both experiencing the same thing?"

What are the odds? My mind reels with questions and implications. Who is my father and where is he? Did he change his name to hide the fact that he gained his vision? How did he gain it? What does that mean for me?

I take a deep breath. *I must see him.* How I went from never wanting to see him to needing to in a single moment surprises me. He rejected me before I was born and now my future clings to him. *I think I'm gonna be sick.*

"Does he have a last known address?"

"He does, but you won't like it."

What's new? My life has turned to shambles over the last two weeks. It wouldn't surprise me if it winds up being a cemetery or some prison. I close my eyes and cringe. "Hit me with it."

"Your mother's house. He's been un-existent ever since."

I sigh loudly. "Non-existent, genius."

"That's what I said."

There's no point in arguing with him, so I don't. "I guess it's time to tangle with the hornet's nest."

"Best you sleep on it. I don't wanna be sent over to your house in the middle of the night for a reported domestic violence call."

"Fine, but you should still take me home. She won't be as uncooperative in the morning if I've slept in my own bed."

"That's for certain." He pats my leg and stands. "Well grab your gear and I'll take you back."

I rise, locate Esther, and head for the door. "I'm ready when you are."

He slaps my butt and I turn rigid. "Race you to the car!"

It's only Seth. I shake away my fear and exit into the hallway. "Funny mister. Real funny."

Seth shuts and locks the door behind me. "I thought it was hysterical."

"Yeah, but you don't have a sense of humor. That was just mean-spirited. No one makes fun of the blind ninja and lives to tell about it."

"Maybe not, but you gotta catch me first."

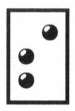

CHAPTER TWENTY-ONE

MY PHONE SAYS IT'S 08:24 on Wednesday morning but my body tells me that it's much earlier. I rise from my bed like a zombie from its grave and drag myself into the kitchen. I put on a pot of coffee, collapse into one of the kitchen chairs, and set my phone on the table.

My head is killing me, so I lay it on the table. The experience I had with Seth last night plays in my mind and continues to haunt me. In my heart I know I was with him, but my mind remembers feeling and smelling the Braille Killer.

Between that and my hallucinations at the hospital, I'm unsure if I can trust myself to decipher reality from fantasy anymore. This case has turned me inside out and I just want it to be over.

The scent of fresh coffee wafts in the air and I breathe deep. No smell in the world is better in the morning. I sit up and my phone starts buzzing.

"Call from… Lieutenant Frost," says the phone. "To answer, press or say one. To dis—"

"One." I pick up the phone. "This is Detective Bergman."

"Morning, Bergman. This is Lieutenant Frost."

"Good morning, sir. What can I do for you?"

"We've had some recent developments in the case you and Detective Ryan were working, and we need some input from you. Come to the station as soon as possible. This is a time-sensitive matter."

Recent developments? Seth hadn't mentioned anything new last night. *What've they've found?* Dread saturates me like a layer of sweat. *Crap, crap, crap! Everyone will find out that I'm blind. Will I lose my job?* I push the thought from my mind.

I stand on shaky legs and walk over to the cabinet where the coffee mugs are. "Yes sir. I'll be there as soon as I can get a ride."

"How you manage without a personal car is beyond me. I'll send someone over to pick you up."

I grab a mug out of the cabinet. "That won't be necessary, sir. I'll be there within the hour."

"When you arrive you can head straight to the second floor conference room."

"Will do. See you soon." I swipe down on my phone and end the call.

I set my phone back down on the table and fill my mug with piping hot coffee. Next to the coffee maker is a bowl with sugar cubes. It's been there as long as I can remember. If Mother were to move it, I'd have a meltdown.

I grab three cubes and drop them into my mug. I set the mug down on the table. Thank God I don't need to think about where things are in Mother's house. She's a stickler for keeping things consistent and muscle memory guides my hands. I fetch two creamers from the fridge, peel them open, and empty their contents into my mug. I grab a spoon from the drawer to the left of the sink and stir my coffee with it.

I press a button on the side of my phone and it prompts me for a command. "Call Seth."

"Calling Seth Ryan on cell," it replies.

The phone rings several times before forwarding to his voicemail. "End call," I say before it prompts me to leave a message. The call ends and my phone prompts me for another command, but I don't give it one. I'd call Veronica and ask her for a ride but she's still at work.

I bring up the Uber ridesharing app on my phone with a voice command and request a ride. I hate relying on people and services like Uber but at least the option exists.

Ten years ago, the only option I had was taxi services and they quite literally charged an arm and leg to go anywhere. Two blocks? Twenty bucks, no joke. Not only that, but I had to worry about them taking the long way to my destination so that they could drive up the fare. With Uber, I know the cost upfront and don't have to worry about which roads and routes they take. I can relax and enjoy the ride.

Ten minutes later, I'm in the car with Enrique and we're barreling down Main Street in some souped-up sedan. The engine roars when we take off at each light and the tires squeal around corners. The tight suspension throws me from the seat with every little bump, leaving me breathless and exuberant.

The tires screech to a halt and the car dings when Enrique opens his door and hops out. By the time I remove my seatbelt and retrieve Esther he's around the car and opening my door for me. "Curbside service, miss. May I offer you a hand?"

I'm trapped in the deep bucket seat, so I offer Enrique my hand. "It would be much appreciated."

He takes my hand in his, grabs hold of my elbow with his other hand, and pulls me from the depths of the seat.

"There's a curb right in front of you and the front steps are straight ahead."

"Thank you." I step up on the curb.

The car door slams behind me. "See you soon, miss."

By the time I reach the front steps Enrique's peeling rubber out of the police station parking lot. I traverse the five steps and head through the front doors. I've spent so much time in this building that navigating its halls is second nature to me but maneuvering through the sea of people proves difficult. Halfway down the main stretch someone grabs my arm. I can tell it's Seth by the smell of his cologne.

"Come on. Everyone's waiting on us." He drags me along, pushing through people without remorse.

I don't like the way Seth's handling me. He's a bit on the hostile side today and his voice reflects it. "What's this about, Seth? Why was I called in?"

"I have no idea. We'll know soon enough." His voice barks at me and his words nip at my heels. "Stairs."

I jerk my arm away from him. "I can manage just fine on my own."

"Fine. Hurry up." He stomps up the stairs.

I follow as fast as I can, and he grabs my arm again when I reach the top landing. I don't understand what's going on, and he's starting to scare me. I try to jerk away again but he holds on tight. "You're hurting my arm."

His grip loosens but he doesn't let go. "Sorry. That wasn't my intention." He pulls me forward again. "It's been a rough morning and I didn't get much sleep last night."

"Are you pissed at me for something?"

He stops. "No." He exhales loudly. "Look, we lost another officer last night. Bradford responded to a B&E in the valley and it went south. The bastard jumped him and slit his throat and now he's in the wind."

"Damn." *What else could I say?*

Seth lets go of my arm and opens the conference room door. "You can take the first seat to your left."

I walk inside the room and the tension sucks the air from my lungs. I locate the chair and sit down. I hold Esther between my knees under the table. Several pairs of brooding eyes drill into me. I know it's not my imagination. *Am I on trial for something?*

The door closes, and I hear Seth settle in a chair somewhere to my right.

"Good, we're all finally here." Based on the projection of his voice I assume that Lieut. Frost sits almost directly across the table from me. "Let's begin."

I grip the armrests of my chair so hard that my fingers ache, but I can't let go. "Sir, I haven't been feeling well and I've temporarily lost my vision. Can you start by letting me know who's present?"

"Temporary vision loss?" Skepticism drips from his words. Can't say I blame him. "Certainly. Detective Ryan, Detective Roland, myself, and you."

I take a deep breath and end my assault on the armrests. The tension eases in my shoulders, arms, and hands. "Thank you."

"Detective Roland you may proceed."

"Thanks, Lieutenant." He clears his throat. "As you know, I joined the

Braille Killer investigation ten days ago. What you may not know is that I have a background in cryptology and spent two decades in the Army as one of the top cryptologists in the world. I find patterns where others have failed and take pride in my discoveries. Early this morning I had one such breakthrough on this case."

My hands tighten on the armrests once again and beads of sweat trickle down my nape. My fingernails dig into the vinyl. I lean forward in my seat tantalized and terrified over what his next words might be.

Detective Roland continues, "We're all aware of the word burned into the thigh of each of the two victims, one spelling 'amerce' and the other 'baling', and we understand their meaning. Each explains the motive for the kill, but neither informs us of the reason behind the motive."

Me! I'm the reason. I want to speak so badly and free myself of this burden I've carried for more than a decade but nothing I say now could help my cause. I am a ship lost at sea and there will be no rescue.

Papers rustle and Detective Roland continues, "However, once you combine the two words you can decrypt the hidden message."

Hidden message? I swallow wrong and cough. My pulse races as I twist the words together in my head. My mind fights to find a solution, but the pressure is too great. I'm an aluminum can crushed under foot. I clear my mind and await Detective Roland's revelation.

"But it's more than a mere message. The killer names the one he deems responsible for evading responsibility and why he punishes them by killing innocent victims." His voice turns cold. "It's you, Detective Bergman."

My body goes numb and my mind reels. I sink back in the chair and chew on his last words. I *am* the reason for the killings, but how did he reach that conclusion?

"Rearrange the letters from amerce and baling and you get Alice Bergman."

His words are a double-hoofed horse kick to the chest. I cannot breathe or think or talk. Had I not already gone blind, this revelation might've taken my vision as well. I'm in a war room and fighting for my life and I think all my alliances have been severed.

"What do you make of that, Detective Bergman?" His words crawl through me like maggots in spoiled meat.

It's the truth. I'm guilty as charged. Lock me up and toss away the key. Their blood is on my hands.

I swallow hard and will my voice to return. "What am I supposed to make of it? It seems like a stretch to me. A mere coincidence."

"As I said, I'm a cryptologist, and in cryptology there are no coincidences." Detective Roland's superiority complex pushes me past my limit.

I fly out of my chair and let Detective Roland have it. "You think you're so smart don't you, you smug prick. Let's say that it isn't some stupid coincidence and the two words intentionally spell my name. Did you ever think that perhaps he knows I'm working the case and that's why he did that? He's screwing with us. Can't you see that or are you too blinded by your own perceived superior intellect?"

Lieut. Frost slams his hand on the table like a gavel. "That's enough, Detective Bergman." If he expected me to flinch, I disappointed him. "I've been in this job for more than a decade and I have a knack for reading people. You're holding back. Why?"

I cross my arms and stare ahead. *What the hell does he expect me to say?*

He continues, "How would the killer have known you'd be working the case when he killed and marked his first victim?"

If I had vision it'd be red with rage. As is, my voice growls through clenched teeth. "Simple—"

"Alice, please take a seat." I'd forgotten Seth was in the room.

Anger rages in my balled fists but I reclaim my chair.

"Thank you. Detective Roland, Lieutenant Frost, what Detective Bergman is trying to say, poorly or otherwise, is that we believe the killer called in the first victim himself. The message was left for Alice on her office phone. No one uses that number anymore."

I huff. "Exactly. He planned it from the start to throw us all off."

"If that's true Detective Bergman, and I'm not implying that it isn't, then we have far bigger issues. A killer with an obsession like that is far more dangerous. He's likely to be watching you. Do you have any issue with us searching your property?"

I reach down and probe the floor until I locate Esther. "I'm sure you won't find anything but go right ahead. Search whatever you want." I push my chair away from the table and stand. "Are we done here?"

"This meeting *is* over, but I'd like you to stay here until we've conducted the search."

I squeeze Esther with all my strength. "You can't expect me to just sit here all day."

"I can't keep you from leaving, but you know it's in your best interest to do so. I imagine it's only a matter of time before he makes a move on you."

I reach back, find the edge of the chair, and sit back down. "Fine, but I expect some food and a drink while you turn my life upside-down. It's the least you can do."

"That can be arranged. I'll send Officer Janis up here in a bit to take your order."

"Good." I lean back in the chair and tilt my head toward the ceiling.

"Detective Ryan. Detective Roland. Go see what you can dig up."

Detective Roland pushes past my chair. "I go where the facts lead me, Bergman. It's not personal."

"Yeah, well I'm not sure you know the meaning of the word because it sure as hell *feels* personal."

Lieut. Frost and his skunk-butt cologne walk past as he exits the room. How anyone can stomach the smell is beyond me. I pity his wife.

Seth walks over to my chair. "I'll make sure your things are handled with care."

He's lucky he didn't try to touch me. He would've received a mouthful of Esther if he had. "Yeah, like you did with my arm earlier. Quite the soft touch you've got."

"I've apologized for that already. Can't we move on?"

"Move on? Yeah, that's exactly what you should be doing right now."

"Fine. I'll be back for you."

"Save your threats."

He huffs and walks away, closing the door behind him. I lean back in the chair again and ponder what the hell just happened.

CHAPTER TWENTY-TWO

HOUR AFTER EXCRUCIATING HOUR crawls by and I continue to wait for the return of the cavalry. It's a form of torture, at least in my book. I might have to press charges. Had I known what I was in for before I came in this morning, I would've at least brought my headphones with me.

Rummaging through my head for hours on end is good for no one, least of all me. I've relived every moment with Sarah and Cara repeatedly, but can't find anything else of significance. What has gotten me thinking though is what Detective Roland said: "There are no coincidences."

I've poured so much of myself into deciphering the letters that I've neglected the items that came with them. Yes, I've considered them thoroughly as well, but what if one is a key to unlocking the other? The Braille Killer has been planning and executing this game for a decade with meticulous detail, so I should assume that he hasn't done anything without express reason. I missed the cypher of my name, so what else have I missed?

The door to the conference room opens and pulls me from my thoughts.

"Bring it all in here, guys. Just set the stuff on the table." Detective Roland's voice grates my nerves.

All what? Did they raid my underwear drawer?

Several minutes of grunting, puffing, sighing, and table shaking occur and then the door closes. The three men sit down in their chairs once more.

Seth sits to my right, Detective Roland to my left, and Lieut. Frost across from me. Each has a unique scent, but only Seth's is pleasant. For several minutes we sit in a silent stalemate—three against one. Normally I'd like the odds, but today I can feel the noose tightening around my neck.

Lieut. Frost breaks the silence. "Is there anything you'd like to tell us before we proceed, Detective Bergman? Perhaps something you've remembered while sitting here?"

My breathing shallows and my pulse rises. What could they have possibly found? "Can't think of anything."

Seth sighs. I'd recognize it from across an airport. "I trusted you, Alice."

I look his direction, my gaze steel but my heart breaking. "That's past-tense. What've I done?"

"There's no point in playing these games. We found the storage unit."

Only the fear felt through Sarah's and Cara's memories rivals this moment. I shake so violently that the chair rattles. I try to take a breath, but the air has escaped the room and I'm left gasping.

"Explain yourself, Alice." There's more hurt in Seth's voice than anger. "Why have you kept all this from me? From us?"

"I... I..." Words form in my head, but their very existence is foreign to me. I can't remember how to put them together into something logical. Every image and thought for the last decade bombard me. Shame and fear well up inside me like lava in a caldera and threaten to explode from my pores. I'm sixteen again and bound with duct tape.

A hand touches my shoulder and I jerk away so hard that I slam my other shoulder into something solid. I cry out and whimper, "Please don't hurt me. I'll do whatever you want." Tears streak my face and run down my neck.

He shakes me violently. "Alice, it's me."

I cry harder. "I don't understand. What do you want from me?"

The smack of his hand on my cheek jars me. "Alice, dammit! It's Seth."

I gasp for air, stunned for a moment and lost as to what's happening. My left cheek stings and someone's arms are wrapped around me. My face and neck are drenched. I lick my lips and taste salt. *Tears.* I'm covered in tears. I believe they're mine.

Seth's cologne fills my nostrils. "Seth? What's happening?"

He releases me. "Are you okay?"

I self-diagnose for a few moments. My heart is pounding, and I'm riddled with fatigue, but everything else seems to be good. "Yeah... I think so. What happened?"

"You were about to explain all the letters and items we found in your storage unit and then you reverted back to another place or something. You freaked me out."

I sit back in the chair and wipe my face on my shoulders. My left shoulder aches, so I rub it. "I'm sorry. I don't know what happened. Give me a minute to collect myself."

I close my eyes and slow my breathing. The world spins in my head like a cyclone. The need to catch this killer overwhelms me and I can't help but obsess over it. It's all I've known for so long. Opening up to Veronica helped.

Maybe it will bring my vision back.

I've lived, breathed, and slept within his twisted mind and I need to find a way out before it's too late. *Let go.* I must tell them what I know so we can reach the end of this nightmare. I need to wake up and live again.

I take a deep breath and exhale slowly. "Before we move forward, I need a guarantee from you, Lieutenant."

"You want a guarantee?" Lieut. Frost scoffs. "You're in no position to demand anything of me or this department."

I nod. "I understand, but I don't think what I want is unreasonable."

"I think we should let her speak, Lieutenant. You can always deny her request." I'm taken aback that Detective Roland would speak up for me.

Lieut. Frost grumbles. "So be it. Give us your demands and make it quick."

I rest my arms on the table and lean forward. "I don't want to lose my job, sir. Guarantee my position. You know how valuable I've been over the last two years. That's all I want."

"You've got a snowball's chance in hell of that happening right now. You'll be lucky if we don't press charges for obstruction of justice. Not only have you hindered this investigation, but you've lied about it as well. You've also lost your vision and seem to be suffering from some sort of psychotic episodes. There's no way I could keep you on the force right now even if I thought you deserved it."

I clasp my hands together. "I will undergo any sort of therapy deemed necessary to keep my job, and I honestly believe my vision loss is due to PTSD from Officer Todd's death, Detective Ryan's injury, and my shooting of the suspect. I will get through this." *If there's a god out there, make this true.*

"We will discuss this at a later date if necessary, but from this moment forward you will comply with our demands and tell us everything you know."

"I'll live with that." My legs are killing me from sitting in the chair for so long, so I stand. "Everything started ten years ago with Denise's death. I was at a doctor's appointment that day and was upset. I hurried out of the office and collided with Denise in the hallway. She fell over the banister and I fell backward, cracking my head on the floor. When I regained consciousness, I could see for the first time in my life."

"And that was when?" asks Detective Roland.

"I assume you brought everything from my storage unit in here or at least what was up on my corkboard."

"Yes," says Seth. "We kept everything on the board as you had it."

"Good. See the picture of Denise splayed on the floor in the top-left corner of the board? That was July seventeenth of two thousand eight. Exactly ten years before Sarah Johnson's death."

"We see the items and dates on the board, but what's the correlation between you and the killer?" asks Lieut. Frost.

"Every year since Denise's death he's sent me a letter and some sort of item that relates to her. He's got it in his head that Denise's death wasn't an accident. He thinks I pushed her over that banister."

"And why didn't you come forward with all of this?" asks Seth.

"I figured the letters and items were his way of mourning her loss. His letters always urged me to find him and confess but he never told me who he was. I thought I could handle catching him myself."

"And he never once spoke of killing you or anyone else?" asks Detective

Roland.

"Only if I told anyone about him and the letters. He never made any direct threats until the letter I received last year."

Papers ruffle and then one slides into my hand.

"Can you read that to us?" asks Seth. "The three of us don't know braille."

I sit down and smooth out the folds in the card stock paper. I don't need to feel it to remember the words, but I glide my finger across the raised bumps anyway. Goosebumps skitter down my nape and arms.

I clear my throat and read it aloud: "With sight reborn a friend is lost, but you didn't mourn so what's the cost? An eye for an eye or something more? Should the innocent die for a sinful whore? Follow the path and meet my demands. Or suffer my wrath; it's all in your hands. It's your curtain call. I've told you what to do. Will you take the fall? The ending's up to you."

"Do you know why he calls you a whore?" asks Lieut. Frost.

My stomach gurgles, and bile rises in my throat. I hold my breath and wait for the feeling to pass. "The picture with the letter from the previous year." A tear rolls down my cheek.

"This picture is of you and Denise?" asks Detective Roland.

"Yes. Denise and the Braille Killer kidnapped me, beat me, and raped me a few months before Denise died."

"My God," exclaims Seth. "Are your hands tied behind your back?"

"Yes... they tortured and abused me for several hours." I let out a sob. "I think the only reason they let me go was because I was blind and couldn't identify them."

"Why would you keep this from me, Alice? I don't understand." Seth's voice quavers. "I could've been there for you and helped you through this if I'd known."

"I couldn't ask that of you and I didn't want you to think I was broken." I sniff and wipe my eyes. "You can't imagine the shame I feel every time I think about what they did to me. It was bad enough reliving it in my mind, but I never had to see it until he sent me that picture. That devastated me for months."

"I'm sorry you had to endure something like that, Detective Bergman," says Detective Roland. "I have a sixteen-year-old daughter and can't imagine her going through something like that."

"Pray she never does." I lean back in the chair and look toward the ceiling. "Part of me died that day and I've never been the same since. He's the entire reason I studied criminology and joined the force. I thought I'd be able to hunt him down if I had the right resources, but he's proven quite elusive."

"From your notes about the killer I see that you mention something about storage unit 109," says Seth. "I gather this is a unit from the same storage facility?"

"Yes, but that turned out to be a wild goose chase. The unit was cleaned out and the name it was rented under wasn't the man who rented it."

"What else can you tell us about these letters and items?" Lieut. Frost's voice is edged with compassion. I didn't think him capable.

I sit back up. "I've given you everything I know, sir. Maybe forensics can shed some light on the rest of it. My resources were quite limited."

"I still can't believe all this. How could you stand to keep it all locked inside?" Seth sounds upset, and I don't blame him.

"I didn't want anyone else to suffer with me or feel sorry for me. I'm a detective, and a damned good one, and I thought I could solve this on my own."

"I don't know how you can be so blind to what's right in front of you. I've been right here for two damn years." Seth's chair bangs against the table. The door opens and then slams shut.

"Denise Eleanor Chavez," says Detective Roland. "Some of the beauties are the most psycho."

Eleanor… My mind races back to the old man in the house across the street from Sarah Johnson's house. "My God… it was him!"

"Who was him?" asks Lieut. Frost.

"The morning of Sarah Johnson's murder I stormed into a house across the street where I thought I saw someone watching from the window. There was an old man in a wheel chair." I return to the scene in my mind, certain his face would match that of the man from storage unit 109, but shadows cover him. I wish my photographic mind came with enhancement tools.

"When I questioned him about anyone else being in the house, he said not for ten years since his Eleanor passed." I smack myself on the forehead. "We had him and didn't even know it."

The door opens again and closes. "Sorry, had a call."

"Seth, we had him. I'm positive he was the old man in the wheelchair."

Seth takes the chair next to mine. "Even if that was him it makes no difference now. When we went back later that day he was gone."

"I know, but that confirms that he likes to watch us investigate. That means he was probably at the second scene as well."

"Maybe, but that means he'd have to kill again before we could try and catch him. I'm not willing to wait for that to happen."

I smack my hands on the table. "That's not what I'm saying."

"Enough," says Lieut. Frost. "I think we've heard enough. Ryan and Roland make sure this stuff gets down to CSI immediately. Roland, take a look at everything and see if you can find a pattern or clues on how to track down this bastard."

"Yes sir," they both reply.

"Bergman, you'll provide Detective Roland translations of all the letters before you leave today so that CSI won't have to do it."

I nod my head slowly. "Yes sir."

"And Bergman you're officially suspended from duty once you finish those translations."

Suspended? A wave of relief sweeps through me. *That's much better than fired.* "I understand, sir."

"Good. Let's move, people. We're a long way from closing this case and I don't want to see any more girls murdered. Understood?"

"Yes sir," we all say.

Ten years of my life have been spent hunting the Braille Killer and now it's out of my hands. Relief passes through me like a fleeting memory and I'm left right where I started. How can I move forward knowing he's still out there? What am I going to do with myself? For once in my life the future is unclear, and it scares the hell out of me.

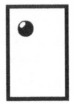

CHAPTER TWENTY-THREE

I AM AN UNINHABITABLE island drifting to and fro in the middle of a vast ocean. Storm waves crash against my rocks and crags and erode my beaches until there's nothing left of me but a hollow shell of what I once was, my beauty and intrigue lost forever.

The drive from the police station to Mother's house proved to me that Seth and I could refrain from conversation for an extended period of time. It also proved that Seth is upset with me. I understand, and I search for the right words to express my sorrow and regret for what I've done to him. Several times I open my mouth to speak but the words fall short of my lips, none of them good enough to justify my betrayal. So much pain could've been avoided had I allowed him in.

How will we move forward?

We sit in his car in Mother's driveway with the windows rolled down. The evening sun hangs low in the sky, a blob of light in my vision. Its brutalizing heat morphs me into a bundle of flesh and blood and sweat inside my clothes. I imagine Seth is much the same but all I can smell is his cologne, that sweet succulent fragrance that I cannot bear to live without.

My heart is a cesspool of grief. It aches in my chest and burns in my throat like acid. My mind is worn and tired, desperate to distance itself from all the lies and hurt and shame that I've received and given.

What I seek is redemption but not by the hand of some god sitting on his throne high in the clouds and pulling my marionette strings. No, my redemption will come when the Braille Killer is brought to justice and I can breathe easy again.

An ocean of silence lies between us and we continue to drift apart. I paddle hard, but the current is swift, and I find myself in a losing battle. The greater the distance, the harder it is to imagine anything but the silence, and the thought of breaking it becomes more awkward.

Seth shifts in his seat, rippling the waters and changing the tide. His voice is an echo in the distance. "Explain yourself, Alice. Explain to me how and why you've lived this double life."

I hug myself for comfort. "Do you think I wanted any of this or that it was easy for me? Every day I tried to find a reason to tell you what was happening to me, but all those reasons always came back to one simple fact: if I let you in you would pity me, and I just couldn't handle the thought of that. I didn't want you to know the vulnerable, shame-filled woman I used to be. I needed you to see me for who I wanted to be so that I could become her for you."

Tears swell in my eyes and I brush them away with the backs of my hands. "I can't tell you how hard it was getting through every day knowing that the man who beat me and raped me and abused me walked freely without fear of retribution, and how he still manipulates me year after year, conditioning me to believe that everything that happened was all my fault and that I brought it upon myself."

Seth clears his throat. "I understand what you're saying, and I'm sorry for what you've gone through, but that's no excuse for shutting me out."

I ball my hands and hold them against my chest. "Everything I am has been wrapped up in this for ten years. I should've gone to the police with the evidence a year ago, but I can't change that now. My rape is different though. That's personal and something I can't shake the shame from."

Seth breathes heavily and sighs loudly. "I get that, and I don't begrudge you for keeping it from me, but I cannot reconcile the connection between you and the woman I grew to love. I can't help but wonder if she ever existed."

I reach out and find his hand, but he moves it away and my heart sinks. "I am the same woman today as I was yesterday. The only thing that has changed is the amount of detail you know about my past."

"No, Alice, there's a big difference." The tone in his voice is harsh but I think it stems from hurt and not anger. "The woman I love would never lie and manipulate me like you've done. God, I feel sorry for what you've been through, but you left me in such an uncomfortable position. Can you imagine my surprise when we find a storage key on your key ring and it leads us to what we found? That devastated me, Alice. Do you understand that?"

My throat tightens, and I want to reach across the car and hold him, but he's an ocean away and my arms cannot stretch that far. "I understand why you feel that way, but you gotta believe me when I tell you that I did it to protect you."

"Protect me?" His anger flares. "No, you did it to protect yourself. You've been manipulating me since the day we met. I've given you my heart and soul and you've left me holding nothing but a bag of rocks. Empty words and lies that I cling to as I fall; vapor between my fingers. I trusted you with my life and my heart. Now you've broken both."

The ground between us fissures and expands to a gaping crevice in a blink. My heart shreds, and sorrow fills its cracks. "I'm so sorry, Seth. Tell me what to do to rectify this and I will. I'd do anything for you."

His silence is far worse than any torture I've ever known. I bawl without restraint, gasping for air between words. "The last two years of my life have been the only ones I'd live again. You found me at my lowest and lifted me from the ashes of my past. You brought stability into a world of chaos and filled me with hope when I thought there was none to be had. You are my heart and my soul and the love of my life. Please don't shut me out."

"I'm sorry, but there's no special phrase you could say or act that you could perform that would reverse the damage you've caused."

If I could get on my knees in the car I would. "I'm not saying that there is. I'm just asking for your forgiveness so that we can move forward."

"Move forward?" He scoffs. "I don't know how we can from here. You've backed me into a corner and left me without options."

My heart beats so loud in my ears that I can hardly hear my own words. "Please, Seth. Don't do this to me. Don't do this to us."

"I cannot be with you." His words are daggers in my chest, twisting and plunging again and again until there is no flesh left untattered.

"Now or ever?" I fear the answer he'll give me, but I have to know.

"Don't ask me that right now because I'm not sure either of us will like the answer." He opens his car door, gets out, and slams it shut.

I wipe my eyes and take several breaths. I know I look like a mess and can only imagine what Mother will think if she sees me this way. Seth opens my door. I grab Esther, pull myself out of the car, and head up the driveway. The car door slams shut and five seconds later another car door slams.

I don't look back. I can't. If I do, I will break down again and might never recover. Seth fires up the engine, pulls out of the drive, and races away, his engine roaring.

I open the front door and go inside. If Mother's here she says nothing to me as I walk through the living room. I head straight to my bedroom, close the door and lock it, and collapse on my bed.

To the ashes I've returned, a dying phoenix, and I don't know if I'll ever rise again.

CHAPTER TWENTY-FOUR

MY BEDROOM DOOR RATTLES on its hinges, battered by Mother's pounding fist. "You best get yourself out of bed and into the kitchen pronto. You've got a lot of explaining to do, young lady."

"I know." My voice croaks. My throat is dry and raw. I must've slept with my mouth open.

My head throbs and the sunbeams through my window are daggers in my swollen eyes. Still fully dressed, I rise from the bed. My phone is still in my pants pocket, so I take it out and plug it into the cable atop my nightstand. I leave the phone there and head for the bedroom door.

Several items are out of place, including my pile of clothes. I imagine everything in the room has been shifted. It's not the best scenario for a blind person, but I've got bigger issues. Or at least one big issue: Mother.

I unlock the door, open it, and head straight to the kitchen. I retrieve a bottle of water from the fridge and sit down in my usual chair at the table. I open the bottle and take a big gulp. It cools my raw throat and brings life back into my parched mouth.

Mother sits across from me. Her foot taps the floor, keeping a perfect four/four beat. She only does it when she's upset, and for once in my life I think she has good reason.

"I had several ladies from church over for tea yesterday afternoon.

Imagine my surprise when Seth and another detective show up at my door. Right in the middle of a deep conversation. And, as if that wasn't awkward enough, they request that I allow them to search through your room and belongings. How could I refuse? They left me completely demoralized in front of my friends. God willing, I might be able to show my face at church on Sunday."

I race my thumb around the top of my water bottle. "I'm sorry, Mother. All of it took me by surprise as well."

"Lord, I prayed all night that He'd give me the strength to hear your explanation, the wisdom to decipher it, and the patience and understanding to keep me from laying into you. Rest assured that it is a struggle, but I will prevail, God willing. So what was it all about? Why were they searching your room? Have you done something wrong? And don't even think of lying to me like you have in the past. I can detect a lie quicker than the strike of a snake."

I take another swig of water and swish it around my mouth before swallowing it. "The search had to do with the case Seth and I were working on. It turns out that the two victims had letters burned into them that spelled my name when arranged properly. Because of that, they thought I might be in some kind of danger."

"Well they had the dickens scared out of me." Mother's foot stops tapping. "I knew you weren't caught up in some illicit scandal."

"I appreciate your vote of confidence, Mother." I screw the lid back on my water bottle. "They wanted to assign an officer to our house, but I declined."

"Good. The Lord will protect us, not some man with a badge and gun."

No matter how hard I try, I can't comprehend her undying faith in a faceless god. *How could anyone?*

The water bottle crumples in my hand when I flex. "If this matter is settled can we talk about another?"

"And what might that be?"

"My father."

"Alice, we've trodden down this road many times. What more can I tell you about him?"

"You continue to berate me about always telling the truth, but you've been lying to me about my father my entire life. Are you exempt from this rule? I believe Revelation 21:8 says no." The damned song plays in my head. *Liars go to hell. Burn, burn, burn.*

Mother stomps her foot. "Alice, you— There's nothing—" She groans.

Score one for Alice.

Her chair squeaks and I know she's squirming in it. "I've hidden the truth about your father from you all these years because I didn't want you hurt by it."

I lean forward and rest my elbows on the table. "Did you ever think that perhaps lying to me might hurt me just as much as telling me the truth? Is anything you've told me about him true?"

"There are certainly truths in what I told you."

I smack the table for effect like the detectives always do in the movies. "I think you've kept the truth from me because it hurts you, not because it would hurt me."

"That's not true, Alice. The truth affects both of us. God, help me in saying this..."

"What? What could be so bad? Is he a murderer? In prison? Dead? What is it?"

"He's crazy, Alice. There's no way around it. When I told him that I was pregnant with you—"

"He wanted you to abort me. Heard that one."

"I did say that, but it isn't true. When I told him... he wanted to move us to some remote island near the Arctic Circle."

"That does sound stupid, but you decided to go with 'he wanted to abort you?' That makes no sense."

"He said you were special like him and that there were people that would hunt you and kill you. When I probed him further, he said your ancestors weren't from this world."

Not from this world? It's absurd, but the thought still chills me.

"He was adamant about all of it so I... I..."

"You what, Mother?" I stand and my chair screeches backward. "Spit it out for God's sake."

"I had him committed. There was nothing else I could do." She sniffles and I'm unsure if it's allergies or self-pity because of what she did to my father. My guess is self-pity.

I unscrew the lid on my water bottle, chug what's left, and toss it and the lid into the recycle bin next to the fridge. I grab my chair and sit back down. "So my father's a mental case. Big deal. So am I. Is he still alive?"

She blows her nose twice and sniffs. "He was the last time I checked."

"And when was that? Better yet, where was that?"

Her chair moans and screeches against the floor when she rises. The tea kettle rattles and then the kitchen sink faucet bursts to life. She fills the kettle and sets it on the stove. The auto-igniter clicks repeatedly, and the smell of gas reaches my nostrils just before the gas ignites with a whoosh.

Mother sits back down at the table. "Ten years ago. Right after you gained your sight, I went to see him. Oh, you should've seen the fury in that man's eyes. Praise God he'd gone blind several years before. I think if he'd seen me, he might've strangled me to death.

"Our conversation led nowhere and ended abruptly when he called security to escort me out of the facility. That's one of the reasons I haven't gone back to see him."

I pull my face down with my hand. "You're telling me he's here in town?"

"Yes, in the St. Thomas Psychiatric Center."

"All this time..."

Daggers of betrayal pierce me, and I thank God I'm blind right now. If I had to look at Mother's face right now, I might puke. *How could she do this to me? I would never...*

Understanding washes over me and leaves my stomach wrecked. *My God, Seth. I'm so sorry.*

I lean back in the chair and let my head dangle behind me. I'd hated my father for so long for abandoning me and wanting me dead that I can hardly reconcile that it was a lie.

I rise from my chair with anger in my heart. "How could you be so calloused? Why would you let me believe that my father didn't want me? Don't you understand how hurt I've been by that fact—no, lie?

"I spent so many years asking God why my father hated me so much that he wanted me dead. I couldn't understand why. Now I find out that it was never true. I've blamed everyone, including God, but never you. The perfect woman, righteous to a fault. You were never on the suspect list. How could I have been so blind to what was right in front of me?"

Those last words harken back to what Seth said to me in the conference room. I *am* my mother, and the thought sickens me.

The tea kettle whistles and Mother rises from the table. She sets the kettle on a different burner and the whistling fades. "You're right, Alice. I had no right to lie to you like that." Her voice is quiet. Meek. "I am as imperfect as anyone. A sinner just like you and every other human on the planet. Can you ever forgive me?"

I want nothing more than to lay into her but all I can think about is Seth and how I hurt him. I hear myself say "yes." To my astonishment, I feel a great burden lifted from me. Mother hugs me. I'm not sure when she crossed the room. Her lavender perfume tickles my nose.

I think this is the most progress Mother and I have ever made toward understanding each other. I decide to push a little further. "Will you take me to see him?"

Mother pulls back from me. "What? No. Why would I do that? He'll never see me again."

"Dr. Strong thinks my vision issues may stem from trauma over my father and recommended that I go see him. I think he might be right. I really need to meet him and talk to him. Please, do this one thing for me."

"Why don't you have Seth or Veronica take you to see him if it's that important to you."

"You lie to me for twenty-six years about my father and you're unwilling to take me to see him?"

"I... I just can't. God forgive me. I can't do it."

"Fine."

I storm out of the kitchen, down the hallway, and into my bedroom. I slam the door and proceed to trip over the pile of laundry that's out of place. I twist around midair and fall right on my tailbone. Pain erupts across my entire butt and lower back. I curse Mother, the clothes, and Seth for moving them.

I crawl over to my nightstand, grab my phone, and call Veronica for a ride.

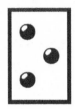

CHAPTER TWENTY-FIVE

I CLUTCH ESTHER IN my right hand and Veronica's arm in my left as we walk through the sliding doors and into the lobby of St. Thomas Medical Center. As of late, it has become a second home to me.

I don't know what it is about hospitals that creeps me out, but my skin crawls every time I walk through their front doors. On the surface they are clean and pristine, but underneath their layers of brown paint and bleached surfaces lies sickness and death.

Veronica nudges my side. "I see what you mean about the info desk guy. He really does look like Eddie from Iron Maiden. A little less dead perhaps but otherwise spot on."

I snort. "Told you so. You owe me lunch now." When we're together we often revert back to teenage girls.

"Whatcha reading, Eddie?" Veronica shouts loud enough to wake the dead in the hospital morgue downstairs. We proceed over to the information desk.

"Well if it isn't Wonderland! Who's this you got hanging on your arm?"

"This is Vee, my bestie."

"Nice to meet you, Vee. I'm sure Wonderland's told you that they call me Eddie. Not sure why, but I kinda like it. Makes me feel like a covert operative or something. Like James Bond or Ethan Hunt, you know?"

"No doubt. Got a page turner on your hands?" Veronica smacks her gum. It's the one thing about her that drives me bonkers.

"Sure do. One of Tosca Lee's thrillers. *The Progeny.* Either of you read it?"

Tosca Lee is one of my all-time favorite authors. "Yeah, read the second one as well. They don't disappoint!"

Veronica pulls on my arm. "You're both too book nerdy for my taste. Let's roll, *Wonderland.*"

I roll my eyes. "See ya, Eddie. Enjoy the book!"

"Oh, I will! See you girls later."

We walk across the main concourse and turn left, toward the East Wing. The hospital is a maze even with sight, so I'm glad I have Veronica at my side to guide me through it. We reach the East Wing elevators and take the third elevator to the third floor. From there, we cross the skybridge over to the St. Thomas Psychiatric Center and take another elevator to the first floor.

By the time we step off the elevator my palms are sweaty, and my pulse is racing. I've never had a father before. In fact I've had very few men in my life at all. With Seth gone, I'm left with no one again.

I've honestly never thought about what I would say to my father if I ever met him. Until two days ago I never did want to meet him. Now that I'm here outside the psychiatric ward I'm not sure I can go through with it.

"Hold up, Vee." My breathing is shallow, my chest is tight, and I think I might start hyperventilating. "I'm not sure I can do this right now. I don't think I'm ready to meet him."

Veronica grabs the side of my head and kisses my cheek. Her lips are silky soft. "You'll be fine, I promise. If he turns out to be some psycho bastard, we'll turn tail and run, but you've gotta give him a chance. After all, he didn't abandon you… exactly. Can't be worse than meeting my father, remember? I'm eight years old and the jerk asks me for money."

I squeeze her arm against my side. "Nice pep talk coach. You sure know how to instill courage and hope in someone."

Veronica smacks her gum again. "I do my best work under pressure."

I wince. "I don't even know what the hell to call him. Father? Dad? Daddy? Pops? Papa? Mr. Mallard? Isaiah?"

"Sperm donor might do the trick."

"I'm being serious, Vee."

"So was I. That's all he's been for you so far. Call it like it is."

"I need his help, not a kick in the pants. I can't go in there without a plan."

"And you didn't devise a plan on the way over here? You're always on top of things like that. What's gotten into you, besides Seth?"

"Sometimes you can be really crude. Besides, Seth and I don't exist anymore."

"Okay, back up the friggin bus. What do you mean you and Seth don't exist anymore? I thought you two were destined to make perfect little babies together. What happened?"

"What didn't happen is the real question. Everything blew up in my face at work and then Seth did too. They raided my storage unit and took everything and then they suspended me from the force."

"Serious? Those bastards don't have a clue. I might have to take my happy butt down there and give 'em a piece of my mind. How you handling it so well? I'd be a total wreck about now."

"Trust me, I was last night. I wanted to call you, and have you come over, but I knew you were working. I'm still upset and pissed about the whole thing, but there's nothing I can do about it right now."

"Yeah there is. You can go through these damned doors and meet your father. They might've raided your storage unit, but they can't take all that knowledge from your head."

"I know, and you're right." I take a deep breath. "Let's do this before I change my mind again."

"Truth." Veronica reaches across me and presses the call button on the wall. A bell sounds.

Moments later a male voice greets us. "Afternoon, ladies. I'm Nurse Vance. How may I be of service?"

"We're here to see Isaiah Mallard." My voice cracks.

"She is. I'm just here for moral support."

I elbow her.

"Got any support needs of your own, big guy?"

I elbow her again.

Vance ignores Veronica. "IDs please. We'll return them to you when you leave."

I retrieve my ID from my front pants pocket and Veronica snatches it out of my hand.

"Okay, I get it. All business. Not a problem. Here's our IDs."

"Thank you," says Nurse Vance.

Veronica releases my arm. "What time you get off work Vance? Ally here is newly single."

"Vee, you're embarrassing me."

Nurse Vance ignores Veronica's question. "Give me a minute or two to get you guys into the visitor's log. Once I've done that, the doors to your left will swing outward. Make sure you're standing behind the red line on the floor so that you don't get hit by them. I will meet you right on the other side."

Veronica whispers in my ear. "Or in a parking lot. Dark alley. Back seat of your car. I don't care where it is."

I roll my eyes. "You're a twisted little perv, Vee."

"Crazy, you say? You might be on to something. At least we're in the right place. Check me in and put me under his care."

"Sometimes I wonder how we ever became friends. How about we focus on my father."

"Oh, don't you worry yourself. This girl can multitask like nobody's business."

"Seriously, Vee. My nerves are frayed already and you're not helping."

"For real? Right here in the hallway? Can someone call diaper patrol? We've got a party pooper on our hands." She kisses my cheek.

"Vee—"

"Don't worry, Ally. I was just messing with Monsieur Vance." She says his name with French flair. "He's so wound and uptight that if he were to squeeze out a fart, he'd take down the entire wing. Seriously, that guy's butt is so puckered that his legs are turned out ninety degrees. He has to sit on his hips. How uncomfortable would that be?"

The mental picture is comedy gold and I can't help but snort.

"Oh, you do have a funny bone. I was beginning to think you might've broken it."

"I can't take you anywhere."

"Yeah, that's the sucky part of being blind again, right? No driving."

Motors groan and whir for ten full seconds and we're met with warm air. "Right through here, ladies." Nurse Vance sounds a bit flustered.

"Thank you." Veronica grabs my arm and pulls me forward.

"Have either of you been here before?" asks Nurse Vance.

"Only as patients. Feels weird being on the other side of things."

I nudge Veronica. "Forgive my friend, Nurse Vance. Neither of us have been here before."

He claps his hands together. "Perfect. I'll just point out a few things really quick and then I'll leave you to your business."

"You're not coming with us?" I ask.

Vance chuckles. "We do things a bit different here than other facilities do. All of our patients are long-term, so we try and give them as much freedom as possible. It tends to keep them in a more manageable state."

"I see." It's an ironic phrase coming from my lips.

He continues, "Restrooms and water fountains are located behind you on your left. Directly to your left is what we call the Gen Pop area. Patients in this area are typically mild-mannered. Be careful though because a few of them are known pickpockets.

"To your right is the area for those who need more direct care, also known as Iso Pop. Some of the patients in there can be erratic and violent at times. Do not venture into that area without a supervising nurse. Straight ahead of you are three hallways lined with Gen Pop resident rooms. Central hallway and the eighth door down on the left is where you'll find Mr. Mallard. Room B15. With the exception of meals, he rarely ventures outside his room. He should be there now. Any questions?"

"Yeah—"

I rib Veronica. "Nope. I think we'll manage just fine from here. Thank you so much for your kindness and patience, Nurse Vance."

"It's been a pleasure, Ms. Bergman. Ms. Gomez." His shoes squeak like squeegees when he walks away.

I take a deep breath. "Let's get this over with."

"Relax, Ally. Otherwise you'll be walking around here like a penguin."

"Is my hair good?"

Veronica chews her gum like a cow chewing its cud. "He's blind, remember? Besides, your hair never looks good."

I smile. "I hate you, jerk."

"Love you, too." She weaves her fingers through mine. "Straight ahead. If the nerves crop up again just think about Nurse Vance farting."

I snort. It's one mental image I'll never stop finding funny.

We walk forward, hand-in-hand. There's no one else I'd rather share this moment with. Mother is Mother, and Seth wouldn't relax me the way Veronica does, but my heart aches for him.

We stop, and Veronica knocks on a door. The sound is hollow.

"Mr. Mallard?" asks Veronica.

My stomach climbs into my throat, leaving a lump I cannot swallow.

"Who's asking?" His voice is gruff.

Not what I expected. Then again, I'm not sure what I expected.

Veronica pulls us into the room. "I'm Veronica. My friend here is Alice."

"Hello." My voice sounds about as strong as a whiff of air.

"Not looking for Girl Scout Cookies," he says with a harrumph.

Veronica lets go of my hand. "That's an odd thing to say."

"Why's that? Sounds like you're both about ten years old. Why else would you visit an old blind man?"

Adrenaline pumps through my veins and kills my fear. I sweep Esther back and forth and move forward several steps. "We're here because you're my father."

He ignores my statement. "I know the sound of a white cane. How long you been blind?"

"Most of my life, like you."

"That so?" He clears his throat and the gurgle of phlegm makes me want to gag. "You're a genuine expert on Isaiah Mallard are ya?"

"Enough to be here." I shift my weight to my right leg and lean on Esther.

Veronica touches my shoulder. "Ally, I'm going to step outside for a bit. Just holler if you need me."

I reach up and touch her hand. "Thanks, Vee."

Veronica exits the room and closes the door behind her.

I take another step forward. "I know who you really are."

"Come to kill me then?" His voice is flat and doesn't quaver. "I've been waiting for this day for quite some time."

I gasp and step backward. "Why would I want to kill you?"

"Don't assume I'm an easy target because I'm old and blind. I killed the last Shadow Priest who came after me and I'll do the same to you if you don't leave."

Mother's right. He is insane, but I can't walk away emptyhanded. "I came here for answers, not to kill you. I know your real name is Philip. You were born blind just like me, but then you changed your name in 1990. How does a blind man obtain a driver's license?"

He coughs and clears his throat again. "Who did you say you were?"

"I'm Alice, the daughter of Gladys Bergman."

He growls, "Name means nothing to me." Inflections in his voice tell me he's lying.

"Like you, I gained my vision, but it only lasted ten years. I'm blind again and want to know why. Can you help me or not?"

"You traipse in here like you own the place, claim you're some long lost child of mine, and demand answers of me because you're smart enough to do a few internet searches about me. What kind of fool do you take me for?" His voice is stern but not angry. "I can't see a thing and I don't know you from Eve, so your word is about as useful as a fart in a hurricane. Unless you've brought proof of who you are you might as well turn around and walk your happy butt right out of here. You'll get nothing from me without proof."

I move my left hand to my hip. "And how am I supposed to bring you proof? It's not like you passed down any family heirlooms to me."

"Darling, I'm sure you'll come up with something. If you don't, then don't bother coming back." He groans and hacks. "Now, if you'll excuse me, I've got a bone to pick with Mother Nature. Lunch is talking back."

I'm so frustrated that I want to unleash Esther on him. "Mark my words, I'll be back."

"You do that, terminator. Can't say I'll be looking forward to it."

I turn around and stomp over to the door. I throw it open and it bangs against the wall. "You out here, Vee?"

"Right beside you." She takes my right hand in her left. "You okay? Your face is flushed."

I shake my fist and Esther. "That bastard is crazy. He's demanding proof of who I am before he'll talk to me."

She lifts my hand and kisses my knuckles. "Look, I don't want to be the voice of reason, especially since I'm terrible at the role, but wouldn't you require the same of him if the roles were reversed?"

"You're siding with him? Turncoat!"

She moves my hand to her right hand and puts her left arm around me. "Love you so much, Ally. Let's go get that proof he wants."

"Damn straight." I lean over and try to kiss her cheek, but my lips wind up on her ear. She giggles.

We walk back down the hallway and over to the nurse's station. Veronica grabs our IDs from Nurse Vance and we exit once the doors fully open. Tension builds in my neck and shoulders.

I've only got three-and-a-half days before the Braille Killer will probably kill again and I've got nothing to go on. I don't even know if my father's sane enough to give me any information that will help either, but first I need proof of who I am.

I hope I'm not wasting my time.

* * * * *

"Do you love me, Mother?"

"Don't be silly, Alice. You know that I do."

"Then take me to see my father."

Mother huffs. "I told you yesterday why I can't do that."

"You have no right to keep me from getting to know him."

"I'm not stopping you, Alice, but I'm not about to help you either."

"And that's what Jesus is telling you? Keep me away from my father? Is that what he teaches?"

"One has nothing to do with the other."

"Doesn't it? My father won't speak to me unless I can prove that I'm his daughter. How else do you expect me to prove that than by bringing you with me to see him?"

"How about a paternity test? Those are pretty accurate, right?"

"Except for the fact that he's blind. I could easily bring him a blank piece of paper and tell him that he's my father, but he'll never believe it. I don't think he'd even believe a nurse if one read it to him. I need more substantial proof. I need you, Mother. You are the only way I'll ever be able to talk to him. Don't you understand how important this is to me?"

"And what will you do for me in return?"

"Anything."

"You start coming to church with me every Sunday and I will take you to see your father."

"That's blackmail!"

"It goes both ways, dear."

"Fine. I promise to start going to church with you if you promise to take me to see him tomorrow."

"Tomorrow? I'm not sure tomorrow will work. I've got a plethora of things to do tomorrow."

I cross my arms. "Tomorrow, or I'll never set foot inside a church again."

"You're an evil little thing." She sighs. "Fine. I promise to take you to see your father tomorrow."

CHAPTER TWENTY-SIX

MOTHER AND I STAND outside the doors of St. Thomas Psychiatric Center. Muffled screams penetrate the thick walls at an almost regular interval. *What in the world is going on in there?*

Yesterday I was a ball of nerves coming here. Today is proving no different. My teeth chatter and my hands tremble.

I hold Mother's hand. Together our shaking might bring down the entire hospital. Buildings aren't built to withstand earthquakes in this region of the country. "We can do this, Mother. Your part is simple. Convince him of who I am and then you can come back out here."

"No, no, no. This is a bad idea. Nothing good will come of you talking to that man. He's insane, Alice. That's why he's in this facility. God saved us from him once. Let's not test God's grace with this."

I squeeze her hand. "You made me a promise, remember?"

"I know I did, but I didn't realize it would be this hard. I haven't seen that man in over ten years. Please don't ask me to do this."

"I would never ask it of you if it wasn't important." I lift her hand to my lips. "I love you, Mother, but I've exhausted all my other options. Besides, you're constantly going on about how God won't allow us to go through something we can't handle. If that's true, then what do you have to fear seeing my father?"

She sighs loudly. "God help me. God help us both."

She presses the call button and we wait almost a minute for one of the nurses to assist us. "May I help you?" The female voice comes through the speaker on the wall.

Mother clears her throat. "We're here to see Isaiah Mallard."

"Certainly. Please place you IDs in the silver tray." Mother and I put our IDs into it. "Thank you. They will be returned to you when you leave."

"Thank you," I say.

"Please stand clear of the door. It will swing outward."

Mother pulls me back a step. The doorlatch clicks and the motor on the automatic door whirs. Another click and Mother guides me through the open door. The nurse is there to greet us.

"Right this way, ladies, and please forgive the noise today. We've got a new resident who's having a difficult time adapting to their environment. We've adjusted their meds, so things should be quiet now."

Adjusting meds is always code for sedation. My nerves are so frayed that I could use a few pills about now. Mother holds my arm and we follow the nurse.

"Mr. Mallard just ate lunch, so your timing is perfect. He tends to be in better spirits on a full stomach."

Wasn't the case yesterday.

Chatter fills the air and I wonder how many of the conversations are one-sided. We stop, and the nurse knocks on a door and opens it. "Mr. Mallard? You have guests."

"If I wanted guests, I would've invited them."

I sigh. *We're definitely in the right place.*

"He's all yours, ladies." I hear the nurse walk away.

Mother doesn't move. Her hand is stone on my arm. I pull on it, but she doesn't budge. I whisper to her. "Two minutes and then you can leave. I promise."

"What's the meaning of this? You just come to stare? This ain't no petting zoo. Animals here are all wild. You got your look. Now get going before I dial up security."

Mother's arm relaxes. "Hello, Isaiah." She leads us into the room.

Bedsprings creak. "Heavens, I know that voice. Gladys? Is that really you?"

Mother releases my arm. "The one and only."

He harrumphs. "For all I know, it could be a voice recording. Can't trust anything with technology these days."

I move forward a step. "I said I'd bring proof. Is she not good enough for you?"

Father snorts. "Tell me something only you'd know, Gladys."

Mother brushes past me. She whispers something to him and I strain my ears to hear it, but I cannot make out any of her words.

Bedsprings creak again. "I didn't think I'd see you again, Gladys. Not after the way things ended between us the last time."

Mother touches my arm. "I'll be out in the lobby. Take as long as you need. I'll be conversing with Jesus."

I grab hold of her elbow. "What did you say to him?"

"Nothing you'll ever know." She pats my hand with her other hand. "Be careful of what he tells you."

"Are we alone in here?" I ask.

"You're alone. I'll close the door behind me."

I let go of her arm. "Thank you, Mother."

She walks away and closes the door behind her.

For several moments, the only sound in the room is heavy breathing. I don't know where to begin. I've never been down this road.

His voice severs the silence. "If she says you're my daughter then you must be, but why are you here? Why now? What do you want from me? I've nothing to offer." There's a softness in his voice that wasn't there yesterday.

I cling to Esther. "I need answers."

"Answers to what?"

I move forward. "Can I sit down?"

"Do whatever you want. I don't make the rules around here." The edge is back in his voice.

I locate the side of the bed and sit down. "Why are you so hostile toward me? I'm your daughter."

"Forgive me. I didn't know I had a daughter until a few minutes ago." Pain tremors in his voice.

My heart aches for him. "She never told you about me?"

Some sounds are distinct, like a tissue scraping against cardboard as it's pulled from its box. I hear it now.

"No. I knew she was pregnant all those years ago, but I'd pushed it from my mind. I thought I'd never meet you." Isaiah blows his nose. "I wasn't prepared for the flood of emotions I'm feeling right now. I don't even know the first thing about you, yet I care deeply for you already. I haven't cared about anything or anyone in a long time."

I'm stunned. Without words. I've spent so long hating him that I can't reconcile the man who sits next to me with the one I created in my mind. He's been dead for as long as I've been alive.

How will I ever forgive Mother?

My throat tightens, and I swallow back tears. "Why did she come see you ten years ago?"

"I don't know. Our conversation never made it that far. I thought she was one of them."

"One of whom?"

"The Shadow Priests. I'd just lost my vision a few months before and I thought she'd come to kill me. It didn't seem like a coincidence at the time. I would've killed her if the nurse hadn't come in."

"You're not making any sense and you're starting to scare me." I want to leave but I can't move.

"Do you have the mark?"

Mother's right. He's insane.

He grabs my left wrist and I jerk it away. "What the hell do you think you're doing?" I can hardly breathe.

He breathes deep. "I can feel it. You're like me. You've got a mark on the inside of your wrist, don't you?"

"If you're talking about my birthmark, then yes." I trace it with my finger.

"That's no birthmark, darling." His voice cuddles, but it only heightens my fear.

"How would you know what it is or isn't?"

"An open eye with a curved sickle blade above it."

My heart leaps about in my chest like a caged animal. "How could you possibly know that?"

He leans forward, cinnamon on his breath. "Because I have a mark of my own just like it."

I rub my wrist. "What does it mean?"

"It means that you're special, like me."

My chest tightens. "Special how?"

"Have you experienced any visions?"

I frown. "What do you mean?"

"Spirit walking. Experiencing memories from those that have moved on from this world."

My legs shake the bed. "You know about that?"

He takes my hand again, this time with a subtle tenderness. "We are the same, Alice. I know many things."

"But why do we only see the last moments before death?"

He laughs. "You must dive deep and give into the experience fully. Once you do, you'll be able to experience memories from any point in their life."

"What else? What is possible?"

He leans close to me and whispers, "There are things we cannot discuss here. Eyes and ears are everywhere. In the shadows."

I nod and ponder everything he's told me. Can it be true? Did Mother know all of this and keep it from me? What reason could she possibly have to do so if she did know?

"Mother never mentioned that you were blind."

"That's because I wasn't blind when she knew me."

My pulse races. "I knew it. I gained my sight ten years ago, but then I lost it again last week and I don't know why."

"And how did you gain your sight?"

"An accident. I hit my head really hard and was knocked unconscious. When I came to, I had limited vision. A few days later my vision was fully restored."

"False." He pats my hand. "Trauma wouldn't have triggered it. What else happened?"

Denise falls to her death in my mind. I've imagined how it happened many times. "A girl died in that accident."

"Ah, and you killed her."

I jerk back, stunned. "No! I didn't kill anyone. We ran into each other and next thing I knew I was waking up and she was dead."

"Intention has no factor. Her death gave you your vision. That's how things work for us in this world. It is a travesty, to be certain, but still a fact."

"You're telling me the only reason I could see was because she died?"

"Yes, and you'll have to kill again if you want to see again."

I gasp. *I'm no killer!* "You're plain crazy. Are you telling me that you're a serial killer? Is that why you're really in here?"

His voice rises several decibels. "You came here asking for answers. If you don't like the answers I'm providing feel free to walk out of here."

"Then how did you maintain your sight? Better yet, how did you gain your sight to begin with?"

"I cannot go into that in here but suffice it to say I never murdered anyone."

"Animals then?"

"For heaven's sake, child. I would never harm innocent creatures. Besides, those kinds of deaths do nothing for us. They must be human or some type of being with a soul."

My heart desperately wants to believe him, but my mind will not climb aboard his crazy train. "This is asinine. I'm starting to see why you're locked up in here. You're as crazy as Mother said."

"Am I? You're more like me than you can imagine. What you have is inherited from me. You're different, Alice, but you already know that. They do too. They'll come after you now that you're blind again. Protect yourself."

"You're insane! No one's after me." I'm lying to myself again, but it doesn't matter. I won't fuel his madness with talk of the Braille Killer.

"Call me what you want, but you'll come around soon enough. We're not from this world, Alice. That's why they want us dead."

I thrust my arms in the air. "This is ridiculous! You're telling me that I'm some kind of alien spawn killing machine. You've watched too many movies and you live in a fantasy world far outside reality."

"And you'd best remember that when you're around your mother or you might wind up locked away in here with me."

I get up, find my way over to the door, open it, and then slam it shut behind me. *Why did I even come here?*

CHAPTER TWENTY-SEVEN

IT'S SATURDAY MORNING AND I find myself back at the police station. My return to the second floor conference room after Wednesday's circus is anything but comfortable. Lieut. Frost, Detective Roland, and Detective Ryan are in the room again as well, along with Deborah from CSI. I sit in the same chair as before.

The tension in the room is thick enough to taste, so I decide to break the ice with a joke. "So why'd you bring me in again? Can't get enough of me? Thought who better to lead a blind investigation than a blind woman?"

"Alice we wouldn't have brought you in if this wasn't important." Seth, my unhorsed knight in tarnished, dull-gray armor speaks. His voice tugs at my heartstrings and I just want to scream. "You might want to brace yourself for what's about to be said."

Brace myself? Why have they brought me in? The tension from the room seeps into my skin and burrows deep inside my bones. I stiffen like a three-day-old cadaver.

"Sorry. Just felt way too uptight in here."

"Deborah and the rest of the CSI team have been analyzing the notes and items from your storage unit for the last several days and uncovered some disturbing information." Lieut. Frost is always serious but something in his tone today sends up warning flares.

I straighten in my seat and plant my feet firmly on the floor.

"The room is yours, Deborah."

"Thank you, Lieutenant Frost." I'm fond of Deborah and have spoken with her on many occasions. Today her voice is laced with caution. "The Braille Killer has sent three packages to Detective Bergman containing friendship bracelets. At first glance they are nothing more than simple hand woven bracelets but as we began to examine them further, we discovered two things of importance.

"The first thing we discovered was that the thread used in these bracelets is very specific and rare. So rare in fact that it was only ever made by a single textile mill, Kyle's Textiles. I'm sure you all remember that's where we found the first victim's mother, Yolanda Johnson, bound to a chair.

"The second thing we discovered was that human hair was woven into each bracelet as well. Once we realized this, we did hair analysis of the three bracelets against our two victims. The science of hair analysis is anything but conclusive with the odds being about one in ten thousand will match but it still allows us to narrow our search significantly. The hair used in the first bracelet he sent a year ago was an identical match to Sarah Johnson and the hair in the second bracelet sent eighteen days ago was an identical match to Cara Strum.

"The third bracelet sent eight days ago is an anomaly. It contains the same type of rare thread, but it also contains human hair from two different individuals. We believe he is planning on killing two people this time and we still have yet to determine who he is, where he is, and who his next victim will be."

I raise my hand and immediately feel like a kid in school again. "Hold up a minute. First you said that you believe he's planning on killing two people but then you say you don't know who his next victim is. You said victim as in singular and not plural. Are you telling me you've identified one of his next potential victims already?"

My mind reels and then realization settles in. I understand why they brought me in.

Lieut. Frost confirms it. "Yes, Detective. We believe it's you for two reasons. The first is that he spelled out your name with the wounds of the first two victims. The second is that we think that one of the sets of hair from the third bracelet may belong to you. It's identical in color to your hair."

Me? How many more ways could he violate me? My stomach gurgles. "You think he took a sample from me when I was younger and kept it all this time?" I chew on the end of my thumbnail. I haven't done that since I was little. "Given his meticulous planning it seems highly probable."

Deborah pipes up. "It could be that or he's gotten it from you more recently."

"More recently?" I search my memories scouring for evidence I find implausible but then I remember the night at the storage facility. Did he cut some hair from my head at that time? I can't remember but I was so distraught that night. "I guess it's possible."

"Would you mind providing us with a hair sample so that we can examine it against the hair from the bracelet?"

"Whatever you need, Deborah. You can take it now."

Deborah's chair groans as she gets up from it. "I'll only need a few hairs. I'll warn you when I'm about to—"

"Ow!" I rub the back of my head.

She pats my shoulder. "Sorry about that. Thought it might not hurt as much if I took it by surprise."

"Well now you know it doesn't help." I lean back in my chair. "There is more evidence that points to me as well."

"Something you just realized or something you've withheld from us?" Detective Roland sure knows how to find a wound and pick at it.

I huff. "Does it really matter at this point? No. What I was going to say is that I noticed the positioning of the first victim held significance as well. Sarah Johnson had her arms folded across her abdomen like an isosceles triangle and her legs spread apart. I believe he placed her that way on purpose, like an 'A' for Alice."

"And the second?" Lieut. Frost's tone is far warmer than a few days ago.

Seth's voice emerges from the depths. "A 'B' for Bergman. I had wondered why he left her that way, but it makes sense now."

Lieut. Frost shifts some papers on the table. "How long will it take to analyze that hair sample, Deborah?"

"An hour or so for a good guess. A day for better accuracy."

"Expedience is key Deborah. Get to it."

"Yes sir." Deborah exits the conference room.

"Detective Bergman I will assign an officer to your home until we determine if you really are in danger."

"No need, sir. I'll take on that responsibility."

Seth? My jaw drops, and I have to force it back shut. *Why would he volunteer to keep watch of me?* I didn't think he wanted to be around me anymore.

"Fine. You and Detective Roland can alternate watching her."

The last thing I need is Detective Roland hanging around. "Sir—"

"My decision isn't up for debate." Lieut. Frost's glare warms my forehead even though I can't see it.

"I'll take first watch." Seth's chair rolls back into the wall. "Alice, you're with me."

I pluck Esther from between my legs and rise from the chair. Seth opens the conference room door and I exit behind him. We walk the length of the hallway and down the two flights of stairs to the first floor.

Seth touches my arm just to stop me. "I'm parked out back."

"Right behind you."

We exit the building and Seth takes my arm. I want to grab him and hold him and tell him how much I love him, but I stay silent and follow his lead. We arrive at his car and he opens the door for me.

"Thank you. I can manage from here." I crawl into the front seat and the backs of my legs are on fire within seconds. I grit my teeth, tuck Esther between the door and the seat, and pull the door closed. The handle burns my fingers.

I can't wait for winter.

Seth drops into the driver's seat and closes his door. "Wow, that's hot."

"I keep telling you to invest in some sunshades."

"High on my list right now."

We pull out of the parking lot and head down the road. I know these streets better than most and within a few turns I realize we're not headed toward my house. "Where are you taking me?"

"My place." I can tell by his tone and how short he's being with me that he's still pissed at me.

I don't understand why he volunteered for Alice duty. There are plenty of officers who would've appreciated the overtime. Sometimes men overly complicate things.

I drum my fingers on the middle console. "Need to pick something up from there?"

"No. You're staying with me."

My fingers freeze mid-drum. "Staying with you? Why would I do that?"

"Because I don't trust anyone else watching you."

Does he miss me? "You know most of the guys on the force. What would make you not trust them?"

"This Braille Killer could be anywhere and anyone."

"Oh. I guess that's true, but I'd smell him coming from a mile away."

"Why? You think he's incapable of cleaning up and brushing his teeth?"

Sometimes Seth does have some good points. Maybe he only eats garlic and pickles right before he kills but I don't think that's the case. Either way, he *could* be anyone.

"Suppose not. And, for the record, I can't think of another place I'd rather be than with you even if you are still pissed at me."

"I'm not pissed at you."

I laugh. "Could've fooled me. I may be blind, but I can still feel your heat vision every time you glance my way."

"Look, you broadsided me with a frickin dump truck on Wednesday and crushed my heart. I'm wounded, Alice, not pissed."

I reach over and put my hand on his thigh. "I'm sorry, Seth. Hurting you was never part of the plan. If I could turn back time and make things right I would."

"I know. You're the smartest damn woman I know and so completely stupid and self-absorbed at times too. I often wonder if you're bipolar and off your meds."

I pull the dagger from my wounded heart and deflect like I always do. "So does Mother."

We make a sharp right, bounce over the speedhump leading into Seth's condo complex, and park. He escorts me up to his condo and we go inside. All I can think about is Tuesday night. Sex gone wrong. At least for me it did. Suddenly I'm in need of a blanket but the cold is much more than skin-deep.

I walk over and crash onto the couch. A TV remote bites into my lower back. I pull it out from underneath me and place it on the coffee table. I exhale and sink into the couch.

Drawers, windows, and doors bang throughout the condo for several minutes and then Seth plops down on the opposite end of the couch. "We're alone, and everything is secure."

The mirror from storage unit 109 creeps into my mind and I cringe. Another thing I've kept from Seth. He doesn't understand the visions I have. If I tell him about the mirror, he'll surely have me committed. Telling him about it wouldn't help anyway since I have no idea where the killer moved it to.

All I know is that no blind girl is safe as long as the Braille Killer is out there. With the mirror, no locked door or window can stop him. The only thing he needs to penetrate lives and gain entry is the shadows, and in the darkness, shadows reign supreme.

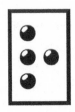

CHAPTER TWENTY-EIGHT

VERONICA AND I LIE on Seth's bed in boxers and tank tops. The AC is cranked as high as it will go, and the ceiling fan is spinning on high, but the heat is unrelenting. Sweat covers my hairline, soaks my hair, and runs down and through every crevice on my body. I imagine it's doing the same to Veronica.

Seth's out working a lead with Detective Roland, so we're alone inside the condo. Officer Dupree stands guard outside the front door in the main hallway. It's even hotter out there and I pity him, but there's no chance of him waiting inside.

Veronica lies on my left side and slowly caresses the inside of my left forearm with her fingertips. It reminds me of when Mother used to rub my back that way during church to keep me from fidgeting. "So how did the second trip to see your father go?"

"Fairly well, all things considered."

"That doesn't sound too positive."

"I know…"

She picks up my arm and kisses my palm. "You know you can tell me anything. Unlike Seth, I'm not going anywhere. I'll love you beyond death. You're like the little sister I never had."

"I love you too, Vee."

"Then spill it. Tell me everything."

"Okay…" I roll on my side and lay my head on her shoulder. "When we arrived, he was ticked that I showed back up and even more so because Mother was there. But then Mother whispered something to him and left the room. From that point forward his entire demeanor was different. I asked him about my blindness and he told me some pretty crazy things. It made me realize why they'd committed him in the first place."

Veronica strokes my head. The thought of her fingers raking through my sweaty locks is a bit repulsive, but she doesn't seem to notice or care. "What did he tell you that was so crazy?"

"First off, he basically told me that my ancestors aren't from this world. Not in so many words, mind you, but seriously? Do I look like I'm from another planet? Don't answer that." I raise my head to look at her. I know I can't see her, but it's hard breaking a habit after ten years.

"Now that you mention it, you are a bit goofy looking. Almost like a Salvador Dali painting. All perky on one side and droopy on the other."

I smack her on the thigh. "You're one to talk with your elvish ears and pointy nose and chin. You look like you came straight out of a *Legend of Zelda* game."

She wraps her arm around my neck and puts me in a headlock. "Don't make me make you cry uncle."

I grab the tender part of her right inside thigh between my forefinger and thumb and twist a little. "You do it and I bruise it."

She releases my head, but I hold onto her thigh. "You want me to finish telling you what happened or not?"

"Yes, mistress. Punish me if you want but leave no details out whilst you do."

I twist my fingers a bit more and then let go. "Where was I even at?"

"You're from another planet, blah blah blah."

"Right. He says we're being hunted and that if I want my vision back, I need to kill someone. He tried to tell me that I killed Denise and that's why I got my vision to start with. How crazy is that?"

"That's top of the list crazy alright. What did Seth think?"

"Same as you. He sided with Mother on having my father committed."

"I can see why she did it too."

"I know… but still. I wonder if some of what he said is true."

"What exactly are you wondering about?" She ruffles my hair. "You haven't said anything that rings true or is even rational for that matter."

"It might sound crazy, but I'm beginning to wonder if Denise's death was really an accident. Could I have killed her?"

"Don't even go there, Ally. You're one of the sweetest people on the planet. There's no way you killed her. You didn't even know her."

"Maybe not, but I remembered the smell of her perfume. It wafted in the hallway outside Dr. Strong's office that day when I came out of my therapy session. I panicked when I smelled it. Next thing I know I'm waking up and she's dead." I sigh and rub my face. "I just don't know Vee. Maybe I did killer her."

"That's absurd and borderline insane." She thumps the top of my head.

"Ow!" I smack her leg and then rub my head. "You're evil!"

"Your thoughts are evil! Get that crap out of there before you start believing it. It's exactly what he wants. You start believing that and he can manipulate you into doing terrible things."

"Ugh. I know but he's had ten years to beat it into me. He's ruined my life and I hate him for it."

Veronica kisses the top of my head where she thumped it. "It'll be okay. We'll get through this together."

"I know. Thanks for being here. I really needed you today with everything going on."

"Speaking of everything going on, what's with the beefcake outside the front door? You on some sort of house arrest or something?"

"Just more trouble in Wonderland. I was called back into the police station this morning. They found some evidence that led them to believe that the killer is targeting me as one of his next victims."

Veronica sits up. "What? When were you planning on dropping that bomb on me?"

I shrug. "Just did. I'm not so sure their intel is credible though."

"And why do you think that?"

I look around out of habit and then shake my head at the absurdity of it. "We're alone, right?"

"We sure as hell better be! I don't traipse around in my boxers and tank top with just anyone." Veronica grabs my arm. "Seth doesn't have some hidden camera that he uses to video you guys having sex, does he?"

"If he does and I find out I will most certainly become a killer."

She lies back down. "Why were you asking if we were alone?"

I lie on my back and bend my knees. "I haven't told anyone what I'm about to tell you, so please keep it between us."

She kisses the top of my head. "I never kiss and tell, Ally."

"I've encountered the killer on multiple occasions. If he wanted me dead, he would've killed me already."

"And how do you know it was him?"

"There are certain things I remember about him from the day he and Denise abducted and raped me. He has a hairy and badly scarred chest—a thick, knotted zipper down his front like Frankenstein's monster." I hug myself.

Veronica squirms next to me. "Damn..."

"I saw him and confronted him at the storage facility, but he got the upper hand on me because I came around a corner too quickly and fell over the top of one of those stupid hand trucks. I gashed my shins and my gun flew out of my hand. It hurt so bad that I could hardly move. He picked up my gun and had it aimed at me but didn't shoot. Instead he picked me up and carried me up to my storage unit and left me there. Why would he do that if he plans to kill me?"

Veronica turns on her side. "I don't know... could he be waiting for something?"

"I suppose, but what? What's changed between then and now?" The answer pops into my mind and I shudder.

"What is it? You okay?"

"I think I know the answer but I'm not sure what it means." I bite my lower lip and search through my memories for meaning but can't find one.

She shakes my shoulder gently. "You going to tell me or keep it to yourself like you've been doing?"

"Yeah, sorry. I've never been blind when I've encountered him other than that first time with Denise."

"So you think he was waiting for you to go blind again? Why? How would he even know that you would?"

"I don't know, but it just feels right."

She pushes my legs over. "I ain't stupid. It's because of something your *insane* father said to you, right? I love you Ally, but it sounds like you're heading off the deep end. There's no life beyond our planet and you're not blind again because you haven't killed anyone. You've just been dealt a crappy hand in life. Deal with it like the rest of us."

The more I think about it the stronger I feel the truth in it. He has been waiting for me to go blind again but why? What purpose does it serve him? Does he have some sort of crazy principle that he adheres to that requires that he only kill blind girls?

I hate lying to Veronica, but I must. "You're right Vee, as always. That's an insane notion. Consider it purged from my mind."

She hugs me tight. "Good. I love you to the moon and back and wouldn't want to see you locked away like your father."

Father... I just can't wrap my mind around the things he told me, but I can't dismiss everything he said either. His words are a two-edged dagger and I'm not sure I'm willing to impale myself on them.

I sit up and hug my legs. "Can I tell you something else?"

Veronica sits up and puts her arm around me. "I'll be anything you need, Ally. Eyes, ears, hands, friend..." Her voice quavers.

I continue, "The other night Seth and I had sex. It was the first time I've ever done it while blind other than when Denise and that bastard raped me. As soon as Seth crawled onto the bed with me my mind reverted back to that horrible day. Every touch repulsed me and shamed me, but I couldn't find a way to tell him."

Tears wet my cheeks. "He didn't seem to notice though until almost the end. I thought I was going to die by the time he finished. I'll never have sex again while I'm blind. I just can't do it."

Veronica puts her hand on my cheek and wipes it with her thumb. "I'm sorry you had to endure that. I've never contemplated how my touching you and kissing you would affect you. I'm such a fool. I never meant to hurt you. I didn't know."

I embrace her and hold her tight. "Never, Vee. You're the sister I never had and my best friend. Don't ever compare yourself to her. She kidnapped me and forced herself on me."

"You don't understand... I..."

I know what she wants to say but I'm glad she doesn't. It would destroy me if I ever had to break her heart. She's one of the best parts of my life and my best friend but we could never be more. To my core I am a woman and I know I was made for a man. Deep inside I think she feels the same, but her uncle abused her and left her broken. I wish I had the words or the power to heal her, but I don't.

I release her. "I know."

"But I—"

The front door squeaks open.

CHAPTER TWENTY-NINE

MY HAND CREEPS TOWARD Esther, and Veronica whimpers next to me as we await the next sound. The front door slams shut and shakes the walls. Veronica jumps and stifles a cry. I roll off the end of the bed, Esther in hand and ready to strike.

"Alice? I'm back."

Seth. My heart starts beating again.

Veronica exhales. "Man you've got me wound so tight."

I lower Esther. "Myself too."

I sit on the end of the bed. "We're in the bedroom, Seth. We'll be out in a minute."

Veronica grunts as she squeezes back into her skintight jeans. I do the same, but mine are far less tight. I prefer them loose so that I can move easier. It's better for the job too.

I slide my shirt back over my head, but it doesn't feel right. Veronica laughs and helps me turn it around the right way. "Thanks." I don't bother with my socks and shoes because I don't plan on going anywhere tonight.

We emerge from the bedroom and the heat hits me again. I'm just a few paces from the gates of hell. One false step and I'll plunge into the depths of the fiery lake.

Water's running full blast in the kitchen sink. A plastic bag rustles.

Veronica gasps and grabs my hand.

"You're a little liar," she whispers. "You told me that Seth didn't cook."

I shrug. "He doesn't. At least I've never witnessed him cook anything in the last two years."

"Well he's cooking now." She nudges my side with her elbow. "I think that's my exit cue."

"The hell it is." I latch onto her arm. "You're not going anywhere."

She leans close and whispers in my ear. "What if he wants to make up with you?"

I yank on her arm. "Exactly! You're not going anywhere."

She sighs. "We're not doing a threesome."

I recoil. "What's wrong with you?"

"Oh! Sorry, Ally." She hugs me. "My mind didn't process that until it'd already left my lips. Sorry I'm so dense at times."

"Forget it." I walk over to the kitchen counter and sit on one of the barstools. "What are you up to, Seth?"

He turns off the water. "Thought I'd make dinner for the three of us. I know the last few weeks have been stressful for all of us and I thought it might be nice for a change."

I lean on my elbow. "Two years and you've never offered to make dinner. Who are you and what have you done with the *real* Seth?"

"Truth be told, I've been taking some online courses." He sounds a bit defensive. "I'm trying to graduate from cold cereal and microwave dinners. Is that a bad thing?"

Veronica sits on the barstool next to me. "Guess we'll find out. Hope you got pizza on speed dial."

Seth scoffs. "Speed dial? What decade do you live in? I've got a one-touch pizza button on my phone and I know all the drivers personally."

I snicker. "It's true."

Veronica's arm brushes mine as she scoots her chair closer to the counter. "So what are you making?"

Seth bangs around in the cabinets. "Spaghetti with red sauce and garlic parmesan breadsticks. Oh, and salad with a few types of lettuce, a carrot or two, spinach, cucumbers, red cabbage, craisins, apples, and some walnuts. Raspberry vinaigrette to top it off."

I nearly fall off my chair. "All from scratch?"

"Baby steps, Alice. I'm boiling water for pasta. The rest is prepackaged."

I sit back up. "Well I'm still impressed."

"It'll be about twenty minutes before it's ready."

Veronica drums the counter. "Sounds good. We'll be right here waiting."

"No, no, no. You two don't need to sit there and watch. I'm nervous enough as it is and you're not helping. Go sit on the couch or something."

I huff. "Fine." I hop off my stool, grab Veronica's arm, and pull her away.

Two hours later, the three of us are lounging on the couch, our stomachs filled with spaghetti and salad. Seth has been anything but cold to me. His hand touched mine several times through dinner and now he's so close I can feel his body heat.

At several points this evening I forgot that we weren't together anymore. As much as I want to be with him, I'm thankful that Veronica's been here. There's no way I could ever suffer through another episode of blind sex and explaining that to Seth would be damn near impossible.

Veronica hops up from the couch and leaves me in a hole. "It's been a fun afternoon, but I need to get home to Guenter before he eats the side of my couch or something worse."

My stomach lurches as I pull myself up. I don't want to be alone with Seth. "You can go get him and come back over. Seth doesn't mind, right?"

"Not at all."

"Appreciate the thought, but no can do bestie. I've got a work thing tomorrow that I can't miss. Some worthless ethics training I believe."

I find her and hug her. I whisper in her ear, "Don't leave me with him."

She whispers back, "I don't think sex is part of his plan this evening. You're safe. Besides, you can always use the migraine or period card. Those never fail to deter." She kisses my cheek. "I'll call you tomorrow." She walks toward the front door. "Bye, Seth. Thanks for dinner and for not killing me!"

Seth gets up and walks past me. "You're welcome, Veronica. Have a good evening and drive safe."

The door opens, closes, and locks, and my pulse soars. I sit back down on the couch and pray that Seth doesn't try and seduce me. All I can think about is sinewy scars, hairy chests, and the smells of garlic, pickles, and cigarettes.

Seth returns to the couch and sits closer to me than I'd like. "We need to talk."

"We do?" My heart thunders. "About what?"

"I think you know."

"I do?" My hands tremble. I slide them under my thighs. I'm about ready to pull my phone out of my pocket and call Veronica to come back. "Seth, I..."

Seth groans and his hand brushes mine. "This case has driven a wedge between us and I hate it. I'm still hurt that you didn't confide in me but at the same time I think I understand why now. I can't begin to imagine what you've gone through over the last decade because of this guy and I wouldn't want to be in your shoes, but I want you to know that I'm here for you.

"I still love you, Alice. I will always love you. However, there's no way we can move forward together until this case is solved. We have too many ties to it and things to work through but once it's behind us I'd like to work on us again... if that's what you want."

My heart soars to the heavens, but my nerves are still frayed. *How could I be with him if my vision doesn't return?* "I've never wanted anything more... to all of it. Let's nail this bastard so we can move on with our lives."

He slides right next to me. "Good. I know you're on suspension, but I'd really like to go over all the evidence with you one last time if you're okay with that. You have more insight into all of it than all the rest of us combined and I think together we can break this case wide open."

I catch myself reaching for his leg and pull my hand back. "I never thought you'd ask."

"Let me grab the case files." He gets up from the couch. "Be right back."

I rub my hands together, suddenly chilled despite the sweltering heat. I think about Mother and the older black woman at the hospital who calmed me down when I was seeing the Braille Killer everywhere I turned. Once again, I find myself praying to the God I've never known. I feel foolish, yet the experience is strangely satisfying as well.

Seth returns, plops down on the couch next to me, and hands me a stack of folders. He begins ransacking a stack of papers of his own.

I sit here in silence. Seth is too engrossed in his task to notice I've done nothing with the folders he handed me. Finally, I speak. "What would you like me to do with these?"

"I tho—damn, I'm sorry. Not used to you being blind. Guess we'll go through all this stuff together."

I hand the folders back to him. "Let's start with the letters and items. The other day you told me I was blind to what was right in front of me. I think you were right, but not exactly in what you were implying at the time. It got me thinking about this case and everything the Braille Killer has sent me. I might have an idea about what we've been missing."

"Really? Great. Let me find that folder." He leafs through several items. "Ah hah, found it. Want me to read you the note?"

"No, I remember it well enough. This one contained the picture of Denise dead on the floor, right?"

"Um... yes."

"I didn't spend much time looking at the photo because it was so disturbing at the time. She's wearing jewelry in the photo, correct?"

"I believe so. Yes, some sort of friendship necklace. A puzzle piece with a heart on it."

"Right." I chew on my thumbnail. "Can you compare that photo to the police photos from the crime scene?"

"Sure, give me a minute."

I know what he's going to find. Or rather what he won't find.

Seth stops rifling through paper. "I'll be damned."

"No necklace. Correct?"

"Right. That means he was at the scene of the crime when it happened and took the necklace after snapping a photo of her."

"Exactly. The question is why were they both there that day?"

"I don't know. Any thoughts?"

"I can't prove anything, but I think they might've been waiting for me.

Why else would they have shown up at my psychiatrist's office?"

Seth rubs his face, stubble grating against flesh. "That's a good question, but where are you headed with this train of thought?"

"The necklace in the photo is the same as the actual necklace he sent me with the second letter."

Seth digs up the second letter and necklace. "Looks like it's the same one to me."

"Can I see the necklace?" Seth hands it to me.

Sometimes I see better with my fingers than I ever did with vision. The front has some writing on it, but it's the back that interests me. It's slightly softer than the front and snags my skin a bit when I rub my finger on it. I scrape my fingernail across the back of the necklace and a clay-like substance rolls up underneath it.

I hand the necklace to Seth and dig the substance from under my nail. "What did I just do?"

"Well… that's interesting." Seth leans across me.

There's a lamp on the end table next to me, so I don't panic. "What is it?"

"Looks like you've uncovered some engraved letters."

My hands tingle and my stomach flutters. How I missed it for nine years is beyond me. "And what are they?"

"Looks like M-R-P."

I grab Seth's arm. "My God, Seth! I bet those are his initials."

"I think you're right. This is a huge find, Alice!"

"Let's keep going. The third envelope contained a newspaper clipping of Denise's obituary, right?"

"Hang on, I'm not there yet."

"I assumed everything he sent me pertained to Denise, but I really was blind to what was in front of me. These things only look like they have something to do with her, but they really point to him somehow."

"Okay, I've got the newspaper clipping. But I'm not seeing anything about him."

I close my eyes and conjure the clipping in my mind. I've read it dozens of times and don't recall anything significant about it either. I'm not sure if it's the prayer I made or sheer brilliance on my part but a thought flashes into the forefront of my mind. "What if it's like the necklace? I've never bothered to look at the back of that clipping."

Seth turns it over. "There's a bunch of classified ads on the back. Doesn't look like there's anything—hold up…"

The anticipation kills me. I'd give nearly anything to see right now. I can't wait any longer. "Well?"

The paper rustles. "There's an ad selling puppies. It says to call Russell at the bottom and there's a phone number as well. 555-0147. You think it could be him?"

I make a mental note of the phone number, but the name Russell niggles in the back of my mind. "Hold on…" I've heard it recently, but where? My eyes grow wide as recollection slaps me in the face. "The old man in the house across the street from Sarah Johnson's house said his name was Russell. He also said that ten years back he lost Eleanor. That's Denise's middle name. That cannot be a coincidence."

"You're on fire with revelations tonight. I should cook for you more often."

I frown. "Oh, you think it's your cooking that's helping me?"

"What else could it be?" I imagine he's smiling at me. I miss his beautiful face, dimpled cheeks, and grayish-blue eyes. "Never mind that. You think I should call the number in the ad?"

I shake my head. "Not yet. You should have Detective Roland run it first and see what pops. If it is the Braille Killer's number, we don't want to tip him off about knowing it. He'd be in the wind before we could track down an address."

"Good call. I'll have him run it first thing in the morning." He shuffles through some more papers. "How about the fourth one? Senior picture from 2008."

"Best guess is that he must've gone to the same high school as Denise and me."

Seth puts his hand on my leg. "You think he's your age?"

"I don't know. His scarred face makes it difficult to determine. Suppose he could've been a teacher or a coach or something."

My heart pounds faster. "Maybe he drew the heart around Denise and me to throw me off. What if he's in that picture as well?"

Seth gasps. "And his name would be in the yearbook!"

I bounce my feet on the floor. "Yes!"

"Do you still have yours?" I've never heard him so excited.

"No, I never bought one. Neither did Vee. I didn't want to purchase a reminder of that hell I lived through."

Seth sobers. "Damn. Maybe the library will have one."

"A good possibility. You should definitely check it out in the morning."

I'm already thinking ahead to the fifth envelope. I remember it contained nothing but the letter. However, unlike any of the other letters, this one was typed on a letterhead for Blackwell's Asylum and Home for Children. Denise spent many years there.

I am such an idiot. "The Braille Killer might've too."

"Hold up, Alice. I see that your brain's working hard, but your mouth isn't relaying all that information it's producing. What about the Braille Killer?"

I drum my fingers on the couch. "I was thinking about the fifth envelope. I looked at everything from the wrong perspective for ten years. I fell right into his trap like a fool. *Everything* is about him. He must've lived at Blackwell's Asylum and Home for Children as well. Or worked there. Why else would he have sent the letter on their letterhead? How would he have had access to it otherwise?"

"He could've stolen it, but your assumption seems reasonable. It could be where he met Denise."

I pat his leg several times, excitement building in my chest. "Do you have Denise's record that I took from the basement of Blackwell's Asylum and Home for Children with you?"

Seth smacks his lips. "I think so. Give me a sec." He clicks his tongue as he searches through the folders and papers. "Yeah, got it. What do you need from it?"

My excitement fades. "I don't know yet." I lean back and close my eyes.

"Maybe nothing. How about the sixth item?"

"The fortune cookie?"

"Yeah. Denise used to work at a Chinese restaurant. I thought he sent it to me as a reminder of her. I don't know what it has to do with him though. Maybe he worked there too?"

"Maybe, but I might have another theory as to why he sent it."

"Oh yeah?"

"You've got a photographic memory, right?"

"I'm good at remembering details, but I wouldn't say that a photographic memory is the correct analogy. Why?"

"Do you remember the lucky numbers inside the fortune cookie?"

I picture it in my mind and chuckle. "Okay, maybe photographic is a good analogy. They were 1, 37, 45, 62, and 89."

"Correct. And do you know what's significant about them?"

"The numbers one through nine are all represented?"

Seth mumbles through the numbers. "Well yes, there's that, but there's more to it."

I search my mind but come up blank. "You've stumped me."

Seth laughs. "Finally! I was looking at Denise's record and noticed that the first four numbers of the fortune cookie are the same first numbers in her ID number from the orphanage. Her ID number is 137456299. I'd be willing to bet that his ID number is—"

"137456289. You are a genius, Seth." I lean over and kiss his cheek. "I never once thought there was a significance to them. I always focused on the message. He kept saying in the letters that he left me a path to find him and I never saw it."

"If the phone number doesn't pan out, we can go find his record and hopefully find him."

"Exactly."

He smacks the papers. "We're getting close to cracking this case. I can feel it."

I long to share his excitement, but so many thoughts still race through my mind. I can hardly keep track of them all before they crash and burn, but one persists through the chaos. *It's me he wants calling that number.*

The hairs on my arms rise. All the emotions of my past flood me: sorrow, guilt, anger, shame, and remorse. "Everything that has happened is my fault. Sarah, Cara, even Denise. I could've stopped this long ago if I'd let you in." I manage to hold back tears, but my body writhes.

Seth leans over and puts his arms around me and tears burst from my eyes. "This isn't your fault, Alice. None of it. He did this to you not the other way around. Don't blame yourself."

I cry harder because he's right. Harder because he smells so good and I need him so bad. It frightens me to think I may never see again. I must get past my fear of that bastard or I'll never be whole again.

Before I know it, I'm in Seth's arms and our lips are locked together. I've no clue if I initiated it or if he did, but I'm not gonna stop kissing him unless he does. His hands crawl under my shirt and unhook my bra in a matter of seconds. I want him so bad, but fear rises in my gut and crushes my lungs.

I pull back, struggling for air. I want to stop, but I know if I do, the Braille Killer wins. He always does because he holds the power.

I don't want to be a victim anymore, so I pull Seth's shirt over his head. He removes his hands from under my shirt just long enough to shrug out of his shirt. My hands glide across his smooth chest and the fragrances of his cologne and deodorant fill my nostrils.

I cannot be a victim again. I smell him and rub my hands under his arms. The coarse curly hairs remind me of the Braille Killer's chest hair and I tense, but only briefly. I push the fear away and pull off my shirt and bra. Seth buries his head between my breasts. Flashes of the past rise in my mind again but I won't give into them. They will no longer define me.

Seth picks me up in his arms and carries me into the bedroom, his lips never leaving my flesh. He lays me on the bed and removes my jeans and panties. The memories press harder, bombarding me like the Braille Killer did my abdomen. I cry, but this time for freedom. Seth moves onto the bed and I tremble. His hands slide up my thighs and to my abdomen. I flinch, but ever so slightly.

I will not be a victim. I am no longer the Braille Killer's to manipulate. I am in control. I take Seth's hands and slide them up to my breasts. I spread my legs, wrap them around his, and pull him onto me.

Memories of my past fade into the distance until nothing remains in my mind but Seth and me. I hold him tight and kiss him deep. He is my lifeline in the darkness. The vanquisher of shadows. The love of my life.

Whether or not this means we're back together means nothing to me right now. I'm right where I want to be, and I am not a victim.

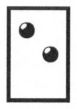

CHAPTER THIRTY

I QUIETLY CRAWL OUT of Seth's bed and grab my phone. It takes me a minute to locate my discarded jeans, and the search disorients me just enough that I stub my toe on the frame as I round the foot of the bed. I hold my tongue and curse profusely in my head. *My ninja skills are slipping.*

The bedroom door moans as it swings open. I pause and wait several moments but Seth doesn't stir. He breathes heavy, and I breathe easier. I step into the living room and slowly pull the bedroom door closed.

The floor is slick under my socks, so I use it to my advantage and scoot across it and over to the couch. I pull on my jeans and then retrieve my bra and shirt from the floor. I check my phone. It tells me that it's 01:15 in its computerized voice. It's loud enough to wake the dead and maybe Seth as well. Thank goodness he's a heavy sleeper.

My nerves are fried, and it takes every ounce of courage I have to tell my phone to dial the number from the classified ad. I put the phone to my ear and it rings several times. I'm about to hang up when the line clicks and stops ringing.

I wait several seconds, listening to the silence. I couldn't speak if I wanted to. Then the silence turns into breathing. Heavy breathing. My skin crawls.

His voice shoves me into the past. "Puppies are all dead, Alice." His laughter lashes at my soul.

I cringe but find my voice and whisper-yell into the phone. "I know who you are, and I'm coming for you."

"Must be hard living with all that blood on your hands. Doesn't wash off like normal things do. But you've got an eye for it."

I ball my fist and almost give in to my rage, but then I remember all my training on how to deal with psychopaths. *Tell him what he wants to hear.* "I think I finally understand and I'm ready to confess."

Silence fills the line again and I wait.

"You'll find me at home, where God is no more. Two hours. *Alone.* If I find anyone else with you everyone dies."

The phone clicks and he's gone.

I exhale. *I'm sorry, Seth…*

* * * * *

Two thirty in the morning on a Sunday and I'm waiting on the curb, Esther in hand, for a car to come pick me up. I've grown reliant on ridesharing services over the last week and it's worked out well so far.

The purr of an engine grows louder as the car approaches. Its brakes squeal as it comes to a halt in front of where I stand. The whir of an electric motor sounds as the car window lowers.

"Are you Alice?" A woman's voice.

I bend down. "I am. You must be Bernice?"

"Sure am. Go ahead and hop on in and I'll get you to your destination."

I use Esther to locate the edge of the curb and then the car. I slide my hand along the side of the car until I find the door handle. I lift up on it, open the door, and climb inside. The interior smells like car-wash cherry. It's better than vanilla; that stuff triggers my headaches faster than almost anything else.

I close the door, locate the seatbelt, and strap myself in. "You know where you're headed, Bernice?"

Her vinyl seat squeaks. I'm guessing she turned in her seat to face me. "Twelve thirty-seven Old Pacific Road, right?"

I give her a nod. "That would be the place. The faster you drive the better I'll tip you."

"You got it." The tires squeal as she pulls away from the curb. I smile. It reminds me of Seth's driving.

Bernice isn't talkative like some of the other drivers I've had, and I appreciate it. However, I need something to distract me from what I'm headed to do. I know it's reckless, but that doesn't mean I want to dwell on it. "How about some music, Bernice? Got anything heavy?"

"I've got some *Devil Wears Prada*. You into them?"

The mental picture I conjure is worthy of a good chuckle. "Not familiar with them. Let's give them a listen."

"You got it!"

A few seconds later, the car is filled with pounding drums, crunching guitars, and growls and screams. I bob my head along with the beat and tap my finger on the side of Esther. In another life, I think Bernice and I could be friends.

I sway back and forth on the seat, both to the music and because Bernice is true to her word about driving fast. Next thing I know the music has faded and we've come to a full stop.

"Good Lord, are you sure this is the right address?" Her seat squeaks, and her voice grows louder. "There's nothing around here but a bunch of creepy, old abandoned buildings. Most of them are all boarded up."

"Sounds like we're at the right address."

"Did they pull this place straight out of a horror film?"

I laugh, but my insides twist in knots. "Might as well have. The property was used as a Catholic boarding school for misbehaved children until the late 1950s."

"Well, it would've set me straight. I'll tell you that much."

I pull a twenty out of my pocket—the only cash I have—and toss it into the front seat. "Thanks for the ride."

"Whoa, that's way too much for a tip. The fare was only twelve bucks."

I open the car door and swing my legs out. "Deal's a deal. I asked for speed and you gave me that plus some terrific music. You earned it."

I climb out of the car, shut the door behind me, and step up onto the curb. I turn back toward the street, wave at Bernice, and wait for her to drive off. She pulls away but then swings back around. Her brakes squeal as she pulls back up in front of me. She rolls down her window. "You sure you don't want me to wait around or something? I really don't mind. I've got no other fares and nowhere to be."

"You're a sweet girl, Bernice. I do appreciate your concern for my safety, but I assure you that I'm meeting someone here. I promise I'll be fine until they arrive. Thank you again."

"You're welcome, Alice." She gives the car some gas and I wait until I can no longer hear the car engine before I turn and face the culmination of the last ten years of my life: Blackwell's Asylum and Home for Children.

I close my eyes and think back to the last time I was here. It was 2013, just after I received the fifth letter. That letter was different than the others because it was typed on letterhead from this orphanage. Why I didn't see the connection back then eludes me. It could've saved two young girls' lives.

I remember every detail of the property, right down to the number of steps up to its front entrance. It's been five years since I was last here, so Esther assists my memory as I traverse the cement walkway. It's overgrown with crabgrass. I reach the six front steps and climb them, but when I get to the top something's there that wasn't before.

I probe the object with Esther. It's about two-and-a-half feet tall and three-and-a-half feet wide and sounds like it's made of metal. I bend down and reach out to see what it is. My fingers touch a meshed metal. It's rough with rust. With a little more probing I conclude that it's an abandoned shopping cart.

The homeless used to hang around this area of town until about three years ago when several of them went missing. It spooked them so bad that they moved their entire makeshift camp to the other side of town. Without suspects, evidence, or bodies the case grew cold.

I stand, step around the cart, and proceed forward to the front entrance. The old doors remain chained and the flanking windows are still boarded up. I move over to the window on the right. Last time I was here the board had been rigged to swing up to the left. I locate its bottom-right corner and pull up to my left. The board moves without hindrance, just as it had before.

Most of the window behind the board lies inside the building, broken into a thousand pieces. I step over and through the framed opening, careful to keep my pants from snagging on the jagged glass jutting up from the bottom and out from the sides of the frame. Previously, I wasn't so cautious and the scar on my outer thigh is proof. I can attest that sight isn't everything. With it you tend to overlook the important details.

The board slips from my hand and bangs against the outside wall. I cringe as the noise fills the front entrance hall like a cannon. Several birds stir, squawk, and then coo. I stand still for several minutes, listening for any sounds beyond those of the birds.

Satisfied I'm still alone, I probe my way through the front entrance hall and to another set of double doors that are propped open. Beyond the doors is a hallway that runs perpendicular to the front entrance hall.

I move into the hallway. At the far left end is a large dayroom where the children studied and played games. At the far right end is a mess hall large enough to seat a hundred. Four administrative offices, two on either side of the hallway, lie between me and the mess hall and four more lie between me and the dayroom. Eight in total.

Straight ahead are stairways that lead up and down. The floor directly above me is split into two wings, one for the boys and one for the girls. Each wing has community bathrooms and showers. The third floor housed the live-in staff, each with their own private facilities.

The basement was filled with classrooms on either side of its central hallway during the years the Catholic school owned the property, but when Blackwell took over, he converted them into holding cells for some of the more unstable residents.

Below the basement lies the subbasement and my destination. Several rooms are located on that level including the one that houses the school and orphanage records. However, the room I'm most interested in is the chapel.

I descend the first flight of stairs and am on the landing between the first floor and basement when I hear a loud bang come from above. My heart gallops in my chest and I freeze. *Should I ascend or descend?* A shout from above followed by a thunderous boom, a loud gasp, and a sickening thud make my mind up for me.

I descend the second flight of stairs and probe my way down the hallway with Esther. The first several doors I try are locked, but the second one on the left isn't. The door moans when I push it open, but not enough to attract attention. I slip inside the room and leave the door cracked so I can hear if someone approaches.

Scraaape!

The sound reminds me of a heavy object being dragged across the floor. It came from the floor above.

Scraaape!

I stand beside the door and hold Esther like a club. My legs tremble and my pulse races.

Thud. Thud. Thud. Thud.

I hold my breath, fearing it will attract attention.

Thud. Thud. Thud. Thud. Thud.

The sound grows louder with each thud.

Scraaape! Scraaape! Scraaape!

I'd give anything right now to have my sight back.

Thud. Thud. Thud.

Thud. Thud. Thud.

I soon realize that something is being dragged down the stairs. But what is it and by whom?

Thud. Thud. Thud. Thud.

Maybe it's the creepy location, but I can't help thinking it's a body. The scraping and thudding continue but the sounds are fading. They must be headed to the subbasement.

I lower Esther, open the door, and step into the hallway. Only the scraping sound continues, but it's muffled through the floor. I step forward and my shoe catches on something and throws me off-balance. I thrust the end of Esther into the floor to keep myself from faceplanting. It works, but the thunderous noise it creates is deafening.

Way to make an entrance, Alice.

It takes me a moment to realize that something quite unexpected is happening. I see a blue circle of light expanding from the point of impact. It crackles and pops like static electricity as it grows ever wider. The floors, walls, doors, and everything else around me light up in my mind like wireframe mesh 3D models. Then my brain begins filling in the mesh with colors and textures and shadows from my memories until the picture is complete. It all happens in the blink of an eye.

Chills envelop me. I turn and can see in every direction. I look down to see what tripped me but it's only a smudge on the floor. I bend down and touch the dark spot. *An old nail head.* The smudge morphs into a nail head. "My God..."

I head back down the hallway and to the stairs that lead down to the subbasement. Below the floor that I stand on there is nothing but complete darkness. An inky void into nothing. My vision as it is. I go back over to the room I'd hidden in and open the door wide. A small portion of the floor exists inside the room but then it turns to perfect darkness as well.

I surmise that this ability of Esther only reveals what I can see from where I'm standing and that my brain only fills in what it knows. The other thing I notice is that I feel weaker than I did before it happened. I recall what Rico told me about the energy Esther uses. *My energy.* I must be strategic in how I use it.

I grab ahold of the railing and descend into the subbasement. It's cooler down here than it was upstairs and smells a bit earthy and musty. I remember how hard it was to traverse the subbasement when I could see, so my chances of getting to the chapel unscathed are slim. Not only that, but I know someone's down here. I must use Esther again and pray that I have enough energy left to take on the Braille Killer when I find him.

I exhale, raise Esther, and strike the floor with her. Again, I see blue sparks, a circle of blue light, and meshing. My brain fills in the details with my memories.

I turn around and there's a dark smudge less than a foot away from me. I start to reach toward it but hesitate. It looks like a large human form.

"Hello, Alice."

In an instant, my mind fills in the details.

Garlic, pickles, and cigarettes.

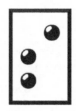

CHAPTER THIRTY-ONE

I ROUSE TO A dark world and a splitting headache. The left side of my face is throbbing, and my jaw feels like it's out of place. My mouth tastes of blood and my lower lip is swollen. Pine-scented candles permeate the air and fill my nostrils, but their scent isn't strong enough to fully mask the nidorous odor beneath it.

I lie on my back on a cold and rough surface. *Concrete?* I push myself up and into a sitting position. *Why am I on the floor?*

A heavy haze distorts my mind and I can't recall where I am or what day it is. But then he speaks. "Welcome to my sanctuary, Alice." His voice reverberates in my chest and sparks my fear. "I've been waiting for you for a very long time. I'd begun to wonder if you'd ever show up."

Sunday. The orphanage.

I work my jaw back and forth. It's stiff but doesn't seem to be broken or dislocated. "I'm here now."

"Yes you are. And you were foolish enough to bring your partner as well."

The contents in my stomach curdle. "Seth?"

Seth doesn't respond.

"Don't waste your breath. He can't hear you."

Fire rages in my heart. "What have you done to him you bastard?" I roll over and onto my hands and knees.

"He's a bit incapacitated right now, but otherwise unharmed."

The thought of Seth dead because of me tortures my soul. "Let him go and I'll do whatever you want."

"Ah, you see, therein lies the problem. You're in no position to bargain. This is my dominion. I make the rules here."

I sit back on my feet. "What do you want from me?"

"Come now, Alice. Don't play the fool. You know what I want. You've always known. Now come forward and make your confession to me."

I try to stand but my legs are weak. I probe the floor with my hands, but Esther isn't there. "What've you done with my cane?"

I hear her familiar tap ahead of me. "You must earn it. Crawl to me if you must, but don't tarry. I've got a schedule to keep."

To my left I find a pew and use it to pull myself up. I turn to my right and hobble toward the front of the chapel, using the pews to keep my balance and bearing. By the time I reach the front pew some of my strength has returned.

"Now what?"

"Get on your knees, confess your sin, and beg me for mercy."

I kneel, and it sickens me, and the words that spew from my mouth taste like vomit on my tongue. "I admit it. I pushed Denise over the banister. I killed her. It should've been me that died that day. God, I am sorry. Please forgive me. I beg of you, show me mercy, Russell."

Whoosh!

Esther slams into my left side and sends me crashing to the floor. I grit my teeth and stifle a scream as pain shoots up both of my arms and into my shoulders. My arms go numb.

He stands over me, nothing but a darker shadow. "You're unworthy to speak my name you blind *freak.*"

I cower and protect my head with my arms. "Why are you doing this to me? What did I ever do to you?"

"You took everything from me!" Spittle rains on me.

He strikes the side of my left leg with Esther. Pain explodes down to my toes and up through my hip and I cannot hold back a scream.

He uses his foot to turn me onto my back, but I keep my arms over my face. "All I ever wanted was to be with a girl, but my father made sure that it would never be with a normal one. No one with sight would ever look past my scarred face.

"Ten years ago, Denise was in love with a blind girl who turned out to be the same girl I was tasked to kill. She thought that I could be with someone blind because they wouldn't care what I looked like. Two birds with one stone. Figured I'd give it a go."

He kicks me in the ribs. Bones crack and I double over, the pain so intense I can't breathe. "You ruined it all. Your vile, deformed blindness left me impotent. Right then I knew that something as disgusting as you could never give me pleasure."

Somehow, I manage to find my voice through the pain. "Then why have you raped the other girls? And why were you tasked to kill me? I don't understand."

"Rape them? You know that's untrue. At least not sexually. What I do to them is punishment for *your* sins. They receive all that *you* deserve."

"If we disgust you so much then why didn't you get together with Denise? Didn't you love each other?"

He retreats several steps. "Even your mind is deformed, you filthy whore! What kind of sick, twisted person would want to be with their sister?"

Sister? She couldn't have been by blood. I need to find a way to get to him, so I adapt to his twisted way of thinking. "You're right, I'm nothing more than a whore but there must be hope for me yet. Tell me what to do. How can I make this right?"

"You killed the only person that ever loved me for who I was. I want you to feel the same kind of loss that I felt. You're going to kill your partner."

Seth... Love of my life. "I'd rather die than do that." I find strength in my defiance and manage to sit up.

"If you refuse to do what I ask, I'll kill everyone that means anything to you, starting with your partner. I'll remove every appendage, one by one, until he finally bleeds to death. Next, I'll put the true fear of God into your dear old mother before I quarter her alive. Then I'll move on to... what do you call her? Ah, yes, Vee. I'll get her and her little dog too. Ever seen someone torn apart by wild pigs? You will. You'll miss nothing."

I'm not the only one he's watched.

Each breath sends shards of pain into my left lung, but I fight through it for Seth. "Even if I agreed to do what you're asking of me how would I kill him?"

"I've taken the liberty of stringing him up like a piñata. It's your job to take your cane and beat him to death with it."

"And what if it doesn't kill him?"

"I won't let you stop until he's dead."

I rise to my knees. "And if I do this, you'll leave me alone and stop killing blind girls?"

"I give you my word. Not another girl will die."

He said nothing of leaving me alone, but it doesn't matter. Nothing from his mouth speaks of truth.

I stare at my hands. "These hands… they've killed once before. But Seth?" I wail, half in earnest. "What choice do I have? One life for many…"

"That's the spirit. Now get up."

I stand but putting pressure on my left leg sends pain coursing through my entire body. He pokes me in the stomach and I realize that it's Esther's end. I take hold of her and the opposite end drops to the ground. I turn her around and lean on her.

"Where is Seth?"

"He's four feet straight ahead of you. Don't even think about taking your time. Every blow better be as hard as you can swing that cane, or I'll beat you with it again."

I step forward, pretend to stumble, and slam Esther's end into the floor. Blue light and crackling air expand in a circle. In an instant the room comes to life in my mind's eye, filled in with details from my photographic mind.

Four columns rise two stories to meet the arched ceiling. Seven small, stained-glass windows stretch across the top of the front wall, each depicting a head from a prominent person from the bible. The center window depicts the head of Jesus Christ wearing his crown of thorns.

A communion table sits to my left and several dark, narrow smudges rise from it. An eight-foot-tall crucifix stands straight in front of me, but most of its vertical beam is smudged with darkness. I know that darkness must be Seth, but the smudge doesn't fill in like the nail did on the floor upstairs. It takes several moments for my brain to make sense of what I'm looking at before the picture in my mind completes itself. Seth hangs upside-down on the crucifix.

I crumble to my knees, weakened both in spirit and in body. I look behind me. Russell stands a good five feet away. His scarred, demonic face and his tan, rubber-soled boots are the only things I see in my mind when I look at him.

He doesn't move to stop me, and I wonder if I'm the only one who sees the light and hears the crackling air.

Russell snarls. "Get back on your feet and fulfill your penance."

It takes every ounce of willpower and strength to rise again but I do. I move forward, my hand outstretched and probing the air even though I can see. I reach Seth and rest my hand on his cheek. Blue light flows from Seth's cheek and into my hand, restoring some of my energy. I stagger back a step. *What did I just do?*

"Now, Alice." Malice warps his voice.

I look down at my shoulder. "Can I at least say goodbye?"

"And why would I allow you to do that? You took Denise from this world without a moment's thought."

"But you're better than me. You exude mercy where I have none. You're a righteous man and I'm a weak and sinful woman. Show me mercy this one last time and I'll give you my life. I'll do anything you ask. You'll be a god to me and I will serve you in any way you see fit."

"I *am* merciful, but I'm not stupid. Do as you're told."

I step back a couple feet, turn to the side, and raise Esther over my shoulder. "I'm sorry, but it must be this way. You shouldn't have come here, Seth. Now you must die."

Seth moans. "Alice? What happened?"

"Yes, yes. Do it!" Russell moves into my peripheral view, a shadowy smudge. "Bash his skull in. Make him bleed the way Denise did."

A plan formulates in my mind, but Seth won't like it. I yell at the top of my lungs like a warrior in battle, arch back and swing Esther full-force at Seth's thigh. She connects with a sickening *thwack* and Seth yells.

Russell moves closer, his eyes locked on Seth. "Lower! Aim for his head. I want to hear the crunch."

I arch back to take a big swing and turn the top of Esther counterclockwise ninety degrees. Esther glows blue and crackles. Russell turns toward me, but I've already committed. I press the button atop Esther and swing her at him with everything I have as I lunge forward.

Russell's eyes widen, and he raises his arm to block the blow, but it makes little difference. Esther morphs into a whip and strikes with such force that it rips into Russell's arm and cracks bone.

Russell's scream echoes through the chapel, but then blue sparks ignite the air and thunder crashes, drowning him out. Russell flies backward, toppling several rows of pews, and comes to a rest atop them. He groans but doesn't move.

I turn Esther's top back ninety degrees clockwise and she ceases to glow. I walk over to Russell, but he doesn't even attempt to move. He breathes raggedly.

My father's words rise in my mind and I can't help but wonder if they're true. *You must kill to regain your sight.* Had it been Denise's death that gave me vision ten years ago and not the blow to the head that I suffered? Or something else? Will my vision truly be restored if I take Russell's life? *Can I take his life?*

I reach into my shirt and take out the cross pendant that hangs from my neck. I wrap my fingers around it, close my eyes, and hold it tight. *This man doesn't deserve to live.*

My entire body quakes as I relive the last minutes of Sarah's and Cara's lives once again. Then my mind takes me back to the mill and Yolanda's stitched-open eyes. He forced her to watch him rape and maim and kill her precious daughter.

Fury swells in my chest, burns within my heart, and begs to be released.

I stare at Russell, the man who ruined my life, and feel nothing but hate for him. "You're a monster and monsters don't deserve to live."

I wrap Esther around Russell's throat and hold both ends loosely. One strong tug and I could end his life. "It's time to put you down, you bastard." I spit in his face.

His lips curl into a snarl. "I'll admit that I didn't see the cane thing coming. You certainly surprised me with that. You're full of surprises, but we both already knew that."

I glare at him. "That's it? No begging for your life?"

His eyes are cold and without fear. "I will tell you one thing. You'll never find the next girl in time."

My pulse kicks into overdrive. *The next girl?*

I twist Esther tighter. "Tell me where the girl is, and I might let you live."

Russell coughs. "You still don't get it, do you Alice?"

"Alice!"

I look up. How had I forgotten about Seth?

"We need him alive."

I turn my attention back on Russell and fight the urge to end him. "What is there to get? You're a sick bastard who likes to kill little girls because you can't get it up. You need to torture them because you were tortured, and they must be blind so that they don't see your ugly face. Did I miss anything?"

Russell laughs and chokes on his own spit and blood. "Vision or not, you'll always be blind to the truth."

I loosen Esther. "Then explain it to me. Help me understand what I'm missing. What is your grand plan? To become famous? Isn't that what you psychos always want? To be understood and heralded as some great mastermind?" I spit on him again. "No, this has been personal from the beginning."

"Not from the beginning. It became personal when you killed Denise." He cocks his head. "Ah, you haven't figured out why we targeted you to begin with, have you?"

I snarl. "Why do sick people do anything? I guess you perverts thought you could take advantage of a blind girl."

He shakes his head. "Does it make you feel superior to call us names and label us? Crazies, psychos, sickos, perverts. Do you sleep better at night thinking it's true?"

My left leg aches, so I shift my weight. "It is true."

"You are blind to everything, Alice. We are no different than you in that we serve a higher purpose."

"How does torturing and killing young girls serve a higher purpose? Do you worship the devil or something?"

He laughs again. "Would it help if I said I belonged to some cult of the damned? I think not. What I am is so much more than that. I'm part of a society of likeminded individuals with a higher calling. Our sole purpose is to rid the world of people like you. You don't belong here."

My fists tremble with rage. "Why is that? Because we were born blind and you find that somehow offensive?"

He scoffs. "No, because *you're* not from *our* world."

In that moment time comes to a screeching halt and I'm left breathless. It's the second time in as many days that I've been told as much. My father believed it so adamantly that they locked him up in a psychiatric ward. Now I can't help but believe it might be true and the implications of such a revelation leave me without words.

"Alice don't listen to him." Twice now I've forgotten about Seth. "He's nothing more than a psychotic killer. He's trying to pull you down into his twisted world to make himself sound rational."

I look up at Seth. "It's okay, Seth. I know what I'm doing."

The world conjured in my mind fades to black once again, leaving me blind. I surmise that Esther's effects only last so long. It doesn't matter though because I have Russell right where I want him.

I focus my attention back on Russell. I need answers. "And how would you know this? What craziness drove you to the conclusion that those like me are from another world?"

"You saw the Shadow Mirror. It doesn't lie. Only your kind can be seen with it."

"What the hell is he talking about, Alice? Can't you hear how crazy he sounds?"

I ignore Seth. "You only see blind people through it?"

"Don't be naïve, Alice. You're far more than just a blind woman."

"My God…" My mind spins with so many questions.

"Yes, Alice. Whether I live or die makes little difference. The killings won't stop until every last one of your kind has been eradicated."

Then this is just the beginning.

I probe deeper. "Who are you?"

He sneers. "I am a Shadow Priest, and you'll never find the rest of us."

Something about his story makes no sense. He's had his chance to kill me on several occasions. "So why didn't you kill me ten years ago?"

"Simple. I hadn't prepared myself to break Denise's heart as well."

He coughs and chokes again before continuing. "She loved you and begged me to wait, so I did. As you know, that decision cost her life. We were going to finish the job the day you killed her. That's why we were there at your doctor's office. But you ruined everything, and I had to wait ten long years."

"Why?"

"I've said enough. You'll learn nothing more from me."

"Back away from him, Alice. He's insane. You're not from some other world. You're no different than me or anyone else."

I shake my head. "You know that's not true, Seth. You've seen what I can do."

"No, Alice. There's a rational explanation for everything. We just haven't found it yet."

"I've found my answer."

"You kill him, and we'll never find her. There's no going back from that. It's not too late."

"You know me, Seth. The thought of killing him in cold blood sickens me, but it's the only way we'll find her. She dies if he lives. That's what I wouldn't be able to come back from. I can't have another girl's blood on my hands."

My soul is on fire and I hate myself for what I must do. I rip off my necklace and toss it on the floor. "It's too late for him."

I pull Esther's ends tight.

Russell gasps and convulses for nearly a minute before going still. I unwrap Esther from around his neck, press the button atop her handle, and she becomes rigid once more. I try to stand but my legs are weak, so I drop Esther and crawl back over to Seth.

Seth's cheeks are wet and he's shivering. "What have you done?"

I kiss his forehead. "What was necessary."

"Listen to yourself, Alice. How are you any better than him?"

"I had to do it to save her… and I wanted to see again."

"See again? You're crazy! How could you let your father fill your head with such nonsense?"

"It's not nonsense!"

"So it worked then? You can see?"

Everything around me is still black as night. *Did my father lie to me?* My heart thunders and I think I might puke. "No…"

"Then you've gained nothing!" His anger drills into my mind.

"That's not true." I hold his face and can feel the heat radiating from his cheeks. "You know he was never going to tell us where to find the girl. Now I can find out, just like I found things out with Sarah and Cara."

Seth shakes his head until I let go of his face. His voice is frantic. "What gives you the right to take the law into your own hands? You aren't judge and jury. You can't just determine someone's fate like that. And you don't know that he wouldn't have told us anything. How are you going to find the girl now that he's dead? Even if you are able to see his last moments before death, they'd only be of you killing him!"

"No, Seth. I don't believe that. I can't allow myself to. My father isn't insane. Everything he told me must be true. Russell confirmed as much. My father says that I have the ability to see into someone's memories far beyond the moments before their death. Not only can I save this next girl, but I can bring down the entire Shadow Priest society Russell spoke of."

Seth groans. "Two insane people in agreement doesn't validate what they tell you. They're both crazy. Russell got one thing right though: you truly are blind. You can't see the truth through your pain. And your father was wrong about you getting your sight back. He's wrong about everything. It's insane to think otherwise."

I understand the logic of what Seth says, but some things are illogical. "I just do. Maybe it takes some time for me to regain my vision."

"Is that what he told you? You'll eventually get your sight back if you kill someone?"

"No, but—"

"There's not buts, Alice. Do you know how crazy all this sounds? How crazy you sound?"

"I do, but I also know it's true. I can feel it in my heart. You need to trust me on this."

"Trust you? I'm not sure I even know you anymore. Did I ever?"

"Don't be like that, Seth."

"Like what? Hurt that you've lied to me for two years?" He growls. "What do you expect? You've changed. You're not the woman I met two years ago."

"Look, I'm sorry I withheld so much from you. I can't change that now, but what I can do is promise you that I will never keep anything from you again. You have my word. You have my love. Don't push me away again. I need you more than ever."

"Dammit! I can't even think straight right now, let alone make life-altering decisions. Can you get me down from here? I think my brain might explode if I hang upside down much longer."

I nod. "Okay, but you'll have to tell me how. I can't see anything."

"The rope I'm hanging from is on a pulley system. It looks like it's tied off on a hook on the wall to your right."

I stand, and Seth guides me over to the wall. I locate the rope.

"That's—Alice look out!"

It's too late. My side explodes with pain and I'm lifted off my feet. We crash into the wall and slide to the floor. Garlic, pickles, and cigarettes sting my nose. My mind reels. *I killed him!*

His weight crushes me. "Should've finished the job when you had the chance."

My mind returns to 2008 but this time it doesn't debilitate me. My ninjutsu training kicks in and I land a palm right up through his nose. He grunts and blood sprays everywhere, but it doesn't stop him from punching me in the face. I land another blow right across his throat and he grabs my arm.

I locate his left shoulder with my free hand and dig my nails and fingers into the wound. I gag, and he screams. He lets go of my other arm and falls to the side. I punch and bite everything I can until I free my legs. I get to my knees, but the pain is excruciating. I can hardly think through it, but I can't let him win.

"Behind you!" yells Seth.

Russell grabs my foot, so I twist and kick as hard as I can with my other leg. My foot connects with his arm and bones crunch. We both cry out and Russell releases my foot. I think I might've broken my foot and I'm certain I broke his arm.

I crawl over to Russell and take his head in my hands. His breathing is shallow, and he doesn't resist. I don't think he has any strength left and I'm not sure I do either. I twist Russell's head with everything I have but it isn't enough. I don't even know why I tried.

I clamp my hand over his mouth and nose but feel no breath. He doesn't stir, so I check his pulse and find none. "He's dead this time."

I collapse on the floor and stare at the vaulted ceiling and the colored light from the stained-glass windows. My heart skips a beat and I scream with joy. "I can see again!"

"Really?"

Ever the skeptic.

I look over at Seth and remember that I hadn't freed him. I crawl over to the wall again and claw my way to my knees. The rope is bound another foot beyond my reach. "I don't think I can do it, Seth. I've got nothing left in me."

"Yes you can. You're the strongest woman I know. You just need to reach a bit deeper and find that last reserve of strength."

I yell as loud as I can and push myself to my feet. I grab the rope, untie it, and Seth drops to the ground with a loud *thud*. He groans.

I collapse against the wall, slide down until my butt rests on the floor, and close my eyes for a moment. "I'm sorry. I didn't mean to drop you. It's all I could do. Are you injured?"

"Bruised, but okay. He injected me with something that knocked me out cold. How about you?"

"I've suffered worse." I lie.

Seth unties the rope from his ankles and hands and gets up. He walks over to me and sits down next to me. "We can't keep doing this."

I turn my head. "Doing what?"

"Lying to each other."

"But I haven't lied... have I?"

"Several of your ribs are probably broken, your foot might be broken, and you're going to have bruises all over your body for weeks. You're telling me that you've suffered worse injuries?"

"It's no lie. I really have suffered far worse. Physical injuries heal over time, but mental ones last forever." I take his hand, but he pulls it away.

He stares at the ceiling. "Look, what happened last night shouldn't have. And what you just did to Russell sickens me."

"*Sickens* you?" I ball my fists and scream. I want to punch him in the face. "You didn't live through what he did to me and to Sarah and to Cara. You have no right to be sickened by what I did. He was a disgusting, twisted monster. And he attacked me and tried to make me kill you. If anything, I killed him in self-defense. I can't help it if you don't understand that, but don't judge me for it. Don't *ever* judge me!"

Seth stands. "I need to go call for backup. Russell smashed my walkie-talkie."

Russell's dead eyes stare at me and the thought of entering his memories scares the hell out of me. The last thing I want is to relive my nightmare through his eyes, but I'll do it if it means saving someone. "Fine, but first I need to find the girl."

"That, and nothing more."

I crawl over next to Russell's head and look back at Seth. There's no way I can stop with just finding the girl and he knows it.

"I'm serious, Alice. You don't know what a mind like his will do to you."

No, but I'm about to find out. I place my hands on Russell's scarred face. It's repulsive and the thought of touching my forehead to his leaves me nauseous. Even worse is the thought of being in his head and experiencing the world the way he saw it. *But I have no choice. Lives are at stake.*

I swallow hard, close my eyes, lean over him, and touch my forehead to his. As with Sarah and Cara, a shift within me occurs, my birthmark on my left wrist burns with fire, and I enter the twisted mind of Russell.

CHAPTER THIRTY-TWO

I AM MYSELF, YET I am Russell. He is dead, yet he lives. I am a bleating lamb lost in the shadowlands, hunted by a dire wolf. Hunted by him.

Time and again he attacks me, slashing and biting at my neck with his razor-sharp claws and teeth. I fend him off and run as fast as my legs will carry me, but the ground turns to quicksand and my little feet sink deeper with every step. I look back and he stands at its edge, teeth gleaming and snout dripping.

"Where is the girl?" I ask.

He growls deep in his throat. "You'll get nothing from me."

* * * * *

I rise from the depths of Russell's mind like Jesus from the grave and gasp.

"Well?" asks Seth.

My mind is numb and fatigued. I can't process what just happened.

"Did you see anything beyond his last moments?" asks Seth.

I shake my head. "Not even that much. It wasn't the same as with the others." I close my eyes and search for the right words to express what happened. I focus on what I felt: *hostility.* "He's got some kind of defense mechanism on his memories or something. I don't even know how to explain it."

"Alice, that can't be it. We need to know how to find the girl and you're the last hope for that."

I groan. "You think I don't know that?"

"Sorry. What can I do?"

I open my eyes. "I just remembered that Bill told me Russell has two other storage units."

"I'll call it in along with everything else, but who is Bill?"

"The manager at the storage facility. It doesn't matter." I wave him off. "I'm gonna try again."

I take a deep breath, and dive deep once again...

* * * * *

Memories rise from the soil of his mind like rotten trees with hollowed trunks and decrepit branches; a landscape of the hell he has made for himself. I dash from tree to tree plucking their leaves of memories, but they rot in my hands as fast as I can grab them.

"What have you done with the girl? Where is she?" I ask.

I am alone.

* * * * *

Once again, I rise from the depths, lost for answers. I lift my head and let go of Russell's face.

Seth still leans against the chapel wall, his eyes trained on me. "Have you found what you're looking for? Do you know where she is?"

"What do you think?" My voice is full of venom and my heart bleeds with hate but not for Seth. "Forgive me, that wasn't aimed at you. He won't let me in."

"What do you mean? He's dead. Perhaps you're trying too hard." Seth holds his side where I beat him with Esther and guilt fills me past full.

Tears fill my eyes. "I'm sorry I had to hit you."

Seth gets up and moves over next to me. He puts his hand on my shoulder. "I forgive you, Alice."

My lips tremble and I look away. "It was the only way I knew to draw him close."

Seth gently takes my chin and turns my head back toward him. "No, Alice, I forgive you for everything." He leans in and touches his lips to my cheek, stirring up a torrent of emotions.

I rest my head against Seth's for several minutes. I breathe deep and allow my heart to settle. "How can I get past Russell's defenses?"

Seth strokes the back of my hand. "Maybe he feeds on your fear. Or your hate. You know, your defensiveness fuels his or something."

Sometimes Seth is a genius, but he'll never hear it from my lips. At least not today. The answer is so simple, yet so very difficult.

I raise my head and look into Seth's grayish-blue eyes. "I know what I must do." He nods and backs away without a word.

I look back to the crucifix and then up to the window where Jesus looks down on me with a crown of thorns upon his head. I'm not sure I'll ever understand why Christians worship a dead man. I take another deep breath and exhale.

I look down at Russell and his scarred face and I pity him for the first time. *I forgive you for everything you did to me, but I'll never forget.* A burden that I could not possibly bear a moment longer lifts from my shoulders. I breathe deep again, this time unencumbered. I've not felt so good in more than a decade.

I wipe my eyes with the backs of my hands and then place my hands on Russell's cheeks once more but this time I'm no longer repulsed by the scars left by his father. I lean forward, press my forehead against his, and dive deep one last time.

* * * * *

I am the wolf and she's invaded my territory once again. Through the woods I chase her until we come to a dead end. I've got her trapped between me and sheer rock walls. I move in for the kill.

"No!" she screams.

Her voice startles me and gives me pause. "Why are you here?"

"To tell you that I'm sorry. You didn't deserve your father's abuse, but I didn't deserve yours either. I'm sorry Denise died as well."

I snarl. "You killed her, Alice."

She steps forward. "Yes. It was an accident, but that doesn't matter. I can't carry this pain and malice anymore. It's tearing me up inside. I forgive you, Russell."

I look closer and truly see her for the first time. She is me and I am he, yet we are not the same. I don't understand how it can be, but her words leave me vulnerable. Forgiveness I never asked for.

"Where is the girl?" she asks.

I am no longer a wolf but a ten-year-old boy. I giggle and rub my hands together. "Hide-and-seek is my favorite game and I never lose." I spring from the couch and I'm out the back door. Papa's land backs up to the Griffith National Reserve, a wooded and mountainous area covering tens of thousands of acres. I know nearly every inch of it backward and forward. I've explored every nook, cranny, crevice, and cave for miles. "Close your eyes and count to twenty."

Alice does and I'm off like the wind; a blur through the trees. Many favorite spots flitter through my mind, but I've got my sights set on my special place. No one's ever found me there and they'll never find the girl either.

I splash across the creek, through a forest of pines and piñon, traverse a ravine dried with the summer heat, and scale the sandstone cliffs. Through the garden of rocks I climb, down another ravine, across several deer trails, and past the forest road.

Straight ahead I see the silver of the cistern cap shining through the wild grass. When I reach the cap, I look around to make sure Alice hasn't followed me. How could she have? She knows nothing of this land. My land.

I lift the cap and crawl down the rope ladder and into the dark cistern. At the bottom I find the girl, her brown hair soiled, and her blue dress torn. She shivers and cries but there's no one to hear her but me. I sit next to her, content knowing we'll never be found.

But my pulse spikes and my heart thunders. Something's not right.

Cloaked in darkness she watches from the shadows, her eyes upon me. Alice.

I stand, fists balled. "You cheated! No one's ever found me here."

Alice smiles. "But I am you, and you are he, and no secrets can be kept."

I stomp the ground. "You'll still never get there in time. The water rises. You cannot win."

Alice leans forward and caresses my scarred face. "I've already won, Russell. Now tell me where I can find the Shadow Mirror and the ones you call the Shadow Priests."

Flashes of mountains and trees and rivers and a monastery bombard me but then everything around me turns black, burns like ashes, and scatters.

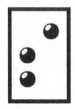

CHAPTER THIRTY-THREE

IT'S LATE AFTERNOON AND I lead a team of police officers through the backwoods of the old Puge property northwest of town. Normally we'd have a forest ranger guide us, but there is too little time to wait for them to arrive.

Two hours into it and we're more than halfway up the side of a mountain but the terrain is slick, and the slope is steep. Several times my footing has slipped, and I've fallen to my knees. Thankfully, I didn't break my foot kicking Russell. Had I, this journey would've proved impossible.

As is, I can't imagine traversing this terrain while carrying someone. There must be another way to where we're headed, but we don't have the time to find it. I'd never forgive myself if we arrived too late and found her drowned.

Sweat pours from me in buckets and my throat is parched but I've drained the last of my water from my canteen. It makes little difference though because there's no going back. I'll continue to push forward until I drop if I must. I cannot stomach the thought of another girl dying because of me and I will not allow it. We'll find her even if it takes all night to do so.

Finding the same paths and markers has been tougher than I had imagined, but we've finally reached the end of the garden of rocks. Forty feet below is the ravine that descends from the backside of the mountain. The path down to the ravine is both narrow and treacherous and borders a twenty-foot drop into a bed of rock and debris. Several sections of the path have fallen away, leaving gaps up to two feet between some of them.

We decide to traverse the path one at a time and wait at the mouth of the ravine until we've all made it down safely. I move toward the path, but Seth grabs my shoulder and turns me around. I look up into his grayish-blue eyes and I can see the world. We share a moment, and I'd give anything to stay in it for a little longer, but we're running out of time.

His brow furrows. "Let me go first and find the safest path down."

He has more hiking experience than the lot of us combined and I'd be a fool to refuse. I step aside. "Be careful."

Within ten minutes, six of us have traversed the narrow path. Only Officer Spalding remains up top. The sun is dipping low and the fear of not finding her or getting to her in time is creeping into my thoughts.

I turn and look down the ravine not a moment before Officer Spalding's cry reaches my ears. By the time I turn around he hits the ground twenty-feet below with a sickening crack, thud, and groan. The others rush to his aid and I just stand there, transfixed by the bloody branch skewering his right thigh.

Officer Spalding will need to be airlifted out of here, but we don't have the time to stand around and wait for help to arrive. I walk over to Seth and pull him around to face me. "I know this sounds harsh, but we need to get moving before we're too late."

Seth grabs his temples between his forefinger and thumb and takes a deep breath. "I know. Give me a minute."

Seth turns back to the others. "Listen up. Officers Dupree and Brex hike back up where you can get a good signal and call for airlift support. Officer Janis stay with Officer Spalding and make sure he stays lucid and doesn't try to remove the tree limb from his leg. Detective Bergman, Detective Roland, and I will continue to search for the cistern and the girl."

I don't wait for a response before traversing the ravine. Crunching leaves and snapping sticks tell me Seth and Detective Roland are close behind. I push forward, driven by determination and fear.

Landmarks I hadn't noticed when chasing Russell bloom in my mind as I pass by them. My shoes pound the ground and I cannot keep myself from moving forward as we rush downhill. Brush and tree limbs whack my chest, arms, and legs but they don't slow me down.

Two deer trails pass by in a blur and the next thing I know I'm stumbling out onto a service road. I skid to a stop and my chest heaves. Moments later, Seth and Detective Roland crash through the bushes and brush and stumble onto the road. They pull up next to me, both winded and chests heaving.

A sign down the road says we're on Forest Road 109. What are the odds of the road number being the same as Russell's storage unit? If left to chance, infinite. However, Russell never left anything to chance. He planned out every last detail for an entire decade. *But he failed to account for Esther.*

I don't really know who I am or where I come from, but I won't stop until I discover the truth. I've got two resources in Rico and my father, and a single clue to follow: find the monastery and find the Shadow Priests. I will find them all and bring them to justice. *But right now I have a girl to find.*

I cannot catch my breath and my lungs are on fire, but I press on across the road, down the embankment, and through the tall grass. The sun descends behind the mountain, its last rays racing away faster than I can move.

I pull up and bend over, my hands on my knees for support. I look up and catch a glimmer of silver just before the last sunbeams fade. "There!" My voice barks and I point straight ahead.

Seth and Detective Roland rush past me. I unscrew the cap on my water canteen and lift it to my mouth. I tilt my head back and the canteen forward but there's not a single drop left in it.

I stagger through the grass until I reach Seth and Detective Roland. The two of them are fighting to get the cistern cap loose, but I know its secret.

"Move aside." I drop to my knees and crawl forward.

In my mind I'm Russell again. I reach underneath the sides of the cap and unlatch the hidden locks. With both hands I lift the cap and it swings back on its hinge.

"Alice!" Seth's voice sounds so distant.

My world turns black in an instant and I feel as though I'm falling. Before I even think to scream, I splash into a body of water. I gasp for air, but water fills my lungs instead. It soothes my dry throat and burns my lungs. I cough, but there's nowhere for the water to go.

My arms and legs flail aimlessly, and I can't remember which way is up, but then something latches onto my shirt. I stop struggling and a slender hand grabs my arm and pulls me back to the surface. I gasp and cough and spit up water.

"You can still stand." It's a girl's voice. A familiar voice.

I lower my feet and rest them on a solid surface.

A dim light shines from above. "Alice! Are you okay?"

"Yes! She's still alive!" I cough and spit up more water.

I find the girl's hand and hold it tight. "Are you okay?"

"I am now. I knew you'd save me from him, Alice."

Priscilla…

CHAPTER THIRTY-FOUR

THE DOORBELL CHIMES DEEP in the house and George Hallard pulls the front door open before it finishes its tune. His eyes are swollen and red but the smile he wears stretches ear-to-ear. "Thank God you found her!" He bends down and embraces Priscilla.

Grace stands inside the door, her arms crossed, and her gaze locked on me. She says nothing, so I follow suit. What's to be said anyway? *I told you so?*

Erma, George's sister, stands farther back in the house, her face nearly consumed by shadows. Her eyes glisten in the low light. She's been crying as well. She dips her head and then moves out of view.

"She's one brave girl," says Seth.

"The bravest," George agrees.

George releases Priscilla and stands. Priscilla walks inside and right past Grace without pause. I smile to myself. *Good girl.*

George's hand extends toward me, so I take it. "I'll never be able to repay you for what you've done."

I shake his hand and nod curtly. "Just doing my job, Mr. Hallard."

His brow wrinkles. "I still don't understand how he got to her." He looks back over his shoulder. "We have an alarm system on the house and it's wired to all the windows and doors. None of them were tripped and the system was never disarmed."

Seth exhales. "I don't think any of us understand what happened, not even Priscilla."

I hand him my card. "If Priscilla remembers anything, give me a call."

He flips the card over and back. "You got it."

Seth shakes George's hand and then we walk back down to Seth's sedan. We climb inside and sit in silence. It's the first moment we've had to sit and relax in weeks.

Seth drums the steering wheel with his thumbs. "How did he get to her?"

The Shadow Mirror looms in the back of my mind. "You wouldn't believe me if I told you."

Seth looks over at me. "I won't deny that there's something different about you, but I'm still skeptical about this whole alien angle. I still don't believe in Roswell, NM or Area 51."

"Yeah, I don't think there are little green men running around either. I'm thinking more along the lines of *Species*. I've come here to mate with the perfect human."

He whistles. "Then you'd better get your senses checked. There ain't nothing perfect about me."

I nudge his shoulder. "Double negatives make a positive."

He shakes his head. "Why you always getting technical on me?"

"Reeducation. You—"

My phone buzzes. I pull it out of my pocket and check the display. I have a new text message from Officer Jaramillo:

Sunday, August 5, 2018

22:37

BJ: We're over here at Dunharrow Storage. There's something you've got to see. Come as quickly as you can. Bring Detective Ryan with you.

Seth has a similar message on his phone. We buckle in, Seth fires up the engine, and we haul butt toward Dunharrow Storage.

* * * * *

Twenty minutes later, Seth and I are riding up to the fifth floor in the Dunharrow Storage elevator. My mind races through endless scenarios of what they might've found in the Braille Killer's refrigerated storage unit.

The elevator doors open, and we step into a long corridor buzzing with activity. Unlike the other floors, there's only one central corridor and it stretches straight ahead. There are three units to each side and one at the far end.

We walk straight ahead toward Lieut. Frost. He's talking with Deborah from forensics. Their conversation ends as we arrive, and she walks back into the unit. The air is thick with his cologne. *The skunks always come out at night.*

Lieut. Frost looks grim as ever. "Detective Ryan. Detective Bergman. We've found a body inside. Deborah says it could be anywhere from a week to twenty days old, but it's hard to tell for certain since the unit is refrigerated."

Seth crosses his arms over his chest. He does it every time he's around Lieut. Frost. I think he's self-conscious about his physique, but he shouldn't be.

"We know anything? Sex, age? Have they ID'd the body?" asks Seth.

Lieut. Frost nods. "Male, late 30s to early 40s. We believe he was an employee here since he's wearing a shirt with the business logo. Facilities manager most likely. Name on the shirt says Bill."

"My God..." *Why would he have killed Bill?*

"We're guessing he must've seen something that he wasn't supposed to. Suffered a single GSW to the left temple. 9mm from the looks of it."

Seth voices what I'm thinking. "GSW? But that isn't the Braille Killer's MO."

I head into the storage unit. Charlie's still photographing evidence and Detective Roland is walking the scene with Deborah. I step around Charlie and bend down to pull back the sheet over the body, but two jars on a shelf at the back of the unit draw my eye.

I stand and walk over to them. Each jar contains a pair of eyes in a clear

THE BRAILLE KILLER 307

liquid I assume to be formaldehyde. The first jar has an "SJ" on its lid and the second one has a "CS."

Sarah and Cara.

I take a deep breath.

Thank God there aren't more jars.

"Alice, over here." Seth's voice comes from my left.

Beyond Seth I see a wall of latex masks. Twelve long faces hang on hooks, stretched with gravity. Several of them trigger memories that pull me deeper into my past.

I point them out to Seth as I recognize them. "That one's the old man from the house across the street from the Johnsons. And that's the doctor from St. Thomas Medical Center that followed me in the stairwell when we went to see Yolanda."

Seth points at another one. "There's the guy Yolanda drew."

I nod. "Yes, and the one with the black goatee was a guest instructor at the police academy. The silver-haired one was a professor from college. And the one with the skull and crossbones neck tattoo was a janitor at my high school. I think he was in the background of my senior class picture where he drew a heart around Denise and me."

Seth moves closer to the wall and lifts the mask off its hook. He shoves his fist inside of it and holds it up. "Yeah, I think you're right."

My heart thunders. "How long had he been watching me?"

"Too long, but it's over now." He hangs the mask back on its hook.

My thoughts turn to Mother and her vile priest. I look through the masks again but don't find Father Rogallo's face among them. I'm more disappointed than shocked by it.

I can't stomach thinking about him watching me anymore, so I return to the covered body and pull the sheet back. My breath catches as I gasp. "Ryan!"

Seth is at my side within a few seconds. "What is it?"

"It's not him," I say.

Lieut. Frost walks over to us and scowls. "What do you mean?"

"The Bill I met. This isn't him." My heart races as my mind searches for clues. Then it hits me. "How did I miss it?"

Seth leans back on his heels. "Miss what?"

"The keys. They were color-coded to the doors, but Bill told me he was color blind. I had assumed someone else who worked here had marked them."

Lieut. Frost's radio squawks. "Sir, I think we've got something. Please come down to the front office when you can. Bring Bergman."

"On our way." Lieut. Frost steps back into the corridor.

I pull the sheet back over the body and then Seth and I follow him to the elevators. This is the last thing I thought I'd be doing today.

The front office door is open wide. We enter, and Officer Jaramillo is sitting at one of the desks in front of a monitor. He's viewing security footage.

The office still smells like old pizza and Funyuns, but the garbage drifts have been shoved into the next room. I shudder as Bill's lips press against mine again. I wipe my mouth on my sleeve, but it won't erase the memory.

Lieut. Frost moves around the far side of the desk. "What've you got for us, Bob?"

Seth and I file in behind Officer Jaramillo. We all stare at the monitor.

"I found the footage from the day Detective Bergman was in the office here."

My stomach gurgles. "No one needs to see that, Jaramillo."

"Don't worry, I'm past the part where he plants one on you."

I can feel Seth's eyes on me, so I focus on the screen. "Then play it."

He does.

On the screen, I leave the office. Thirty seconds later, Bill makes a phone call. His back is to the camera, but the audio is clear:

> "It's Reagan. Everything's in place. As you suspected, Alice doesn't have a clue about any of it. She won't have her vision much longer, either. Once it's gone, you can eliminate her."

There are several seconds of silence, and then he continues:

"Yes, the Shadow Mirror is on its way. Morgan and the others should expect its arrival soon. We are so close, Russell. Only a handful of them remain. The Shadow Priests will prevail."

Bill—or Reagan—ends the call and steps out of the frame.

Jaramillo stops the playback and leans back in the chair. "Anyone have a clue as to what he's talking about?"

Conversation ensues, but my mind is far beyond these walls. There are so many questions that need answers and only two people in the world that can help me find them. Neither of them is in this room.

With Rico's and my father's help, I'm certain I can locate and take down the Shadow Priests. However, there's one question that outweighs all the others and must be answered before I can move forward.

How do I get Father out of the St. Thomas Psychiatric Center?

TO BE CONTINUED...

Alice's story continues in *The Night Mauler*. Visit **danielkuhnley.com** for more information.

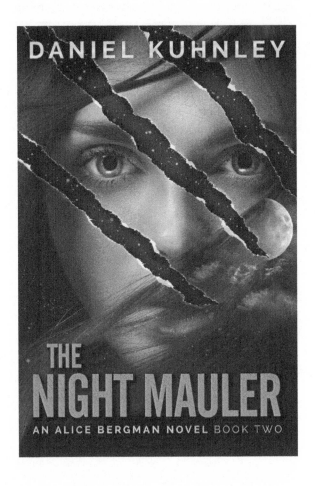

PLEASE TELL OTHERS WHAT YOU THOUGHT

Thank you for taking this journey with me. If you'd like to show your support for my work, please leave a review wherever you purchased this book. It's free to do so, and it'll only take you a minute to write a quick sentence expressing your thoughts about the book.

Your review is very important to independent, self-published authors like me. Internet and online bookstore algorithms favor books with reviews. They display in search results and at the top of search results more often than books without reviews.

Did you know that there's a minimum number of reviews needed to purchase certain advertising? It's true. Help me reach that threshold by leaving a review. Doing so will help more people find this book and will in turn help me sell more books, which means I can keep writing more books for you.

Go to danielkuhnley.com/reviews if you need a link to where you can leave a review.

Thank you!

READ *BIRTH OF A KILLER* FOR FREE

Curious how Alice gained her sight as a teen?
Want to read about the attack that started it all?

danielkuhnley.com/become-a-conqueror

Sign up and read *Birth Of A Killer*, An Alice Bergman Novella, and also get **EXCLUSIVE** access to additional Alice Bergman series content. Be the **FIRST** to get sneak peaks at my upcoming novels and the chance to win **FREE** stuff, like signed books.

Thank you for reading!

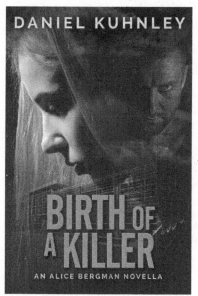

Be careful what you dream…

…when murder is on your mind.

Sixteen-year-old Alice is a ghost. Although born blind, the world is more blind to her than she is to it. Until the day she's noticed. By a bully.

She did what any girl would do…

…and wished him dead.

When a body is discovered, Alice fears the worst. Could she be to blame? No one would believe her even if she confessed. Because nightmares don't come true…do they?

You'll enjoy this supernatural serial killer thriller, because everyone enjoys a nail-biting mystery they can't put down.

Get it now.

Birth Of A Killer is the prequel to *The Braille Killer*.

EXPLORE CENTAURIA

Alice's father said their ancestors were from another world. You can explore that world, Centauria, in Daniel Kuhnley's fantasy series, *The Dark Heart Chronicles*.

Read *The Dragon's Stone*, book one in the series.

Available on Amazon. Visit danielkuhnley.com for more details.

ABOUT THE AUTHOR

Daniel Kuhnley is an American author of Dragon Fantasy and Supernatural Serial Killer stories. Some of his novels include *The Dragon's Stone, Reborn, Rended Souls,* and *The Braille Killer.* He enjoys watching movies, reading novels, and programming. He lives in Albuquerque, NM with his wife who is also an author.

CONNECT WITH DANIEL

danielkuhnley.com/connect

ACKNOWLEDGEMENTS

Catherine, Donna, Geoff, Marsha, and Phylls—thank you so much for your invaluable feedback. You helped make a good book great!

Alisha, thank you for providing me with invaluable insight.

To my fans—thank you so much for your support and for reading through to the very end.

Made in the USA
Coppell, TX
28 June 2020